DESERT GOLD

ZANE GREY

Desert
Gold

Reg. U. S. Pat. Off.

WALTER J. BLACK, INC.

ROSLYN, NEW YORK

CONTENTS

DESERT GOLD

PROLOGUE

I

A FACE haunted Cameron—a woman's face. It was there in the white heart of the dying campfire; it hung in the shadows that hovered over the flickering light; it drifted in the darkness beyond.

This hour, when the day had closed and the lonely desert night set in with its dead silence, was one in which Cameron's mind was thronged with memories of a time long past—of a home back in Peoria, of a woman he had wronged and lost, and loved too late. He was a prospector for gold, a hunter of solitude, a lover of the drear, rock-ribbed infinitude, because he wanted to be alone to remember.

A sound disturbed Cameron's reflections. He bent his head, listening. A soft wind fanned the paling embers, blew sparks and white ashes and thin smoke away into the enshrouding circle of blackness. His burro did not appear to be moving about. The quiet split to the cry of a coyote. It rose strange, wild, mournful—not the howl of a prowling upland beast baying the campfire or barking at a lonely prospector, but the wail of a wolf, full-voiced, crying out the meaning of the desert and the night. Hunger throbbed in it—hunger for a mate, for offspring, for life. When it ceased, the terrible desert silence smote Cameron, and the cry echoed in his soul. He and that wandering wolf were brothers.

Then a sharp clink of metal on stone and soft pads of hoofs in sand prompted Cameron to reach for his gun, and to move out of the light of waning campfire. He was somewhere along the wild border line between Sonora and Arizona; and the prospector who dared the heat and barrenness of that region risked other dangers sometimes as menacing.

Figures darker than the gloom approached and took shape, and in the light turned out to be those of a white man and a heavily packed burro.

"Hello there," the man called, as he came to a halt and gazed about him. "I saw your fire. May I make camp here?"

Cameron came forth out of the shadow and greeted his visitor, whom he took for a prospector like himself. Cameron resented the breaking of his lonely campfire vigil, but he respected the law of the desert.

The stranger thanked him, and then slipped the pack from his burro. Then he rolled out his pack and began preparations for a meal. His movements were slow and methodical.

Cameron watched him, still with resentment, yet with a curious and growing interest. The campfire burst into a bright blaze, and by its light Cameron saw a man whose gray hair somehow did not seem to make him old, and whose stooped shoulders did not detract from an impression of rugged strength.

"Find any mineral?" asked Cameron, presently.

His visitor looked up quickly, as if startled by the sound of a human voice. He replied, and then the two men talked a little. But the stranger evidently preferred silence. Cameron understood that. He laughed grimly and bent a keener gaze upon the furrowed, shadowy face. Another of those strange desert prospectors in whom there was some relentless driving power besides the lust for gold! Cameron felt that between this man and himself there was a subtle affinity, vague and undefined, perhaps born of the divination that here was a desert wanderer like himself, perhaps born of a deeper, an unintelligible relation having its roots back in the past. A long-forgotten sensation stirred in Cameron's breast, one so long forgotten that he could not recognize it. But it was akin to pain.

II

When he awakened he found, to his surprise, that his companion had departed. A trail in the sand led off to the north. There was no water in that direction. Cameron shrugged his shoulders; it was not his affair; he had his own problems. And straightway he forgot his strange visitor.

Cameron began his day, grateful for the solitude that was now unbroken, for the cañon-furrowed and cactus-spired scene that now showed no sign of life. He traveled southwest, never straying far from the dry stream bed; and in a desultory way, without eagerness, he hunted for signs of gold.

The work was toilsome, yet the periods of rest in which he indulged were not taken because of fatigue. He rested to look, to listen, to feel. What the vast silent world meant to him had always been a mystical thing, which he felt in all its incalculable power, but never understood.

That day, while it was yet light, and he was digging in a moist white-bordered wash for water, he was brought sharply up by hearing the crack of hard hoofs on stone. There down the cañon came a man and a burro. Cameron recognized them.

"Hello, friend," called the man, halting. "Our trails crossed again. That's good."

"Hello," replied Cameron, slowly. "Any mineral sign to-day?"

"No."

They made camp together, ate their frugal meal, smoked a pipe, and rolled in their blankets without exchanging many words. In the morning the same reticence, the same aloofness characterized the manner of both. But Cameron's companion, when he had packed his burro and was ready to start, faced about and said: "We might stay together, if it's all right with you."

"I never take a partner," replied Cameron.

"You're alone; I'm alone," said the other, mildly. "It's a big place. If we find gold there'll be enough for two."

"I don't go down into the desert for gold alone," rejoined Cameron, with a chill note in his swift reply.

His companion's deep-set, luminous eyes emitted a singular flash. It moved Cameron to say that in the years of his wandering he had met no man who could endure equally with him the blasting heat, the blinding dust storms, the wilderness of sand and rock and lava and cactus, the terrible silence and desolation of the desert. Cameron waved a hand toward the wide, shimmering, shadowy descent of plain and range. "I may strike through the Sonora Desert. I may head for Pinacate or north for the Colorado Basin. You are an old man."

"I don't know the country, but to me one place is the same as another," replied his companion. For moments he seemed to forget himself, and swept his far-reaching gaze out over the colored gulf of stone and sand. Then with gentle slaps he drove his burro in behind Cameron. "Yes, I'm old. I'm lonely, too. It's come to me just lately. But, friend, I can still travel, and for a few days my company won't hurt you."

"Have it your way," said Cameron.

They began a slow march down into the desert. At

PROLOGUE

sunset they camped under the lee of a low mesa. Cameron was glad his comrade had the Indian habit of silence. Another day's travel found the prospectors deep in the wilderness. Then there came a breaking of reserve, noticeable in the elder man, almost imperceptibly gradual in Cameron. Besides the meager mesquite campfire this gray-faced, thoughtful old prospector would remove his black pipe from his mouth to talk a little; and Cameron would listen, and sometimes unlock his lips to speak a word. And so, as Cameron began to respond to the influence of a desert less lonely than habitual, he began to take keener note of his comrade, and found him different from any other he had ever encountered in the wilderness. This man never grumbled at the heat, the glare, the driving sand, the sour water, the scant fare. During the daylight hours he was seldom idle. At night he sat dreaming before the fire or paced to and fro in the gloom. He slept but little, and that long after Cameron had had his own rest. He was tireless, patient, brooding.

Cameron's awakened interest brought home to him the realization that for years he had shunned companionship. In those years only three men had wandered into the desert with him, and these had left their bones to bleach in the shifting sands. Cameron had not cared to know their secrets. But the more he studied this latest comrade the more he began to suspect that he might have missed something in the others. In his own driving passion to take his secret into the limitless abode of silence and desolation, where he could be alone with it, he had forgotten that life dealt shocks to other men. Somehow this silent comrade reminded him.

One afternoon late, after they had toiled up a white, winding wash of sand and gravel, they came upon a dry waterhole. Cameron dug deep into the sand, but without avail. He was turning to retrace weary steps back to the last water when his comrade asked him to wait. Cameron watched him search in his pack and bring forth

5

what appeared to be a small, forked branch of a peach tree. He grasped the prongs of the fork and held them before him with the end standing straight out, and then he began to walk along the stream bed. Cameron, at first amused, then amazed, then pitying and at last curious, kept pace with the prospector. He saw a strong tension of his comrade's wrists, as if he was holding hard against a considerable force. The end of the peach branch began to quiver and turn. Cameron reached out a hand to touch it, and was astounded at feeling a powerful vibrant force pulling the branch downward. He felt it as a magnetic shock. The branch kept turning, and at length pointed to the ground.

"Dig here," said the prospector.

"What!" ejaculated Cameron. Had the man lost his mind?

Then Cameron stood by while his comrade dug in the sand. Three feet he dug—four—five, and the sand grew dark, then moist. At six feet water began to seep through.

"Get the little basket in my pack," he said.

Cameron complied, and saw his comrade drop the basket into the deep hole, where it kept the sides from caving in and allowed the water to seep through. While Cameron watched, the basket filled. Of all the strange incidents of his desert career this was the strangest. Curiously he picked up the peach branch and held it as he had seen it held. The thing, however, was dead in his hands.

"I see you haven't got it," remarked his comrade. "Few men have."

"Got what?" demanded Cameron.

"A power to find water that way. Back in Illinois an old German used to do that to locate wells. He showed me I had the same power. I can't explain. But you needn't look so dumfounded. There's nothing supernatural about it."

"You mean it's a simple fact—that some men have a

PROLOGUE

magnetism, a force or power to find water as you did?"

"Yes. It's not unusual on the farms back in Illinois, Ohio, Pennsylvania. The old German I spoke of made money traveling round with his peach fork."

"What a gift for a man in the desert!"

Cameron's comrade smiled—the second time in all those days.

They entered a region where mineral abounded, and their march became slower. Generally they took the course of a wash, one on each side, and let the burros travel leisurely along nipping at the bleached blades of scant grass, or at sage or cactus, while they searched in the cañons and under the ledges for signs of gold. When they found any rock that hinted of gold they picked off a piece and gave it a chemical test. The search was fascinating. They interspersed the work with long, restful moments when they looked afar down the vast reaches and smoky shingles to the line of dim mountains. Some impelling desire. not all the lure of gold, took them to the top of mesas and escarpments; and here, when they had dug and picked, they rested and gazed out at the wide prospect. Then, as the sun lost its heat and sank lowering to dent its red disk behind far-distant spurs, they halted in a shady cañon or likely spot in a dry wash and tried for water. When they found it they unpacked, gave drink to the tired burros, and turned them loose. Dead mesquite served for the campfire. While the strange twilight deepened into weird night they sat propped against stones, with eyes on the dying embers of the fire, and soon they lay on the sand with the light of white stars on their dark faces.

Each succeeding day and night Cameron felt himself more and more drawn to this strange man. He found that after hours of burning toil he had insensibly grown nearer to his comrade. He reflected that after a few weeks in the desert he had always.become a different man.

7

In civilization, in the rough mining camps, he had been a prey to unrest and gloom. But once down on the great billowing sweep of this lonely world, he could look into his unquiet soul without bitterness. Did not the desert magnify men? Cameron believed that wild men in wild places, fighting cold, heat, starvation, thirst, barrenness, facing the elements in all their ferocity, usually retrograded, descended to the savage, lost all heart and soul and became mere brutes. Likewise he believed that men wandering or lost in the wilderness often reversed that brutal order of life and became noble, wonderful, superhuman. So now he did not marvel at a slow stir stealing warmer along his veins, and at the premonition that perhaps he and this man, alone on the desert, driven there by life's mysterious and remorseless motive, were to see each other through God's eyes.

His companion was one who thought of himself last. It humiliated Cameron that in spite of growing keenness he could not hinder him from doing more than an equal share of the day's work. The man was mild, gentle, quiet, mostly silent, yet under all his softness he seemed to be made of the fiber of steel. Cameron could not thwart him. Moreover, he appeared to want to find gold for Cameron, not for himself. Cameron's hands always trembled at the turning of rock that promised gold; he had enough of the prospector's passion for fortune to thrill at the chance of a strike. But the other never showed the least trace of excitement.

One night they were encamped at the head of a cañon. The day had been exceedingly hot, and long after sundown the radiation of heat from the rocks persisted. A desert bird whistled a wild, melancholy note from a dark cliff, and a distant coyote wailed mournfully. The stars shone white until the huge moon rose to burn out all their whiteness. And on this night Cameron watched his comrade, and yielded to interest he had not heretofore voiced.

8

PROLOGUE

"Pardner, what drives you into the desert?"

"Do I seem to be a driven man?"

"No. But I feel it. Do you come to forget?"

"Yes."

"Ah!" softly exclaimed Cameron. Always he seemed to have known that. He said no more. He watched the old man rise and begin his nightly pace to and fro, up and down. With slow, soft tread, forward and back, tirelessly and ceaselessly, he paced that beat. He did not look up at the stars or follow the radiant track of the moon along the cañon ramparts. He hung his head. He was lost in another world. It was a world which the lonely desert made real. He looked a dark, sad, plodding figure, and somehow impressed Cameron with the helplessness of men.

Cameron grew acutely conscious of the pang in his own breast, of the fire in his heart, the strife and torment of his passion-driven soul. He had come into the desert to remember a woman. She appeared to him then as she had looked when first she entered his life—a golden-haired girl, blue-eyed, white-skinned, red-lipped, tall and slender and beautiful. He had never forgotten, and an old, sickening remorse knocked at his heart. He rose and climbed out of the cañon and to the top of a mesa, where he paced to and fro and looked down into the weird and mystic shadows, like the darkness of his passion, and farther on down the moon track and the glittering stretches that vanished in the cold, blue horizon. The moon soared radiant and calm, the white stars shone serene. The vault of heaven seemed illimitable and divine. The desert surrounded him, silver-streaked and black-mantled, a chaos of rock and sand, silent, austere, ancient, always waiting. It spoke to Cameron. It was a naked corpse, but it had a soul. In that wild solitude the white stars looked down upon him pitilessly and pityingly. They had shone upon a desert that might once have been alive and was now dead, and might again throb with life, only to die.

9

It was a terrible ordeal for him to stand there alone and realize that he was only a man facing eternity. But that was what gave him strength to endure. Somehow he was a part of it all, some atom in that vastness, somehow necessary to an inscrutable purpose, something indestructible in that desolate world of ruin and death and decay, something perishable and changeable and growing under all the fixity of heaven. In that endless, silent hall of desert there was a spirit; and Cameron felt hovering near him what he imagined to be phantoms of peace.

He returned to camp and sought his comrade.

"I reckon we're two of a kind," he said. "It was a woman who drove me into the desert. But I come to remember. The desert's the only place I can do that."

"Was she your wife?" asked the elder man.

"No."

A long silence ensued. A cool wind blew up the cañon sifting the sand through the dry sage, driving away the last of the lingering heat. The campfire wore down to a ruddy ashen heap.

"I had a daughter," said Cameron's comrade. "She lost her mother at birth. And I—I didn't know how to bring up a girl. She was pretty and gay. It was the—the old story."

His words were peculiarly significant to Cameron. They distressed him. He had been wrapped up in his remorse. If ever in the past he had thought of any one connected with the girl he had wronged he had long forgotten. But the consequences of such wrong were far-reaching. They struck at the roots of a home. Here in the desert he was confronted by the spectacle of a splendid man, a father, wasting his life because he could not forget—because there was nothing left to live for. Cameron understood better now why his comrade was drawn by the desert.

"Well, tell me more?" asked Cameron, earnestly.

"It was the old, old story. My girl was pretty and

free. The young bucks ran after her. I guess she did not run away from them. And I was away a good deal—working in another town. She was in love with a wild fellow. I knew nothing of it till too late. He was engaged to marry her. But he didn't come back. And when the disgrace became plain to all, my girl left home. She went West. After a while I heard from her. She was well—working—living for her baby. A long time passed. I had no ties. I drifted West. Her lover had also gone West. In those days everybody went West. I trailed him, intending to kill him. But I lost his trail. Neither could I find any trace of her. She had moved on, driven, no doubt, by the hound of her past. Since then I have taken to the wilds, hunting gold on the desert."

"Yes, it's the old, old story, only sadder, I think," said Cameron; and his voice was strained and unnatural. "Pardner, what Illinois town was it you hailed from?"

"Peoria."

"And your—your name?" went on Cameron, huskily.

"Warren—Jonas Warren."

That name might as well have been a bullet. Cameron stood erect, motionless, as men sometimes stand momentarily when shot straight through the heart. In an instant, when thoughts resurged like blinding flashes of lightning through his mind, he was a swaying, quivering, terror-stricken man. He mumbled something hoarsely and backed into the shadow. But he needed not have feared discovery, however surely his agitation might have betrayed him. Warren sat brooding over the campfire, oblivious of his comrade, absorbed in the past.

Cameron swiftly walked away in the gloom, with the blood thrumming thick in his ears, whispering over and over:

"Merciful God! Nell was *his* daughter!"

As thought and feeling multiplied, Cameron was overwhelmed. Beyond belief, indeed, was it that out of the millions of men in the world two who had never seen each other could have been driven into the desert by memory of the same woman. It brought the past so close. It showed Cameron how inevitably all his spiritual life was governed by what had happened long ago. That which made life significant to him was a wandering in silent places where no eye could see him with his secret. Some fateful chance had thrown him with the father of the girl he had wrecked. It was incomprehensible; it was terrible. It was the one thing of all possible happenings in the world of chance that both father and lover would have found unendurable.

Cameron's pain reached to despair when he felt this relation between Warren and himself. Something within him cried out to him to reveal his identity. Warren would kill him; but it was not fear of death that put Cameron on the rack. He had faced death too often to be afraid. It was the thought of adding torture to this long-suffering man. All at once Cameron swore that he would not augment Warren's trouble, or let him stain his hands with blood. He would tell the truth of Nell's sad story and his own, and make what amends he could.

Then Cameron's thought shifted from father to daughter. She was somewhere beyond the dim horizon line. In those past lonely hours by the campfire his fancy had tortured him with pictures of Nell. But his remorseful and cruel fancy had lied to him. Nell had struggled upward out of menacing depths. She had reconstructed a broken life. And now she was fighting for the name and happiness of her child. Little Nell! Cameron experienced a shuddering ripple in all his being—the physical rack of an emotion born of a new and strange consciousness.

As Cameron gazed out over the blood-red, darkening desert suddenly the strife in his soul ceased. The moment was one of incalculable change, in which his eyes seemed to pierce the vastness of cloud and range, and mystery of gloom and shadow—to see with strong vision the illimitable space before him. He felt the grandeur of the desert, its simplicity, its truth. He had learned at last the lesson it taught. No longer strange was his meeting and wandering with Warren. Each had marched in the steps of destiny; and as the lines of their fates had been inextricably tangled in the years that were gone, so now their steps had crossed and turned them toward one common goal. For years they had been two men marching alone, answering to an inward driving search, and the desert had brought them together. For years they had wandered alone in silence and solitude, where the sun burned white all day and the stars burned white all night, blindly following the whisper of a spirit. But now Cameron knew that he was no longer blind, and in this flash of revelation he felt that it had been given him to help Warren with his burden.

He returned to camp trying to evolve a plan. As always at that long hour when the afterglow of sunset lingered in the west, Warren plodded to and fro in the gloom. All night Cameron lay awake thinking.

In the morning, when Warren brought the burros to camp and began preparations for the usual packing, Cameron broke silence.

"Pardner, your story last night made me think. I want to tell you something about myself. It's hard enough to be driven by sorrow for some one you've loved, as you've been driven; but to suffer sleepless and eternal remorse for the *ruin* of one you've loved as I have suffered —that is hell....Listen. In my younger days—it seems long now, yet it's not so many years—I was wild. I wronged the sweetest and loveliest girl I ever knew. I went away not dreaming that any disgrace might come to her. Along about that time I fell into terrible moods —I changed—I learned I really loved her. Then came a letter I should have gotten months before. It told of her trouble—importuned me to hurry to save her. Half frantic with shame and fear, I got a marriage certificate and rushed back to her town. She was gone—had been gone for weeks, and her disgrace was known. Friends warned me to keep out of reach of her father. I trailed her—found her. I married her. But too late!...She would not live with me. She left me—I followed her west, but never found her."

Warren leaned forward a little and looked into Cameron's eyes, as if searching there for the repentance that might make him less deserving of a man's scorn.

Cameron met the gaze unflinchingly, and again began to speak:

"You know, of course, how men out here somehow lose old names, old identities. It won't surprise you much to learn my name really isn't Cameron, as I once told you."

Warren stiffened upright. It seemed that there might have been a blank, a suspension, between his grave interest and some strange mood to come.

Cameron felt his heart bulge and contract in his breast; all his body grew cold; and it took tremendous effort for him to make his lips form words.

"Warren, I'm the man you're hunting. I'm Burton. I was Nell's lover!"

The old man rose and towered over Cameron, and then plunged down upon him, and clutched at his throat with terrible stifling hands. The harsh contact, the pain awakened Cameron to his peril before it was too late. Desperate fighting saved him from being hurled to the ground and stamped and crushed. Warren seemed a maddened giant. There was a reeling, swaying, wrestling struggle before the elder man began to weaken. Then Cameron, buffeted, bloody, half-stunned, panted for speech.

"Warren—hold on! Give me—a minute. I married Nell. Didn't you know that?...I saved the child!"

Cameron felt the shock that vibrated through Warren.

PROLOGUE

He repeated the words again and again. As if compelled by some resistless power, Warren released Cameron, and, staggering back, stood with uplifted, shaking hands. In his face was a horrible darkness.

"Warren! Wait—listen!" panted Cameron. "I've got that marriage certificate—I've had it by me all these years. I kept it—to prove to myself I did right."

The old man uttered a broken cry.

Cameron stole off among the rocks. How long he absented himself or what he did he had no idea. When he returned Warren was sitting before the campfire, and once more he appeared composed. He spoke, and his voice had a deeper note; but otherwise he seemed as usual.

They packed the burros and faced the north together.

Cameron experienced a singular exaltation. He had lightened his comrade's burden. Wonderfully it came to him that he had also lightened his own. From that hour it was not torment to think of Nell. Walking with his comrade through the silent places, lying beside him under the serene luminous light of the stars, Cameron began to feel the haunting presence of invisible things that were real to him—phantoms whispering peace. In the moan of the cool wind, in the silken seep of sifting sand, in the distant rumble of a slipping ledge, in the faint rush of a shooting star he heard these phantoms of peace coming with whispers of the long pain of men at the last made endurable. Even in the white noonday, under the burning sun, these phantoms came to be real to him. In the dead silence of the midnight hours he heard them breathing nearer on the desert wind—nature's voices of motherhood, whispers of God, peace in the solitude.

IV

There came a morning when the sun shone angry and red through a dull, smoky haze.

"We're in for sandstorms," said Cameron.

They had scarcely covered a mile when a desert-wide, moaning, yellow wall of flying sand swooped down upon them. Seeking shelter in the lee of a rock, they waited, hoping the storm was only a squall, such as frequently whipped across the open places. The moan increased to a roar, and the dull red slowly dimmed, to disappear in the yellow pall, and the air grew thick and dark. Warren slipped the packs from the burros. Cameron feared the sandstorms had arrived some weeks ahead of their usual season.

The men covered their heads and patiently waited. The long hours dragged, and the storm increased in fury. Cameron and Warren wet scarfs with water from their canteens, and bound them round their faces, and then covered their heads. The steady, hollow bellow of flying sand went on. It flew so thickly that enough sifted down under the shelving rock to weight the blankets and almost bury the men. They were frequently compelled to shake off the sand to keep from being borne to the ground. And it was necessary to keep digging out the packs. The floor of their shelter gradually rose higher and higher. They tried to eat, and seemed to be grinding only sand between their teeth. They lost the count of time. They dared not sleep, for that would have meant being buried alive. They could only crouch close to the leaning rock, shake off the sand, blindly dig out their packs, and every moment gasp and cough and choke to fight suffocation.

The storm finally blew itself out. It left the prospectors heavy and stupid for want of sleep. Their burros had wandered away, or had been buried in the sand. Far as eye could reach the desert had marvelously changed; it was now a rippling sea of sand dunes. Away to the north rose the peak that was their only guiding mark. They headed toward it, carrying a shovel and part of their packs.

At noon the peak vanished in the shimmering glare of

the desert. The prospectors pushed on, guided by the sun. In every wash they tried for water. With the forked peach branch in his hands Warren always succeeded in locating water. They dug, but it lay too deep. At length, spent and sore, they fell and slept through that night and part of the next day. Then they succeeded in getting water, and quenched their thirst, and filled the canteens, and cooked a meal.

The burning day found them in an interminably wide plain, where there was no shelter from the fierce sun. The men were exceedingly careful with their water, though there was absolute necessity of drinking a little every hour. Late in the afternoon they came to a cañon that they believed was the lower end of the one in which they had last found water. For hours they traveled toward its head, and, long after night had set, found what they sought. Yielding to exhaustion, they slept, and next day were loath to leave the waterhole. Cool night spurred them on with canteens full and renewed strength.

Morning told Cameron that they had turned back miles into the desert, and it was desert new to him. The red sun, the increasing heat, and especially the variety and large size of the cactus plants warned Cameron that he had descended to a lower level. Mountain peaks loomed on all sides, some near, others distant; and one, a blue spur, splitting the glaring sky far to the north, Cameron thought he recognized as a landmark. The ascent toward it was heartbreaking, not in steepness, but in its league-and-league-long monotonous rise. Cameron knew there was only one hope—to make the water hold out and never stop to rest. Warren began to weaken. Often he had to halt. The burning white day passed, and likewise the night, with its white stars shining so pitilessly cold and bright.

Cameron measured the water in his canteen by its weight. Evaporation by heat consumed as much as he drank. During one of the rests, when he had wetted his parched mouth and throat, he found opportunity to pour a little water from his canteen into Warren's.

At first Cameron had curbed his restless activity to accommodate the pace of his elder comrade. But now he felt that he was losing something of his instinctive and passionate zeal to get out of the desert. The thought of water came to occupy his mind. He began to imagine that his last little store of water did not appreciably diminish. He knew he was not quite right in his mind regarding water; nevertheless, he felt this to be more of fact than fancy, and he began to ponder.

When next they rested he pretended to be in a kind of stupor; but he covertly watched Warren. The man appeared far gone, yet he had cunning. He cautiously took up Cameron's canteen and poured water into it from his own.

This troubled Cameron. The old irritation at not being able to thwart Warren returned to him. Cameron reflected, and concluded that he had been unwise not to expect this very thing. Then, as his comrade dropped into weary rest, he lifted both canteens. If there were any water in Warren's, it was only very little. Both men had been enduring the terrible desert thirst, concealing it, each giving his water to the other, and the sacrifice had been useless.

Instead of ministering to the parched throats of one or both, the water had evaporated. When Cameron made sure of this, he took one more drink, the last, and poured the little water left into Warren's canteen. He threw his own away.

Soon afterward Warren discovered the loss.

"Where's your canteen?" he asked.

"The heat was getting my water, so I drank what was left."

"My son!" said Warren.

The day opened for them in a red and green hell of rock and cactus. Like a flame the sun scorched and peeled

PROLOGUE

their faces. Warren went blind from the glare, and Cameron had to lead him. At last Warren plunged down, exhausted, in the shade of a ledge.

Cameron rested and waited, hopeless, with hot, weary eyes gazing down from the height where he sat. The ledge was the top step of a ragged gigantic stairway. Below stretched a sad, austere, and lonely valley. A dim, wide streak, lighter than the bordering gray, wound down the valley floor. Once a river had flowed there, leaving only a forlorn trace down the winding floor of this forlorn valley.

Movement on the part of Warren attracted Cameron's attention. Evidently the old prospector had recovered his sight and some of his strength. For he had arisen, and now began to walk along the arroyo bed with his forked peach branch held before him. He had clung to that precious bit of wood. Cameron considered the prospect for water hopeless, because he saw that the arroyo had once been a cañon, and had been filled with sands by desert winds. Warren, however, stopped in a deep pit, and, cutting his canteen in half, began to use one side of it as a scoop. He scooped out a wide hollow, so wide that Cameron was certain he had gone crazy. Cameron gently urged him to stop, and then forcibly tried to make him. But these efforts were futile. Warren worked with slow, ceaseless, methodical movement. He toiled for what seemed hours. Cameron, seeing the darkening, damp-ening sand, realized a wonderful possibility of water, and he plunged into the pit with the other half of the canteen. Then both men toiled, round and round the wide hole, down deeper and deeper. The sand grew moist, then wet. At the bottom of the deep pit the sand coarsened, gave place to gravel. Finally water welled in, a stronger vol-ume than Cameron ever remembered finding on the desert. It would soon fill the hole and run over. He marveled at the circumstance. The time was near the end of the dry season. Perhaps an underground stream flowed from the range behind down to the valley floor, and at this point came near to the surface. Cameron had heard of such desert miracles.

The finding of water revived Cameron's flagging hopes. But they were short-lived. Warren had spent himself utterly.

"I'm done. Don't linger," he whispered. "My son, go—go!"

Then he fell. Cameron dragged him out of the sand pit to a sheltered place under the ledge. While sitting beside the failing man Cameron discovered painted images on the wall. Often in the desert he had found these evidences of a prehistoric people. Then, from long habit, he picked up a piece of rock and examined it. Its weight made him closely scrutinize it. The color was a peculiar black. He scraped through the black rust to find a piece of gold. Around him lay scattered heaps of black pebbles and bits of black, weathered rock and pieces of broken ledge, and they showed gold.

"Warren! Look! See it! Feel it! Gold!"

But Warren had never cared, and now he was too blind to see.

"Go—go!" he whispered.

Cameron gazed down the gray reaches of that forlorn valley, and something within him that was neither intelligence nor emotion—something inscrutably strange—impelled him to promise.

Then Cameron built up stone monuments to mark his gold strike. That done, he tarried beside the unconscious Warren. Moments passed—grew into hours. Cameron still had strength left to make an effort to get out of the desert. But that same inscrutable something which had ordered his strange involuntary promise to Warren held him beside his fallen comrade. He watched the white sun turn to gold, and then to red, and sink behind mountains in the west. Twilight stole into the arroyo. It lingered, slowly turning to gloom. The vault of blue-

PROLOGUE

black lightened to the blinking of stars. Then fell the serene, silent, luminous desert night.

Cameron kept his vigil. As the long hours wore on he felt creep over him the comforting sense that he need not forever fight sleep. A wan glow flared behind the dark, uneven horizon, and a melancholy misshapen moon rose to make the white night one of shadows. Absolute silence claimed the desert. It was mute. Then that inscrutable something breathed to him, telling him when he was alone. He need not have looked at the dark, still face beside him.

Another face haunted Cameron's—a woman's face. It was there in the white moonlit shadows; it drifted in the darkness beyond; it softened, changed to that of a young girl, sweet, with the same dark, haunting eyes of her mother. Cameron prayed to that nameless thing within him, the spirit of something deep and mystical as life. He prayed to that nameless thing outside, of which the rocks and the sand, the spiked cactus and the ragged lava, the endless waste, with its vast star-fired mantle, were but atoms. He prayed for mercy to a woman—for happiness to her child. Both mother and daughter were close to him then. Time and distance were annihilated. He had faith—he saw into the future. The fateful threads of the past, so inextricably woven with his error, wound out their tragic length here in this forlorn desert.

Cameron then took a little tin box from his pocket, and, opening it, removed a folded certificate. He had kept a pen, and now he wrote something upon the paper, and in lieu of ink he wrote with blood. The moon afforded him enough light to see; and, having replaced the paper, he laid the little box upon a shelf of rock. It would remain there unaffected by dust, moisture, heat, time. How long had those painted images been there clear and sharp on the dry stone walls? There were no trails in that desert, and always there were incalculable changes. Cameron saw this mutable mood of nature—

21

the sands would fly and seep and carve and bury; the floods would dig and cut; the ledges would weather in the heat and rain; the avalanches would slide; the cactus seeds would roll in the wind to catch in a niche and split the soil with thirsty roots. Years would pass. Cameron seemed to see them, too; and likewise destiny leading a child down into this forlorn waste, where she would find love and fortune, and the grave of her father.

Cameron covered the dark, still face of his comrade from the light of the waning moon.

That action was the severing of his hold on realities. They fell away from him in final separation. Vaguely, dreamily he seemed to behold his soul. Night merged into gray day; and night came again, weird and dark. Then up out of the vast void of the desert, from the silence and illimitableness, trooped his phantoms of peace. Majestically they formed around him, marshaling and mustering in ceremonious state, and moved to lay upon him their passionless serenity.

I

R ICHARD GALE reflected that his sojourn in the
    West had been what his disgusted father had pre-
dicted—idling here and dreaming there, with no objective
point or purpose.

It was reflection such as this, only more serious and
perhaps somewhat desperate, that had brought Gale
down to the border. For some time the newspapers had
been printing news of Mexican revolution, guerrilla warfare, United States cavalry patrolling the international
line, American cowboys fighting with the rebels, and wild
stories of bold raiders and bandits. Regarding these
rumors Gale was skeptical. But as opportunity, and adventure, too, had apparently given him a wide berth in
Montana, Wyoming, Colorado, he had struck southwest
for the Arizona border, where he hoped to see some
stirring life. He did not care very much what happened.
Months of futile wandering in the hope of finding a place
where he fitted had inclined Richard to his father's
opinion.

It was after dark one evening in early October when
Richard arrived in Casita. He was surprised to find that
it was evidently a town of importance. There was a
jostling, jabbering, sombreroed crowd of Mexicans around
the railroad station. He felt as if he were in a foreign
country. After a while he saw several men of his nation-
ality, one of whom he engaged to carry his luggage to a
hotel. They walked up a wide, well-lighted street lined
with buildings in which were bright windows. Of the

many people encountered by Gale most were Mexicans. His guide explained that the smaller half of Casita lay in Arizona, the other half in Mexico, and of several thousand inhabitants the majority belonged on the southern side of the street, which was the boundary line. He also said that rebels had entered the town that day, causing a good deal of excitement.

Gale was almost at the end of his financial resources, which fact occasioned him to turn away from a pretentious hotel and ask his guide for a cheaper lodging-house. When this was found, a sight of the loungers in the office, and also a desire for comfort, persuaded Gale to change his traveling-clothes for rough outing garb and boots.

"Well, I'm almost broke," he soliloquized, thoughtfully. "The governor said I wouldn't make any money. He's right—so far. And he said I'd be coming home beaten. There he's wrong. I've got a hunch that something 'll happen to me in this Greaser town."

He went out into a wide, whitewashed, high-ceiled corridor, and from that into an immense room which, but for pool tables, bar, and benches, would have been like a courtyard. The floor was cobblestoned, the walls were of adobe, and the large windows opened like doors. A blue cloud of smoke filled the place. Gale heard the click of pool balls and the clink of glasses along the crowded bar. Bare-legged, sandal-footed Mexicans in white rubbed shoulders with Mexicans mantled in black and red. There were others in tight-fitting blue uniforms with gold fringe or tassels at the shoulders. These men wore belts with heavy, bone-handled guns, and evidently were the rurales, or native policemen. There were black-bearded, coarse-visaged Americans, some gambling round the little tables, others drinking. The pool tables were the center of a noisy crowd of younger men, several of whom were unsteady on their feet. There were khaki-clad cavalrymen strutting in and out.

OLD FRIENDS

At one end of the room, somewhat apart from the general melee, was a group of six men round a little table, four of whom were seated, the other two standing. These last two drew a second glance from Gale. The sharp-featured, bronzed faces and piercing eyes, the tall, slender, loosely jointed bodies, the quiet, easy, reckless air that seemed to be a part of the men—these things would plainly have stamped them as cowboys without the buckled sombreros, the colored scarfs, the high-topped, high-heeled boots with great silver-roweled spurs. Gale did not fail to note, also, that these cowboys wore guns, and this fact was rather a shock to his idea of the modern West. It caused him to give some credence to the rumors of fighting along the border, and he felt a thrill.

He satisfied his hunger in a restaurant adjoining, and as he stepped back into the saloon a man wearing a military cape jostled him. Apologies from both were instant. Gale was moving on when the other stopped short as if startled, and, leaning forward, exclaimed:

"Dick Gale?"

"You've got me," replied Gale, in surprise. "But I don't know you."

He could not see the stranger's face, because it was wholly shaded by a wide-brimmed hat pulled well down.

"By Jove! It's Dick! If this isn't great! Don't you know me?"

"I've heard your voice somewhere," replied Gale. "Maybe I'll recognize you if you come out from under that bonnet."

For answer the man, suddenly manifesting thought of himself, hurriedly drew Gale into the restaurant, where he thrust back his hat to disclose a handsome, sunburned face.

"George Thorne! So help me—"

" 'S-s-ssh. You needn't yell," interrupted the other, as he met Gale's outstretched hand. There was a close, hard, straining grip. "I must **not be** recognized here.

There are reasons. I'll explain in a minute. Say, but it's fine to see you! Five years, Dick, five years since I saw you run down University Field and spread-eagle the whole Wisconsin football team."

"Don't recollect that," replied Dick, laughing. "George, I'll bet you I'm gladder to see you than you are to see me. It seems so long. You went into the army, didn't you?"

"I did. I'm here now with the Ninth Cavalry. But —never mind me. What're you doing way down here? Say, I just noticed your togs. Dick, you can't be going in for mining or ranching, not in this God-forsaken desert?"

"On the square, George, I don't know any more why I'm here than—than you know."

"Well, that beats me!" ejaculated Thorne, sitting back in his chair, amaze and concern in his expression. "What the devil's wrong? Your old man's got too much money for you ever to be up against it. Dick, you couldn't have gone to the bad?"

A tide of emotion surged over Gale. How good it was to meet a friend—some one to whom to talk! He had never appreciated his loneliness until that moment.

"George, how I ever drifted down here I don't know. I didn't exactly quarrel with the governor. But—damn it, Dad hurt me—shamed me, and I dug out for the West. It was this way. After leaving college I tried to please him by tackling one thing after another that he set me to do. On the square, I had no head for business. I made a mess of everything. The governor got sore. He kept ramming the harpoon into me till I just couldn't stand it. What little ability I possessed deserted me when I got my back up, and there you are. Dad and I had a rather uncomfortable half hour. When I quit— when I told him straight out that I was going West to fare for myself, why, it wouldn't have been so tough if he hadn't laughed at me. He called me a rich man's son—an idle, easy-going, spineless swell. He said I didn't even have character enough to be out and out bad. He said I didn't have sense enough to marry one of the nice girls in my sister's crowd. He said I couldn't earn a dollar—that I'd starve out West, and couldn't get back home unless I sent to him for money. He said he didn't believe I could fight—could really make a fight for anything under the sun. Oh—he—he shot it into me, all right."

Dick dropped his head upon his hands, somewhat ashamed of the smarting dimness in his eyes. He had not meant to say so much. Yet what a relief to let out that long-congested burden!

"Fight!" cried Thorne, hotly. "What's ailing him? Didn't they call you Biff Gale in college? Dick, you were one of the best men Stagg ever developed. I heard him say so—that you were the fastest one-hundred-and-seventy-five-pound man he'd ever trained, the hardest to stop."

"The governor didn't count football," said Dick. "He didn't mean that kind of a fight. When I left home I don't think I had an idea what was wrong with me. But George, I think I know now. I was a rich man's son—spoiled, dependent, absolutely ignorant of the value of money. I haven't yet discovered any earning capacity in me. I seem to be unable to do anything with my hands. That's the trouble. But I'm at the end of my tether now. And I'm going to punch cattle or be a miner, or do some real stunt—like joining the rebels."

"Aha! I thought you'd spring that last one on me," declared Thorne, wagging his head. "Well, you just forget it. Say, old boy, there's something doing in Mexico. The United States in general doesn't realize it. But across that line there are crazy revolutionists, ill-paid soldiers, guerrilla leaders, raiders, robbers, outlaws, bandits galore, starving peons by the thousand, girls and women in terror. Mexico is like some of her volcanoes —ready to erupt fire and hell! Don't make the awful mistake of joining the rebel forces. Americans are hated by Mexicans of the lower class—the fighting class, both rebel and federal. Half the time these crazy Greasers are on one side, then on the other. If you didn't starve or get shot in ambush, or die of thirst, some Greaser would knife you in the back for your belt buckle or boots. There are a good many Americans with the rebels eastward toward Agua Prieta and Juarez. Orozco is operating in Chihuahua, and I guess he has some idea of warfare. But this is Sonora, a mountainous desert, the home of the slave and the Yaqui. There's unorganized revolt everywhere. The American miners and ranchers, those who could get away, have fled across into the States, leaving property. Those who couldn't or wouldn't come must fight for their lives, are fighting now."

"That's bad," said Gale. "It's news to me. Why doesn't the government take action, do something?"

"Afraid of international complications. Don't want to offend the Maderists, or be criticized by jealous foreign nations. It's a delicate situation, Dick. The Washington officials know the gravity of it, you can bet. But the United States in general is in the dark, and the army—well, you ought to hear the inside talk back at San Antonio. We're patrolling the boundary line. We're making a grand bluff. I could tell you of a dozen instances where cavalry should have pursued raiders on the other side of the line. But we won't do it. The officers are a grouchy lot these days. You see, of course, what significance would attach to United States cavalry going into Mexican territory. There would simply be hell. My own colonel is the sorest man on the job. We're all sore. It's like sitting on a powder magazine. We can't keep the rebels and raiders from crossing the line. Yet we don't fight. My commission expires soon. I'll be discharged in three months. You can bet I'm glad for more reasons than I've mentioned."

Thorne was evidently laboring under strong, suppressed excitement. His face showed pale under the tan, and his

eyes gleamed with a dark fire. Occasionally his delight
at meeting, talking with Gale, dominated the other emotions, but not for long. He had seated himself at a table
near one of the doorlike windows leading into the street,
and every little while he would glance sharply out. Also
he kept consulting his watch.

These details gradually grew upon Gale as Thorne talked.

"George, it strikes me that you're upset," said Dick,
presently. "I seem to remember you as a cool-headed
fellow whom nothing could disturb. Has the army
changed you?"

Thorne laughed. It was a laugh with a strange, high
note. It was reckless—it hinted of exaltation. He rose
abruptly; he gave the waiter money to go for drinks; he
looked into the saloon, and then into the street. On this
side of the house there was a porch opening on a plaza
with trees and shrubbery and branches. Thorne peered
out one window, then another. His actions were rapid.
Returning to the table, he put his hands upon it and
leaned over to look closely into Gale's face.

"I'm away from camp without leave," he said.

"Isn't that a serious offense?" asked Dick.

"Serious? For me, if I'm discovered, it means ruin.
There are rebels in town. Any moment we might have
trouble. I ought to be ready for duty—within call. If
I'm discovered it means arrest. That means delay—the
failure of my plans—ruin."

Gale was silenced by his friend's intensity. Thorne
bent over closer with his dark eyes searchingly bright.

"We were old pals—once?"

"Surely," replied Dick.

"What would you say, Dick Gale, if I told you that
you're the one man I'd rather have had come along than
any other at this crisis of my life?"

The earnest gaze, the passionate voice with its deep
tremor drew Dick upright, thrilling and eager, conscious
of strange, unfamiliar impetuosity.

"Thorne, I should say I was glad to be the fellow," replied Dick.

Their hands locked for a moment, and they sat down again with heads close over the table.

"Listen," began Thorne, in low, swift whisper, "a few days, a week ago—it seems like a year!—I was of some assistance to refugees fleeing from Mexico into the States. They were all women, and one of them was dressed as a nun. Quite by accident I saw her face. It was that of a beautiful girl. I observed she kept aloof from the others. I suspected a disguise, and, when opportunity afforded, spoke to her, offered my services. She replied to my poor efforts at Spanish in fluent English. She had fled in terror from her home, some place down in Sinaloa. Rebels are active there. Her father was captured and held for ransom. When the ransom was paid the rebels killed him. The leader of these rebels was a bandit named Rojas. Long before the revolution began he had been feared by people of class—loved by the peons. Bandits are worshiped by the peons. All of the famous bandits have robbed the rich and given to the poor. Rojas saw the daughter, made off with her. But she contrived to bribe her guards, and escaped almost immediately before any harm befell her. She hid among friends. Rojas nearly tore down the town in his efforts to find her. Then she disguised herself, and traveled by horseback, stage, and train to Casita.

"Her story fascinated me, and that one fleeting glimpse I had of her face I couldn't forget. She had no friends here, no money. She knew Rojas was trailing her. This talk I had with her was at the railroad station, where all was bustle and confusion. No one noticed us, so I thought. I advised her to remove the disguise of a nun before she left the waiting-room. And I got a boy to guide her. But he fetched her to this house. I had promised to come in the evening to talk over the situation with her.

OLD FRIENDS

"I found her, Dick, and when I saw her—I went stark, staring, raving mad over her. She is the most beautiful, wonderful girl I ever saw. Her name is Mercedes Castañeda, and she belongs to one of the old wealthy Spanish families. She has lived abroad and in Havana. She speaks French as well as English. She is—but I must be brief.

"Dick, think, think! With Mercedes also it was love at first sight. My plan is to marry her and get her farther to the interior, away from the border. It may not be easy. She's watched. So am I. It was impossible to see her without the women of this house knowing. At first, perhaps, they had only curiosity—an itch to gossip. But the last two days there has been a change. Since last night there's some powerful influence at work. Oh, these Mexicans are subtle, mysterious! After all, they are Spaniards. They work in secret, in the dark. They are dominated first by religion, then by gold, then by passion for a woman. Rojas must have got word to his friends here; yesterday his gang of cutthroat rebels arrived, and to-day he came. When I learned that, I took my chance and left camp; I hunted up a priest. He promised to come here. It's time he's due. But I'm afraid he'll be stopped."

"Thorne, why don't you take the girl and get married without waiting, without running these risks?" said Dick.

"I fear it's too late now. I should have done that last night. You see, we're over the line—"

"Are we in Mexican territory now?" queried Gale, sharply.

"I guess yes, old boy. That's what complicates it. Rojas and his rebels have Casita in their hands. But Rojas without his rebels would be able to stop me, get the girl, and make for his mountain haunts. If Mercedes is really watched—if her identity is known, which I am sure is the case—we couldn't get far from this house before I'd be knifed and she seized."

"Good Heavens! Thorne, can that sort of thing happen less than a stone's throw from the United States line?" asked Gale, incredulously.

"It *can* happen, and don't you forget it. You don't seem to realize the power these guerrilla leaders, these rebel captains, and particularly these bandits, exercise over the mass of Mexicans. A bandit is a man of honor in Mexico. He is feared, envied, loved. In the hearts of the people he stands next to the national idol—the bull-fighter, the matador. The race has a wild, barbarian, bloody strain. Take Quinteros, for instance. He was a peon, a slave. He became a famous bandit. At the outbreak of the revolution he proclaimed himself a leader, and with a band of followers he devastated whole counties. The opposition to federal forces was only a blind to rob and riot and carry off women. The motto of this man and his followers was: 'Let us enjoy ourselves while we may!'

"There are other bandits besides Quinteros, not so famous or such great leaders, but just as bloodthirsty. I've seen Rojas. He's a handsome, bold, sneering devil, vainer than any peacock. He decks himself in gold lace and silver trappings, in all the finery he can steal. He was one of the rebels who helped sack Sinaloa and carry off half a million in money and valuables. Rojas spends gold like he spills blood. But he is chiefly famous for abducting women. The peon girls consider it an honor to be ridden off with. Rojas has shown a penchant for girls of the better class."

Thorne wiped the perspiration from his pale face and bent a dark gaze out of the window before he resumed his talk.

"Consider what the position of Mercedes really is. I can't get any help from our side of the line. If so, I don't know where. The population on that side is mostly Mexican, absolutely in sympathy with whatever actuates those on this side. The whole caboodle of Greasers on both sides belong to the class in sympathy with the rebels, the class that secretly respects men like Rojas, and hates an aristocrat like Mercedes. They would conspire to throw her into his power. Rojas can turn all the hidden underground influences to his ends. Unless I thwart him he'll get Mercedes as easily as he can light a cigarette. But I'll kill him or some of his gang or her before I let him get her.... This is the situation, old friend. I've little time to spare. I face arrest for desertion. Rojas is in town. I think I was followed to this hotel. The priest has betrayed me or has been stopped. Mercedes is here alone, waiting, absolutely dependent upon me to save her from—from.... She's the sweetest, loveliest girl!.... In a few moments—sooner or later there'll be hell here! Dick, are you with me?"

Dick Gale drew a long, deep breath. A coldness, a lethargy, and indifference that had weighed upon him for months had passed out of his being. On the instant he could not speak, but his hand closed powerfully upon his friend's. Thorne's face changed wonderfully, the distress, the fear, the appeal all vanishing in a smile of passionate gratefulness.

Then Dick's gaze, attracted by some slight sound, shot over his friend's shoulder to see a face at the window—a handsome, bold, sneering face, with glittering dark eyes that flashed in sinister intentness.

Dick stiffened in his seat. Thorne, with sudden clenching of hands, wheeled toward the window.

"Rojas!" he whispered.

MERCEDES CASTAÑEDA

THE dark face vanished. Dick Gale heard footsteps and the tinkle of spurs. He strode to the window, and was in time to see a Mexican swagger into the front door of the saloon. Dick had only a glimpse; but in that he saw a huge black sombrero with a gaudy band, the back of a short, tight-fitting jacket, a heavy pearl-handled gun swinging with a fringe of sash, and close-fitting trousers spreading wide at the bottom. There were men passing in the street, also several Mexicans lounging against the hitching-rail at the curb.

"Did you see him? Where did he go?" whispered Thorne, as he joined Gale. "Those Greasers out there with the cartridge belts crossed over their breasts—they are rebels."

"I think he went into the saloon," replied Dick. "He had a gun, but for all I can see the Greasers out there are unarmed."

"Never believe it! There! Look, Dick! That fellow's a guard, though he seems so unconcerned. See, he has a short carbine, almost concealed.....There's another Greaser farther down the path. I'm afraid Rojas has the house spotted."

"If we could only be sure."

"I'm sure, Dick. Let's cross the hall; I want to see how it looks from the other side of the house."

Gale followed Thorne out of the restaurant into the high-ceiled corridor which evidently divided the hotel, opening into the street and running back to a patio. A few dim, yellow lamps flickered. A Mexican with a blanket round his shoulders stood in the front entrance. Back toward the patio there were sounds of boots on the stone floor. Shadows flitted across that end of the corridor. Thorne entered a huge chamber which was even more poorly lighted than the hall. It contained a table littered with papers, a few high-backed chairs, a couple of couches, and was evidently a parlor.

"Mercedes has been meeting me here," said Thorne. "At this hour she comes every moment or so to the head of the stairs there, and if I am here she comes down. Mostly there are people in this room a little later. We go out into the plaza. It faces the dark side of the house, and that's the place I must slip out with her if there's any chance at all to get away."

They peered out of the open window. The plaza was gloomy, and at first glance apparently deserted. In a moment, however, Gale made out a slow-pacing dark form on the path. Farther down there was another. No particular keenness was required to see in these forms a sentinel-like stealthiness.

Gripping Gale's arm, Thorne pulled back from the window.

"You saw them," he whispered. "It's just as I feared. Rojas has the place surrounded. I should have taken Mercedes away. But I had no time—no chance! I'm bound!....There's Mercedes now! My God!....Dick, think—think if there's a way to get her out of this trap!"

Gale turned as his friend went down the room. In the dim light at the head of the stairs stood the slim, muffled figure of a woman. When she saw Thorne she flew noiselessly down the stairway to him. He caught her in his arms. Then she spoke softly, brokenly, in a low, swift voice. It was a mingling of incoherent Spanish and English; but to Gale it was mellow, deep, unutterably tender, a voice full of joy, fear, passion, hope, and love.

Upon Gale it had an unaccountable effect. He found himself thrilling, wondering.

Thorne led the girl to the center of the room, under the light where Gale stood. She had raised a white hand, holding a black-lace mantilla half aside. Dick saw a small, dark head, proudly held, an oval face half hidden, white as a flower, and magnificent black eyes.

Then Thorne spoke.

"Mercedes—Dick Gale, an old friend—the best friend I ever had."

She swept the mantilla back over her head, disclosing a lovely face, strange and striking to Gale in its pride and fire, its intensity.

"Señor Gale—ah! I cannot speak my happiness. His friend!"

"Yes, Mercedes; my friend and yours," said Thorne, speaking rapidly. "We'll have need of him. Dear, there's bad news and no time to break it gently. The priest did not come. He must have been detained. And listen—be brave, dear Mercedes—Rojas is here!"

She uttered an inarticulate cry, the poignant terror of which shook Gale's nerve, and swayed as if she would faint. Thorne caught her, and in husky voice importuned her to bear up.

"My darling! For God's sake don't faint—don't go to pieces! We'd be lost! We've got a chance. We'll think of something. Be strong! Fight!"

It was plain to Gale that Thorne was distracted. He scarcely knew what he was saying. Pale and shaking, he clasped Mercedes to him. Her terror had struck him helpless. It was so intense—it was so full of horrible certainty of what fate awaited her.

She cried out in Spanish, beseeching him; and as he shook his head, she changed to English:

"Señor, my lover, I will be strong—I will fight—I will obey. But swear by my Virgin, if need be to save me from Rojas—you will kill me!"

36

"Mercedes! Yes, I'll swear," he replied, hoarsely. "I know—I'd rather have you dead than— But don't give up. Rojas can't be sure of you, or he wouldn't wait. He's in there. He's got his men there—all round us. But he hesitates. A beast like Rojas doesn't stand idle for nothing. I tell you we've a chance. Dick, here, will think of something. We'll slip away. Then he'll take you somewhere. Only—speak to him—show him you won't weaken. Mercedes, this is more than love and happiness for us. It's life or death."

She became quiet, and slowly recovered control of herself.

Suddenly she wheeled to face Gale with proud dark eyes, tragic sweetness of appeal, an exquisite grace.

"Señor, you are an American. You cannot know the Spanish blood—the peon bandit's hate and cruelty. I wish to die before Rojas's hand touches me. If he takes me alive, then the hour, the little day that my life lasts afterward will be torture—torture of hell. If I live two days his brutal men will have me. If I live three, the dogs of his camp....Señor, have you a sister whom you love? Help Señor Thorne to save me. He is a soldier. He is bound. He must not betray his honor, his duty, for me....Ah, you two splendid Americans—so big, so strong, so fierce! What is that little black half-breed slave Rojas to such men? Rojas is a coward. Now, let me waste no more precious time. I am ready. I will be brave."

She came close to Gale, holding out her white hands, a woman all fire and soul and passion. To Gale she was wonderful. His heart leaped. As he bent over her hands and kissed them he seemed to feel himself renewed, remade.

"Señorita," he said, "I am happy to be your servant. I can conceive of no greater pleasure than giving the service you require."

"And what is that?" inquired Thorne, hurriedly.

"That of incapacitating Señor Rojas for to-night, and perhaps several nights to come," replied Gale.

"Dick, what will you do?" asked Thorne, now in alarm.

"I'll make a row in that saloon," returned Dick, bluntly. "I'll start something. I'll rush Rojas and his crowd. I'll—"

"Lord, no; you mustn't, Dick—you'll be knifed!" cried Thorne. He was in distress, yet his eyes were shining.

"I'll take a chance. Maybe I can surprise that slow Greaser bunch and get away before they know what's happened.....You be ready watching at the window. When the row starts those fellows out there in the plaza will run into the saloon. Then you slip out, go straight through the plaza down the street. It's a dark street, I remember. I'll catch up with you before you get far."

Thorne gasped, but did not say a word. Mercedes leaned against him, her white hands now at her breast, her great eyes watching Gale as he went out.

In the corridor Gale stopped long enough to pull on a pair of heavy gloves, to muss his hair, and disarrange his collar. Then he stepped into the restaurant, went through, and halted in the door leading into the saloon. His five feet eleven inches and one hundred and eighty pounds were more noticeable there, and it was part of his plan to attract attention to himself. No one, however, appeared to notice him. The pool-players were noisily intent on their game, the same crowd of motley-robed Mexicans hung over the reeking bar. Gale's roving glance soon fixed upon the man he took to be Rojas. He recognized the huge, high-peaked, black sombrero with its ornamented band. The Mexican's face was turned aside. He was in earnest, excited colloquy with a dozen or more comrades, most of whom were sitting round a table. They were listening, talking, drinking. The fact that they wore cartridge belts crossed over their breasts satisfied Gale that these were the rebels. He had noted the belts of the Mexicans outside, who were apparently guards. A waiter brought more drinks to this group at the table, and this caused the leader to turn so Gale could see his face. It was indeed the sinister, sneering face of the bandit Rojas. Gale gazed at the man with curiosity. He was under medium height, and striking in appearance only because of his dandified dress and evil visage. He wore a lace scarf, a tight, bright-buttoned jacket, a buckskin vest embroidered in red, a sash and belt joined by an enormous silver clasp. Gale saw again the pearl-handled gun swinging at the bandit's hip. Jewels flashed in his scarf. There were gold rings in his ears and diamonds on his fingers.

Gale became conscious of an inward fire that threatened to overrun his coolness. Other emotions harried his self-control. It seemed as if sight of the man liberated or created a devil in Gale. And at the bottom of his feelings there seemed to be a wonder at himself, a strange satisfaction for the something that had come to him.

He stepped out of the doorway, down the couple of steps to the floor of the saloon, and he staggered a little, simulating drunkenness. He fell over the pool tables, jostled Mexicans at the bar, laughed like a maudlin fool, and, with his hat slouched down, crowded here and there. Presently his eye caught sight of the group of cowboys whom he had before noticed with such interest.

They were still in a corner somewhat isolated. With fertile mind working, Gale lurched over to them. He remembered his many unsuccessful attempts to get acquainted with cowboys. If he were to get any help from these silent aloof rangers it must be by striking fire from them in one swift stroke. Planting himself squarely before the two tall cowboys who were standing, he looked straight into their lean, bronzed faces. He spared a full moment for that keen, cool gaze before he spoke.

"I'm not drunk. I'm throwing a bluff, and I mean to start a rough house. I'm going to rush that damned bandit Rojas. It's to save a girl—to give her lover, who is my friend, a chance to escape with her. She's in the house. Rojas is here to get her. When I start a row my friend will try to slip out with her. Every door and window is watched. I've got to raise hell to draw the guards in.....Well, you're my countrymen. We're in Mexico. A beautiful girl's honor and life are at stake. Now, gentlemen, watch me!"

One cowboy's eyes narrowed, blinking a little, and his lean jaw dropped; the other's hard face rippled with a fleeting smile.

Gale backed away, and his pulse leaped when he saw the two cowboys, as if with one purpose, slowly stride after him. Then Gale swerved, staggering along, brushed against the tables, kicked over the empty chairs. He passed Rojas and his gang, and out of the tail of his eye saw that the bandit was watching him, waving his hands and talking fiercely. The hum of the many voices grew louder, and when Dick lurched against a table, overturning it and spilling glasses into the laps of several Mexicans, there arose a shrill cry. He had succeeded in attracting attention; almost every face turned his way. One of the insulted men, a little tawny fellow, leaped up to confront Gale, and in a frenzy screamed a volley of Spanish, of which Gale distinguished "Gringo!" The Mexican stamped and made a threatening move with his right hand. Dick swung his leg and with a swift side kick knocked the fellow's feet from under him, whirling him down with a thud.

The action was performed so suddenly, so adroitly, it made the Mexican such a weakling, so like a tumbled tenpin, that the shrill jabbering hushed. Gale knew this to be the significant moment.

Wheeling, he rushed at Rojas. It was his old line-breaking plunge. Neither Rojas nor his men had time to move. The black-skinned bandit's face turned a dirty white; his jaw dropped; he would have shrieked if Gale had not hit him. The blow swept him backward against his men. Then Gale's heavy body, swiftly following with the momentum of that rush, struck the little group of rebels. They went down with table and chairs in a sliding crash.

Gale, carried by his plunge, went with them. Like a cat he landed on top. As he rose his powerful hands fastened on Rojas. He jerked the little bandit off the tangled pile of struggling, yelling men, and, swinging him with terrific force, let go his hold. Rojas slid along the floor, knocking over tables and chairs. Gale bounded back, dragged Rojas up, handling him as if he were a limp sack.

A shot rang out above the yells. Gale heard the jingle of breaking glass. The room darkened perceptibly. He flashed a glance backward. The two cowboys were between him and the crowd of frantic rebels. One cowboy held two guns low down, level in front of him. The other had his gun raised and aimed. On the instant it spouted red and white. With the crack came the crashing of glass, another darkening shade over the room. With a cry Gale slung the bleeding Rojas from him. The bandit struck a table, toppled over it, fell, and lay prone.

Another shot made the room full of moving shadows, with light only back of the bar. A white-clad figure rushed at Gale. He tripped the man, but had to kick hard to disengage himself from grasping hands. Another figure closed in on Gale. This one was dark, swift. A blade glinted—described a circle aloft. Simultaneously with a close, red flash the knife wavered; the man wielding it stumbled backward. In the din Gale did not hear a report, but the Mexican's fall was significant. Then pandemonium broke loose. The din became a roar. Gale heard shots that sounded like dull spats in the distance. The big lamp behind the bar seemingly split, then sputtered and went out, leaving the room in darkness.

Gale leaped toward the restaurant door, which was outlined faintly by the yellow light within. Right and left he pushed the groping men who jostled with him. He vaulted a pool table, sent tables and chairs flying, and gained the door, to be the first of a wedging mob to squeeze through. One sweep of his arm knocked the restaurant lamp from its stand; and he ran out, leaving darkness behind him. A few bounds took him into the parlor. It was deserted. Thorne had gotten away with Mercedes!

It was then Gale slowed up. For the space of perhaps sixty seconds he had been moving with startling velocity. He peered cautiously out into the plaza. The paths, the benches, the shady places under the trees contained no skulking men. He ran out, keeping to the shade, and did not go into the path till he was halfway through the plaza. Under a street lamp at the far end of the path he thought he saw two dark figures. He ran faster, and soon reached the street. The uproar back in the hotel began to diminish, or else he was getting out of hearing. The few people he saw close at hand were all coming his way, and only the foremost showed any excitement. Gale walked swiftly, peering ahead for two figures. Presently he saw them—one tall, wearing a cape; the other slight, mantled. Gale drew a sharp breath of relief. Thorne and Mercedes were not far ahead.

From time to time Thorne looked back. He strode swiftly, almost carrying Mercedes, who clung closely to him. She, too, looked back. Once Gale saw her white face flash in the light of a street lamp. He began to overhaul them; and soon, when the last lamp had been passed and the street was dark, he ventured a whistle. Thorne heard it, for he turned, whistled a low reply, and went on. Not for some distance beyond, where the street ended in open country, did they halt to wait. The desert began here. Gale felt the soft sand under his feet and saw the grotesque forms of cactus. Then he came up with the fugitives.

"Dick! Are you—all right?" panted Thorne, grasping Gale.

"I'm—out of breath—but—O. K.," replied Gale.

"Good! Good!" choked Thorne. "I was scared—helpless.....Dick, it worked splendidly. We had no trouble. What on earth did you do?"

"I made the row, all right," said Dick.

"Good Heavens! It was like a row I once heard made by a mob. But the shots, Dick—were they at you? They paralyzed me. Then the yells. What happened? Those guards of Rojas ran round in front at the first shot. Tell me what happened."

"While I was rushing Rojas a couple of cowboys shot out the lamplights. A Mexican who pulled a knife on me got hurt, I guess. Then I think there was some shooting from the rebels after the room was dark."

"Rushing Rojas?" queried Thorne, leaning close to Dick. His voice was thrilling, exultant, deep with a joy that yet needed confirmation. "What did you do to him?"

"I handed him one off side, tackled, then tried a forward pass," replied Dick, lightly speaking the football vernacular so familiar to Thorne.

Thorne leaned closer, his fine face showing fierce and corded in the starlight. "Tell me straight," he demanded, in thick voice.

Gale then divined something of the suffering Thorne had undergone—something of the hot, wild, vengeful passion of a lover who must have brutal truth.

It stilled Dick's lighter mood, and he was about to reply when Mercedes pressed close to him, touched his hands, looked up into his face with wonderful eyes. He thought he would not soon forget their beauty—the shadow of pain that had been, the hope dawning so fugitively.

"Dear lady," said Gale, with voice not wholly steady, "Rojas himself will hound you no more to-night, nor for many nights."

She seemed to shake, to thrill, to rise with the intelligence. She pressed his hand close over her heaving breast. Gale felt the quick throb of her heart.

"Señor! Señor Dick!" she cried. Then her voice failed. But her hands flew up; quick as a flash she raised her face—kissed him. Then she turned and with a sob fell into Thorne's arms.

There ensued a silence broken only by Mercedes's sobbing. Gale walked some paces away. If he were not stunned, he certainly was agitated. The strange, sweet fire of that girl's lips remained with him. On the spur of the moment he imagined he had a jealousy of Thorne. But presently this passed. It was only that he had been deeply moved—stirred to the depths during the last hour—had become conscious of the awakening of a spirit. What remained with him now was the splendid glow of gladness that he had been of service to Thorne. And by the intensity of Mercedes's abandon of relief and gratitude he measured her agony of terror and the fate he had spared her.

"Dick, Dick, come here!" called Thorne, softly. "Let's pull ourselves together now. We've got a problem yet. What to do? Where to go? How to get any place? We don't dare risk the station—the corrals where Mexicans hire out horses. We're on good old U. S. ground this minute, but we're not out of danger."

As he paused, evidently hoping for a suggestion from Gale, the silence was broken by the clear, ringing peal of a bugle. Thorne gave a violent start. Then he bent over, listening. The beautiful notes of the bugle floated out of the darkness, clearer, sharper, faster.

"It's a call, Dick! It's a call!" he cried.

Gale had no answer to make. Mercedes stood as if stricken. The bugle call ended. From a distance another faintly pealed. There were other sounds too remote to recognize. Then scattering shots rattled out.

"Dick, the rebels are fighting somebody," burst out

Thorne, excitedly. "The little federal garrison still holds its stand. Perhaps it is attacked again. Anyway, there's something doing over the line. Maybe the crazy Greasers are firing on our camp. We've feared it—in the dark.... And here I am, away without leave—practically a deserter!"

"Go back! Go back, before you're too late!" cried Mercedes.

"Better make tracks, Thorne," added Gale. "It can't help our predicament for you to be arrested. I'll take care of Mercedes."

"No, no, no," replied Thorne. "I can get away—avoid arrest."

"That'd be all right for the immediate present. But it's not best for the future. George, a deserter is a deserter!....Better hurry. Leave the girl to me till tomorrow."

Mercedes embraced her lover, begged him to go. Thorne wavered.

"Dick, I'm up against it," he said. "You're right. If only I can run back in time. But, oh, I hate to leave her! Old fellow, you've saved her! I already owe you everlasting gratitude. Keep out of Casita, Dick The U. S. side might be safe, but I'm afraid to trust it at night. Go out in the desert, up in the mountains, in some safe place. Then come to me in camp. We'll plan. I'll have to confide in Colonel Weede. Maybe he'll help us. Hide her from the rebels—that's all."

He wrung Dick's hand, clasped Mercedes tightly in his arms, kissed her, and murmured low over her, then released her to rush off into the darkness. He disappeared in the gloom. The sound of his dull footfalls gradually died away.

For a moment the desert silence oppressed Gale. He was unaccustomed to such strange stillness. There was a low stir of sand, a rustle of stiff leaves in the wind. How white the stars burned! Then a coyote barked, to be bayed by a dog. Gale realized that he was between the edge of an unknown desert and the edge of a hostile town. He had to choose the desert, because, though he had no doubt that in Casita there were many Americans who might befriend him, he could not chance the risks of seeking them at night.

He felt a slight touch on his arm, felt it move down, felt Mercedes slip a trembling cold little hand into his. Dick looked at her. She seemed a white-faced girl now, with staring, frightened black eyes that flashed up at him. If the loneliness, the silence, the desert, the unknown dangers of the night affected him, what must they be to this hunted, driven girl? Gale's heart swelled. He was alone with her. He had no weapon, no money, no food, no drink, no covering, nothing except his two hands. He had absolutely no knowledge of the desert, of the direction or whereabouts of the boundary line between the republics; he did not know where to find the railroad, or any road or trail, or whether or not there were towns near or far. It was a critical, desperate situation. He thought first of the girl, and groaned in spirit, prayed that it would be given him to save her. When he remembered himself it was with the stunning consciousness that he could conceive of no situation which he would have exchanged for this one—where fortune had set him a perilous task of loyalty to a friend, to a helpless girl.

"Señor, señor!" suddenly whispered Mercedes, clinging to him. "Listen! I hear horses coming!"

III

UNEASY and startled, Gale listened and, hearing nothing, wondered if Mercedes's fears had not worked upon her imagination. He felt a trembling seize her, and he held her hands tightly.

"You were mistaken, I guess," he whispered.

"No, no, señor."

Dick turned his ear to the soft wind. Presently he heard, or imagined he heard, low beats. Like the first faint, far-off beats of a drumming grouse, they recalled to him the Illinois forests of his boyhood. In a moment he was certain the sounds were the padlike steps of hoofs in yielding sand. The regular tramp was not that of grazing horses.

On the instant, made cautious and stealthy by alarm, Gale drew Mercedes deeper into the gloom of the shrubbery. Sharp pricks from thorns warned him that he was pressing into a cactus growth, and he protected Mercedes as best he could. She was shaking as one with a severe chill. She breathed with little hurried pants and leaned upon him almost in collapse. Gale ground his teeth in helpless rage at the girl's fate. If she had not been beautiful she might still have been free and happy in her home. What a strange world to live in—how unfair was fate!

The sounds of hoofbeats grew louder. Gale made out a dark moving mass against a background of dull gray. There was a line of horses. He could not discern whether or not all the horses carried riders. The murmur of a voice struck his ear—then a low laugh. It made him

47

tingle, for it sounded American. Eagerly he listened. There was an interval when only the hoofbeats could be heard.

"It shore was, Laddy, it shore was," came a voice out of the darkness. "Rough house! Laddy, since wire fences drove us out of Texas we ain't seen the like of that. An' we never had such a call."

"Call? It was a burnin' roast," replied another voice. "I felt low down. He vamoosed some sudden, an' I hope he an' his friends shook the dust of Casita. That's a rotten town, Jim."

Gale jumped up in joy. What luck! The speakers were none other than the two cowboys whom he had accosted in the Mexican hotel.

"Hold on, fellows," he called out, and strode into the road.

The horses snorted and stamped. Then followed swift rustling sounds—a clinking of spurs, then silence. The figures loomed clearer in the gloom. Gale saw five or six horses, two with riders, and one other, at least, carrying a pack. When Gale got within fifteen feet of the group the foremost horseman said:

"I reckon that's close enough, stranger."

Something in the cowboy's hand glinted darkly bright in the starlight.

"You'd recognize me, if it wasn't so dark," replied Gale, halting. "I spoke to you a little while ago—in the saloon back there."

"Come over an' let's see you," said the cowboy, curtly.

Gale advanced till he was close to the horse. The cowboy leaned over the saddle and peered into Gale's face. Then, without a word, he sheathed the gun and held out his hand. Gale met a grip of steel that warmed his blood. The other cowboy got off his nervous, spirited horse and threw the bridle. He, too, peered closely into Gale's face.

A FLIGHT INTO THE DESERT

"My name's Ladd," he said. "Reckon I'm some glad to meet you again."

Gale felt another grip as hard and strong as the other had been. He realized he had found friends who belonged to a class of men whom he had despaired of ever knowing.

"Gale—Dick Gale is my name," he began, swiftly. "I dropped into Casita to-night hardly knowing where I was. A boy took me to that hotel. There I met an old friend whom I had not seen for years. He belongs to the cavalry stationed here. He had befriended a Spanish girl—fallen in love with her. Rojas had killed this girl's father—tried to abduct her.....You know what took place at the hotel. Gentlemen, if it's ever possible, I'll show you how I appreciate what you did for me there. I got away, found my friend with the girl. We hurried out here beyond the edge of the town. Then Thorne had to make a break for camp. We heard bugle calls, shots, and he was away without leave. That left the girl with me. I don't know what to do. Thorne swears Casita is no place for Mercedes at night."

"The girl ain't no peon, no common Greaser?" interrupted Ladd.

"No. Her name is Castañeda. She belongs to an old Spanish family, once rich and influential."

"Reckoned as much," replied the cowboy. "There's more than Rojas's wantin' to kidnap a pretty girl. Shore he does that every day or so. Must be somethin' political or feelin' against class. Well, Casita ain't no place for your friend's girl at night or day, or any time. Shore, there's Americans who'd take her in an' fight for her, if necessary. But it ain't wise to risk that. Lash, what do you say?"

"It's been gettin' hotter round this Greaser corral for some weeks," replied the other cowboy. "If that two-bit of a garrison surrenders, there's no tellin' what 'll happen. Orozco is headin' west from Agua Prieta with

49

his guerrillas. Campo is burnin' bridges an' tearin' up the railroad south of Nogales. Then there's all these bandits callin' themselves revolutionists just for an excuse to steal, burn, kill, an' ride off with women. It's plain facts, Laddy, an' bein' across the U. S. line a few inches or so don't make no hell of a difference. My advice is, don't let Miss Castañeda ever set foot in Casita again."

"Looks like you've shore spoke sense," said Ladd. "I reckon, Gale, you an' the girl ought to come with us. Casita shore would be a little warm for us to-morrow. We didn't kill anybody, but I shot a Greaser's arm off, an' Lash strained friendly relations by destroyin' property. We know people who'll take care of the señorita till your friend can come for her."

Dick warmly spoke his gratefulness, and, inexpressibly relieved and happy for Mercedes, he went toward the clump of cactus where he had left her. She stood erect, waiting, and, dark as it was, he could tell she had lost the terror that had so shaken her.

"Señor Gale, you are my good angel," she said, tremulously.

"I've been lucky to fall in with these men, and I'm glad with all my heart," he replied. "Come."

He led her into the road up to the cowboys, who now stood bareheaded in the starlight. They seemed shy, and Lash was silent while Ladd made embarrassed, unintelligible reply to Mercedes's thanks.

There were five horses—two saddled, two packed and the remaining one carried only a blanket. Ladd shortened the stirrups on his mount, and helped Mercedes up into the saddle. From the way she settled herself and took the few restive prances of the mettlesome horse Gale judged that she could ride. Lash urged Gale to take his horse. But this Gale refused to do.

"I'll walk," he said "I'm used to walking. I know cowboys are not."

They tried again to persuade him, without avail. Then

A FLIGHT INTO THE DESERT

Ladd started off, riding bareback. Mercedes fell in behind, with Gale walking beside her. The two pack animals came next, and Lash brought up the rear.

Once started with protection assured for the girl and a real objective point in view, Gale relaxed from the tense strain he had been laboring under. How glad he would have been to acquaint Thorne with their good fortune! Later, of course, there would be some way to get word to the cavalryman. But till then what torments his friend would suffer!

It seemed to Dick that a very long time had elapsed since he stepped off the train; and one by one he went over every detail of incident which had occurred between that arrival and the present moment. Strange as the facts were, he had no doubts. He realized that before that night he had never known the deeps of wrath undisturbed in him; had never conceived even a passing idea that it was possible for him to try to kill a man. His right hand was swollen stiff, so sore that he could scarcely close it. His knuckles were bruised and bleeding, and ached with a sharp pain. Considering the thickness of his heavy glove, Gale was of the opinion that so to bruise his hand he must have struck Rojas a powerful blow. He remembered that for him to give or take a blow had been nothing. This blow to Rojas, however, had been a different matter. The hot wrath which had been his motive was not puzzling; but the effect on him after he had cooled off, a subtle difference, something puzzled and eluded him. The more it baffled him the more he pondered. All those wandering months of his had been filled with dissatisfaction, yet he had been too apathetic to understand himself. So he had not been much of a person to try. Perhaps it had not been the blow to Rojas any more than other things that had wrought some change in him.

His meeting with Thorne; the wonderful black eyes of a Spanish girl; her appeal to him; the hate inspired by

51

Rojas, and the rush, the blow, the action; sight of Thorne and Mercedes hurrying safely away; the girl's hands pressing his to her heaving breast; the sweet fire of her kiss; the fact of her being alone with him, dependent upon him—all these things Gale turned over and over in his mind, only to fail of any definite conclusion as to which had affected him so remarkably, or to tell what had really happened to him.

Had he fallen in love with Thorne's sweetheart? The idea came in a flash. Was he, all in an instant, and by one of those incomprehensible reversals of character, jealous of his friend? Dick was almost afraid to look up at Mercedes. Still he forced himself to do so, and as it chanced Mercedes was looking down at him. Somehow the light was better, and he clearly saw her white face, her black and starry eyes, her perfect mouth. With a quick, graceful impulsiveness she put her hand upon his shoulder. Like her appearance, the action was new, strange, striking to Gale; but it brought home suddenly to him the nature of gratitude and affection in a girl of her blood. It was sweet and sisterly. He knew then that he had not fallen in love with her. The feeling that was akin to jealousy seemed to be of the beautiful something for which Mercedes stood in Thorne's life. Gale then grasped the bewildering possibilities, the infinite wonder of what a girl could mean to a man.

The other haunting intimations of change seemed to be elusively blended with sensations—the heat and thrill of action, the sense of something done and more to do, the utter vanishing of an old weary hunt for he knew not what. Maybe it had been a hunt for work, for energy, for spirit, for love, for his real self. Whatever it might be, there appeared to be now some hope of finding it.

The desert began to lighten. Gray openings in the border of shrubby growths changed to paler hue. The road could be seen some rods ahead, and it had become a stony descent down, steadily down. Dark, ridged backs of mountains bounded the horizon, and all seemed near at hand, hemming in the plain. In the east a white glow grew brighter and brighter, reaching up to a line of cloud, defined sharply below by a rugged notched range. Presently a silver circle rose behind the black mountain, and the gloom of the desert underwent a transformation. From a gray mantle it changed to a transparent haze. The moon was rising.

"Señor, I am cold," said Mercedes.

Dick had been carrying his coat upon his arm. He had felt warm, even hot, and had imagined that the steady walk had occasioned it. But his skin was cool. The heat came from an inward burning. He stopped the horse and raised the coat up, and helped Mercedes put it on.

"I should have thought of you," he said. "But I seemed to feel warm....The coat's a little large; we might wrap it around you twice."

Mercedes smiled and lightly thanked him in Spanish. The flash of mood was in direct contrast to the appealing, passionate, and tragic states in which he had successively viewed her; and it gave him a vivid impression of what vivacity and charm she might possess under happy conditions. He was about to start when he observed that Ladd had halted and was peering ahead in evident caution. Mercedes's horse began to stamp impatiently, raised his ears and head, and acted as if he was about to neigh.

A warning "hist" from Ladd bade Dick put a quieting hand on the horse. Lash came noiselessly forward to join his companion. The two then listened and watched.

An uneasy yet thrilling stir ran through Gale's veins. This scene was not fancy. These men of the ranges had heard or seen or scented danger. It was all real, as tangible and sure as the touch of Mercedes's hand upon his arm. Probably for her the night had terrors beyond Gale's power to comprehend. He looked down into the

desert, and would have felt no surprise at anything hidden
away among the bristling cactus, the dark, winding
arroyos, the shadowed rocks with their moonlit tips, the
ragged plain leading to the black bold mountains. The
wind appeared to blow softly, with an almost imperceptible moan, over the desert. That was a new sound to
Gale. But he heard nothing more.

Presently Lash went to the rear and Ladd started
ahead. The progress now, however, was considerably
slower, not owing to a bad road—for that became better
—but probably owing to caution exercised by the cowboy
guide. At the end of a half hour this marked deliberation changed, and the horses followed Ladd's at a gait
that put Gale to his best walking-paces.

Meanwhile the moon soared high above the black
corrugated peaks. The gray, the gloom, the shadow
whitened. The clearing of the dark foreground appeared
to lift a distant veil and show endless aisles of desert
reaching down between dim horizon-bounding ranges.

Gale gazed abroad, knowing that as this night was the
first time for him to awake to consciousness of a vague,
wonderful other self, so it was one wherein he began to be
aware of an encroaching presence of physical things—
the immensity of the star-studded sky, the soaring moon,
the bleak, mysterious mountains, and limitless slope, and
plain, and ridge, and valley. These things in all their
magnificence had not been unnoticed by him before; only
now they spoke a different meaning. A voice that he
had never heard called him to see, to feel the vast hard
externals of heaven and earth, all that represented the
open, the free, silence and solitude and space.

Once more his thoughts, like his steps, were halted by
Ladd's actions. The cowboy reined in his horse, listened
a moment, then swung down out of the saddle. He
raised a cautioning hand to the others, then slipped into
the gloom and disappeared. Gale marked that the halt
had been made in a ridged and cut-up pass between low

mesas. He could see the columns of cactus standing out black against the moon-white sky. The horses were evidently tiring, for they showed no impatience. Gale heard their panting breaths, and also the bark of some animal—a dog or a coyote. It sounded like a dog, and this led Gale to wonder if there was any house near at hand. To the right, up under the ledges some distance away, stood two square black objects, too uniform, he thought, to be rocks. While he was peering at them, uncertain what to think, the shrill whistle of a horse pealed out, to be followed by the rattling of hoofs on hard stone. Then a dog barked. At the same moment that Ladd hurriedly appeared in the road a light shone out and danced before one of the square black objects.

"Keep close an' don't make no noise," he whispered, and led his horse at right angles off the road.

Gale followed, leading Mercedes's horse. As he turned he observed that Lash also had dismounted.

To keep closely at Ladd's heels without brushing the cactus or stumbling over rocks and depressions was a task Gale found impossible. After he had been stabbed several times by the bayonetlike spikes, which seemed invisible, the matter of caution became equally one of self-preservation. Both the cowboys, Dick had observed, wore leather chaps. It was no easy matter to lead a spirited horse through the dark, winding lanes walled by thorns. Mercedes's horse often balked and had to be coaxed and carefully guided. Dick concluded that Ladd was making a wide detour. The position of certain stars grown familiar during the march veered round from one side to another. Dick saw that the travel was fast, but by no means noiseless. The pack animals at times crashed and ripped through the narrow places. It seemed to Gale that any one within a mile could have heard these sounds. From the tops of knolls or ridges he looked back, trying to locate the mesas where the light had danced and the dog had barked alarm. He could not distinguish these two rocky eminences from among many rising in the background.

Presently Ladd led out into a wider lane that appeared to run straight. The cowboy mounted his horse, and this fact convinced Gale that they had circled back to the road. The march proceeded then once more at a good, steady, silent walk. When Dick consulted his watch he was amazed to see the hour was still early. How much had happened in little time! He now began to be aware that the night was growing colder; and, strange to him, he felt something damp that in a country he knew he would have recognized as dew. He had not been aware there was dew on the desert. The wind blew stronger, the stars shone whiter, the sky grew darker, and the moon climbed toward the zenith. The road stretched level for miles, then crossed arroyos and ridges, wound between mounds of broken ruined rock, found a level again, and then began a long ascent. Dick asked Mercedes if she was cold, and she answered that she was, speaking especially of her feet, which were growing numb. Then she asked to be helped down to walk awhile. At first she was cold and lame, and accepted the helping hand Dick proffered. After a little, however, she recovered and went on without assistance. Dick could scarcely believe his eyes, as from time to time he stole a sidelong glance at this silent girl, who walked with lithe and rapid stride. She was wrapped in his long coat, yet it did not hide her slender grace. He could not see her face, which was concealed by the black mantle.

A low-spoken word from Ladd recalled Gale to the question of surroundings and of possible dangers. Ladd had halted a few yards ahead. They had reached the summit of what was evidently a high ridge which sloped with much greater steepness on the far side. It was only after a few more forward steps, however, that Dick could see down the slope. Then full in view flashed a bright campfire around which clustered a group of dark figures. They were encamped in a wide arroyo, where horses could be seen grazing in black patches of grass between clusters of trees. A second look at the campers told Gale they were Mexicans. At this moment Lash came forward to join Ladd, and the two spent a long, uninterrupted moment studying the arroyo. A hoarse laugh, faint yet distinct, floated up on the cool wind.

"Well, Laddy, what 'r you makin' of that outfit?" inquired Lash, speaking softly.

"Same as any of them raider outfits," replied Ladd. "They're across the line for beef. But they'll run off any good stock. As hoss thieves these rebels have got 'em all beat. That outfit is waitin' till it's late. There's a ranch up the arroyo."

Gale heard the first speaker curse under his breath.

"Sure, I feel the same," said Ladd. "But we've got a girl an' the young man to look after, not to mention our pack outfit. An' we're huntin' for a job, not a fight, old hoss. Keep on your chaps!"

"Nothin' to it but head south for the Rio Forlorn."

"You're talkin' sense now, Jim. I wish we'd headed that way long ago. But it ain't strange I'd want to travel away from the border, thinkin' of the girl. Jim, we can't go round this Greaser outfit an' strike the road again. Too rough. So we'll have to give up gettin' to San Felipe."

"Perhaps it's just as well, Laddy. Rio Forlorn is on the border line, but it's country where these rebels ain't been yet."

"Wait till they learn of the oasis an' Beldin's hosses!" exclaimed Laddy. "I'm not anticipatin' peace anywhere along the border, Jim. But we can't go ahead; we can't go back."

"What 'll we do, Laddy? It's a hike to Beldin's ranch. An' if we get there in daylight some Greaser will see the girl before Beldin' can hide her. It'll get talked about. The news 'll travel to Casita like sage balls before the wind."

"Shore we won't ride into Rio Forlorn in the daytime. Let's slip the packs, Jim. We can hide them off in the cactus an' come back after them. With the young man ridin' we—"

The whispering was interrupted by a loud ringing neigh that whistled up from the arroyo. One of the horses had scented the travelers on the ridge top. The indifference of the Mexicans changed to attention.

Ladd and Lash turned back and led the horses into the first opening on the south side of the road. There was nothing more said at the moment, and manifestly the cowboys were in a hurry. Gale had to run in the open places to keep up. When they did stop it was welcome to Gale, for he had begun to fall behind.

The packs were slipped, securely tied and hidden in a mesquite clump. Ladd strapped a blanket around one of the horses. His next move was to take off his chaps.

"Gale, you're wearin' boots, an' by liftin' your feet you can beat the cactus," he whispered. "But the—the—Miss Castañeda, she'll be torn all to pieces unless she puts these on. Please tell her—an' hurry."

Dick took the chaps, and, going up to Mercedes, he explained the situation. She laughed, evidently at his embarrassed earnestness, and slipped out of the saddle.

"Señor, chapparejos and I are not strangers," she said.

Deftly and promptly she equipped herself, and then Gale helped her into the saddle, called to her horse, and started off. Lash directed Gale to mount the other saddled horse and go next.

Dick had not ridden a hundred yards behind the trotting leaders before he had sundry painful encounters with reaching cactus arms. The horse missed these by a narrow margin. Dick's knees appeared to be in line, and it became necessary for him to lift them high and let his boots take the onslaught of the spikes. He was at home in the saddle, and the accomplishment was about the only one he possessed that had been of any advantage during his sojourn in the West.

Ladd pursued a zigzag course southward across the desert, trotting down the aisles, cantering in wide, bare patches, walking through the clumps of cacti. The desert seemed all of a sameness to Dick—a wilderness of rocks and jagged growths hemmed in by lowering ranges, always looking close, yet never growing any nearer. The moon slanted back toward the west, losing its white radiance, and the gloom of the earlier evening began to creep into the washes and to darken under the mesas. By and by Ladd entered an arroyo, and here the travelers turned and twisted with the meanderings of a dry stream bed. At the head of the cañon they had to take once more to the rougher ground. Always it led down, always it grew rougher, more rolling, with wider bare spaces, always the black ranges loomed close.

Gale became chilled to the bone, and his clothes were damp and cold. His knees smarted from the wounds of the poisoned thorns, and his right hand was either swollen stiff or too numb to move. Moreover, he was tiring. The excitement, the long walk, the miles on miles of jolting trot—these had wearied him. Mercedes must be made of steel, he thought, to stand all that she had been subjected to and yet, when the stars were paling and dawn perhaps not far away, stay in the saddle.

So Dick Gale rode on, drowsier for each mile, and more and more giving the horse a choice of ground. Sometimes a prod from a murderous spine roused Dick. A grayness had blotted out the waning moon in the west and the clear, dark, starry sky overhead. Once when Gale, thinking to fight his weariness, raised his head, he saw that one of the horses in the lead was riderless. Ladd was carrying Mercedes. Dick marveled that her collapse had not come sooner. Another time, rousing himself again, he imagined they were now on a good hard road.

It seemed that hours passed, though he knew only little time had elapsed, when once more he threw off the spell of weariness. He heard a dog bark. Tall trees lined the open lane down which he was riding. Presently in the gray gloom he saw low, square houses with flat roofs. Ladd turned off to the left down another lane, gloomy between trees. Every few rods there was one of the squat houses. This lane opened into wider, lighter space. The cold air bore a sweet perfume—whether of flowers or fruit Dick could not tell. Ladd rode on for perhaps a quarter of a mile, though it seemed interminably long to Dick. A grove of trees loomed dark in the gray of morning. Ladd entered it and was lost in the shade. Dick rode on among trees. Presently he heard voices, and soon another house, low and flat like the others, but so long he could not see the farther end, stood up blacker than the trees. As he dismounted, cramped and sore, he could scarcely stand. Lash came alongside. He spoke, and some one with a big, hearty voice replied to him. Then it seemed to Dick that he was led into blackness like pitch, where, presently, he felt blankets thrown on him, and then his drowsy faculties faded

IV

WHEN Dick opened his eyes a flood of golden sunshine streamed in at the open window under which
he lay. His first thought was one of blank wonder as to
where in the world he happened to be. The room was
large, square, adobe-walled. It was littered with saddles,
harness, blankets. Upon the floor was a bed spread out
upon a tarpaulin. Probably this was where some one
had slept. The sight of huge dusty spurs, a gun belt
with sheath and gun, and a pair of leather chaps bristling
with broken cactus thorns recalled to Dick the cowboys,
the ride, Mercedes, and the whole strange adventure that
had brought him there.

He did not recollect having removed his boots; indeed,
upon second thought, he knew he had not done so. But
there they stood upon the floor. Ladd and Lash must
have taken them off when he was so exhausted and sleepy
that he could not tell what was happening. He felt a dead
weight of complete lassitude, and he did not want to
move. A sudden pain in his hand caused him to hold
it up. It was black and blue, swollen to almost twice
its normal size, and stiff as a board. The knuckles were
skinned and crusted with dry blood. Dick soliloquized
that it was the worst-looking hand he had seen since
football days, and that it would inconvenience him for
some time.

A warm, dry, fragrant breeze came through the window. Dick caught again the sweet smell of flowers or
fruit. He heard the fluttering of leaves, the murmur of

running water, the twittering of birds, then the sound of approaching footsteps and voices. The door at the far end of the room was open. Through it he saw poles of peeled wood upholding a porch roof, a bench, rose bushes in bloom, grass, and beyond these bright-green foliage of trees.

"He shore was sleepin' when I looked in an hour ago," said a voice that Dick recognized as Ladd's.

"Let him sleep," came the reply in deep, good-natured tones. "Mrs. B. says the girl's never moved. Must have been a tough ride for them both. Forty miles through cactus!"

"Young Gale hoofed darn near half the way," replied Ladd. "We tried to make him ride one of our hosses. If we had, we'd never got here. A walk like that'd killed me an' Jim."

"Well, Laddy, I'm right down glad to see you boys, and I'll do all I can for the young couple," said the other. "But I'm doing some worry here; don't mistake me."

"About your stock?"

"I've got only a few head of cattle at the oasis now. I'm worrying some, mostly about my horses. The U. S. is doing some worrying, too, don't mistake me. The rebels have worked west and north as far as Casita. There are no cavalrymen along the line beyond Casita, and there can't be. It's practically waterless desert. But these rebels are desert men. They could cross the line beyond the Rio Forlorn and smuggle arms into Mexico. Of course, my job is to keep tab on Chinese and Japs trying to get into the U. S. from Magdalena Bay. But I'm supposed to patrol the border line. I'm going to hire some rangers. Now, I'm not so afraid of being shot up, though out in this lonely place there's danger of it; what I'm afraid of most is losing that bunch of horses. If any rebels come this far, or if they ever hear of my horses, they're going to raid me. You know what those guerrilla

Mexicans will do for horses. They're crazy on horse flesh. They know fine horses. They breed the finest in the world. So I don't sleep nights any more."

"Reckon me an' Jim might as well tie up with you for a spell, Beldin'. We've been ridin' up an' down Arizona tryin' to keep out of sight of wire fences."

"Laddy, it's open enough around Forlorn River to satisfy even an old-time cowpuncher like you," laughed Belding. "I'd take your staying on as some favor, don't mistake me. Perhaps I can persuade the young man Gale to take a job with me."

"That's shore likely. He said he had no money, no friends. An' if a scrapper's all you're lookin' for he'll do," replied Ladd, with a dry chuckle.

"Mrs. B. will throw some broncho capers round this ranch when she hears I'm going to hire a stranger."

"Why?"

"Well, there's Nell— And you said this Gale was a young American. My wife will be scared to death for fear Nell will fall in love with him."

Laddy choked off a laugh, then evidently slapped his knee or Belding's, for there was a resounding smack.

"He's a fine-spoken, good-looking chap, you said?" went on Belding.

"Shore he is," said Laddy, warmly. "What do you say, Jim?"

By this time Dick Gale's ears began to burn and he was trying to make himself deaf when he wanted to hear every little word.

"Husky young fellow, nice voice, steady, clear eyes, kinda proud, I thought, an' some handsome, he was," replied Jim Lash.

"Maybe I ought to think twice before taking a stranger into my family," said Belding, seriously. "Well, I guess he's all right, Laddy, being the cavalryman's friend. No bum or lunger? He must be all right?"

"Bum? Lunger? Say, didn't I tell you I shook hands

with this boy an' was plumb glad to meet him?" demanded Laddy, with considerable heat. Manifestly he had been affronted. "Tom Beldin', he's a gentleman, an' he could lick you in—in half a second. How about that, Jim?"

"Less time," replied Lash. "Tom, here's my stand. Young Gale can have my hoss, my gun, anythin' of mine."

"Aw, I didn't mean to insult you, boys, don't mistake me," said Belding. "Course he's all right."

The object of this conversation lay quiet upon his bed, thrilling and amazed at being so championed by the cowboys, delighted with Belding's idea of employing him, and much amused with the quaint seriousness of the three.

"How's the young man?" called a woman's voice. It was kind and mellow and earnest.

Gale heard footsteps on flagstones.

"He's asleep yet, wife," replied Belding. "Guess he was pretty much knocked out. . . . I'll close the door there so we won't wake him."

There were slow, soft steps, then the door softly closed. But the fact scarcely made a perceptible difference in the sound of the voices outside.

"Laddy and Jim are going to stay," went on Belding. "It'll be like the old Panhandle days a little. I'm powerful glad to have the boys, Nellie. You know I meant to send to Casita to ask them. We'll see some trouble before the revolution is ended. I think I'll make this young man Gale an offer."

"He isn't a cowboy?" asked Mrs. Belding, quickly.

"No."

"Shore he'd make a darn good one," put in Laddy.

"What is he? Who is he? Where did he come from? Surely you must be—"

"Laddy swears he's all right," interrupted the husband. "That's enough reference for me. Isn't it enough for you?"

"Humph! Laddy knows a lot about young men, now

64

doesn't he, especially strangers from the East? . . . Tom, you must be careful!"

"Wife, I'm only too glad to have a nervy young chap come along. What sense is there in your objection, if Jim and Laddy stick up for him?"

"But, Tom—he'll fall in love with Nell!" protested Mrs. Belding.

"Well, wouldn't that be regular? Doesn't every man who comes along fall in love with Nell? Hasn't it always happened? When she was a schoolgirl in Kansas didn't it happen? Didn't she have a hundred moon-eyed ninnies after her in Texas? I've had some peace out here in the desert, except when a Greaser or a prospector or a Yaqui would come along. Then same old story—in love with Nell!"

"But, Tom, Nell might fall in love with this young man!" exclaimed the wife, in distress.

"Laddy, Jim, didn't I tell you?" cried Belding. "I knew she'd say that. . . . My dear wife, I would be simply overcome with joy if Nell did fall in love once. Real good and hard! She's wilder than any antelope out there on the desert. Nell's nearly twenty now, and so far as we know she's never cared a rap for any fellow. And she's just as gay and full of the devil as she was at fourteen. Nell's as good and lovable as she is pretty, but I'm afraid she'll never grow into a woman while we live out in this lonely land. And you've always hated towns where there was a chance for the girl—just because you were afraid she'd fall in love. You've always been strange, even silly, about that. I've done my best for Nell—loved her as if she were my own daughter. I've changed many business plans to suit your whims. There are rough times ahead, maybe. I need men. I'll hire this chap Gale if he'll stay. Let Nell take her chance with him, just as she'll have to take chances with men when we get out of the desert. She'll be all the better for it."

"I hope Laddy's not mistaken in his opinion of this newcomer," replied Mrs. Belding, with a sigh of resignation.

"Shore I never made a mistake in my life figger'n' people," said Laddy, stoutly.

"Yes, you have, Laddy," replied Mrs. Belding. "You're wrong about Tom. . . . Well, supper is to be got. That young man and the girl will be starved. I'll go in now. If Nell happens around don't—don't flatter her, Laddy, like you did at dinner. Don't make her think of her looks."

Dick heard Mrs. Belding walk away.

"Shore she's powerful particular about that girl," observed Laddy. "Say, Tom, Nell knows she's pretty, doesn't she?"

"She's liable to find it out unless you shut up, Laddy. When you visited us out here some weeks ago, you kept paying cowboy compliments to her."

"An' it's your idee that cowboy compliments are plumb bad for girls?"

"Downright bad, Laddy, so my wife says."

"I'll be darned if I believe any girl can be hurt by a little sweet talk. It pleases 'em. . . . But say, Beldin', speaking of looks, have you got a peek yet at the Spanish girl?"

"Not in the light."

"Well, neither have I in daytime. I had enough by moonlight. Nell is some on looks, but I'm regretful passin' the ribbon to the lady from Mex. Jim, where are you?"

"My money's on Nell," replied Lash. "Gimme a girl with flesh an' color, an' blue eyes a-laughin'. Miss Castañeda is some peach, I'll not gainsay. But her face seemed too white. An' when she flashed those eyes on me, I thought I was shot! When she stood up there at first, thankin' us, I felt as if a—a princess was round somewhere. Now, Nell is kiddish an' sweet an'—"

"Chop it," interrupted Belding. "Here comes Nell now."

Dick's tingling ears took in the pattering of light footsteps, the rush of some one running.

"Here you are," cried a sweet, happy voice. "Dad, the Señorita is perfectly lovely. I've been peeping at her. She sleeps like—like death. She's so white. Oh, I hope she won't be ill."

"Shore she's only played out," said Laddy. "But she had spunk while it lasted. . . . I was just arguin' with Jim an' Tom about Miss Castañeda."

"Gracious! Why, she's beautiful. I never saw any one so beautiful. . . . How strange and sad, that about her! Tell me more, Laddy. You promised. I'm dying to know. I never hear anything in this awful place. Didn't you say the Señorita had a sweetheart?"

"Shore I did."

"And he's a cavalryman?"

"Yes."

"Is he the young man who came with you?"

"Nope. That fellow's the one who saved the girl from Rojas."

"Ah! Where is he, Laddy?"

"He's in there asleep."

"Is he hurt?"

"I reckon not. He walked about fifteen miles."

"Is he—nice, Laddy?"

"Shore."

"What is he like?"

"Well, I'm not long acquainted, never saw him by day, but I was some tolerable took with him. An' Jim here, Jim says the young man can have his gun an' his hoss."

"Wonderful! Laddy, what on earth did this stranger do to win you cowboys in just one night?"

"I'll shore have to tell you. Me an' Jim was watchin' a game of cards in the Del Sol saloon in Casita. That's across the line. We had acquaintances—four fellows from the Cross Bar outfit, where we worked a while back. This Del Sol is a billiard hall, saloon, restaurant, an' the like. An' it was full of Greasers. Some of Campo's rebels were there drinkin' an' playin' games. Then pretty soon in come Rojas with some of his outfit. They were packin' guns an' kept to themselves off to one side. I didn't give them a second look till Jim said he reckoned there was somethin' in the wind. Then, careless-like, I began to peek at Rojas. They call Rojas the 'dandy rebel,' an' he shore looked the part. It made me sick to see him in all that lace an' glitter, knowin' him to be the cutthroat robber he is. It's no oncommon sight to see excited Greasers. They're all crazy. But this bandit was shore some agitated. He kept his men in a tight bunch round a table. He talked an' waved his hands. He was actually shakin'. His eyes had a wild glare. Now I figgered that trouble was brewin', most likely for the little Casita garrison. People seemed to think Campo an' Rojas would join forces to oust the federals. Jim thought Rojas' excitement was at the hatchin' of some plot. Anyway, we didn't join no card games, an' without pretendin' to, we was some watchful.

"A little while afterward I seen a fellow standin' in the restaurant door. He was a young American dressed in corduroys an' boots, like a prospector. You know it's no onusual fact to see prospectors in these parts. What made me think twice about this one was how big he seemed, how he filled up that door. He looked round the saloon, an' when he spotted Rojas he sorta jerked up. Then he pulled his slouch hat lopsided an' began to stagger down, down the steps. First off I made shore he was drunk. But I remembered he didn't seem drunk before. It was some queer. So I watched that young man.

"He reeled around the room like a fellow who was drunker'n a lord. Nobody but me seemed to notice him. Then he began to stumble over pool-players an' get his feet tangled up in chairs an' bump against tables. He got some pretty hard looks. He came round our way, an' all of a sudden he seen us cowboys. He gave another start, like the one when he first seen Rojas, then he made for us. I tipped Jim off that somethin' was doin'.

"When he got close he straightened up, put back his slouch hat, an' looked at us. Then I saw his face. It sorta electrified yours truly. It was white, with veins standin' out an' eyes flamin'—a face of fury. I was plumb amazed, didn't know what to think. Then this queer young man shot some cool, polite words at me an' Jim.

"He was only bluffin' at bein' drunk—he meant to rush Rojas, to start a rough house. The bandit was after a girl. This girl was in the hotel, an' she was the sweetheart of a soldier, the young fellow's friend. The hotel was watched by Rojas's guards, an' the plan was to make a fuss an' get the girl away in the excitement. Well, Jim an' me got a hint of our bein' Americans—that cowboys generally had a name for loyalty to women. Then this amazin' chap—you can't imagine how scornful—said for me an' Jim to watch him.

"Before I could catch my breath an' figger out what he meant by 'rush' an' 'rough house' he had knocked over a table an' crowded some Greaser half off the map. One little funny man leaped up like a wild monkey an' began to screech. An' in another second he was in the air upside down. When he lit, he laid there. Then, quicker'n I can tell you, the young man dove at Rojas. Like a mad steer on the rampage he charged Rojas an' his men. The whole outfit went down—smash! I figgered then what 'rush' meant. The young fellow came up out of the pile with Rojas, an' just like I'd sling an empty sack along the floor he sent the bandit. But swift as that went he was on top of Rojas before the chairs an' tables had stopped rollin'.

"I woke up then, an' made for the center of the room,

Jim with me. I began to shoot out the lamps. Jim threwed his guns on the crazy rebels, an' I was afraid there'd be blood spilled before I could get the room dark. Bein' shore busy, I lost sight of the young fellow for a second or so, an' when I got an eye free for him I seen a Greaser about to knife him. Think I was some considerate of the Greaser by only shootin' his arm off. Then I cracked the last lamp, an' in the hullabaloo me an' Jim vamoosed.

"We made tracks for our hosses an' packs, an' was hittin' the San Felipe road when we run right plumb into the young man. Well, he said his name was Gale—Dick Gale. The girl was with him safe an' well; but her sweetheart, the soldier, bein' away without leave, had to go back sudden. There shore was some trouble, for Jim an' me heard shootin'. Gale said he had no money, no friends, was a stranger in a desert country; an' he was distracted to know how to help the girl. So me an' Jim started off with them for San Felipe, got switched, an' then we headed for the Rio Forlorn."

"Oh, I think he was perfectly splendid!" exclaimed the girl.

"Shore he was. Only, Nell, you can't lay no claim to bein' the original discoverer of that fact."

"But, Laddy, you haven't told me what he looks like."

At this juncture Dick Gale felt it absolutely impossible for him to play the eavesdropper any longer. Quietly he rolled out of bed. The voices still sounded close outside, and it was only by effort that he kept from further listening. Belding's kindly interest, Laddy's blunt and sincere cowboy eulogy, the girl's sweet eagerness and praise—these warmed Gale's heart. He had fallen among simple people, into whose lives the advent of an unknown man was welcome. He found himself in a singularly agitated mood. The excitement, the thrill, the difference felt in himself, experienced the preceding night, had extended on into his present. And the possibilities suggested by the conversation he had unwittingly overheard added sufficiently to the other feelings to put him into a peculiarly receptive state of mind. He was wild to be one of Belding's rangers. The idea of riding a horse in the open desert, with a dangerous duty to perform, seemed to strike him with an appealing force. Something within him went out to the cowboys, to this blunt and kind Belding. He was afraid to meet the girl. If every man who came along fell in love with this sweet-voiced Nell, then what hope had he to escape—now, when his whole inner awakening betokened a change of spirit, hope, a finding of real worth, real good, real power in himself? He did not understand wholly; yet he felt ready to ride, to fight, to love the desert, to love these outdoor men, to love a woman. That beautiful Spanish girl had spoken to something dead in him, and it had quickened to life. The sweet voice of an audacious, unseen girl warned him that presently a still more wonderful thing would happen to him.

Gale imagined he made noise enough as he clumsily pulled on his boots; yet the voices, split by a merry laugh, kept on murmuring outside the door. It was awkward for him, having only one hand available to lace up his boots. He looked out of the window. Evidently this was at the end of the house. There was a flagstone walk, beside which ran a ditch full of swift, muddy water. It made a pleasant sound. There were trees strange of form and color to him. He heard bees, birds, chickens, saw the red of roses and green of grass. Then he saw, close to the wall, a tub full of water, and a bench upon which lay basin, soap, towel, comb, and brush. The window was also a door, for under it there was a step.

Gale hesitated a moment, then went out. He stepped naturally, hoping and expecting that the cowboys would hear him. But nobody came. Awkwardly, with left hand, he washed his face. Upon a nail in the wall hung a little mirror, by the aid of which Dick combed and brushed his hair. He imagined he looked a most hag-

gard wretch. With that he faced forward, meaning to
go round the corner of the house to greet the cowboys
and these new-found friends.

Dick had taken but one step when he was halted by
laughter and the patter of light feet.

From close around the corner pealed out that sweet
voice. "Dad, you'll have your wish, and mama will
be wild!"

Dick saw a little foot sweep into view, a white dress,
then the swiftly moving form of a girl. She was looking
backward.

"Dad, I shall fall in love with your new ranger. I
will—I have—"

Then she plumped squarely into Dick's arms.

She started back violently.

Dick saw a fair face and dark-blue, audaciously flashing eyes. Swift as lightning their expression changed to
surprise, fear, wonder. For an instant they were level
with Dick's grave questioning. Suddenly, sweetly, she
blushed.

"Oh-h!" she faltered.

Then the blush turned to a scarlet fire. She whirled
past him, and like a white gleam was gone.

Dick became conscious of the quickened beating of his
heart. He experienced a singular exhilaration. That
moment had been the one for which he had been ripe,
the event upon which strange circumstances had been
rushing him.

With a couple of strides he turned the corner. Laddy
and Lash were there talking to a man of burly form.
Seen by day, both cowboys were gray-haired, red-skinned,
and weather-beaten, with lean, sharp features, and gray
eyes so much alike that they might have been brothers.

"Hello, there's the young fellow," spoke up the burly
man. "Mr. Gale, I'm glad to meet you. My name's
Belding."

His greeting was as warm as his handclasp was long and

hard. Gale saw a heavy man of medium height. His head was large and covered with grizzled locks. He wore a short-cropped mustache and chin beard. His skin was brown, and his dark eyes beamed with a genial light.

The cowboys were as cordial as if Dick had been their friend for years.

"Young man, did you run into anything as you came out?" asked Belding, with twinkling eyes.

"Why, yes; I met something white and swift flying by," replied Dick.

"Did she see you?" asked Laddy.

"I think so; but she didn't wait for me to introduce myself."

"That was Nell Burton, my girl—step-daughter, I should say," said Belding. "She's sure some whirlwind, as Laddy calls her. Come, let's go in and meet the wife."

The house was long, like a barracks, with porch extending all the way, and doors every dozen paces. When Dick was ushered into a sitting-room, he was amazed at the light and comfort. This room had two big windows and a door opening into a patio, where there were luxuriant grass, roses in bloom, and flowering trees. He heard a slow splashing of water.

In Mrs. Belding, Gale found a woman of noble proportions and striking appearance. Her hair was white. She had a strong, serious, well-lined face that bore haunting evidences of past beauty. The gaze she bent upon him was almost piercing in its intensity. Her greeting, which seemed to Dick rather slow in coming, was kind though not cordial. Gale's first thought, after he had thanked these good people for their hospitality, was to inquire about Mercedes. He was informed that the Spanish girl had awakened with a considerable fever and nervousness. When, however, her anxiety had been allayed and her thirst relieved, she had fallen asleep again. Mrs. Belding said the girl had suffered no great hardship, other than mental, and would very soon be rested and well.

"Now, Gale," said Belding, when his wife had excused herself to get supper, "the boys, Jim and Laddy, told me about you and the mix-up at Casita. I'll be glad to take care of the girl till it's safe for your soldier friend to get her out of the country. That won't be very soon, don't mistake me.... I don't want to seem over-curious about you—Laddy has interested me in you—and straight out I'd like to know what you propose to do now."

"I haven't any plans," replied Dick; and, taking the moment as propitious, he decided to speak frankly concerning himself. "I just drifted down here. My home is in Chicago. When I left school some years ago —I'm twenty-five now—I went to work for my father. He's—he has business interests there. I tried all kinds of inside jobs. I couldn't please my father. I guess I put no real heart in my work. The fact was I didn't know how to work. The governor and I didn't exactly quarrel; but he hurt my feelings, and I quit. Six months or more ago I came West, and have knocked about from Wyoming southwest to the border. I tried to find congenial work, but nothing came my way. To tell you frankly, Mr. Belding, I suppose I didn't much care. I believe, though, that all the time I didn't know what I wanted. I've learned—well, just lately—"

"What do you want to do?" interposed Belding.

"I want a man's job. I want to do things with my hands. I want action. I want to be outdoors."

Belding nodded his head as if he understood that, and he began to speak again, cut something short, then went on, hesitatingly:

"Gale—you could go home again—to the old man— it'd be all right?"

"Mr. Belding, there's nothing shady in my past. The governor would be glad to have me home. That's the only consolation I've got. But I'm not going. I'm broke. I won't be a tramp. And it's up to me to do something."

"How'd you like to be a border ranger?" asked Belding, laying a hand on Dick's knee. "Part of my job here is United States Inspector of Immigration. I've got that boundary line to patrol—to keep out Chinks and Japs. This revolution has added complications, and I'm looking for smugglers and raiders here any day. You'll not be hired by the U. S. You'll simply be my ranger, same as Laddy and Jim, who have promised to work for me. I'll pay you well, give you a room here, furnish everything down to guns, and the finest horse you ever saw in your life. Your job won't be safe and healthy, sometimes, but it 'll be a man's job—don't mistake me! You can gamble on having things to do outdoors. Now, what do you say?"

"I accept, and I thank you—I can't say how much," replied Gale, earnestly.

"Good! That's settled. Let's go out and tell Laddy and Jim."

Both boys expressed satisfaction at the turn of affairs, and then with Belding they set out to take Gale around the ranch. The house and several outbuildings were constructed of adobe, which, according to Belding, retained the summer heat on into winter, and the winter cold on into summer. These gray-red mud habitations were hideous to look at, and this fact, perhaps, made their really comfortable interiors more vividly a contrast. The wide grounds were covered with luxuriant grass and flowers and different kinds of trees. Gale's interest led him to ask about fig trees and pomegranates, and especially about a beautiful specimen that Belding called *palo verde*.

Belding explained that the luxuriance of this desert place was owing to a few springs and the dammed-up waters of the Rio Forlorn. Before he had come to the oasis it had been inhabited by a Papago Indian tribe and a few peon families. The oasis lay in an arroyo a mile wide, and sloped southwest for some ten miles or more.

The river went dry most of the year; but enough water was stored in flood season to irrigate the gardens and alfalfa fields.

"I've got one never-failing spring on my place," said Belding. "Fine, sweet water! You know what that means in the desert. I like this oasis. The longer I live here the better I like it. There's not a spot in southern Arizona that'll compare with this valley for water or grass or wood. It's beautiful and healthy. Forlorn and lonely, yes, especially for women like my wife and Nell; but I like it.... And between you and me, boys, I've got something up my sleeve. There's gold dust in the arroyos, and there's mineral up in the mountains. If we only had water! This hamlet has steadily grown since I took up a station here. Why, Casita is no place beside Forlorn River. Pretty soon the Southern Pacific will shoot a railroad branch out here. There are possibilities, and I want you boys to stay with me and get in on the ground floor. I wish this rebel war was over. . . . Well, here are the corrals and the fields. Gale, take a look at that bunch of horses!"

Belding's last remark was made as he led his companions out of shady gardens into the open. Gale saw an adobe shed and a huge pen fenced by strangely twisted and contorted branches or trunks of mesquite, and, beyond these, wide, flat fields, green—a dark, rich green—and dotted with beautiful horses. There were whites and blacks, and bays and grays. In his admiration Gale searched his memory to see if he could remember the like of these magnificent animals, and had to admit that the only ones he could compare with them were the Arabian steeds.

"Every rancher loves his horses," said Belding. "When I was in the Panhandle I had some fine stock. But these are Mexican. They came from Durango, where they were bred. Mexican horses are the finest in the world, bar none."

"Shore I reckon I savvy why you don't sleep nights,"

drawled Laddy. "I see a Greaser out there—no, it's an Indian."

"That's my Papago herdsman. I keep watch over the horses now day and night. Lord, how I'd hate to have Rojas or Salazar—any of those bandit rebels—find my horses!... Gale, can you ride?"

Dick modestly replied that he could, according to the Eastern idea of horsemanship.

"You don't need to be half horse to ride one of that bunch. But over there in the other field I've iron-jawed bronchos I wouldn't want you to tackle—except to see the fun. I've an outlaw I'll gamble even Laddy can't ride."

"So. How much'll you gamble?" asked Laddy, instantly.

The ringing of a bell, which Belding said was a call to supper, turned the men back toward the house. Facing that way, Gale saw dark, beetling ridges rising from the oasis and leading up to bare, black mountains. He had heard Belding call them No Name Mountains, and somehow the appellation suited those lofty, mysterious, frowning peaks.

It was not until they reached the house and were about to go in that Belding chanced to discover Gale's crippled hand.

"What an awful hand!" he exclaimed. "Where the devil did you get that?"

"I stove in my knuckles on Rojas," replied Dick.

"You did that in one punch? Say, I'm glad it wasn't me you hit! Why didn't you tell me? That's a bad hand. Those cuts are full of dirt and sand. Inflammation's setting in. It's got to be dressed. Nell!" he called.

There was no answer. He called again, louder.

"Mother, where's the girl?"

"She's there in the dining-room," replied Mrs. Belding.

"Did she hear me?" he inquired, impatiently.

"Of course."

"Nell!" roared Belding.

This brought results. Dick saw a glimpse of golden hair and a white dress in the door. But they were not visible longer than a second.

"Dad, what's the matter?" asked a voice that was still as sweet as formerly, but now rather small and constrained.

"Bring the antiseptics, cotton, bandages—and things out here. Hurry now."

Belding fetched a pail of water and a basin from the kitchen. His wife followed him out, and, upon seeing Dick's hand, was all solicitude. Then Dick heard light, quick footsteps, but he did not look up.

"Nell, this is Mr. Gale—Dick Gale, who came with the boys last night," said Belding. "He's got an awful hand. Got it punching that greaser Rojas. I want you to dress it.... Gale, this is my step-daughter, Nell Burton, of whom I spoke. She's some good when there's somebody sick or hurt. Shove out your fist, my boy, and let her get at it. Supper's nearly ready."

Dick felt that same strange, quickening heart throb, yet he had never been cooler in his life. More than anything else in the world he wanted to look at Nell Burton; however, divining that the situation might be embarrassing to her, he refrained from looking up. She began to bathe his injured knuckles. He noted the softness, the deftness of her touch, and then it seemed her fingers were not quite as steady as they might have been. Still, in a moment they appeared to become surer in their work. She had beautiful hands, not too large, though certainly not small, and they were strong, brown, supple. He observed next, with stealthy, upward-stealing glance, that she had rolled up her sleeves, exposing fine, round arms graceful in line. Her skin was brown—no, it was more gold than brown. It had a wonderful clear tint. Dick stoically lowered his eyes then, putting off as long as possible the alluring moment when he was to look into her

face. That would be a fateful moment. He played with a certain strange joy of anticipation. When, however, she sat down beside him and rested his injured hand in her lap as she cut bandages, she was so thrillingly near that he yielded to an irrepressible desire to look up. She had a sweet, fair face warmly tinted with that same healthy golden-brown sunburn. Her hair was light gold and abundant, a waving mass. Her eyes were shaded by long, downcast lashes, yet through them he caught a gleam of blue.

Despite the stir within him, Gale, seeing she was now absorbed in her task, critically studied her with a second closer gaze. She was a sweet, wholesome, joyous, pretty girl.

"Shore it musta hurt?" inquired Laddy, who sat an interested spectator.

"Yes, I confess it did," replied Dick, slowly, with his eyes on Nell's face. "But I didn't mind."

The girl's lashes swept up swiftly in surprise. She had taken his words literally. But the dark-blue eyes met his for only a fleeting second. Then the warm tint in her cheeks turned as red as her lips. Hurriedly she finished tying the bandage and rose to her feet.

"I thank you," said Gale, also rising.

With that Belding appeared in the doorway, and, finding the operation concluded, called them in to supper. Dick had the use of only one arm, and he certainly was keenly aware of the shy, silent girl across the table; but in spite of these considerable handicaps he eclipsed both hungry cowboys in the assault upon Mrs. Belding's bounteous supper. Belding talked, the cowboys talked more or less, Mrs. Belding put in a word now and then, and Dick managed to find brief intervals when it was possible for him to say yes or no. He observed gratefully that no one round the table seemed to be aware of his enormous appetite.

After supper, having a favorable opportunity when for

a moment no one was at hand, Dick went out through the yard, past the gardens and fields, and climbed the first knoll. From that vantage point he looked out over the little hamlet, somewhat to his right, and was surprised at its extent, its considerable number of adobe houses. The overhanging mountains, ragged and darkened, a great heave of splintered, sundered rock, rather chilled and affronted him.

Westward the setting sun gilded a spiked, frost-colored, limitless expanse of desert. It awed Gale. Everywhere rose blunt, broken ranges or isolated groups of mountains. Yet the desert stretched away down between and beyond them. When the sun set and Gale could not see so far, he felt a relief.

That grand and austere attraction of distance gone, he saw the desert nearer at hand—the valley at his feet. What a strange, gray, somber place! There was a lighter strip of gray winding down between darker hues. This he realized presently was the river bed, and he saw how the pools of water narrowed and diminished in size till they lost themselves in gray sand. This was the rainy season, near its end, and here a little river struggled hopelessly, forlornly to live in the desert. He received a potent impression of the nature of that blasted age-worn waste which he had divined was to give him strength and work and love.

V

BELDING assigned Dick to a little room which had no windows but two doors, one opening into the patio, the other into the yard on the west side of the house. It contained only the barest necessities for comfort. Dick mentioned the baggage he had left in the hotel at Casita, and it was Belding's opinion that to try to recover this property would be rather risky; on the moment Richard Gale was probably not popular with the Mexicans at Casita. So Dick bade good-bye to fine suits of clothes and linen with a feeling that, as he had said farewell to an idle and useless past, it was just as well not to have any old luxuries as reminders. As he possessed, however, not a thing save the clothes on his back, and not even a handkerchief, he expressed regret that he had come to Forlorn River a beggar.

"Beggar hell!" exploded Belding, with his eyes snapping in the lamplight. "Money's the last thing we think of out here. All the same, Gale, if you stick you'll be rich."

"It wouldn't surprise me," replied Dick, thoughtfully. But he was not thinking of material wealth. Then, as he viewed his stained and torn shirt, he laughed and said: "Belding, while I'm getting rich I'd like to have some respectable clothes."

"We've a little Mex store in town, and what you can't get there the women folks will make for you."

When Dick lay down he was dully conscious of pain and headache, that he did not feel well. Despite this, and a mind thronging with memories and anticipations, he succumbed to weariness and soon fell asleep.

It was light when he awoke, but a strange brightness seen through what seemed blurred eyes. A moment passed before his mind worked clearly, and then he had to make an effort to think. He was dizzy. When he essayed to lift his right arm, an excruciating pain made him desist. Then he discovered that his arm was badly swollen, and the hand had burst its bandages. The injured member was red, angry, inflamed, and twice its normal size. He felt hot all over, and a raging headache consumed him.

Belding came stamping into the room.

"Hello, Dick. Do you know it's late? How's the busted fist this morning?"

Dick tried to sit up, but his effort was a failure. He got about half up, then felt himself weakly sliding back.

"I guess—I'm pretty sick," he said.

He saw Belding lean over him, feel his face, and speak, and then everything seemed to drift, not into darkness, but into some region where he had dim perceptions of gray moving things, and of voices that were remote. Then there came an interval when all was blank. He knew not whether it was one of minutes or hours, but after it he had a clearer mind. He slept, awakened during night-time, and slept again. When he again unclosed his eyes the room was sunny, and cool with a fragrant breeze that blew through the open door. Dick felt better; but he had no particular desire to move or talk or eat. He had, however, a burning thirst. Mrs. Belding visited him often; her husband came in several times, and once Nell slipped in noiselessly. Even this last event aroused no interest in Dick.

On the next day he was very much improved.

"We've been afraid of blood poisoning," said Belding. "But my wife thinks the danger's past. You'll have to rest that arm for a while."

A DESERT ROSE

Ladd and Jim came peeping in at the door.

"Come in, boys. He can have company—the more the better—if it 'll keep him content. He mustn't move, that's all."

The cowboys entered, slow, easy, cool, kind-voiced.

"Shore it's tough," said Ladd, after he had greeted Dick. "You look used up."

Jim Lash wagged his half-bald, sunburned head. "Musta been more'n tough for Rojas."

"Gale, Laddy tells me one of our neighbors, fellow named Carter, is going to Casita," put in Belding. "Here's a chance to get word to your friend the soldier."

"Oh, that will be fine!" exclaimed Dick. "I declare I'd forgotten Thorne.... How is Miss Castañeda? I hope—"

"She's all right, Gale. Been up and around the patio for two days. Like all the Spanish—the real thing—she's made of Damascus steel. We've been getting acquainted. She and Nell made friends at once. I'll call them in."

He closed the door leading out into the yard, explaining that he did not want to take chances of Mercedes's presence becoming known to neighbors. Then he went to the patio and called.

Both girls came in, Mercedes leading. Like Nell, she wore white, and she had a red rose in her hand. Dick would scarcely have recognized anything about her except her eyes and the way she carried her little head, and her beauty burst upon him strange and anew. She was swift, impulsive in her movements to reach his side.

"Señor, I am so sorry you were ill—so happy you are better."

Dick greeted her, offering his left hand, gravely apologizing for the fact that, owing to a late infirmity, he could not offer the right. Her smile exquisitely combined sympathy, gratitude, admiration. Then Dick spoke to Nell, likewise offering his hand, which she took shyly. Her reply was a murmured, unintelligible one; but her eyes were glad, and the tint in her cheeks threatened to rival the hue of the rose she carried.

Everybody chatted then, except Nell, who had apparently lost her voice. Presently Dick remembered to speak of the matter of getting news to Thorne.

"Señor, may I write to him? Will some one take a letter? . . . I shall hear from him!" she said; and her white hands emphasized her words.

"Assuredly. I guess poor Thorne is almost crazy. I'll write to him. . . . No, I can't with this crippled hand."

"That'll be all right, Gale," said Belding. "Nell will write for you. She writes all my letters."

So Belding arranged it; and Mercedes flew away to her room to write, while Nell fetched pen and paper and seated herself beside Gale's bed to take his dictation.

What with watching Nell and trying to catch her glance, and listening to Belding's talk with the cowboys, Dick was hard put to it to dictate any kind of a creditable letter. Nell met his gaze once, then no more. The color came and went in her cheeks, and sometimes, when he told her to write so and so, there was a demure smile on her lips. She was laughing at him. And Belding was talking over the risks involved in a trip to Casita.

"Shore I'll ride in with the letters," Ladd said.

"No you won't," replied Belding. "That bandit outfit will be laying for you."

"Well, I reckon if they was I wouldn't be oncommon grieved."

"I'll tell you, boys, I'll ride in myself with Carter. There's business I can see to, and I'm curious to know what the rebels are doing. Laddy, keep one eye open while I'm gone. See the horses are locked up. . . . Gale, I'm going to Casita myself. Ought to get back to-morrow some time. I'll be ready to start in an hour. Have your letter ready. And say—if you want to write home it's a chance. Sometimes we don't go to the P. O. in a month."

A DESERT ROSE

He tramped out, followed by the tall cowboys, and then Dick was enabled to bring his letter to a close. Mercedes came back, and her eyes were shining. Dick imagined a letter received from her would be something of an event for a fellow. Then, remembering Belding's suggestion, he decided to profit by it.

"May I trouble you to write another for me?" asked Dick, as he received the letter from Nell.

"It's no trouble, I'm sure—I'd be pleased," she replied.

That was altogether a wonderful speech of hers, Dick thought, because the words were the first coherent ones she had spoken to him.

"May I stay?" asked Mercedes, smiling.

"By all means," he answered, and then he settled back and began.

Presently Gale paused, partly because of genuine emotion, and stole a look from under his hand at Nell. She wrote swiftly, and her downcast face seemed to be softer in its expression of sweetness. If she had in the very least been drawn to him— But that was absurd—impossible!

When Dick finished dictating, his eyes were upon Mercedes, who sat smilingly curious and sympathetic. How responsive she was! He heard the hasty scratch of Nell's pen. He looked at Nell. Presently she rose, holding out his letter. He was just in time to see a wave of red recede from her face. She gave him one swift gaze, unconscious, searching, then averted it and turned away. She left the room with Mercedes before he could express his thanks.

But that strange, speaking flash of eyes remained to haunt and torment Gale. It was indescribably sweet, and provocative of thoughts that he believed were wild without warrant. Something within him danced for very joy, and the next instant he was conscious of wistful doubt, a gravity that he could not understand. It dawned upon him that for the brief instant when Nell had met his gaze she had lost her shyness. It was a woman's questioning eyes that had pierced through him.

During the rest of the day Gale was content to lie still on his bed thinking and dreaming, dozing at intervals, and watching the lights change upon the mountain peaks, feeling the warm, fragrant desert wind that blew in upon him. He seemed to have lost the faculty of estimating time. A long while, strong in its effect upon him, appeared to have passed since he had met Thorne. He accepted things as he felt them, and repudiated his intelligence. His old inquisitive habit of mind returned. Did he love Nell? Was he only attracted for the moment? What was the use of worrying about her or himself? He refused to answer, and deliberately gave himself up to dreams of her sweet face and of that last dark-blue glance.

Next day he believed he was well enough to leave his room; but Mrs. Belding would not permit him to do so. She was kind, soft-handed, motherly, and she was always coming in to minister to his comfort. This attention was sincere, not in the least forced; yet Gale felt that the friendliness so manifest in the others of the household did not extend to her. He was conscious of something that a little thought persuaded him was antagonism. It surprised and hurt him. He had never been much of a success with girls and young married women, but their mothers and old people had generally been fond of him. Still, though Mrs. Belding's hair was snow-white, she did not impress him as being old. He reflected that there might come a time when it would be desirable, far beyond any ground of every-day friendly kindliness, to have Mrs. Belding be well disposed toward him. So he thought about her, and pondered how to make her like him. It did not take very long for Dick to discover that he liked her. Her face, except when she smiled, was thoughtful and sad. But it seemed too strong, too intense, too nobly lined. It was a face to make one serious. Like a haunting shadow, like a phantom of happier years, the sweetness of Nell's face was there, and infinitely more of beauty than had been transmitted to the daughter. Dick believed Mrs. Belding's friendship and motherly love were worth much striving to win, entirely aside from any more selfish motive. He decided both would be hard to get. Often he felt her deep, penetrating gaze upon him; and, though this in no wise embarrassed him—for he had no shameful secrets of past or present—it showed him how useless it would be to try to conceal anything from her. Naturally, on first impulse, he wanted to hide his interest in the daughter; but he resolved to be absolutely frank and true, and through that win or lose. Moreover, if Mrs. Belding asked him any questions about his home, his family, his connections, he would not avoid direct and truthful answers.

Toward evening Gale heard the tramp of horses and Belding's hearty voice. Presently the rancher strode in upon Gale, shaking the gray dust from his broad shoulders and waving a letter.

"Hello, Dick! Good news and bad!" he said, putting the letter in Dick's hand. "Had no trouble finding your friend Thorne. Looked like he'd been drunk for a week! Say, he nearly threw a fit. I never saw a fellow so wild with joy. He made sure you and Mercedes were lost in the desert. He wrote two letters which I brought. Don't mistake me, boy, it was some fun with Mercedes just now. I teased her, wouldn't give her the letter. You ought to have seen her eyes. If ever you see a black-and-white desert hawk swoop down upon a quail, then you'll know how Mercedes pounced upon her letter.... Well, Casita is one hell of a place these days. I tried to get your baggage, and think I made a mistake. We're going to see travel toward Forlorn River. The federal garrison got reinforcements from somewhere, and is holding out. There's been fighting for three days. The rebels have a string of flat railroad cars, all iron, and they ran this up within range of the barricades. They've got some machine guns, and they're going to lick the federals sure. There are dead soldiers in the ditches, Mexican non-combatants lying dead in the streets—and buzzards everywhere! It's reported that Campo, the rebel leader, is on the way up from Sinaloa, and Huerta, a federal general, is coming to relieve the garrison. I don't take much stock in reports. But there's hell in Casita, all right."

"Do you think we'll have trouble out here?" asked Dick, excitedly.

"Sure. Some kind of trouble sooner or later," replied Belding, gloomily. "Why, you can stand on my ranch and step over into Mexico. Laddy says we'll lose horses and other stock in night raids. Jim Lash doesn't look for any worse. But Jim isn't as well acquainted with Greasers as I am. Anyway, my boy, as soon as you can hold a bridle and a gun you'll be on the job, don't mistake me."

"With Laddy and Jim?" asked Dick, trying to be cool.

"Sure. With them and me, and by yourself."

Dick drew a deep breath, and even after Belding had departed he forgot for a moment about the letter in his hand. Then he unfolded the paper and read:

DEAR DICK,—You've more than saved my life. To the end of my days you'll be the one man to whom I owe everything. Words fail to express my feelings.

This must be a brief note. Belding is waiting, and I used up most of the time writing to Mercedes. I like Belding. He was not unknown to me, though I never met or saw him before. You'll be interested to learn that he's the unadulterated article, the real Western goods. I've heard of some of his stunts, and they made my hair curl. Dick, your luck is staggering. The way Belding spoke of you was great. But you deserve it, old man.

I'm leaving Mercedes in your charge, subject, of course, to advice from Belding. Take care of her, Dick, for my life is wrapped up in her. By all means keep her from being seen by Mexicans. We are sitting tight here—nothing doing. If some action doesn't come soon, it'll be darned strange. Things are centering this way. There's scrapping right along, and people have begun to move. We're still patrolling the line eastward of Casita. It'll be impossible to keep any tab on the line west of Casita, for

A DESERT ROSE

it's too rough. That cactus desert is awful. Cowboys or rangers
with desert-bred horses might keep raiders and smugglers from
crossing. But if cavalrymen could stand that waterless wilderness, which I doubt much, their horses would drop under them.

If things do quiet down before my commission expires, I'll
get leave of absence, run out to Forlorn River, marry my beautiful Spanish princess, and take her to a civilized country, where,
I opine, every son of a gun who sees her will lose his head, and
drive me mad. It's my great luck, old pal, that you are a fellow
who never seemed to care about pretty girls. So you won't give
me the double cross and run off with Mercedes—carry her off,
like the villain in the play, I mean.

That reminds me of Rojas. Oh, Dick, it was glorious! You
didn't do anything to the Dandy Rebel! Not at all! You merely
caressed him—gently moved him to one side. Dick, harken to
these glad words: Rojas is in the hospital. I was interested to
inquire. He had a smashed finger, a dislocated collar bone, three
broken ribs, and a fearful gash on his face. He'll be in the hospital for a month. Dick, when I meet that pig-headed dad of
yours I'm going to give him the surprise of his life.

Send me a line whenever any one comes in from F. R., and in-
close Mercedes's letter in yours. Take care of her, Dick, and may
the future hold in store for you some of the sweetness I know now!

Faithfully yours,

THORNE.

Dick reread the letter, then folded it and placed it
under his pillow.

"Never cared for pretty girls, huh?" he soliloquized.
"George, I never saw any till I struck Southern Arizona!
Guess I'd better make up for lost time."

While he was eating his supper, with appetite rapidly
returning to normal, Ladd and Jim came in, bowing their
tall heads to enter the door. Their friendly advances
were singularly welcome to Gale, but he was still backward. He allowed himself to show that he was glad to
see them, and he listened. Jim Lash had heard from
Belding the result of the mauling given to Rojas by Dick.
And Jim talked about what a grand thing that was.
Ladd had a good deal to say about Belding's horses. It
took no keen judge of human nature to see that horses
constituted Ladd's ruling passion.

"I've had wimmen go back on me, but never no hoss!"
declared Ladd, and manifestly that was a controlling
truth with him.

"Shore it's a cinch Beldin' is agoin' to lose some of
them hosses," he said. "You can search me if I don't
think there'll be more doin' on the border here than
along the Rio Grande. We're just the same as on Greaser
soil. Mebbe we don't stand no such chance of bein'
shot up as we would across the line. But who's goin' to
give up his hosses without a fight? Half the time when
Beldin's stock is out of the alfalfa it's grazin' over the
line. He thinks he's careful about them hosses, but he
ain't."

"Look a-here, Laddy; you cain't believe all you hear,"
replied Jim, seriously. "I reckon we mightn't have any
trouble."

"Back up, Jim. Shore you're standin' on your bridle.
I ain't goin' much on reports. Remember that American
we met in Casita, the prospector who'd just gotten out of
Sonora? He had some story, he had. Swore he'd killed
seventeen Greasers breakin' through the rebel line round
the mine where he an' other Americans were corralled.
The next day when I met him again, he was drunk, an'
then he told me he'd shot thirty Greasers. The chances
are he did kill some. But reports are exaggerated.
There are miners fightin' for life down in Sonora, you can
gamble on that. An' the truth is bad enough. Take
Rojas's harryin' of the Señorita, for instance. Can you
beat that? Shore, Jim, there's more doin' than the raid-
in' of a few hosses. An' Forlorn River is goin' to get
hers!"

Another dawn found Gale so much recovered that he
arose and looked after himself, not, however, without
considerable difficulty and rather disheartening twinges
of pain.

Some time during the morning he heard the girls in the
patio and called to ask if he might join them. He re-

ceived one response, a mellow, "*Si,* señor." It was not as much as he wanted, but considering that it was enough, he went out. He had not as yet visited the patio, and surprise and delight were in store for him. He found himself lost in a labyrinth of green and rose-bordered walks. He strolled around, discovering that the patio was a courtyard, open at an end; but he failed to discover the young ladies. So he called again. The answer came from the center of the square. After stooping to get under shrubs and wading through bushes he entered an open sandy circle, full of magnificent and murderous cactus plants, strange to him. On the other side, in the shade of a beautiful tree, he found the girls, Mercedes sitting in a hammock, Nell upon a blanket.

"What a beautiful tree!" he exclaimed. "I never saw one like that. What is it?"

"*Palo verde,*" replied Nell.

"Señor, *palo verde* means 'green tree,'" added Mercedes.

This desert tree, which had struck Dick as so new and strange and beautiful, was not striking on account of size, for it was small, scarcely reaching higher than the roof; but rather because of its exquisite color of green, trunk and branch alike, and owing to the odd fact that it seemed not to possess leaves. All the tree from ground to tiny flat twigs was a soft polished green. It bore no thorns.

Right then and there began Dick's education in desert growths; and he felt that even if he had not had such charming teachers he would still have been absorbed. For the patio was full of desert wonders. A twisting-trunked tree with full foliage of small gray leaves Nell called a mesquite. Then Dick remembered the name, and now he saw where the desert got its pale-gray color. A huge, lofty, fluted column of green was a *saguaro,* or giant cactus. Another odd-shaped cactus, resembling the legs of an inverted devil-fish, bore the name *ocatillo.* Each branch rose high and symmetrical, furnished with sharp blades that seemed to be at once leaves and thorns. Yet another cactus interested Gale, and it looked like a huge, low barrel covered with green-ribbed cloth and long thorns. This was the *bisnaga,* or barrel cactus. According to Nell and Mercedes, this plant was a happy exception to its desert neighbors, for it secreted water which had many times saved the lives of men. Last of the cacti to attract Gale, and the one to make him shiver, was a low plant, consisting of stem and many rounded protuberances of a frosty, steely white, and covered with long, murderous spikes. From this plant the desert got its frosty glitter. It was as stiff, as unyielding as steel, and bore the name *choya.*

Dick's enthusiasm was contagious, and his earnest desire to learn was flattering to his teachers. When it came to assimilating Spanish, however, he did not appear to be so apt a pupil. He managed, after many trials, to acquire *"buenos dias"* and *"buenos tardes,"* and "señorita" and *"gracias,"* and a few other short terms. Dick was indeed eager to get a little smattering of Spanish, and perhaps he was not really quite so stupid as he pretended to be. It was delightful to be taught by a beautiful Spaniard who was so gracious and intense and magnetic of personality, and by a sweet American girl who moment by moment forgot her shyness. Gale wished to prolong the lessons.

So that was the beginning of many afternoons in which he learned desert lore and Spanish verbs, and something else that he dared not name.

Nell Burton had never shown to Gale that daring side of her character which had been so suggestively defined in Belding's terse description and Ladd's encomiums, and in her own audacious speech and merry laugh and flashing eye of that never-to-be-forgotten first meeting. She might have been an entirely different girl. But Gale remembered; and when the ice had been somewhat broken between them, he was always trying to surprise

her into her real self. There were moments that fairly
made him tingle with expectation. Yet he saw little
more than a ghost of her vivacity, and never a gleam of
that individuality which Belding had called a devil. On
the few occasions that Dick had been left alone with her
in the patio Nell had grown suddenly unresponsive and
restrained, or she had left him on some transparent pretext. On the last occasion Mercedes returned to find
Dick staring disconsolately at the rose-bordered path,
where Nell had evidently vanished. The Spanish girl
was wonderful in her divination.

"Señor Dick!" she cried.

Dick looked at her, soberly nodded his head, and then
he laughed. Mercedes had seen through him in one swift
glance. Her white hand touched his in wordless sympathy and thrilled him. This Spanish girl was all fire and
passion and love. She understood him, she was his friend,
she pledged him what he felt would be the most subtle
and powerful influence.

Little by little he learned details of Nell's varied life.
She had lived in many places. As a child she remembered
moving from town to town, of going to school among
schoolmates whom she never had time to know. Lawrence, Kansas, where she studied for several years, was
the later exception to this changeful nature of her school-
ing. Then she moved to Stillwater, Oklahoma, from
there to Austin, Texas, and on to Waco, where her
mother met and married Belding. They lived in New
Mexico awhile, in Tucson, Arizona, in Douglas, and
finally had come to lonely Forlorn River.

"Mother could never live in one place any length of
time," said Nell. "And since we've been in the Southwest she has never ceased trying to find some trace of her
father. He was last heard of in Nogales fourteen years
ago. She thinks grandfather was lost in the Sonora
Desert.... And every place we go is worse. Oh, I love
the desert. But I'd like to go back to Lawrence—or to

see Chicago or New York—some of the places Mr. Gale speaks of.... I remember the college at Lawrence, though I was only twelve. I saw races—and once real football. Since then I've read magazines and papers about big football games, and I was always fascinated .... Mr. Gale, of course, you've seen games?"

"Yes, a few," replied Dick; and he laughed a little. It was on his lips then to tell her about some of the famous games in which he had participated. But he refrained from exploiting himself. There was little, however, of the color and sound and cheer, of the violent action and rush and battle incidental to a big college football game that he did not succeed in making Mercedes and Nell feel just as if they had been there. They hung breathless and wide-eyed upon his words.

Some one else was present at the latter part of Dick's narrative. The moment he became aware of Mrs. Belding's presence he remembered fancying he had heard her call, and now he was certain she had done so. Mercedes and Nell, however, had been and still were oblivious to everything except Dick's recital. He saw Mrs. Belding cast a strange, intent glance upon Nell, then turn and go silently through the patio. Dick concluded his talk, but the brilliant beginning was not sustained.

Dick was haunted by the strange expression he had caught on Mrs. Belding's face, especially the look in her eyes. It had been one of repressed pain liberated in a flash of certainty. The mother had seen just as quickly as Mercedes how far he had gone on the road of love. Perhaps she had seen more—even more than he dared hope. The incident roused Gale. He could not understand Mrs. Belding, nor why that look of hers, that seeming baffled, hopeless look of a woman who saw the inevitable forces of life and could not thwart them, should cause him perplexity and distress. He wanted to go to her and tell her how he felt about Nell, but fear of absolute destruction of his hopes held him back. He would wait.

A DESERT ROSE

Nevertheless, an instinct that was perhaps akin to self-preservation prompted him to want to let Nell know the state of his mind. Words crowded his brain seeking utterance. Who and what he was, how he loved her, the work he expected to take up soon, his longings, hopes, and plans—there was all this and more. But something checked him. And the repression made him so thoughtful and quiet, even melancholy, that he went outdoors to try to throw off the mood. The sun was yet high, and a dazzling white light enveloped valleys and peaks. He felt that the wonderful sunshine was the dominant feature of that arid region. It was like white gold. It had burned its color in a face he knew. It was going to warm his blood and brown his skin. A hot, languid breeze, so dry that he felt his lips shrink with its contact, came from the desert; and it seemed to smell of wide-open, untainted places where sand blew and strange, pungent plants gave a bitter-sweet tang to the air.

When he returned to the house, some hours later, his room had been put in order. In the middle of the white coverlet on his table lay a fresh red rose. Nell had dropped it there. Dick picked it up, feeling a throb in his breast. It was a bud just beginning to open, to show between its petals a dark-red, unfolding heart. How fragrant it was, how exquisitely delicate, how beautiful its inner hue of red, deep and dark, the crimson of life blood!

Had Nell left it there by accident or by intent? Was it merely kindness or a girl's subtlety? Was it a message couched elusively, a symbol, a hope in a half-blown desert rose?

VI

TOWARD evening of a lowering December day, some fifty miles west of Forlorn River, a horseman rode along an old, dimly defined trail. From time to time he halted to study the lay of the land ahead. It was bare, somber, ridgy desert, covered with dun-colored grease-wood and stunted prickly pear. Distant mountains hemmed in the valley, raising black spurs above the round lomas and the square-walled mesas.

This lonely horseman bestrode a steed of magnificent build, perfectly white except for a dark bar of color running down the noble head from ears to nose. Sweat-caked dust stained the long flanks. The horse had been running. His mane and tail were laced and knotted to keep their length out of reach of grasping cactus and brush. Clumsy home-made leather shields covered the front of his forelegs and ran up well to his wide breast. What otherwise would have been muscular symmetry of limb was marred by many a scar and many a lump. He was lean, gaunt, worn, a huge machine of muscle and bone, beautiful only in head and mane, a weight-carrier, a horse strong and fierce like the desert that had bred him.

The rider fitted the horse as he fitted the saddle. He was a young man of exceedingly powerful physique, wide-shouldered, long-armed, big-legged. His lean face, where it was not red, blistered and peeling, was the hue of bronze. He had a dark eye, a falcon gaze, roving and keen. His jaw was prominent and set, mastiff-like; his lips were stern. It was youth with its softness not yet quite burned and hardened away that kept the whole cast of his face from being ruthless.

This young man was Dick Gale, but not the listless traveler, nor the lounging wanderer who, two months before, had by chance dropped into Casita. Friendship, chivalry, love—the deep-seated, unplumbed emotions that had been stirred into being with all their incalculable power for spiritual change, had rendered different the meaning of life. In the moment almost of their realization the desert had claimed Gale, and had drawn him into its crucible. The desert had multiplied weeks into years. Heat, thirst, hunger, loneliness, toil, fear, ferocity, pain —he knew them all. He had felt them all—the white sun, with its glazed, coalescing, lurid fire; the caked split lips and rasping, dry-puffed tongue; the sickening ache in the pit of his stomach; the insupportable silence, the empty space, the utter desolation, the contempt of life; the weary ride, the long climb, the plod in sand, the search, search, search for water; the sleepless night alone, the watch and wait, the dread of ambush, the swift flight; the fierce pursuit of men wild as Bedouins and as fleet, the willingness to deal sudden death, the pain of poison thorn, the stinging tear of lead through flesh; and that strange paradox of the burning desert, the cold at night, the piercing icy wind, the dew that penetrated to the marrow, the numbing desert cold of the dawn.

Beyond any dream of adventure he had ever had, beyond any wild story he had ever read, had been his experience with those hard-riding rangers, Ladd and Lash. Then he had traveled alone the hundred miles of desert between Forlorn River and the Sonoyta Oasis. Ladd's prophecy of trouble on the border had been mild compared to what had become the actuality. With rebel occupancy of the garrison at Casita, outlaws, bandits, raiders in rioting bands had spread westward. Like troops of Arabs, magnificently mounted, they were here, there, everywhere along the line; and if murder and worse were confined to the Mexican side, pillage and raiding were perpetrated across the border. Many a dark-skinned raider bestrode one of Belding's fast horses; and, indeed, all except his selected white thoroughbreds had been stolen. So the job of the rangers had become more than a patrolling of the boundary line to keep Japanese and Chinese from being smuggled into the United States. Belding kept close at home to protect his family and to hold his property. But the three rangers, in fulfilling their duty, had incurred risks on their own side of the line, had been outraged, robbed, pursued, and injured on the other. Some of the few waterholes that had to be reached lay far across the border in Mexican territory. Horses had to drink, men had to drink; and Ladd and Lash were not of the stripe that forsook a task because of danger. Slow to wrath at first, as became men who had long lived peaceful lives, they had at length revolted; and desert vultures could have told a gruesome story. Made a comrade and ally of these bordermen, Dick Gale had leaped at the desert action and strife with an intensity of heart and a rare physical ability which accounted for the remarkable fact that he had not yet fallen by the way.

On this December afternoon the three rangers, as often, were separated. Lash was far to the westward of Sonoyta, somewhere along Camino del Diablo, that terrible Devil's Road, where many desert wayfarers had perished. Ladd had long been overdue in a prearranged meeting with Gale. The fact that Ladd had not shown up miles west of the Papago Well was significant.

The sun had hidden behind clouds all the latter part of that day, an unusual occurrence for that region even in winter. And now, as the light waned suddenly, telling of the hidden sunset, a cold, dry, penetrating wind sprang up and blew in Gale's face. Not at first, but by imperceptible degrees it chilled him. He untied his coat from the back of the saddle and put it on. A few cold drops of rain touched his cheek.

THE YAQUI

He halted upon the edge of a low escarpment. Below him the narrowing valley showed bare, black ribs of rock, long, winding gray lines leading down to a central floor where mesquite and cactus dotted the barren landscape. Moving objects, diminutive in size, gray and white in color, arrested Gale's roving sight. They bobbed away for a while, then stopped. They were antelope, and they had seen his horse. When he rode on they started once more, keeping to the lowest level. These wary animals were often desert watchdogs for the ranger; they would betray the proximity of horse or man. With them trotting forward, he made better time for some miles across the valley. When he lost them, caution once more slowed his advance.

The valley sloped up and narrowed, to head into an arroyo where grass began to show gray between the clumps of mesquite. Shadows formed ahead in the hollows, along the walls of the arroyo, under the trees, and they seemed to creep, to rise, to float into a veil cast by the background of bold mountains, at last to claim the skyline. Night was not close at hand; but it was there in the east, lifting upward, drooping downward, encroaching upon the west.

Gale dismounted to lead his horse, to go forward more slowly. He had ridden sixty miles since morning, and he was tired, and a not entirely healed wound in his hip made one leg drag a little. A mile up the arroyo, near its head, lay the Papago Well. The need of water for his horse entailed a risk that otherwise he could have avoided. The well was on Mexican soil. Gale distinguished a faint light flickering through the thin, sharp foliage. Campers were at the well, and, whoever they were, no doubt they had prevented Ladd from meeting Gale. Ladd had gone back to the next waterhole, or maybe he was hiding in an arroyo to the eastward, awaiting developments.

Gale turned his horse, not without urge of iron arm and persuasive speech, for the desert steed scented water, and plodded back to the edge of the arroyo, where in a secluded circle of mesquite he halted. The horse snorted his relief at the removal of the heavy, burdened saddle and accoutrements, and sagging, bent his knees, lowered himself with slow heave, and plunged down to roll in the sand. Gale poured the contents of his larger canteen into his hat and held it to the horse's nose.

"Drink, Sol," he said.

It was but a drop for a thirsty horse. However, Blanco Sol rubbed a wet muzzle against Gale's hand in appreciation. Gale loved the horse, and was loved in return. They had saved each other's lives, and had spent long days and nights of desert solitude together. Sol had known other masters, though none so kind as this new one; but it was certain that Gale had never before known a horse.

The spot of secluded ground was covered with bunches of galleta grass upon which Sol began to graze. Gale made a long halter of his lariat to keep the horse from wandering in search of water. Next Gale kicked off the cumbersome chapparejos, with their flapping, tripping folds of leather over his feet, and drawing a long rifle from its saddle sheath, he slipped away into the shadows.

The coyotes were howling, not here and there, but in concerted volume at the head of the arroyo. To Dick this was no more reassuring than had been the flickering light of the campfire. The wild desert dogs, with their characteristic insolent curiosity, were baying men round a campfire. Gale proceeded slowly, halting every few steps, careful not to brush against the stiff greasewood. In the soft sand his steps made no sound. The twinkling light vanished occasionally, like a Jack-o'-lantern, and when it did show it seemed still a long way off. Gale was not seeking trouble or inviting danger. Water was the thing that drove him. He must see who these campers were, and then decide how to give Blanco Sol a drink.

A rabbit rustled out of brush at Gale's feet and thumped

away over the sand. The wind pattered among dry, broken stalks of dead *ocatilla*. Every little sound brought Gale to a listening pause. The gloom was thickening fast into darkness. It would be a night without starlight. He moved forward up the pale, zigzag aisles between the mesquite. He lost the light for a while, but the coyotes' chorus told him he was approaching the campfire. Presently the light danced through the black branches, and soon grew into a flame. Stooping low, with bushy mesquites between him and the fire, Gale advanced. The coyotes were in full cry. Gale heard the tramping, stamping thumps of many hoofs. The sound worried him. Foot by foot he advanced, and finally began to crawl. The wind favored his position, so that neither coyotes nor horses could scent him. The nearer he approached the head of the arroyo, where the well was located, the thicker grew the desert vegetation. At length a dead *palo verde,* with huge, black clumps of its parasite mistletoe thick in the branches, marked a distance from the well that Gale considered close enough. Noiselessly he crawled here and there until he secured a favorable position, and then rose to peep from behind his covert.

He saw a bright fire, not a cooking-fire, for that would have been low and red, but a crackling blaze of mesquite. Three men were in sight, all close to the burning sticks. They were Mexicans and of the coarse type of raiders, rebels, bandits that Gale had expected to see. One stood up, his back to the fire; another sat with shoulders enveloped in a blanket, and the third lounged in the sand, his feet almost in the blaze. They had cast off belts and weapons. A glint of steel caught Gale's eye. Three short, shiny carbines leaned against a rock. A little to the left, within the circle of light, stood a square house made of adobe bricks. Several untrimmed poles upheld a roof of brush, which was partly fallen in. This house was a Papago Indian habitation, and a month before had been occupied by a family that had been murdered or driven off by a roving band of outlaws. A rude corral showed dimly in the edge of firelight, and from a black mass within came the snort and stamp and whinny of horses.

Gale took in the scene in one quick glance, then sank down at the foot of the mesquite. He had naturally expected to see more men. But the situation was by no means new. This was one, or part of one, of the raider bands harrying the border. They were stealing horses, or driving a herd already stolen. These bands were more numerous than the waterholes of northern Sonora; they never camped long at one place; like Arabs, they roamed over the desert all the way from Nogales to Casita. If Gale had gone peaceably up to this campfire there were a hundred chances that the raiders would kill and rob him to one chance that they might not. If they recognized him as a ranger comrade of Ladd and Lash, if they got a glimpse of Blanco Sol, then Gale would have no chance.

These Mexicans had evidently been at the well some time. Their horses being in the corral meant that grazing had been done by day. Gale revolved questions in mind. Had this trio of outlaws run across Ladd? It was not likely, for in that event they might not have been so comfortable and care-free in camp. Were they waiting for more members of their gang? That was very probable. With Gale, however, the most important consideration was how to get his horse to water. Sol must have a drink if it cost a fight. There was stern reason for Gale to hurry eastward along the trail. He thought it best to go back to where he had left his horse and not make any decisive move until daylight.

With the same noiseless care he had exercised in the advance, Gale retreated until it was safe for him to rise and walk on down the arroyo. He found Blanco Sol contentedly grazing. A heavy dew was falling, and, as the grass was abundant, the horse did not show the usual restlessness and distress after a dry and exhausting day. Gale carried his saddle, blankets, and bags into the lee of a little greasewood-covered mound, from around which the wind had cut the soil; and here, in a wash, he risked building a small fire. By this time the wind was piercingly cold. Gale's hands were numb, and he moved them to and fro in the little blaze. Then he made coffee in a cup, cooked some slices of bacon on the end of a stick, and took a couple of hard biscuits from a saddlebag. Of these his meal consisted. After that he removed the halter from Blanco Sol, intending to leave him free to graze for a while.

Then Gale returned to his little fire, replenished it with short sticks of dead greasewood and mesquite, and, wrapping his blanket round his shoulders, he sat down to warm himself and to wait till it was time to bring in the horse and tie him up.

The fire was inadequate, and Gale was cold and wet with dew. Hunger and thirst were with him. His bones ached, and there was a dull, deep-seated pain throbbing in his unhealed wound. For days unshaven, his beard seemed like a million pricking needles in his blistered skin. He was so tired that, once having settled himself, he did not move hand or foot. The night was dark, dismal, cloudy, windy, growing colder. A moan of wind in the mesquites was occasionally pierced by the high-keyed yelp of a coyote. There were lulls in which the silence seemed to be a thing of stifling, encroaching substance—a thing that enveloped, buried the desert.

Judged by the great average of ideals and conventional standards of life, Dick Gale was a starved, lonely, suffering, miserable wretch. But in his case the judgment would have hit only externals, would have missed the vital inner truth. For Gale was happy with a kind of strange, wild glory in the privations, the pains, the perils, and the silence and solitude to be endured on this desert land. In the past he had not been of any use to himself or others; and he had never known what it meant to be hungry, cold, tired, lonely. He had never worked for anything. The needs of the day had been provided, and to-morrow and the future looked the same. Danger, peril, toil—these had been words read in books and papers.

In the present he used his hands, his senses, and his wits. He had a duty to a man who relied on his services. He was a comrade, a friend, a valuable ally to riding, fighting rangers. He had spent endless days, weeks that seemed years, alone with a horse, trailing over, climbing over, hunting over a desert that was harsh and hostile by nature, and perilous by the invasion of savage men. That horse had become human to Gale. And with him Gale had learned to know the simple needs of existence. Like dead scales the superficialities, the falsities, the habits that had once meant all of life dropped off, useless things in this stern waste of rock and sand.

Gale's happiness, as far as it concerned the toil and strife, was perhaps a grim and stoical one. But love abided with him, and it had engendered and fostered other undeveloped traits—romance and a feeling for beauty, and a keen observation of nature. He felt pain, but he was never miserable. He felt the solitude, but he was never lonely.

As he rode across the desert, even though keen eyes searched for the moving black dots, the rising puffs of white dust that were warnings, he saw Nell's face in every cloud. The clean-cut mesas took on the shape of her straight profile, with its strong chin and lips, its fine nose and forehead. There was always a glint of gold or touch of red or graceful line or gleam of blue to remind him of her. Then at night her face shone warm and glowing, flushing and paling, in the campfire.

To-night, as usual, with a keen ear to the wind, Gale listened as one on guard; yet he watched the changing phantom of a sweet face in the embers, and as he watched he thought. The desert developed and multiplied thought. A thousand sweet faces glowed in the pink and white ashes of his campfire, the faces of other sweethearts or wives that had gleamed for other men. Gale was happy in his thought of Nell, for something, when he was alone this way in the wilderness, told him she was near him, she thought of him, she loved him. But there were many men alone on that vast southwestern plateau, and when they saw dream faces, surely for some it was a fleeting flash, a gleam soon gone, like the hope and the name and the happiness that had been and was now no more. Often Gale thought of those hundreds of desert travelers, prospectors, wanderers who had ventured down the Camino del Diablo, never to be heard of again. Belding had told him of that most terrible of all desert trails—a trail of shifting sands. Lash had traversed it, and brought back stories of buried waterholes, of bones bleaching white in the sun, of gold mines as lost as were the prospectors who had sought them, of the merciless Yaqui and his hatred for the Mexican. Gale thought of this trail and the men who had camped along it. For many there had been one night, one campfire that had been the last. This idea seemed to creep in out of the darkness, the loneliness, the silence, and to find a place in Gale's mind, so that it had strange fascination for him. He knew now as he had never dreamed before how men drifted into the desert, leaving behind graves, wrecked homes, ruined lives, lost wives and sweethearts. And for every wanderer every campfire had a phantom face. Gale measured the agony of these men at their last campfire by the joy and promise he traced in the ruddy heart of his own.

By and by Gale remembered what he was waiting for; and, getting up, he took the halter and went out to find Blanco Sol. It was pitch-dark now, and Gale could not see a rod ahead. He felt his way, and presently as he rounded a mesquite he saw Sol's white shape outlined against the blackness. The horse jumped and wheeled, ready to run. It was doubtful if any one unknown to Sol could ever have caught him. Gale's low call reassured him, and he went on grazing. Gale haltered him in the likeliest patch of grass and returned to his camp. There he lifted his saddle into a protected spot under a low wall of the mound, and, laying one blanket on the sand, he covered himself with the other and stretched himself for the night.

Here he was out of reach of the wind; but he heard its melancholy moan in the mesquite. There was no other sound. The coyotes had ceased their hungry cries. Gale dropped to sleep, and slept soundly during the first half of the night; and after that he seemed always to be partially awake, aware of increasing cold and damp. The dark mantle turned gray, and then daylight came quickly. The morning was clear and nipping cold. He threw off the wet blanket and got up cramped and half frozen. A little brisk action was all that was necessary to warm his blood and loosen his muscles, and then he was fresh, tingling, eager. The sun rose in a golden blaze, and the descending valley took on wondrous changing hues. Then he fetched up Blanco Sol, saddled him, and tied him to the thickest clump of mesquite.

"Sol, we'll have a drink pretty soon," he said, patting the splendid neck.

Gale meant it. He would not eat till he had watered his horse. Sol had gone nearly forty-eight hours without a sufficient drink, and that was long enough, even for a desert-bred beast. No three raiders could keep Gale away from that well. Taking his rifle in hand, he faced up the arroyo. Rabbits were frisking in the short willows, and some were so tame he could have kicked them. Gale walked swiftly for a goodly part of the distance, and then, when he saw blue smoke curling up above the trees, he proceeded slowly, with alert eye and ear. From the lay of the land and position of trees seen by daylight, he found an easier and safer course than the one he had taken in the dark. And by careful work he was enabled to get closer to the well, and somewhat above it.

The Mexicans were leisurely cooking their morning meal. They had two fires, one for warmth, the other to cook over. Gale had an idea these raiders were familiar to him. It seemed all these border hawks resembled one another—being mostly small of build, wiry, angular, swarthy-faced, and black-haired, and they wore the oddly styled Mexican clothes and sombreros. A slow wrath stirred in Gale as he watched the trio. They showed not the slightest indication of breaking camp. One fellow, evidently the leader, packed a gun at his hip, the only weapon in sight. Gale noted this with speculative eyes. The raiders had slept inside the little adobe house, and had not yet brought out the carbines. Next Gale swept his gaze to the corral, in which he saw more than a dozen horses, some of them fine animals. They were stamping and whistling, fighting one another, and pawing the dirt. This was entirely natural behavior for desert horses penned in when they wanted to get at water and grass.

But suddenly one of the blacks, a big, shaggy fellow, shot up his ears and pointed his nose over the top of the fence. He whistled. Other horses looked in the same direction, and their ears went up, and they, too, whistled. Gale knew that other horses or men, very likely both, were approaching. But the Mexicans did not hear the alarm, or show any interest if they did. These mescal-drinking raiders were not scouts. It was notorious how easily they could be surprised or ambushed. Mostly they were ignorant, thick-skulled peons. They were wonderful horsemen, and could go long without food or water; but they had no other accomplishments or attributes calculated to help them in desert warfare. They had poor sight, poor hearing, poor judgment, and when excited they resembled crazed ants running wild.

Gale saw two Indians on burros come riding up the

other side of the knoll upon which the adobe house stood; and apparently they were not aware of the presence of the Mexicans, for they came on up the path. One Indian was a Papago. The other, striking in appearance for other reasons than that he seemed to be about to fall from the burro, Gale took to be a Yaqui. These travelers had absolutely nothing for an outfit except a blanket and a half-empty bag. They came over the knoll and down the path toward the well, turned a corner of the house, and completely surprised the raiders.

Gale heard a short, shrill cry, strangely high and wild, and this came from one of the Indians. It was answered by hoarse shouts. Then the leader of the trio, the Mexican who packed a gun, pulled it and fired point-blank. He missed once—and again. At the third shot the Papago shrieked and tumbled off his burro to fall in a heap. The other Indian swayed, as if the taking away of the support lent by his comrade had brought collapse, and with the fourth shot he, too, slipped to the ground.

The reports had frightened the horses in the corral; and the vicious black, crowding the rickety bars, broke them down. He came plunging out. Two of the Mexicans ran for him, catching him by nose and mane, and the third ran to block the gateway.

Then, with a splendid vaulting mount, the Mexican with the gun leaped to the back of the horse. He yelled and waved his gun, and urged the black forward. The manner of all three was savagely jocose. They were having sport. The two on the ground began to dance and jabber. The mounted leader shot again, and then stuck like a leech upon the bare back of the rearing black. It was a vain show of horsemanship. Then this Mexican, by some strange grip, brought the horse down, plunging almost upon the body of the Indian that had fallen last.

Gale stood aghast with his rifle clutched tight. He could not divine the intention of the raider, but suspected something strikingly brutal. The horse answered to that cruel, guiding hand, yet he swerved and bucked. He reared aloft, pawing the air, wildly snorting, then he plunged down upon the prostrate Indian. Even in the act the intelligent animal tried to keep from striking the body with his hoofs. But that was not possible. A yell, hideous in its passion, signaled this feat of horsemanship.

The Mexican made no move to trample the body of the Papago. He turned the black to ride again over the other Indian. That brought into Gale's mind what he had heard of a Mexican's hate for a Yaqui. It recalled the barbarism of these savage peons, and the war of extermination being waged upon the Yaquis.

Suddenly Gale was horrified to see the Yaqui writhe and raise a feeble hand. The action brought renewed and more savage cries from the Mexicans. The horse snorted in terror.

Gale could bear no more. He took a quick shot at the rider. He missed the moving figure, but hit the horse. There was a bound, a horrid scream, a mighty plunge, then the horse went down, giving the Mexican a stunning fall. Both beast and man lay still.

Gale rushed from his cover to intercept the other raiders before they could reach the house and their weapons. One fellow yelled and ran wildly in the opposite direction; the other stood stricken in his tracks. Gale ran in close and picked up the gun that had dropped from the raider leader's hand. This fellow had begun to stir, to come out of his stunned condition. Then the frightened horses burst the corral bars, and in a thundering, dust-mantled stream fled up the arroyo.

The fallen raider sat up, mumbling to his saints in one breath, cursing in his next. The other Mexican kept his stand, intimidated by the threatening rifle.

"Go, Greasers! Run!" yelled Gale. Then he yelled it in Spanish. At the point of his rifle he drove the two raiders out of the camp. His next move was to run into the house and fetch out the carbines. With a heavy

stone he dismantled each weapon. That done, he set out
on a run for his horse. He took the shortest cut down the
arroyo, with no concern as to whether or not he would
encounter the raiders. Probably such a meeting would
be all the worse for them, and they knew it. Blanco Sol
heard him coming and whistled a welcome, and when
Gale ran up the horse was snorting war. Mounting, Gale
rode rapidly back to the scene of the action, and his first
thought, when he arrived at the well, was to give Sol a
drink and to fill his canteens.

Then Gale led his horse up out of the waterhole, and
decided before remounting to have a look at the Indians.
The Papago had been shot through the heart, but the
Yaqui was still alive. Moreover, he was conscious and
staring up at Gale with great, strange, somber eyes, black
as volcanic slag.

"Gringo good—no kill," he said, in husky whisper.

His speech was not affirmative so much as questioning.

"Yaqui, you're done for," said Gale, and his words
were positive. He was simply speaking aloud his mind.

"Yaqui—no hurt—much," replied the Indian, and then
he spoke a strange word—repeated it again and again.

An instinct of Gale's, or perhaps some suggestion in the
husky, thick whisper or dark face, told Gale to reach for
his canteen. He lifted the Indian and gave him a drink,
and if ever in all his life he saw gratitude in human eyes
he saw it then. Then he examined the injured Yaqui,
not forgetting for an instant to send wary, fugitive
glances on all sides. Gale was not to be surprised. The
Indian had three wounds—a bullet hole in his shoulder,
a crushed arm, and a badly lacerated leg. What had been
the matter with him before being set upon by the raider
Gale could not be certain.

The ranger thought rapidly. This Yaqui would live
unless left there to die or be murdered by the Mexicans
when they found courage to sneak back to the well. It
never occurred to Gale to abandon the poor fellow. That

was where his old training, the higher order of human feeling, made impossible the following of any elemental instinct of self-preservation. All the same, Gale knew he multiplied his perils a hundredfold by burdening himself with a crippled Indian. Swiftly he set to work, and with rifle ever under his hand, and shifting glance spared from his task, he bound up the Yaqui's wounds. At the same time he kept keen watch.

The Indians' burros and the horses of the raiders were all out of sight. Time was too valuable for Gale to use any in what might be vain search. Therefore, he lifted the Yaqui upon Sol's broad shoulders and climbed into the saddle. At a word Sol dropped his head and started eastward up the trail, walking swiftly, without resentment for his double burden.

Far ahead, between two huge mesas where the trail mounted over a pass, a long line of dust clouds marked the position of the horses that had escaped from the corral. Those that had been stolen would travel straight and true for home, and perhaps would lead the others with them. The raiders were left on the desert without guns or mounts.

Blanco Sol walked or jog-trotted six miles to the hour. At that gait fifty miles would not have wet or turned a hair of his dazzling white coat. Gale, bearing in mind the ever-present possibility of encountering more raiders and of being pursued, saved the strength of the horse. Once out of sight of Papago Well, Gale dismounted and walked beside the horse, steadying with one firm hand the helpless, dangling Yaqui.

The sun cleared the eastern ramparts, and the coolness of morning fled as if before a magic foe. The whole desert changed. The grays wore bright; the mesquites glistened; the cactus took the silver hue of frost, and the rocks gleamed gold and red. Then, as the heat increased, a wind rushed up out of the valley behind Gale, and the hotter the sun blazed down the swifter rushed the wind.

The wonderful transparent haze of distance lost its bluish hue for one with tinge of yellow. Flying sand made the peaks dimly outlined.

Gale kept pace with his horse. He bore the twinge of pain that darted through his injured hip at every stride. His eye roved over the wide, smoky prospect seeking the landmarks he knew. When the wild and bold spurs of No Name Mountains loomed through a rent in flying clouds of sand he felt nearer home. Another hour brought him abreast of a dark, straight shaft rising clear from a beetling escarpment. This was a monument marking the international boundary line. When he had passed it he had his own country under foot. In the heat of midday he halted in the shade of a rock, and, lifting the Yaqui down, gave him a drink. Then, after a long, sweeping survey of the surrounding desert, he removed Sol's saddle and let him roll, and took for himself a welcome rest and a bite to eat.

The Yaqui was tenacious of life. He was still holding his own. For the first time Gale really looked at the Indian to study him. He had a large head nobly cast, and a face that resembled a shrunken mask. It seemed chiseled in the dark-red, volcanic lava of his Sonora wilderness. The Indian's eyes were always black and mystic, but this Yaqui's encompassed all the tragic desolation of the desert. They were fixed on Gale, moved only when he moved. The Indian was short and broad, and his body showed unusual muscular development, although he seemed greatly emaciated from starvation or illness.

Gale resumed his homeward journey. When he got through the pass he faced a great depression, as rough as if millions of gigantic spikes had been driven by the hammer of Thor into a seamed and cracked floor. This was Altar Valley. It was a chaos of arroyos, cañons, rocks, and ridges all mantled with cactus, and at its eastern end it claimed the dry bed of Forlorn River and water when there was any.

THE YAQUI

With a wounded, helpless man across the saddle, this stretch of thorny and contorted desert was practically impassable. Yet Gale headed into it unflinchingly. He would carry the Yaqui as far as possible, or until death made the burden no longer a duty. Blanco Sol plodded on over the dragging sand, up and down the steep, loose banks of washes, out on the rocks, and through the rows of white-toothed *choyas*.

The sun sloped westward, bending fiercer heat in vengeful, parting reluctance. The wind slackened. The dust settled. And the bold, forbidding front of No Name Mountains changed to red and gold. Gale held grimly by the side of the tireless, implacable horse, holding the Yaqui on the saddle, taking the brunt of the merciless thorns. In the end it became heartrending toil. His heavy chaps dragged him down; but he dared not go on without them, for, thick and stiff as they were, the terrible, steel-bayoneted spikes of the *choyas* pierced through to sting his legs.

To the last mile Gale held to Blanco Sol's gait and kept ever-watchful gaze ahead on the trail. Then, with the low, flat houses of Forlorn River shining red in the sunset, Gale flagged and rapidly weakened. The Yaqui slipped out of the saddle and dropped limp in the sand. Gale could not mount his horse. He clutched Sol's long tail and twisted his hand in it and staggered on.

Blanco Sol whistled a piercing blast. He scented cool water and sweet alfalfa hay. Twinkling lights ahead meant rest. The melancholy desert twilight rapidly succeeded the sunset. It accentuated the forlorn loneliness of the gray, winding river of sand and its grayer shores. Night shadows trooped down from the black and looming mountains.

VII

WHITE HORSES

" A CRIPPLED Yaqui! Why the hell did you saddle
yourself with him?" roared Belding, as he laid
Gale upon the bed.

Belding had grown hard these late, violent weeks.

"Because I chose," whispered Gale, in reply. "Go
after him—he dropped in the trail—across the river—
near the first big *saguaro.*"

Belding began to swear as he fumbled with matches
and the lamp; but as the light flared up he stopped short
in the middle of a word.

"You said you weren't hurt?" he demanded, in sharp
anxiety, as he bent over Gale.

"I'm only—all in.... Will you go—or send some one—
for the Yaqui?"

"Sure, Dick, sure," Belding replied, in softer tones.
Then he stalked out; his heels rang on the flagstones;
he opened a door and called: "Mother—girls, here's Dick
back. He's done up.... Now—no, no, he's not hurt or
in bad shape. You women!... Do what you can to make
him comfortable. I've got a little job on hand."

There were quick replies that Gale's dulling ears did
not distinguish. Then it seemed Mrs. Belding was beside his bed, her very presence so cool and soothing and
helpful; and Mercedes and Nell, wide-eyed and white-
faced, were fluttering around him. He drank thirstily,
but refused food. He wanted rest. And with their faces
drifting away in a kind of haze, with the feeling of gentle
hands about him, he lost consciousness.

114

WHITE HORSES

He slept twenty hours. Then he arose, thirsty, hungry, lame, overworn, and presently went in search of Belding and the business of the day.

"Your Yaqui was near dead, but guess we'll pull him through," said Belding. "Dick, the other day that Indian came here by rail and foot and Lord only knows how else, all the way from New Orleans! He spoke English better than most Indians, and I know a little Yaqui. I got some of his story and guessed the rest. The Mexican government is trying to root out the Yaquis. A year ago his tribe was taken in chains to a Mexican port on the Gulf. The fathers, mothers, children, were separated and put in ships bound for Yucatan. There they were made slaves on the great henequen plantations. They were driven, beaten, starved. Each slave had for a day's rations a hunk of sour dough, no more. Yucatan is low, marshy, damp, hot. The Yaquis were bred on the high, dry Sonoran plateau, where the air is like a knife. They dropped dead in the henequen fields, and their places were taken by more. You see, the Mexicans won't kill outright in their war of extermination of the Yaquis. They get use out of them. It's a horrible thing. . . . Well, this Yaqui you brought in escaped from his captors, got aboard ship, and eventually reached New Orleans. Somehow he traveled way out here. I gave him a bag of food, and he went off with a Papago Indian. He was a sick man then. And he must have fallen foul of some Greasers."

Gale told of his experience at Papago Well.

"That raider who tried to grind the Yaqui under a horse's hoofs—he was a hyena!" concluded Gale, shuddering. "I've seen some blood spilled and some hard sights, but that inhuman devil took my nerve. Why, as I told you, Belding, I missed a shot at him—not twenty paces!"

"Dick, in cases like that the sooner you clean up the bunch the better," said Belding, grimly. "As for hard sights—wait till you've seen a Yaqui do up a Mexican.

Bar none, that is the limit! It's blood lust, a racial hate, deep as life, and terrible. The Spaniards crushed the Aztecs four or five hundred years ago. That hate has had time to grow as deep as a cactus root. The Yaquis are mountain Aztecs. Personally, I think they are noble and intelligent, and if let alone would be peaceable and industrious. I like the few I've known. But they are a doomed race. Have you any idea what ailed this Yaqui before the raider got in his work?"

"No, I haven't. I noticed the Indian seemed in bad shape; but I couldn't tell what was the matter with him."

"Well, my idea is another personal one. Maybe it's off color. I think that Yaqui was, or is, for that matter, dying of a broken heart. All he wanted was to get back to his mountains and die. There are no Yaquis left in that part of Sonora he was bound for."

"He had a strange look in his eyes," said Gale, thoughtfully.

"Yes, I noticed that. But all Yaquis have a wild look. Dick, if I'm not mistaken, this fellow was a chief. It was a waste of strength, a needless risk for you to save him, pack him back here. But, damn the whole Greaser outfit generally, I'm glad you did!"

Gale remembered then to speak of his concern for Ladd.

"Laddy didn't go out to meet you," replied Belding. "I knew you were due in any day, and, as there's been trouble between here and Casita, I sent him that way. Since you've been out our friend Carter lost a bunch of horses and a few steers. Did you get a good look at the horses those raiders had at Papago Well?"

Dick had learned, since he had become a ranger, to see everything with keen, sure, photographic eye; and, being put to the test so often required of him, he described the horses as a dark-colored drove, mostly bays and blacks, with one spotted sorrel.

WHITE HORSES

"Some of Carter's—sure as you're born!" exclaimed Belding. "His bunch has been split up, divided among several bands of raiders. He has a grass ranch up here in Three Mile Arroyo. It's a good long ride in U. S. territory from the border."

"Those horses I saw will go home, don't you think?" asked Dick.

"Sure. They can't be caught or stopped."

"Well, what shall I do now?"

"Stay here and rest," bluntly replied Belding. "You need it. Let the women fuss over you—doctor you a little. When Jim gets back from Sonoyta I'll know more about what we ought to do. By Lord! it seems our job now isn't keeping Japs and Chinks out of the U. S. It's keeping our property from going into Mexico."

"Are there any letters for me?" asked Gale.

"Letters! Say, my boy, it'd take something pretty important to get me or any man here back Casita way. If the town is safe these days the road isn't. It's a month now since any one went to Casita."

Gale had received several letters from his sister Elsie, the last of which he had not answered. There had not been much opportunity for writing on his infrequent returns to Forlorn River; and, besides, Elsie had written that her father had stormed over what he considered Dick's falling into wild and evil ways.

"Time flies," said Dick. "George Thorne will be free before long, and he'll be coming out. I wonder if he'll stay here or try to take Mercedes away?"

"Well, he'll stay right here in Forlorn River, if I have any say," replied Belding. "I'd like to know how he'd ever get that Spanish girl out of the country now, with all the trails overrun by rebels and raiders. It'd be hard to disguise her. Say, Dick, maybe we can get Thorne to stay here. You know, since you've discovered the possibility of a big water supply, I've had dreams of a future for Forlorn River.... If only this war was over!

Dick, that's what it is—war—scattered war along the northern border of Mexico from gulf to gulf. What if it isn't our war? We're on the fringe. No, we can't develop Forlorn River until there's peace."

The discovery that Belding alluded to was one that might very well lead to the making of a wonderful and agricultural district of Altar Valley. While in college Dick Gale had studied engineering, but he had not set the scientific world afire with his brilliance. Nor after leaving college had he been able to satisfy his father that he could hold a job. Nevertheless, his smattering of engineering skill bore fruit in the last place on earth where anything might have been expected of it—in the desert. Gale had always wondered about the source of Forlorn River. No white man or Mexican, or, so far as known, no Indian, had climbed those mighty broken steps of rock called No Name Mountains, from which Forlorn River was supposed to come. Gale had discovered a long, narrow, rock-bottomed and rock-walled gulch that could be dammed at the lower end by the dynamiting of leaning cliffs above. An inexhaustible supply of water could be stored there. Furthermore, he had worked out an irrigation plan to bring the water down for mining uses, and to make a paradise out of that part of Altar Valley which lay in the United States. Belding claimed there was gold in the arroyos, gold in the gulches, not in quantities to make a prospector rejoice, but enough to work for. And the soil on the higher levels of Altar Valley needed only water to make it grow anything the year round. Gale, too, had come to have dreams of a future for Forlorn River.

On the afternoon of the following day Ladd unexpectedly appeared leading a lame and lathered horse into the yard. Belding and Gale, who were at work at the forge, looked up and were surprised out of speech. The legs of the horse were raw and red, and he seemed about to drop. Ladd's sombrero was missing; he wore a bloody scarf

round his head; sweat and blood and dust had formed
a crust on his face; little streams of powdery dust slid
from him; and the lower half of his scarred chaps were
full of broken white thorns.

"Howdy, boys," he drawled. "I shore am glad to see
you all."

"Where 'n hell's your hat?" demanded Belding, furi-
ously. It was a ridiculous greeting. But Belding's words
signified little. The dark shade of worry and solicitude
crossing his face told more than his blank amaze.

The ranger stopped unbuckling the saddle girths, and,
looking at Belding, broke into his slow, cool laugh.

"Tom, you recollect that whopper of a *saguaro* up here
where Carter's trail branches off the main trail to Casita?
Well, I climbed it an' left my hat on top for a wood-
pecker's nest."

"You've been running—fighting?" queried Belding, as
if Ladd had not spoken at all.

"I reckon it 'll dawn on you after a while," replied
Ladd, slipping the saddle.

"Laddy, go in the house to the women," said Belding.
"I'll tend to your horse."

"Shore, Tom, in a minute. I've been down the road.
An' I found hoss tracks an' steer tracks goin' across the
line. But I seen no sign of raiders till this mornin'.
Slept at Carter's last night. That raid the other day
cleaned him out. He's shootin' mad. Well, this mornin'
I rode plumb into a bunch of Carter's hosses, runnin' wild
for home. Some Greasers were tryin' to head them round
an' chase them back across the line. I rode in between
an' made matters embarrassin'. Carter's hosses got
away. Then me an' the Greasers had a little game of
hide an' seek in the cactus. I was on the wrong side, an'
had to break through their line to head toward home.
We run some. But I had a closer call than I'm stuck on
havin'."

"Laddy, you wouldn't have any such close calls if

you'd ride one of my horses," expostulated Belding. "This broncho of yours can run, and Lord knows he's game. But you want a big, strong horse, Mexican bred, with cactus in his blood. Take one of the bunch— Bull, White Woman, Blanco José."

"I had a big, fast horse a while back, but I lost him," said Ladd. "This bronch ain't so bad. Shore Bull an' that white devil with his Greaser name—they could run down my bronch, kill him in a mile of cactus. But, somehow, Tom, I can't make up my mind to take one of them grand white hosses. Shore I reckon I'm kinda soft. An' mebbe I'd better take one before the raiders clean up Forlorn River."

Belding cursed low and deep in his throat, and the sound resembled muttering thunder. The shade of anxiety on his face changed to one of dark gloom and passion. Next to his wife and daughter there was nothing so dear to him as those white horses. His father and his grandfather—all his progenitors of whom he had trace—had been lovers of horses. It was in Belding's blood.

"Laddy, before it's too late can't I get the whites away from the border?"

"Mebbe it ain't too late; but where can we take them?"

"To San Felipe?"

"No. We've more chance to hold them here."

"To Casita and the railroad?"

"Afraid to risk gettin' there. An' the town's full of rebels who need hosses."

"Then straight north?"

"Shore man, you're crazy. There's no water, no grass for a hundred miles. I'll tell you, Tom, the safest plan would be to take the white bunch south into Sonora, into some wild mountain valley. Keep them there till the raiders have traveled on back east. Pretty soon there won't be any rich pickin' left for these Greasers. An' then they'll ride on to new ranges."

"Laddy, I don't know the trails into Sonora. An' I can't trust a Mexican or a Papago. Between you and me, I'm afraid of this Indian who herds for me."

"I reckon we'd better stick here, Tom.... Dick, it's some good to see you again. But you seem kinda quiet. Shore you get quieter all the time. Did you see any sign of Jim out Sonoyta way?"

Then Belding led the lame horse toward the watering-trough, while the two rangers went toward the house. Dick was telling Ladd about the affair at Papago Well when they turned the corner under the porch. Nell was sitting in the door. She rose with a little scream and came flying toward them.

"Now I'll get it," whispered Ladd. "The women" make a baby of me. An' shore I can't help myself."

"Oh, Laddy, you've been hurt!" cried Nell, as with white cheeks and dilating eyes she ran to him and caught his arm.

"Nell, I only run a thorn in my ear."

"Oh, Laddy, don't lie! You've lied before. I know you're hurt. Come in to mother."

"Shore, Nell, it's only a scratch. My bronch throwed me."

"Laddy, no horse ever threw you." The girl's words and accusing eyes only hurried the ranger on to further duplicity.

"Mebbe I got it when I was ridin' hard under a mesquite, an' a sharp snag——"

"You've been shot!... Mamma, here's Laddy, and he's been shot!.... Oh, these dreadful days we're having! I can't bear them! Forlorn River used to be so safe and quiet. Nothing happened. But now! Jim comes home with a bloody hole in him—then Dick—then Laddy!... Oh, I'm afraid some day they'll *never* come home."

The morning was bright, still, and clear as crystal. The heat waves had not yet begun to rise from the desert.

A soft gray, white, and green tint perfectly blended lay like a mantle over mesquite and sand and cactus. The cañons of distant mountain showed deep and full of lilac haze.

Nell sat perched high upon the topmost bar of the corral gate. Dick leaned beside her, now with his eyes on her face, now gazing out into the alfalfa field where Belding's thoroughbreds grazed and pranced and romped and whistled. Nell watched the horses. She loved them, never tired of watching them. But her gaze was too consciously averted from the yearning eyes that tried to meet hers to be altogether natural.

A great fenced field of velvety green alfalfa furnished a rich background for the drove of about twenty white horses. Even without the horses the field would have presented a striking contrast to the surrounding hot, glaring blaze of rock and sand. Belding had bred a hundred or more horses from the original stock he had brought up from Durango. His particular interest was in the almost unblemished white, and these he had given especial care. He made a good deal of money selling this strain to friends among the ranchers back in Texas. No mercenary consideration, however, could have made him part with the great, rangy white horses he had gotten from the Durango breeder. They were named Blanco Diablo (White Devil), Blanco Sol (White Sun), Blanca Reina (White Queen), Blanca Mujer (White Woman), and El Grande Blanco Torres (The Big White Bull). Belding had been laughed at by ranchers for preserving the sentimental Durango names, and he had been unmercifully ridiculed by cowboys. But the names had never been changed.

Blanco Diablo was the only horse in the field that was not free to roam and graze where he listed. A stake and a halter held him to one corner, where he was severely let alone by the other horses. He did not like this isolation. Blanco Diablo was not happy unless he was run-

WHITE HORSES

ning, or fighting a rival. Of the two he would rather fight. If anything white could resemble a devil, this horse surely did. He had nothing beautiful about him, yet he drew the gaze and held it. The look of him suggested discontent, anger, revolt, viciousness. When he was not grazing or prancing, he held his long, lean head level, pointing his nose and showing his teeth. Belding's favorite was almost all the world to him, and he swore Diablo could stand more heat and thirst and cactus than any other horse he owned, and could run down and kill any horse in the Southwest. The fact that Ladd did not agree with Belding on these salient points was a great disappointment, and also a perpetual source for argument. Ladd and Lash both hated Diablo; and Dick Gale, after one or two narrow escapes from being brained, had inclined to the cowboys' side of the question.

El Grande Blanco Torres upheld his name. He was a huge, massive, thick-flanked stallion, a kingly mate for his full-bodied, glossy consort, Blanca Reina. The other mare, Blanca Mujer, was dazzling white, without a spot, perfectly pointed, racy, graceful, elegant, yet carrying weight and brawn and range that suggested her relation to her forebears.

The cowboys admitted some of Belding's claims for Diablo, but they gave loyal and unshakable allegiance to Blanco Sol. As for Dick, he had to fight himself to keep out of arguments, for he sometimes imagined he was unreasonable about the horse. Though he could not understand himself, he knew he loved Sol as a man loved a friend, a brother. Free of heavy saddle and the clumsy leg shields, Blanco Sol was somehow all-satisfying to the eyes of the rangers. As long and big as Diablo was, Sol was longer and bigger. Also, he was higher, more powerful. He looked more a thing for action—speedier. At a distance the honorable scars and lumps that marred his muscular legs were not visible. He grazed aloof from the others, and did not cavort nor prance; but when he lifted his head to whistle, how wild he appeared, and proud and splendid! The dazzling whiteness of the desert sun shone from his coat; he had the fire and spirit of the desert in his noble head, its strength and power in his gigantic frame.

"Belding swears Sol never beat Diablo," Dick was saying.

"He believes it," replied Nell. "Dad is queer about that horse."

"But Laddy rode Sol once—made him beat Diablo. Jim saw the race."

Nell laughed. "I saw it, too. For that matter, even I have made Sol put his nose before Dad's favorite."

"I'd like to have seen that. Nell, aren't you ever going to ride with me?"

"Some day—when it's safe."

"Safe!"

"I—I mean when the raiders have left the border."

"Oh, I'm glad you mean that," said Dick, laughing. "Well, I've often wondered how Belding ever came to give Blanco Sol to me."

"He was jealous. I think he wanted to get rid of Sol."

"No? Why, Nell, he'd give Laddy or Jim one of the whites any day."

"Would he? Not Devil or Queen or White Woman. Never in this world! But Dad has lots of fast horses the boys could pick from. Dick, I tell you Dad wants Blanco Sol to run himself out—lose his speed on the desert. Dad is just jealous for Diablo."

"Maybe. He surely has strange passion for horses. I think I understand better than I used to. I owned a couple of racers once. They were just animals to me, I guess. But Blanco Sol!"

"Do you love him?" asked Nell; and now a warm, blue flash of eyes swept his face.

"Do I? Well, rather."

"I'm glad. Sol has been finer, a better horse since you

owned him. He loves you, Dick. He's always watching for you. See him raise his head. That's for you. I know as much about horses as Dad or Laddy any day. Sol always hated Diablo, and never had much use for Dad."

Dick looked up at her.

"It'll be—be pretty hard to leave Sol—when I go away."

Nell sat perfectly still.

"Go away?" she asked, presently, with just the faintest tremor in her voice.

"Yes. Sometimes when I get blue—as I am to-day—I think I'll go. But, in sober truth, Nell, it's not likely that I'll spend all my life here."

There was no answer to this. Dick put his hand softly over hers; and, despite her half-hearted struggle to free it, he held on.

"Nell!"

Her color fled. He saw her lips part. Then a heavy step on the gravel, a cheerful, complaining voice interrupted him, and made him release Nell and draw back. Belding strode into view round the adobe shed.

"Hey, Dick, that darned Yaqui Indian can't be driven or hired or coaxed to leave Forlorn River. He's well enough to travel. I offered him horse, gun, blanket, grub. But no go."

"That's funny," replied Gale, with a smile. "Let him stay—put him to work."

"It doesn't strike me funny. But I'll tell you what I think. That poor, homeless, heartbroken Indian has taken a liking to you, Dick. These desert Yaquis are strange folk. I've heard strange stories about them. I'd believe 'most anything. And that's how I figure his case. You saved his life. That sort of thing counts big with any Indian, even with an Apache. With a Yaqui maybe it's of deep significance. I've heard a Yaqui say that with his tribe no debt to friend or foe ever went unpaid. Perhaps that's what ails this fellow."

"Dick, don't laugh," said Nell. "I've noticed the Yaqui. It's pathetic the way his great gloomy eyes follow you."

"You've made a friend," continued Belding. "A Yaqui could be a real friend on this desert. If he gets his strength back he'll be of service to you, don't mistake me. He's welcome here. But you're responsible for him, and you'll have trouble keeping him from massacring all the Greasers in Forlorn River."

The probability of a visit from the raiders, and a dash bolder than usual on the outskirts of a ranch, led Belding to build a new corral. It was not sightly to the eye, but it was high and exceedingly strong. The gate was a massive affair, swinging on huge hinges and fastening with heavy chains and padlocks. On the outside it had been completely covered with barb wire, which would make it a troublesome thing to work on in the dark.

At night Belding locked his white horses in this corral. The Papago herdsman slept in the adobe shed adjoining. Belding did not imagine that any wooden fence, however substantially built, could keep determined raiders from breaking it down. They would have to take time, however, and make considerable noise; and Belding relied on these facts. Belding did not believe a band of night raiders would hold out against a hot rifle fire. So he began to make up some of the sleep he had lost. It was noteworthy, however, that Ladd did not share Belding's sanguine hopes.

Jim Lash rode in, reporting that all was well out along the line toward the Sonoyta Oasis. Days passed, and Belding kept his rangers home. Nothing was heard of raiders at hand. Many of the newcomers, both American and Mexican, who came with wagons and pack trains from Casita stated that property and life were cheap back in that rebel-infested town.

One January morning Dick Gale was awakened by a

shrill, menacing cry. He leaped up bewildered and frightened. He heard Belding's booming voice answering shouts, and rapid steps on flagstones. But these had not awakened him. Heavy breaths, almost sobs, seemed at his very door. In the cold and gray dawn Dick saw something white. Gun in hand, he bounded across the room. Just outside his door stood Blanco Sol.

It was not unusual for Sol to come poking his head in at Dick's door during daylight. But now in the early dawn, when he had been locked in the corral, it meant raiders—no less. Dick called softly to the snorting horse; and, hurriedly getting into clothes and boots, he went out with a gun in each hand. Sol was quivering in every muscle. Like a dog he followed Dick around the house. Hearing shouts in the direction of the corrals, Gale bent swift steps that way.

He caught up with Jim Lash, who was also leading a white horse.

"Hello, Jim! Guess it's all over but the fireworks," said Dick.

"I cain't say just what has come off," replied Lash. "I've got the Bull. Found him runnin' in the yard."

They reached the corral to find Belding shaking, roaring like a madman. The gate was open, the corral was empty. Ladd stooped over the ground, evidently trying to find tracks.

"I reckon we might jest as well cool off an' wait for daylight," suggested Jim.

"Shore. They've flown the coop, you can gamble on that. Tom, where's the Papago?" said Ladd.

"He's gone, Laddy—gone!"

"Double-crossed us, eh? I see here's a crowbar lyin' by the gatepost. That Indian fetched it from the forge. It was used to pry out the bolts an' steeples. Tom, I reckon there wasn't much time lost forcin' that gate."

Belding, in shirt sleeves and barefooted, roared with

rage. He said he had heard the horses running as he leaped out of bed.

"What woke you?" asked Laddy.

"Sol. He came whistling for Dick. Didn't you hear him before I called you?"

"Hear him! He came thunderin' right under my window. I jumped up in bed, an' when he let out that blast Jim lit square in the middle of the floor, an' I was scared stiff. Dick, seein' it was your room he blew into, what did you think?"

"I couldn't think. I'm shaking yet, Laddy."

"Boys, I'll bet Sol spilled a few raiders if any got hands on him," said Jim. "Now, let's sit down an' wait for daylight. It's my idea we'll find some of the hosses runnin' loose. Tom, you go an' get some clothes on. It's freezin' cold. An' don't forget to tell the women folks we're all right."

Daylight made clear some details of the raid. The cowboys found tracks of eight raiders coming up from the river bed where their horses had been left. Evidently the Papago had been false to his trust. His few personal belongings were gone. Lash was correct in his idea of finding more horses loose in the fields. The men soon rounded up eleven of the whites, all more or less frightened, and among the number were Queen and Blanka Mujer. The raiders had been unable to handle more than one horse for each man. It was bitter irony of fate that Belding should lose his favorite, the one horse more dear to him than all the others. Somewhere out on the trail a raider was fighting the iron-jawed savage Blanco Diablo.

"I reckon we're some lucky," observed Jim Lash.

"Lucky ain't enough word," replied Ladd. "You see, it was this way. Some of the raiders piled over the fence while the others worked on the gate. Mebbe the Papago went inside to pick out the best hosses. But it didn't work except with Diablo, an' how they ever got him I don't know. I'd have gambled it'd take all of eight men to steal him. But Greasers have got us skinned on handlin' hosses."

Belding was unconsolable. He cursed and railed, and finally declared he was going to trail the raiders.

"Tom, you just ain't agoin' to do nothin' of the kind," said Laddy, coolly.

Belding groaned and bowed his head.

"Laddy, you're right," he replied, presently. "I've got to stand it. I can't leave the women and my property. But it's sure tough. I'm sore way down deep, and nothin' but blood would ever satisfy me."

"Leave that to me an' Jim," said Ladd.

"What do you mean to do?" demanded Belding, starting up.

"Shore I don't know yet.... Give me a light for my pipe. An' Dick, go fetch out your Yaqui."

VIII

THE RUNNING OF BLANCO SOL

THE Yaqui's strange dark glance roved over the corral, the swinging gate with its broken fastenings, the tracks in the road, and then rested upon Belding.

"Malo," he said, and his Spanish was clear.

"Shore Yaqui, about eight bad men, an' a traitor Indian," said Ladd.

"I think he means my herder," added Belding. "If he does, that settles any doubt it might be decent to have—Yaqui—malo Papago—Si?"

The Yaqui spread wide his hands. Then he bent over the tracks in the road. They led everywhither, but gradually he worked out of the thick net to take the trail that the cowboys had followed down to the river. Belding and the rangers kept close at his heels. Occasionally Dick lent a helping hand to the still feeble Indian. He found a trampled spot where the raiders had left their horses. From this point a deeply defined narrow trail led across the dry river bed.

Belding asked the Yaqui where the raiders would head for in the Sonora Desert. For answer the Indian followed the trail across the stream of sand, through willows and mesquite, up to the level of rock and cactus. At this point he halted. A sand-filled, almost obliterated trail led off to the left, and evidently went round to the east of No Name Mountains. To the right stretched the road toward Papago Well and the Sonoyta Oasis. The trail of the raiders took a southeasterly course over untrodden desert. The Yaqui spoke in his own tongue, then in Spanish.

"Think he means slow march," said Belding. "Laddy, from the looks of that trail the Greasers are having trouble with the horses."

"Tom, shore a boy could see that," replied Laddy. "Ask Yaqui to tell us where the raiders are headin', an' if there's water."

It was wonderful to see the Yaqui point. His dark hand stretched; he sighted over his stretched finger at a low white escarpment in the distance. Then with a stick he traced a line in the sand, and then at the end of that another line at right angles. He made crosses and marks and holes, and as he drew the rude map he talked in Yaqui, in Spanish; with a word here and there in English. Belding translated as best he could. The raiders were heading southeast toward the railroad that ran from Nogales down into Sonora. It was four days' travel, bad trail, good sure waterhole one day out; then water not sure for two days. Raiders traveling slow; bothered by too many horses, not looking for pursuit; were never pursued, could be headed and ambushed that night at the first waterhole, a natural trap in a valley.

The men returned to the ranch. The rangers ate and drank while making hurried preparations for travel. Blanco Sol and the cowboys' horses were fed, watered, and saddled. Ladd again refused to ride one of Belding's whites. He was quick and cold.

"Get me a long-range rifle an' lots of shells. Rustle now," he said.

"Laddy, you don't want to be weighted down?" protested Belding.

"Shore I want a gun that'll outshoot the dinky little carbines an' muskets used by the rebels. Trot one out an' be quick."

"I've got a .405, a long-barreled heavy rifle that'll

shoot a mile. I use it for mountain sheep. But Laddy, it'll break that bronch's back."

"His back won't break so easy.... Dick, take plenty of shells for your Remington. An' don't forget your field glass."

In less than an hour after the time of the raid the three rangers, heavily armed and superbly mounted on fresh horses, rode out on the trail. As Gale turned to look back from the far bank of Forlorn River, he saw Nell waving a white scarf. He stood high in his stirrups and waved his sombrero. Then the mesquite hid the girl's slight figure, and Gale wheeled grim-faced to follow the rangers.

They rode in single file with Ladd in the lead. He did not keep to the trail of the raiders all the time. He made short cuts. The raiders were traveling leisurely, and they evinced a liking for the most level and least cactus-covered stretches of ground. But the cowboy took a bee-line course for the white escarpment pointed out by the Yaqui; and nothing save deep washes and impassable patches of cactus or rocks made him swerve from it. He kept the broncho at a steady walk over the rougher places and at a swinging Indian canter over the hard and level ground. The sun grew hot and the wind began to blow. Dust clouds rolled along the blue horizon. Whirling columns of sand, like water spouts at sea, circled up out of white arid basins, and swept away and spread aloft before the wind. The escarpment began to rise, to change color, to show breaks upon its rocky face.

Whenever the rangers rode out on the brow of a knoll or ridge or an eminence, before starting to descend, Ladd required of Gale a long, careful, sweeping survey of the desert ahead through the field glass. There were streams of white dust to be seen, streaks of yellow dust, trailing low clouds of sand over the glistening dunes, but no steadily rising, uniformly shaped puffs that would tell a tale of moving horses on the desert.

RUNNING OF BLANCO SOL

At noon the rangers got out of the thick cactus. More-over, the gravel-bottomed washes, the low weathering, rotting ledges of yellow rock gave place to hard sandy rolls and bare clay knolls. The desert resembled a round-ed hummocky sea of color. All light shades of blue and pink and yellow and mauve were there dominated by the glaring white sun. Mirages glistened, wavered, faded in the shimmering waves of heat. Dust as fine as powder whiffed from under the tireless hoofs.

The rangers rode on and the escarpment began to loom. The desert floor inclined perceptibly upward. When Gale got an unobstructed view of the slope of the escarp-ment he located the raiders and horses. In another hour's travel the rangers could see with naked eyes a long, faint moving streak of black and white dots.

"They're headin' for that yellow pass," said Ladd, pointing to a break in the eastern end of the escarp-ment. "When they get out of sight we'll rustle. I'm thinkin' that waterhole the Yaqui spoke of lays in the pass."

The rangers traveled swiftly over the remaining miles of level desert leading to the ascent of the escarpment. When they achieved the gateway of the pass the sun was low in the west. Dwarfed mesquite and greasewood appeared among the rocks. Ladd gave the word to tie up horses and go forward on foot.

The narrow neck of the pass opened and descended into a valley half a mile wide, perhaps twice that in length. It had apparently unscalable slopes of weathered rock leading up to beetling walls. With floor bare and hard and white, except for a patch of green mesquite near the far end, it was a lurid and desolate spot, the barren bot-tom of a desert bowl.

"Keep down, boys," said Ladd. "There's the water-hole, an' hosses have sharp eyes. Shore the Yaqui figgered this place. I never seen its like for a trap."

Both white and black horses showed against the green,

and a thin curling column of blue smoke rose lazily from amid the mesquites.

"I reckon we'd better wait till dark, or mebby daylight," said Jim Lash.

"Let me figger some. Dick, what do you make of the outlet to this hole? Looks rough to me."

With his glass Gale studied the narrow construction of walls and roughened rising floor.

"Laddy, it's harder to get out at that end than here," he replied.

"Shore that's hard enough. Let me have a look.... Well, boys, it don't take no figgerin' for this job. Jim, I'll want you at the other end blockin' the pass when we're ready to start."

"When 'll that be?" inquired Jim.

"Soon as it's light enough in the mornin'. That Greaser outfit will hang till to-morrow. There's no sure water ahead for two days, you remember."

"I reckon I can slip through to the other end after dark," said Lash, thoughtfully. "It might get me in bad to go round."

The rangers stole back from the vantage point and returned to their horses, which they untied and left farther round among broken sections of cliff. For the horses it was a dry, hungry camp, but the rangers built a fire and had their short though strengthening meal.

The location was high, and through a break in the jumble of rocks the great colored void of desert could be seen rolling away endlessly to the west. The sun set, and after it had gone down the golden tips of mountains dulled, their lower shadows creeping upward.

Jim Lash rolled in his saddle blanket, his feet near the fire, and went to sleep. Ladd told Gale to do likewise while he kept the fire up and waited until it was late enough for Jim to undertake circling round the raiders. When Gale awakened the night was dark, cold, windy. The stars shone with white brilliance. Jim was up saddling his horse, and Ladd was talking low. When Gale rose to accompany them both rangers said he need not go. But Gale wanted to go, because that was the thing Ladd or Jim would have done.

With Ladd leading, they moved away into the gloom. Advance was exceedingly slow, careful, silent. Under the walls the blackness seemed impenetrable. The horse was as cautious as his master. Ladd did not lose his way, nevertheless he wound between blocks of stone and clumps of mesquite, and often tried a passage to abandon it. Finally the trail showed pale in the gloom, and eastern stars twinkled between the lofty ramparts of the pass.

The advance here was still as stealthily made as before, but not so difficult or slow. When the dense gloom of the pass lightened, and there was a wide space of sky and stars overhead, Ladd halted and stood silent a moment.

"Luck again!" he whispered. "The wind's in your face, Jim. The horses won't scent you. Go slow. Don't crack a stone. Keep close under the wall. Try to get up as high as this at the other end. Wait till daylight before riskin' a loose slope. I'll be ridin' the job early. That's all."

Ladd's cool, easy speech was scarcely significant of the perilous undertaking. Lash moved very slowly away, leading his horse. The soft pads of hoofs ceased to sound about the time the gray shape merged into the black shadows. Then Ladd touched Dick's arm, and turned back up the trail.

But Dick tarried a moment. He wanted a fuller sense of that ebony-bottomed abyss, with its pale encircling walls reaching up to the dusky blue sky and the brilliant stars. There was absolutely no sound.

He retraced his steps down, soon coming up with Ladd; and together they picked a way back through the winding recesses of cliff. The campfire was smoldering. Ladd replenished it and lay down to get a few hours' sleep, while Gale kept watch. The after part of the night wore on till the paling of stars, the thickening of gloom indicated the dark hour before dawn. The spot was secluded from wind, but the air grew cold as ice. Gale spent the time stripping wood from a dead mesquite, in pacing to and fro, in listening. Blanco Sol stamped occasionally, which sound was all that broke the stillness. Ladd awoke before the faintest gray appeared. The rangers ate and drank. When the black did lighten to gray they saddled the horses and led them out to the pass and down to the point where they had parted with Lash. Here they awaited daylight.

To Gale it seemed long in coming. Such a delay always aggravated the slow fire within him. He had nothing of Ladd's patience. He wanted action. The gray shadow below thinned out, and the patch of mesquite made a blot upon the pale valley. Then day dawned.

Still Ladd waited. He grew more silent, grimmer as the time of action approached. Gale wondered what the plan of attack would be. Yet he did not ask. He waited ready for orders.

The valley grew clear of gray shadow except under leaning walls on the eastern side. Then a straight column of smoke rose from among the mesquites. Manifestly this was what Ladd had been awaiting. He took the long .405 from its sheath and tried the lever. Then he lifted a cartridge belt from the pommel of his saddle. Every ring held a shell and these shells were four inches long. He buckled the belt round him.

"Come on, Dick."

Ladd led the way down the slope until he reached a position that commanded the rising of the trail from a level. It was the only place a man or horse could leave the valley for the pass.

"Dick, here's your stand. If any raider rides in range take a crack at him.... Now I want the lend of your hoss."

"Blanco Sol!" exclaimed Gale, more in amaze that

RUNNING OF BLANCO SOL

Ladd should ask for the horse than in reluctance to lend him.

"Will you let me have him?" Ladd repeated, almost curtly.

"Certainly, Laddy."

A smile momentarily chased the dark cold gloom that had set upon the ranger's lean face.

"Shore I appreciate it, Dick. I know how you care for that hoss. I guess mebbe Charley Ladd has loved a hoss! An' one not so good as Sol. I was only tryin' your nerve, Dick, askin' you without tellin' my plan. Sol won't get a scratch, you can gamble on that! I'll ride him down into the valley an' pull the Greasers out in the open. They've got short-ranged carbines. They can't keep out of range of the .405, an' I'll be takin' the dust of their lead. Sabe, señor?"

"Laddy! You'll run Sol away from the raiders when they chase you? Run him after them when they try to get away?"

"Shore. I'll run all the time. They can't gain on Sol, an' he'll run them down when I want. Can you beat it?"

"No. It's great!... But suppose a raider comes out on Blanco Diablo?"

"I reckon that's the one weak place in my plan. I'm figgerin' they'll never think of that till it's too late. But if they do, well, Sol can outrun Diablo. An' I can always kill the white devil!"

Ladd's strange hate of the horse showed in the passion of his last words, in his hardening jaw and grim set lips.

Gale's hand went swiftly to the ranger's shoulder.

"Laddy. Don't kill Diablo unless it's to save your life."

"All right. But, by God, if I get a chance I'll make Blanco Sol run him off his legs!"

He spoke no more and set about changing the length of Sol's stirrups. When he had them adjusted to suit he mounted and rode down the trail and out upon the level. He rode leisurely as if merely going to water his horse. The long black rifle lying across his saddle, however, was ominous.

Gale securely tied the other horse to a mesquite at hand, and took a position behind a low rock over which he could easily see and shoot when necessary. He imagined Jim Lash in a similar position at the far end of the valley blocking the outlet. Gale had grown accustomed to danger and the hard and fierce feelings peculiar to it. But the coming drama was so peculiarly different in promise from all he had experienced, that he awaited the moment of action with thrilling intensity. In him stirred long, brooding wrath at these border raiders—affection for Belding, and keen desire to avenge the outrages he had suffered—warm admiration for the cold, implacable Ladd and his absolute fearlessness, and a curious throbbing interest in the old, much-discussed and never-decided argument as to whether Blanco Sol was a fleeter, stronger horse than Blanco Diablo. Gale felt that he was to see a race between these great rivals—the kind of race that made men and horses terrible.

Ladd rode a quarter of a mile out upon the flat before anything happened. Then a whistle rent the still, cold air. A horse had seen or scented Blanco Sol. The whistle was prolonged, faint, but clear. It made the blood thrum in Gale's ears. Sol halted. His head shot up with the old, wild, spirited sweep. Gale leveled his glass at the patch of mesquites. He saw the raiders running to an open place, pointing, gesticulating. The glass brought them so close that he saw dark faces. Suddenly they broke and fled back among the trees. Then he got only white and dark gleams of moving bodies. Evidently that moment was one of boots, guns, and saddles for the raiders.

Lowering the glass, Gale saw that Blanco Sol had started forward again. His gait was now a canter, and

he had covered another quarter of a mile before horses
and raiders appeared upon the outskirts of the mesquites.
Then Blanco Sol stopped. His shrill, ringing whistle
came distinctly to Gale's ears. The raiders were mounted
on dark horses, and they stood abreast in a motionless
line. Gale chuckled as he appreciated what a puzzle the
situation presented for them. A lone horseman in the
middle of the valley did not perhaps seem so menacing
himself as the possibilities his presence suggested.

Then Gale saw a raider gallop swiftly from the group
toward the farther outlet of the valley. This might have
been owing to characteristic cowardice; but it was more
likely a move of the raiders to make sure of retreat.
Undoubtedly Ladd saw this galloping horseman. A
few waiting moments ensued. The galloping horseman
reached the slope, began to climb. With naked eyes
Gale saw a puff of white smoke spring out of the rocks.
Then the raider wheeled his plunging horse back to the
level, and went racing wildly down the valley.

The compact bunch of bays and blacks seemed to break
apart and spread rapidly from the edge of the mesquites.
Puffs of white smoke indicated firing, and showed the
nature of the raiders' excitement. They were far out of
ordinary range; but they spurred toward Ladd, shooting
as they rode. Ladd held his ground; the big white horse
stood like a rock in his tracks. Gale saw little spouts of
dust rise in front of Blanco Sol and spread swift as sight
to his rear. The raiders' bullets, striking low, were skip-
ping along the hard, bare floor of the valley. Then Ladd
raised the long rifle. There was no smoke, but three
high, spanging reports rang out. A gap opened in the
dark line of advancing horsemen; then a riderless steed
sheered off to the right. Blanco Sol seemed to turn as
on a pivot and charged back toward the lower end of the
valley. He circled over to Gale's right and stretched out
into his run. There were now five raiders in pursuit,
and they came sweeping down, yelling and shooting,

evidently sure of their quarry. Ladd reserved his fire. He kept turning from back to front in his saddle.

Gale saw how the space widened between pursuers and pursued, saw distinctly when Ladd eased up Sol's running. Manifestly Ladd intended to try to lead the raiders round in front of Gale's position, and, presently, Gale saw he was going to succeed. The raiders, riding like vaqueros, swept on in a curve, cutting off what distance they could. One fellow, a small, wiry rider, high on his mount's neck like a jockey, led his companions by many yards. He seemed to be getting the range of Ladd, or else he shot high, for his bullets did not strike up the dust behind Sol. Gale was ready to shoot. Blanco Sol pounded by, his rapid, rhythmic hoofbeats plainly to be heard. He was running easily.

Gale tried to still the jump of heart and pulse, and turned his eye again on the nearest pursuer. This raider was crossing in, his carbine held muzzle up in his right hand, and he was coming swiftly. It was a long shot, upward of five hundred yards. Gale had not time to adjust the sights of the Remington, but he knew the gun and, holding coarsely upon the swiftly moving blot, he began to shoot. The first bullet sent up a great splash of dust beneath the horse's nose, making him leap as if to hurdle a fence. The rifle was automatic; Gale needed only to pull the trigger. He saw now that the raiders behind were in line. Swiftly he worked the trigger. Suddenly the leading horse leaped convulsively, not up nor aside, but straight ahead, and then he crashed to the ground throwing his rider like a catapult, and then slid and rolled. He half got up, fell back, and kicked; but his rider never moved.

The other rangers sawed the reins of plunging steeds and whirled to escape the unseen battery. Gale slipped a fresh clip into the magazine of his rifle. He restrained himself from useless firing and gave eager eye to the duel below. Ladd began to shoot while Sol was running.

The .405 rang out sharply—then again. The heavy bullets streaked the dust all the way across the valley. Ladd aimed deliberately and pulled slowly, unmindful of the kicking dust-puffs behind Sol, and to the side. The raiders spurred madly in pursuit, loading and firing. They shot ten times while Ladd shot once, and all in vain; and on Ladd's sixth shot a raider toppled backward, threw his carbine and fell with his foot catching in a stirrup. The frightened horse plunged away, dragging him in a path of dust.

Gale had set himself to miss nothing of that fighting race, yet the action passed too swiftly for clear sight of all. Ladd had emptied a magazine, and now Blanco Sol quickened and lengthened his running stride. He ran away from his pursuers. Then it was that the ranger's ruse was divined by the raiders. They hauled sharply up and seemed to be conferring. But that was a fatal mistake. Blanco Sol was seen to break his gait and slow down in several jumps, then square away and stand stock-still. Ladd fired at the closely grouped raiders. An instant passed. Then Gale heard the spat of a bullet out in front, saw a puff of dust, then heard the lead strike the rocks and go whining away. And it was after this that one of the raiders fell prone from his saddle. The steel-jacketed .405 had gone through him on its uninterrupted way to hum past Gale's position.

The remaining two raiders frantically spurred their horses and fled up the valley. Ladd sent Sol after them. It seemed to Gale, even though he realized his excitement, that Blanco Sol made those horses seem like snails. The raiders split, one making for the eastern outlet, the other circling back of the mesquites. Ladd kept on after the latter. Then puffs of white smoke and rifle shots faintly crackling told of Jim Lash's hand in the game. However, he succeeded only in driving the raider back into the valley. But Ladd had turned the other horseman, and now it appeared the two raiders were between Lash above on

the stony slope and Ladd below on the level. There was
desperate riding on part of the raiders to keep from being
hemmed in closer. Only one of them got away, and he
came riding for life down under the eastern wall. Blanco
Sol settled into his graceful, beautiful swing. He gained
steadily, though he was far from extending himself. By
Gale's actual count the raider fired eight times in that
race down the valley, and all his bullets went low and
wide. He pitched the carbine away and lost all control
in headlong flight.

Some few hundred rods to the left of Gale the raider
put his horse to the weathered slope. He began to climb.
The horse was superb, infinitely more courageous than
his rider. Zigzag they went up and up, and when Ladd
reached the edge of the slope they were high along the
cracked and guttered rampart. Once—twice Ladd raised
the long rifle, but each time he lowered it. Gale divined
that the ranger's restraint was not on account of the
Mexican, but for that valiant and faithful horse. Up
and up he went, and the yellow dust clouds rose, and an
avalanche rolled rattling and cracking down the slope.
It was beyond belief that a horse, burdened or unburdened,
could find footing and hold it upon that wall of narrow
ledges and inverted, slanting gullies. But he climbed on,
sure-footed as a mountain goat, and, surmounting the last
rough steps, he stood a moment silhouetted against the
white sky. Then he disappeared. Ladd sat astride
Blanco Sol gazing upward. How the cowboy must have
honored that raider's brave steed!

Gale, who had been too dumb to shout the admiration
he felt, suddenly leaped up, and his voice came with a
shriek:

"Look out, Laddy!"

A big horse, like a white streak, was bearing down to
the right of the ranger. Blanco Diablo! A matchless
rider swung with the horse's motion. Gale was stunned.
Then he remembered the first raider, the one Lash had

shot at and driven away from the outlet. This fellow had made for the mesquite and had put a saddle on Belding's favorite. In the heat of the excitement, while Ladd had been intent upon the climbing horse, this last raider had come down with the speed of the wind straight for the western outlet. Perhaps, very probably, he did not know Gale was there to block it; and certainly he hoped to pass Ladd and Blanco Sol.

A touch of the spur made Sol lunge forward to head off the raider. Diablo was in his stride, but the distance and angle favored Sol. The raider had no carbine. He held aloft a gun ready to level it and fire. He sat the saddle as if it were a stationary seat. Gale saw Ladd lean down and drop the .405 in the sand. He would take no chances of wounding Belding's best-loved horse.

Then Gale sat transfixed with suspended breath watching the horses thundering toward him. Blanco Diablo was speeding low, fleet as an antelope, fierce and terrible in his devilish action, a horse for war and blood and death. He seemed unbeatable. Yet to see the magnificently running Blanco Sol was but to court a doubt. Gale stood spellbound. He might have shot the raider; but he never thought of such a thing. The distance swiftly lessened. Plain it was the raider could not make the opening ahead of Ladd. He saw it and swerved to the left, emptying his six-shooter as he turned. His dark face gleamed as he flashed by Gale.

Blanco Sol thundered across. Then the race became straight away up the valley. Diablo was cold and Sol was hot: therein lay the only handicap and vantage. It was a fleet, beautiful, magnificent race. Gale thrilled and exulted and yelled as his horse settled into a steadily swifter run and began to gain. The dust rolled in a funnel-shaped cloud from the flying hoofs. The raider wheeled with gun puffing white, and Ladd ducked low over the neck of his horse.

The gap between Diablo and Sol narrowed yard by

yard. At first it had been a wide one. The raider beat his mount and spurred, beat and spurred, wheeled round to shoot, then bent forward again. In his circle at the upper end of the valley he turned far short of the jumble of rocks.

All the devil that was in Blanco Diablo had its running on the downward stretch. The strange, cruel urge of bit and spur, the crazed rider who stuck like a burr upon him, the shots and smoke added terror to his natural violent temper. He ran himself off his feet. But he could not elude that relentless horse behind him. The running of Blanco Sol was that of a sure, remorseless driving power—steadier—stronger—swifter with every long and wonderful stride.

The raider tried to sheer Diablo off closer under the wall, to make the slope where his companion had escaped. But Diablo was uncontrollable. He was running wild, with breaking gait. Closer and closer crept that white, smoothly gliding, beautiful machine of speed.

Then, like one white flash following another, the two horses gleamed down the bank of a wash and disappeared in clouds of dust.

Gale watched with strained and smarting eyes. The thick throb in his ears was pierced by faint sounds of gunshots. Then he waited in almost unendurable suspense.

Suddenly something whiter than the background of dust appeared above the low roll of valley floor. Gale leveled his glass. In the clear circle shone Blanco Sol's noble head with its long black bar from ears to nose. Sol's head was drooping now. Another second showed Ladd still in the saddle.

The ranger was leading Blanco Diablo—spent—broken —dragging—riderless.

IX

NO man ever had a more eloquent and beautiful plead-
er for his cause than had Dick Gale in Mercedes
Castañeda. He peeped through the green, shining twigs
of the *palo verde* that shaded his door. The hour was
high noon, and the patio was sultry. The only sounds
were the hum of bees in the flowers and the low murmur
of the Spanish girl's melodious voice. Nell lay in the
hammock, her hands behind her head, with rosy cheeks
and arch eyes. Indeed she looked rebellious. Certain
it was, Dick reflected, that the young lady had fully
recovered the wilful personality which had lain dormant
for a while. Equally certain it seemed that Mercedes's
earnestness was not apparently having the effect it should
have had.

Dick was inclined to be rebellious himself. Belding had
kept the rangers in off the line, and therefore Dick had
been idle most of the time, and, though he tried hard, he
had been unable to stay far from Nell's vicinity. He believed she cared for him; but he could not catch her alone
long enough to verify his tormenting hope. When alone
she was as illusive as a shadow, as quick as a flash, as
mysterious as a Yaqui. When he tried to catch her in
the garden or fields, or corner her in the patio, she eluded
him, and left behind a memory of dark-blue, haunting
eyes. It was that look in her eyes which lent him hope.
At other times, when it might have been possible for
Dick to speak, Nell clung closely to Mercedes. He had
long before enlisted the loyal Mercedes in his cause; but

in spite of this Nell had been more than a match for
them both.

Gale pondered over an idea he had long revolved in
mind, and which now suddenly gave place to a decision
that made his heart swell and his cheek burn. He peeped
again through the green branches to see Nell laughing
at the fiery Mercedes.

"*Quién sabe,*" he called, mockingly, and was delighted
with Nell's quick, amazed start.

Then he went in search of Mrs. Belding, and found
her busy in the kitchen.

The relation between Gale and Mrs. Belding had subtly
and incomprehensively changed. He understood her less
than when at first he divined an antagonism in her. If
such a thing were possible she had retained the antagonism while seeming to yield to some influence that must
have been fondness for him. Gale was in no wise sure
of her affection, and he had long imagined she was afraid
of him, or of something that he represented. He had gone
on, openly and fairly, though discreetly, with his rather
one-sided love affair; and as time passed he had grown
less conscious of what had seemed her unspoken opposition. Gale had come to care greatly for Nell's mother.
Not only was she the comfort and strength of her home,
but also of the inhabitants of Forlorn River. Indian, Mexican, American were all the same to her in trouble or
illness; and then she was nurse, doctor, peacemaker,
helper. She was good and noble, and there was not a
child or grownup in Forlorn River who did not love and
bless her. But Mrs. Belding did not seem happy. She was
brooding, intense, deep, strong, eager for the happiness
and welfare of others; and she was dominated by a wor-
ship of her daughter that was as strange as it was pathetic. Mrs. Belding seldom smiled, and never laughed.
There was always a soft, sad, hurt look in her eyes. Gale
often wondered if there had been other tragedy in her
life than the supposed loss of her father in the desert.

Perhaps it was the very unsolved nature of that loss which made it haunting.

Mrs. Belding heard Dick's step as he entered the kitchen, and, looking up, greeted him.

"Mother," began Dick, earnestly. Belding called her that, and so did Ladd and Lash, but it was the first time for Dick. "Mother—I want to speak to you."

The only indication Mrs. Belding gave of being startled was in her eyes, which darkened, shadowed with multiplying thought.

"I love Nell," went on Dick, simply, "and I want you to let me ask her to be my wife."

Mrs. Belding's face blanched to a deathly white. Gale, thinking with surprise and concern that she was going to faint, moved quickly toward her, took her arm.

"Forgive me. I was blunt. . . . But I thought you knew."

"I've known for a long time," replied Mrs. Belding. Her voice was steady, and there was no evidence of agitation except in her pallor. "Then you—you haven't spoken to Nell?"

Dick laughed. "I've been trying to get a chance to tell her. I haven't had it yet. But she knows. There are other ways besides speech. And Mercedes has told her. I hope, I almost believe Nell cares a little for me."

"I've known that, too, for a long time," said Mrs. Belding, low almost as a whisper.

"You know!" cried Dick, with a glow and rush of feeling.

"Dick, you must be very blind not to see what has been plain to all of us. . . . I guess—it couldn't have been helped. You're a splendid fellow. No wonder she loves you."

"Mother! You'll give her to me?"

She drew him to the light and looked with strange, piercing intentness into his face. Gale had never dreamed a woman's eyes could hold such a world of thought and feeling. It seemed all the sweetness of life was there, and all the pain.

"Do you love her?" she asked.

"With all my heart."

"You want to marry her?"

"Ah, I want to! As much as I want to live and work for her."

"*When* would you marry her?"

"Why! . . . Just as soon as she will do it. To-morrow!" Dick gave a wild, exultant little laugh.

"Dick Gale, you want my Nell? You love her just as she is—her sweetness—her goodness? Just herself, body and soul? . . . There's nothing could change you—nothing?"

"Dear Mrs. Belding, I love Nell for herself. If she loves me I'll be the happiest of men. There's absolutely nothing that could make any difference in me."

"But your people? Oh, Dick, you come of a proud family. I can tell. I—I once knew a young man like you. A few months can't change pride—blood. Years can't change them. You've become a ranger. You love the adventure—the wild life. That won't last. Perhaps you'll settle down to ranching. I know you love the West. But, Dick, there's your family—"

"If you want to know anything about my family, I'll tell you," interrupted Dick, with strong feeling. "I've no secrets about them or myself. My future and happiness are Nell's to make. No one else shall count with me."

"Then, Dick—you may have her. God—bless—you —both."

Mrs. Belding's strained face underwent a swift and mobile relaxation, and suddenly she was weeping in strangely mingled happiness and bitterness.

"Why, mother!" Gale could say no more. He did not comprehend a mood seemingly so utterly at variance with Mrs. Belding's habitual temperament. But he put his arm around her. In another moment she had gained command over herself, and, kissing him, she pushed him out of the door.

"There! Go tell her, Dick. . . . And have some spunk about it!"

Gale went thoughtfully back to his room. He vowed that he would answer for Nell's happiness, if he had the wonderful good fortune to win her. Then remembering the hope Mrs. Belding had given him, Dick lost his gravity in a flash, and something began to dance and ring within him. He simply could not keep his steps turned from the patio. Every path led there. His blood was throbbing, his hopes mounting, his spirit soaring. He knew he had never before entered the patio with that inspirited presence.

"Now for some spunk!" he said, under his breath.

Plainly he meant his merry whistle and his buoyant step to interrupt this first languorous stage of the siesta which the girls always took during the hot hours. Nell had acquired the habit long before Mercedes came to show how fixed a thing it was in the life of the tropics. But neither girl heard him. Mercedes lay under the *palo verde,* her beautiful head dark and still upon a cushion. Nell was asleep in the hammock. There was an abandonment in her deep repose, and a faint smile upon her face. Her sweet, red lips, with the soft, perfect curve, had always fascinated Dick, and now drew him irresistibly. He had always been consumed with a desire to kiss her, and now he was overwhelmed with his opportunity. It would be a terrible thing to do, but if she did not awaken at once— No, he would fight the temptation. That would be more than spunk. It would— Suddenly an ugly green fly sailed low over Nell, appeared about to alight on her. Noiselessly Dick stepped close to the hammock bent under the tree, and with a sweep of his hand chased the intruding fly away. But he found himself powerless to straighten up. He

was close to her—bending over her face—near the sweet
lips. The insolent, dreaming smile just parted them.
Then he thought he was lost. But she stirred—he feared
she would awaken.

He had stepped back erect when she opened her eyes.
They were sleepy, yet surprised until she saw him. Then
she was wide awake in a second, bewildered, uncertain.

"Why—you here?" she asked, slowly.

"Large as life!" replied Dick, with unusual gayety.

"How long have you been here?"

"Just got here this fraction of a second," he replied,
lying shamelessly.

It was evident that she did not know whether or not
to believe him, and as she studied him a slow blush dyed
her cheek.

"You are absolutely truthful when you say you just
stepped there?"

"Why, of course," answered Dick, right glad he did not
have to lie about that.

"I thought—I was—dreaming," she said, and evidently
the sound of her voice reassured her.

"Yes, you looked as if you were having pleasant
dreams," replied Dick. "So sorry to wake you. I can't
see how I came to do it, I was so quiet. Mercedes didn't
wake. Well, I'll go and let you have your siesta and
dreams."

But he did not move to go. Nell regarded him with
curious, speculative eyes.

"Isn't it a lovely day?" queried Dick.

"I think it's hot."

"Only ninety in the shade. And you've told me the
mercury goes to one hundred and thirty in midsummer.
This is just a glorious golden day."

"Yesterday was finer, but you didn't notice it."

"Oh, yesterday was somewhere back in the past—the
inconsequential past."

Nell's sleepy blue eyes opened a little wider. She did

not know what to make of this changed young man. Dick felt gleeful and tried hard to keep the fact from becoming manifest.

"What's the inconsequential past? You seem remarkably happy to-day."

"I certainly am happy. *Adios*. Pleasant dreams."

Dick turned away then and left the patio by the opening into the yard. Nell was really sleepy, and when she had fallen asleep again he would return. He walked around for a while. Belding and the rangers were shoeing a broncho. Yaqui was in the field with the horses. Blanco Sol grazed contentedly, and now and then lifted his head to watch. His long ears went up at sight of his master, and he whistled. Presently Dick, as if magnet-drawn, retraced his steps to the patio and entered noiselessly.

Nell was now deep in her siesta. She was inert, relaxed, untroubled by dreams. Her hair was damp on her brow.

Again Nell stirred, and gradually awakened. Her eyes unclosed, humid, shadowy, unconscious. They rested upon Dick for a moment before they became clear and comprehensive. He stood back fully ten feet from her, and to all outside appearances regarded her calmly.

"I've interrupted your siesta again," he said. "Please forgive me. I'll take myself off."

He wandered away, and when it became impossible for him to stay away any longer he returned to the patio.

The instant his glance rested upon Nell's face he divined she was feigning sleep. The faint rose-blush had paled. The warm, rich, golden tint of her skin had fled. Dick dropped upon his knees and bent over her. Though his blood was churning in his veins, his breast laboring, his mind whirling with the wonder of that moment and its promise, he made himself deliberate. He wanted more than anything he had ever wanted in his life to see if she would keep up that pretense of sleep and let him kiss her. She must have felt his breath, for her hair waved off her brow. Her cheeks were now white. Her breast swelled and sank. He bent down closer—closer. But he must have been maddeningly slow, for as he bent still closer Nell's eyes opened, and he caught a swift purple gaze of eyes as she whirled her head. Then, with a little cry, she rose and fled.

X

NO word from George Thorne had come to Forlorn
River in weeks. Gale grew concerned over the fact,
and began to wonder if anything serious could have
happened to him. Mercedes showed a slow, wearing
strain.

Thorne's commission expired the end of January, and
if he could not get his discharge immediately, he surely
could obtain leave of absence. Therefore, Gale waited,
not without growing anxiety, and did his best to cheer
Mercedes. The first of February came bringing news of
rebel activities and bandit operations in and around
Casita, but not a word from the cavalryman.

Mercedes became silent, mournful. Her eyes were
great black windows of tragedy. Nell devoted herself
entirely to the unfortunate girl; Dick exerted himself to
persuade her that all would yet come well; in fact, the
whole household could not have been kinder to a sister
or a daughter. But their united efforts were unavailing.
Mercedes seemed to accept with fatalistic hopelessness
a last and crowning misfortune.

A dozen times Gale declared he would ride in to Casita
and find out why they did not hear from Thorne; however, older and wiser heads prevailed over his impetuosity.
Belding was not sanguine over the safety of the Casita
trail. Refugees from there arrived every day in Forlorn
River, and if the tales they told were true, real war would
have been preferable to what was going on along the
border. Belding and the rangers and the Yaqui held a

DESERT GOLD

consultation. Not only had the Indian become a faithful servant to Gale, but he was also of value to Belding. Yaqui had all the craft of his class, and superior intelligence. His knowledge of Mexicans was second only to his hate of them. And Yaqui, who had been scouting on all the trails, gave information that made Belding decide to wait some days before sending any one to Casita. He required promises from his rangers, particularly Gale, not to leave without his consent.

It was upon Gale's coming from this conference that he encountered Nell. Since the interrupted siesta episode she had been more than ordinarily elusive, and about all he had received from her was a tantalizing smile from a distance. He got the impression now, however, that she had awaited him. When he drew close to her he was certain of it, and he experienced more than surprise.

"Dick," she began, hurriedly. "Dad's not going to send any one to see about Thorne?"

"No, not yet. He thinks it best not to. We all think so. I'm sorry. Poor Mercedes!"

"I knew it. I tried to coax him to send Laddy or even Yaqui. He wouldn't listen to me. Dick, Mercedes is dying by inches. Can't you see what ails her? It's more than love or fear. It's uncertainty—suspense. Oh, can't we find out for her?"

"Nell, I feel as badly as you about her. I wanted to ride in to Casita. Belding shut me up quick, the last time."

Nell came close to Gale, clasped his arm. There was no color in her face. Her eyes held a dark, eager excitement.

"Dick, will you slip off without Dad's consent? Risk it! Go to Casita and find out what's happened to Thorne—at least if he ever started for Forlorn River?"

"No, Nell, I won't do that."

She drew away from him with passionate suddenness. "Are you afraid?"

This certainly was not the Nell Burton that Gale knew.

"No, I'm not afraid," Gale replied, a little nettled.

"Will you go—for my sake?" Like lightning her mood changed and she was close to him again, hands on his, her face white, her whole presence sweetly alluring.

"Nell, I won't disobey Belding," protested Gale. "I won't break my word."

"Dick, it 'll not be so bad as that. But—what if it is?... Go, Dick, if not for poor Mercedes's sake, then for mine—to please me. I'll—I'll .... you won't lose anything by going. I think I know how Mercedes feels. Just a word from Thorne or about him would save her. Take Blanco Sol and go, Dick. What rebel outfit could ever ride you down on that horse? Why, Dick, if I was up on Sol I wouldn't be afraid of the whole rebel army."

"My dear girl, it's not a question of being afraid. It's my word—my duty to Belding."

"You said you loved me. If you do love me you will go.... You don't love me!"

Gale could only stare at this transformed girl.

"Dick, listen!... If you go—if you fetch some word of Thorne to comfort Mercedes, you—well, you will have your reward."

"*Nell!*"

Her dangerous sweetness was as amazing as this newly revealed character.

"Dick, will you go?"

"No—no!" cried Gale, in violence, struggling with himself. "Nell Burton, I'll tell you this. To have the reward I want would mean pretty near heaven for me. But not even for that will I break my word to your father."

She seemed the incarnation of girlish scorn and willful passion.

"*Gracias,* señor," she replied, mockingly. "*Adios.*" Then she flashed out of his sight.

Gale went to his room at once, disturbed and thrilling, and did not soon recover from that encounter.

The following morning at the breakfast table Nell was not present. Mrs. Belding evidently considered the fact somewhat unusual, for she called out into the patio and then into the yard. Then she went to Mercedes's room. But Nell was not there, either.

"She's in one of her tantrums lately," said Belding. "Wouldn't speak to me this morning. Let her alone, mother. She's spoiled enough, without running after her. She's always hungry. She'll be on hand presently, don't mistake me."

Notwithstanding Belding's conviction, which Gale shared, Nell did not appear at all during the hour. When Belding and the rangers went outside, Yaqui was eating his meal on the bench where he always sat.

"Yaqui—*Lluvia d' oro, si?*" asked Belding, waving his hand toward the corrals. The Indian's beautiful name for Nell meant "shower of gold," and Belding used it in asking Yaqui if he had seen her. He received a negative reply.

Perhaps half an hour afterward, as Gale was leaving his room, he saw the Yaqui running up the path from the fields. It was markedly out of the ordinary to see the Indian run. Gale wondered what was the matter. Yaqui ran straight to Belding, who was at work at his bench under the wagon shed. In less than a moment Belding was bellowing for his rangers. Gale got to him first, but Ladd and Lash were not far behind.

"Blanco Sol gone!" yelled Belding, in a rage.

"Gone? In broad daylight, with the Indian a-watchin'?" queried Ladd.

"It happened while Yaqui was at breakfast. That's sure. He'd just watered Sol."

"Raiders!" exclaimed Jim Lash.

"Lord only knows. Yaqui says it wasn't raiders."

"Mebbe Sol's just walked off somewheres."

"He was haltered in the corral."

"Send Yaqui to find the hoss's trail, an' let's figger," said Ladd. "Shore this 's no raider job."

In the swift search that ensued Gale did not have anything to say; but his mind was forming a conclusion. When he found his old saddle and bridle missing from the peg in the barn his conclusion became a positive conviction, and it made him, for the moment, cold and sick and speechless.

"Hey, Dick, don't take it so much to heart," said Belding. "We'll likely find Sol, and if we don't, there's other good horses."

"I'm not thinking of Sol," replied Gale.

Ladd cast a sharp glance at Gale, snapped his fingers, and said:

"Damn me if I ain't guessed it, too!"

"What's wrong with you locoed gents?" bluntly demanded Belding.

"Nell has slipped away on Sol," answered Dick.

There was a blank pause, which presently Belding broke.

"Well, that's all right, if Nell's on him. I was afraid we'd lost the horse."

"Belding, you're trackin' bad," said Ladd, wagging his head.

"Nell has started for Casita," burst out Gale. "She has gone to fetch Mercedes some word about Thorne. Oh, Belding, you needn't shake your head. I know she's gone. She tried to persuade me to go, and was furious when I wouldn't."

"I don't believe it," replied Belding, hoarsely. "Nell may have her temper. She's a little devil at times, but she always had good sense."

"Tom, you can gamble she's gone," said Ladd.

"Aw, hell, no! Jim, what do you think?" implored Belding.

"I reckon Sol's white head is pointed level an' straight

down the Casita trail. An' Nell can ride. We're losin' time."

That roused Belding to action.

"I say you're all wrong," he yelled, starting for the corrals. "She's only taking a little ride, same as she's done often. But rustle now. Find out. Dick, you ride cross the valley. Jim, you hunt up and down the river. I'll head up San Felipe way. And you, Laddy, take Diablo and hit the Casita trail. If she really has gone after Thorne you can catch her in an hour or so."

"Shore I'll go," replied Ladd. "But, Beldin', if you're not plumb crazy you're close to it. That big white devil can't catch Sol. Not in an hour or a day or a week! What's more, at the end of any runnin' time, with an even start, Sol will be farther in the lead. An' now Sol's got an hour's start."

"Laddy, you mean to say Sol is a faster horse than Diablo?" thundered Belding, his face purple.

"Shore. I mean to tell you just that there," replied the ranger.

"I'll—I'll bet a—"

"We're wastin' time," curtly interrupted Ladd. "You can gamble on this if you want to. I'll ride your Blanco Devil as he never was rid before, 'cept once when a damn sight better hossman than I am couldn't make him out-run Sol."

Without more words the men saddled and were off, not waiting for the Yaqui to come in with possible information as to what trail Blanco Sol had taken. It certainly did not show in the clear sand of the level valley where Gale rode to and fro. When Gale returned to the house he found Belding and Lash awaiting him. They did not mention their own search, but stated that Yaqui had found Blanco Sol's tracks in the Casita trail. After some consultation Belding decided to send Lash along after Ladd.

The interminable time that followed contained for

Gale about as much suspense as he could well bear. What astonished him and helped him greatly to fight off actual distress was the endurance of Nell's mother.

Early on the morning of the second day, Gale, who had acquired an unbreakable habit of watching, saw three white horses and a bay come wearily stepping down the road. He heard Blanco Sol's familiar whistle, and he leaped up wild with joy. The horse was riderless. Gale's sudden joy received a violent check, then resurged when he saw a limp white form in Jim Lash's arms. Ladd was supporting a horseman who wore a military uniform.

Gale shouted with joy and ran into the house to tell the good news. It was the ever-thoughtful Mrs. Belding who prevented him from rushing in to tell Mercedes. Then he hurried out into the yard, closely followed by the Beldings.

Lash handed down a ragged, travel-stained, wan girl into Belding's arms.

"Dad! Mama!"

It was indeed a repentant Nell, but there was spirit yet in the tired blue eyes. Then she caught sight of Gale and gave him a faint smile.

"Hello—Dick."

"Nell!" Gale reached for her hand, held it tightly, and found speech difficult.

"You needn't worry—about your old horse," she said, as Belding carried her toward the door. "Oh, Dick! Blanco Sol is—glorious!"

Gale turned to greet his friend. Indeed, it was but a haggard ghost of the cavalryman. Thorne looked ill or wounded. Gale's greeting was also a question full of fear.

Thorne's answer was a faint smile. He seemed ready to drop from the saddle. Gale helped Ladd hold Thorne upon the horse until they reached the house. Belding came out again. His welcome was checked as he saw the condition of the cavalryman. Thorne reeled into Dick's arms. But he was able to stand and walk.

"I'm not—hurt. Only weak—starved," he said. "Is Mercedes— Take me to her."

"She'll be well the minute she sees him," averred Belding, as he and Gale led the cavalryman to Mercedes's room. There they left him; and Gale, at least, felt his ears ringing with the girl's broken cry of joy.

When Belding and Gale hurried forth again the rangers were tending the tired horses. Upon returning to the house Jim Lash calmly lit his pipe, and Ladd declared that, hungry as he was, he had to tell his story.

"Shore, Beldin'," began Ladd, "that was funny about Diablo catchin' Blanco Sol. Funny ain't the word. I nearly laughed myself to death. Well, I rode in Sol's tracks all the way to Casita. Never seen a rebel or a raider till I got to town. Figgered Nell made the trip in five hours. I went straight to the camp of the cavalrymen, an' found them just coolin' off an' dressin' down their hosses after what looked to me like a big ride. I got there too late for the fireworks.

"Some soldier took me to an officer's tent. Nell was there, some white an' all in. She just said, 'Laddy!' Thorne was there, too, an' he was bein' worked over by the camp doctor. I didn't ask no questions, because I seen quiet was needed round that tent. After satisfying myself that Nell was all right, an' Thorne in no danger, I went out.

"Shore there was so darn many fellers who wanted to an' tried to tell me what'd come off, I thought I'd never find out. But I got the story piece by piece. An' here's what happened.

"Nell rode Blanco Sol a-tearin' into camp, an' had a crowd round her in a jiffy. She told who she was, where she'd come from, an' what she wanted. Well, it seemed a day or so before Nell got there the cavalrymen had heard word of Thorne. You see, Thorne had left camp on leave of absence some time before. He was shore mysterious, they said, an' told nobody where he was goin'.

ROJAS

A week or so after he left camp some Greaser give it away that Rojas had a prisoner in a dobe shack near his camp. Nobody paid much attention to what the Greaser said. He wanted money for mescal. An' it was usual for Rojas to have prisoners. But in a few more days it turned out pretty sure that for some reason Rojas was holdin' Thorne.

"Now it happened when this news came Colonel Weede was in Nogales with his staff, an' the officer left in charge didn't know how to proceed. Rojas's camp was across the line in Mexico, an' ridin' over there was serious business. It meant a whole lot more than just scatterin' one Greaser camp. It was what had been botherin' more'n one colonel along the line. Thorne's feller soldiers was anxious to get him out of a bad fix, but they had to wait for orders.

"When Nell found out Thorne was bein' starved an' beat in a dobe shack no more'n two mile across the line, she shore stirred up that cavalry camp. Shore! She told them soldiers Rojas was holdin' Thorne—torturin' him to make him tell where Mercedes was. She told about Mercedes—how sweet an' beautiful she was—how her father had been murdered by Rojas—how she had been hounded by the bandit—how ill an' miserable she was, waitin' for her lover. An' she begged the cavalrymen to rescue Thorne.

"From the way it was told to me I reckon them cavalrymen went up in the air. Fine fiery lot of young bloods, I thought, achin' for a scrap. But the officer in charge, bein' in a ticklish place, still held out for higher orders.

"Then Nell broke loose. You-all know Nell's tongue is sometimes like a *choya* thorn. I'd have give somethin' to see her work up that soldier outfit. Nell's never so pretty as when she's mad. An' this last stunt of hers was no girly tantrum, as Beldin' calls it. She musta been ragin' with all the hell there's in a woman.... Can't you fellers see her on Blanco Sol with her eyes turnin' black?"

Ladd mopped his sweaty face with his dusty scarf. He was beaming. He was growing excited, hurried in his narrative.

"Right out then Nell *swore* she'd go after Thorne. If them cavalrymen couldn't ride with a Western girl to save a brother American—let them hang back! One feller, under orders, tried to stop Blanco Sol. An' that feller invited himself to the hospital. Then the cavalrymen went flyin' for their hosses. Mebbe Nell's move was just foxy—woman's cunnin'. But I'm thinkin' as she felt then she'd have sent Blanco Sol straight into Rojas's camp, which, I'd forgot to say, was in plain sight.

"It didn't take long for every cavalryman in that camp to get wind of what was comin' off. Shore they musta been wild. They strung out after Nell in a thunderin' troop.

"Say, I wish you fellers could see the lane that bunch of hosses left in the greasewood an' cactus. Looks like there'd been a cattle stampede on the desert.... Blanco Sol stayed out in front, you can gamble on that. Right into Rojas's camp! *Sabe,* you señors? Gawd Almighty! I never had a grief that 'd hold a candle to this one of bein' too late to see Nell an' Sol in their one best race.

"Rojas an' his men vamoosed without a shot. That ain't surprisin'. There wasn't a shot fired by anybody. The cavalrymen soon found Thorne an' hurried with him back on Uncle Sam's land. Thorne was half naked, black an' blue all over, thin as a rail. He looked mighty sick when I seen him first. That was a little after midday. He was given food an' drink. Shore he seemed a starved man. But he picked up wonderful, an' by the time Jim came along he was wantin' to start for Forlorn River. So was Nell. By main strength as much as persuasion we kept the two of them quiet till next evenin' at dark.

"Well, we made as sneaky a start in the dark as Jim an' me could manage, an' never hit the trail till we was miles from town. Thorne's nerve held him up for a

while. Then all at once he tumbled out of his saddle.
We got him back, an' Lash held him on. Nell didn't
give out till daybreak."

As Ladd paused in his story Belding began to stutter,
and finally he exploded. His mighty utterances were incoherent. But plainly the wrath he had felt toward the
wilful girl was forgotten. Gale remained gripped by
silence.

"I reckon you'll all be some surprised when you see
Casita," went on Ladd. "It's half burned an' half tore
down. An' the rebels are livin' fat. There was rumors
of another federal force on the road from Case Grandes.
I seen a good many Americans from interior Mexico, an'
the stories they told would make your hair stand up.
They all packed guns, was fightin' mad at Greasers, an'
sore on the good old U. S. But shore glad to get over
the line! Some were waitin' for trains, which don't run
reg'lar no more, an' others were ready to hit the trails
north."

"Laddy, what knocks me is Rojas holding Thorne
prisoner, trying to make him tell where Mercedes had
been hidden," said Belding.

"Shore. It 'd knock anybody."

"The bandit's crazy over her. That's the Spanish of
it," replied Belding, his voice rolling. "Rojas is a peon.
He's been a slave to the proud Castilian. He loves Mercedes as he hates her. When I was down in Durango I
saw something of these peons' insane passions. Rojas
wants this girl only to have her, then kill her. It's damn
strange, boys, and even with Thorne here our troubles
have just begun."

"Tom, you spoke correct," said Jim Ladd, in his cool
drawl.

"Shore I'm not sayin' what I think," added Ladd. But
the look of him was not indicative of a tranquil optimism.

Thorne was put to bed in Gale's room. He was very
weak, yet he would keep Mercedes's hand and gaze at

her with unbelieving eyes. Mercedes's failing hold on hope and strength seemed to have been a fantasy; she was again vivid, magnetic, beautiful, shot through and through with intense and throbbing life. She induced him to take food and drink. Then, fighting sleep with what little strength he had left, at last he succumbed.

For all Dick could ascertain his friend never stirred an eyelash nor a finger for twenty-seven hours. When he awoke he was pale, weak, but the old Thorne.

"Hello, Dick; I didn't dream it then," he said. "There you are, and my darling with the proud, dark eyes—she's here?"

"Why, yes, you locoed cavalryman."

"Say, what's happened to you? It can't be those clothes and a little bronze on your face.... Dick, you're older—you've changed. You're not so thickly built. By Gad, if you don't look fine!"

"Thanks. I'm sorry I can't return the compliment. You're about the seediest, hungriest-looking fellow I ever saw.... Say, old man, you must have had a tough time."

A dark and somber fire burned out the happiness in Thorne's eyes.

"Dick, don't make me—don't let me think of that fiend Rojas!... I'm here now. I'll be well in a day or two. Then!..."

Mercedes came in, radiant and soft-voiced. She fell upon her knees beside Thorne's bed, and neither of them appeared to see Nell enter with a tray. Then Gale and Nell made a good deal of unnecessary bustle in moving a small table close to the bed. Mercedes had forgotten for the moment that her lover had been a starving man. If Thorne remembered it he did not care. They held hands and looked at each other without speaking.

"Nell, I thought I had it bad," whispered Dick. "But I'm not—"

"Hush. It's beautiful,' replied Nell, softly; and she tried to coax Dick from the room.

Dick, however, thought he ought to remain at least long enough to tell Thorne that a man in his condition could not exist solely upon love.

Mercedes sprang up blushing with pretty, penitent manner and moving white hands eloquent of her condition.

"Oh, Mercedes—don't go!" cried Thorne, as she stepped to the door.

"Señor Dick will stay. He is not *mucha malo* for you —as I am."

Then she smiled and went out.

"Good Lord!" exclaimed Thorne. "How I love her! Dick, isn't she the most beautiful, the loveliest, the finest—"

"George, I share your enthusiasm," said Dick, dryly, "but Mercedes isn't the only girl on earth."

Manifestly this was a startling piece of information, and struck Thorne in more than one way.

"George," went on Dick, "did you happen to observe the girl who saved your life—who incidentally just fetched in your breakfast?"

"Nell Burton! Why, of course. She's brave, a wonderful girl, and really nice-looking."

"You long, lean, hungry beggar! That was the young lady who might answer the raving eulogy you just got out of your system....I—well, you haven't cornered the love market!"

Thorne uttered some kind of a sound that his weakened condition would not allow to be a whoop.

"Dick! Do you mean it?"

"I shore do, as Laddy says."

"I'm glad, Dick, with all my heart. I wondered at the changed look you wear. Why, boy, you've got a different front....Call the lady in, and you bet I'll look her over right. I can see better now."

"Eat your breakfast. There's plenty of time to dazzle you afterward."

Thorne fell to upon his breakfast and made it vanish

with magic speed. Meanwhile Dick told him something
of a ranger's life along the border.

"You needn't waste your breath," said Thorne. "I
guess I can see. Belding and those rangers have made
you the real thing—the real Western goods.... What I
want to know is all about the girl."

"Well, Laddy swears she's got your girl roped in the
corral for looks."

"That's not possible. I'll have to talk to Laddy....
But she must be a wonder, or Dick Gale would never
have fallen for her.... Isn't it great, Dick? I'm here!
Mercedes is well—safe! You've got a girl! Oh! . . .
But say, I haven't a dollar to my name. I had a lot of
money, Dick, and those robbers stole it, my watch—
everything. Damn that little black Greaser! He got
Mercedes's letters. I wish you could have seen him trying to read them. He's simply nutty over her, Dick. I
could have borne the loss of money and valuables—but
those beautiful, wonderful letters—they're gone!"

"Cheer up. You have the girl. Belding will make
you a proposition presently. The future smiles, old
friend. If this rebel business was only ended!"

"Dick, you're going to be my savior twice over....
Well, now, listen to me." His gay excitement changed
to earnest gravity. "I want to marry Mercedes at once.
Is there a padre here?"

"Yes. But are you wise in letting any Mexican, even
a priest, know Mercedes is hidden in Forlorn River?"

"It couldn't be kept much longer."

Gale was compelled to acknowledge the truth of this
statement.

"I'll marry her first, then I'll face my problem. Fetch
the padre, Dick. And ask our kind friends to be wit-
nesses at the ceremony."

Much to Gale's surprise neither Belding nor Ladd ob-
jected to the idea of bringing a padre into the household,
and thereby making known to at least one Mexican the

whereabouts of Mercedes Castañeda. Belding's caution was wearing out in wrath at the persistent unsettled condition of the border, and Ladd grew only the cooler and more silent as possibilities of trouble multiplied.

Gale fetched the padre, a little, weazened, timid man who was old and without interest or penetration. Apparently he married Mercedes and Thorne as he told his beads or mumbled a prayer. It was Mrs. Belding who kept the occasion from being a merry one, and she insisted on not exciting Thorne. Gale marked her unusual pallor and the singular depth and sweetness of her voice.

"Mother, what's the use of making a funeral out of a marriage?" protested Belding. "A chance for some fun doesn't often come to Forlorn River. You're a fine doctor. Can't you see the girl is what Thorne needed? He'll be well to-morrow, don't mistake me."

"George, when you're all right again we'll add something to present congratulations," said Gale.

"We shore will," put in Ladd.

So with parting jests and smiles they left the couple to themselves.

Belding enjoyed a laugh at his good wife's expense, for Thorne could not be kept in bed, and all in a day, it seemed, he grew so well and so hungry that his friends were delighted, and Mercedes was radiant. In a few days his weakness disappeared and he was going the round of the fields and looking over the ground marked out in Gale's plan of water development. Thorne was highly enthusiastic, and at once staked out his claim for one hundred and sixty acres of land adjoining that of Belding and the rangers. These five tracts took in all the ground necessary for their operations, but in case of the success of the irrigation project the idea was to increase their squatter holding by purchase of more land down the valley. A hundred families had lately moved to Forlorn River; more were coming all the time; and Belding vowed he could see a vision of the whole Altar Valley green with farms.

Meanwhile everybody in Belding's household, except the quiet Ladd and the watchful Yaqui, in the absence of disturbance of any kind along the border, grew freer and more unrestrained, as if anxiety was slowly fading in the peace of the present. Jim Lash made a trip to the Sonoyta Oasis, and Ladd patrolled fifty miles of the line eastward without incident or sight of raiders. Evidently all the border hawks were in at the picking of Casita.

The February nights were cold, with a dry, icy, penetrating coldness that made a warm fire most comfortable. Belding's household usually congregated in the sitting-room, where burning mesquite logs crackled in the open fireplace. Belding's one passion besides horses was the game of checkers, and he was always wanting to play. On this night he sat playing with Ladd, who never won a game and never could give up trying. Mrs. Belding worked with her needle, stopping from time to time to gaze with thoughtful eyes into the fire. Jim Lash smoked his pipe by the hearth and played with the cat on his knee. Thorne and Mercedes were at the table with pencil and paper; and he was trying his best to keep his attention from his wife's beautiful, animated face long enough to read and write a little Spanish. Gale and Nell sat in a corner watching the bright fire.

There came a low knock on the door. It may have been an ordinary knock, for it did not disturb the women; but to Belding and his rangers it had a subtle meaning.

"Who's that?" asked Belding, as he slowly pushed back his chair and looked at Ladd.

"Yaqui," replied the ranger.

"Come in," called Belding.

The door opened, and the short, square, powerfully built Indian entered. He had a magnificent head, strangely staring, somber black eyes, and very darkly bronzed face. He carried a rifle and strode with impressive dignity.

"Yaqui, what do you want?" asked Belding, and repeated his question in Spanish.

"Señor Dick," replied the Indian.

Gale jumped up, stifling an exclamation, and he went outdoors with Yaqui. He felt his arm gripped, and allowed himself to be led away without asking a question. Yaqui's presence was always one of gloom, and now his stern action boded catastrophe. Once clear of trees he pointed to the level desert across the river, where a row of campfires shone bright out of the darkness.

"Raiders!" ejaculated Gale.

Then he cautioned Yaqui to keep sharp lookout, and, hurriedly returning to the house, he called the men out and told them there were rebels or raiders camping just across the line.

Ladd did not say a word. Belding, with an oath, slammed down his cigar.

"I knew it was too good to last.... Dick, you and Jim stay here while Laddy and I look around."

Dick returned to the sitting-room. The women were nervous and not to be deceived. So Dick merely said Yaqui had sighted some lights off in the desert, and they probably were campfires. Belding did not soon return, and when he did he was alone, and, saying he wanted to consult with the men, he sent Mrs. Belding and the girls to their rooms. His gloomy anxiety had returned.

"Laddy's gone over to scout around and try to find out who the outfit belongs to and how many are in it," said Belding.

"I reckon if they're raiders with bad intentions we wouldn't see no fires," remarked Jim, calmly.

"It 'd be useless, I suppose, to send for the cavalry," said Gale. "Whatever's coming off would be over before the soldiers could be notified, let alone reach here."

"Hell, fellows! I don't look for an attack on Forlorn

River," burst out Belding. "I can't believe that possible. These rebel-raiders have a little sense. They wouldn't spoil their game by pulling U. S. soldiers across the line from Yuma to El Paso. But, as Jim says, if they wanted to steal a few horses or cattle they wouldn't build fires. I'm afraid it's—"

Belding hesitated and looked with grim concern at the cavalryman.

"What?" queried Thorne.

"I'm afraid it's Rojas."

Thorne turned pale but did not lose his nerve.

"I thought of that at once. If true, it 'll be terrible for Mercedes and me. But Rojas will never get his hands on my wife. If I can't kill him, I'll kill her!... Belding, this is tough on you—this risk we put upon your family. I regret—"

"Cut that kind of talk," replied Belding, bluntly. "Well, if it is Rojas he's acting damn strange for a raider. That's what worries me. We can't do anything but wait. With Laddy and Yaqui out there we won't be surprised. Let's take the best possible view of the situation until we know more. That 'll not likely be before to-morrow."

The women of the house might have gotten some sleep that night, but it was certain the men did not get any. Morning broke cold and gray, the 19th of February. Breakfast was prepared earlier than usual, and an air of suppressed waiting excitement pervaded the place. Otherwise the ordinary details of the morning's work continued as on any other day. Ladd came in hungry and cold, and said the Mexicans were not breaking camp. He reported a good-sized force of rebels, and was taciturn as to his idea of forthcoming events.

About an hour after sunrise Yaqui ran in with the information that part of the rebels were crossing the river.

"That can't mean a fight yet," declared Belding. "But get in the house, boys, and make ready anyway. I'll meet them."

"Drive them off the place same as if you had a company of soldiers backin' you," said Ladd. "Don't give them an inch. We're in bad, and the bigger bluff we put up the more likely our chance."

"Belding, you're an officer of the United States. Mexicans are much impressed by show of authority. I've seen that often in camp," said Thorne.

"Oh, I know the white-livered Greasers better than any of you, don't mistake me," replied Belding. He was pale with rage, but kept command over himself.

The rangers, with Yaqui and Thorne, stationed themselves at the several windows of the sitting-room. Rifles and smaller arms and boxes of shells littered the tables and window seats. No small force of besiegers could overcome a resistance such as Belding and his men were capable of making.

"Here they come, boys," called Gale, from his window. "Rebel-raiders I should say, Laddy."

"Shore. An' a fine outfit for buzzards!"

"Reckon there's about a dozen in the bunch," observed the calm Lash. "Some hosses they're ridin'. Where'n the hell do they get such hosses, anyhow?"

"Shore, Jim, they work hard an' buy 'em with real silver pesos," replied Ladd, sarcastically.

"Do any of you see Rojas?" whispered Thorne.

"Nix. No dandy bandit in that outfit."

"It's too far to see," said Gale.

The horsemen halted at the corrals. They were orderly and showed no evidence of hostility. They were, however, fully armed. Belding stalked out to meet them. Apparently a leader wanted to parley with him, but Belding would hear nothing. He shook his head, waved his arms, stamped to and fro, and his loud, angry voice could be heard clear back at the house. Whereupon the detachment of rebels retired to the bank of the river, beyond the white post that marked the boundary line, and there they once more drew rein. Belding remained by the corrals watching them, evidently still in threatening mood. Presently a single rider left the troop and trotted his horse back down the road. When he reached the corrals he was seen to halt and pass something to Belding. Then he galloped away to join his comrades.

Belding looked at whatever it was he held in his hand, shook his burly head, and started swiftly for the house. He came striding into the room holding a piece of soiled paper.

"Can't read it and don't know as I want to," he said, savagely.

"Beldin', shore we'd better read it," replied Ladd. "What we want is a line on them Greasers. Whether they're Campo's men or Salazar's, or just a wanderin' bunch of rebels—or Rojas's bandits. *Sabe*, señor?"

Not one of the men was able to translate the garbled scrawl.

"Shore Mercedes can read it," said Ladd.

Thorne opened a door and called her. She came into the room followed by Nell and Mrs. Belding. Evidently all three divined a critical situation.

"My dear, we want you to read what's written on this paper," said Thorne, as he led her to the table. "It was sent in by rebels, and—and we fear contains bad news for us."

Mercedes gave the writing one swift glance, then fainted in Thorne's arms. He carried her to a couch, and with Nell and Mrs. Belding began to work over her.

Belding looked at his rangers. It was characteristic of the man that, now when catastrophe appeared inevitable, all the gloom and care and angry agitation passed from him.

"Laddy, it's Rojas all right. How many men has he out there?"

"Mebbe twenty. Not more."

"We can lick twice that many Greasers."

"Shore."

Jim Lash removed his pipe long enough to speak.

"I reckon. But it ain't sense to start a fight when mebbe we can avoid it."

"What's your idea?"

"Let's stave the Greaser off till dark. Then Laddy an' me an' Thorne will take Mercedes an' hit the trail for Yuma."

"Camino del Diablo! That awful trail with a woman! Jim, do you forget how many *hundreds of men* have perished on the Devil's Road?"

"I reckon I ain't forgettin' nothin'," replied Jim. "The waterholes are full now. There's grass, an' we can do the job in six days."

"It's three hundred miles to Yuma."

"Beldin', Jim's idea hits me pretty reasonable," interposed Ladd. "Lord knows that's about the only chance we've got except fightin'."

"But suppose we do stave Rojas off, and you get safely away with Mercedes. Isn't Rojas going to find it out quick? Then what'll he try to do to us who're left here?"

"I reckon he'd find out by daylight," replied Jim. "But, Tom, he ain't agoin' to start a scrap then. He'd want time an' hosses an' men to chase us out on the trail. You see, I'm figgerin' on the crazy Greaser wantin' the girl. I reckon he'll try to clean up here to get her. But he's too smart to fight you for nothin'. Rojas may be nutty about women, but he's afraid of the U. S. Take my word for it he'd discover the trail in the mornin' an' light out on it. I reckon with ten hours' start we could travel comfortable."

Belding paced up and down the room. Jim and Ladd whispered together. Gale walked to the window and looked out at the distant group of bandits, and then turned his gaze to rest upon Mercedes. She was conscious now, and her eyes seemed all the larger and blacker for the whiteness of her face. Thorne held her hands, and the other women were trying to still her tremblings.

No one but Gale saw the Yaqui in the background looking down upon the Spanish girl. All of Yaqui's looks
were strange; but this was singularly so. Gale marked
it, and felt he would never forget. Mercedes's beauty
had never before struck him as being so exquisite, so
alluring as now when she lay stricken. Gale wondered
if the Indian was affected by her loveliness, her helplessness, or her terror. Yaqui had seen Mercedes only a
few times, and upon each of these he had appeared to
be fascinated. Could the strange Indian, because his
hate for Mexicans was so great, be gloating over her
misery? Something about Yaqui—a noble austerity of
countenance—made Gale feel his suspicion unjust.

Presently Belding called his rangers to him, and then
Thorne.

"Listen to this," he said, earnestly. "I'll go out and
have a talk with Rojas. I'll try to reason with him; tell
him to think a long time before he sheds blood on Uncle
Sam's soil. That he's now after an American's wife!
I'll not commit myself, nor will I refuse outright to consider his demands, nor will I show the least fear of him.
I'll play for time. If my bluff goes through . . . well and
good. . . . After dark the four of you, Laddy, Jim, Dick
and Thorne, will take Mercedes and my best white horses,
and, with Yaqui as guide, circle round through Altar Valley to the trail, and head for Yuma. . . . Wait now, Laddy.
Let me finish. I want you to take the white horses for
two reasons—to save them and to save you. Savvy?
If Rojas should follow on my horses he'd be likely to
catch you. Also, you can pack a great deal more than
on the bronchs. Also, the big horses can travel faster
and farther on little grass and water. I want you to take
the Indian, because in a case of this kind he'll be a godsend. If you get headed or lost or have to circle off the
trail, think what it 'd mean to have a Yaqui with you.
He knows Sonora as no Greaser knows it. He could
hide you, find water and grass, when you would abso-

lutely believe it impossible. The Indian is loyal. He has his debt to pay, and he'll pay it, don't mistake me. When you're gone I'll hide Nell so Rojas won't see her if he searches the place. Then I think I could sit down and wait without any particular worry."

The rangers approved of Belding's plan, and Thorne choked in his effort to express his gratitude.

"All right, we'll chance it," concluded Belding. "I'll go out now and call Rojas and his outfit over.... Say, it might be as well for me to know just what he said in that paper."

Thorne went to the side of his wife.

"Mercedes, we've planned to outwit Rojas. Will you tell us just what he wrote?"

The girl sat up, her eyes dilating, and with her hands clasping Thorne's. She said:

"Rojas swore—by his saints and his virgin—that if I wasn't given—to him—in twenty-four hours—he would set fire to the village—kill the men—carry off the women —hang the children on cactus thorns!"

A moment's silence followed her last halting whisper.

"By his saints an' his virgin!" echoed Ladd. He laughed—a cold, cutting, deadly laugh—significant and terrible.

Then the Yaqui uttered a singular cry. Gale had heard this once before, and now he remembered it was at the Papago Well.

"Look at the Indian," whispered Belding, hoarsely. "Damn if I don't believe he understood every word Mercedes said. And, gentlemen, don't mistake me, if he ever gets near Señor Rojas there'll be some gory Aztec knife work."

Yaqui had moved close to Mercedes, and stood beside her as she leaned against her husband. She seemed impelled to meet the Indian's gaze, and evidently it was so powerful or hypnotic that it wrought irresistibly upon her. But she must have seen or divined what was beyond the others, for she offered him her trembling hand. Yaqui took it and laid it against his body in a strange motion, and bowed his head. Then he stepped back into the shadow of the room.

Belding went outdoors while the rangers took up their former position at the west window. Each had his own somber thoughts, Gale imagined, and knew his own were dark enough. A slow fire crept along his veins. He saw Belding halt at the corrals and wave his hand. Then the rebels mounted and came briskly up the road, this time to rein in abreast.

Wherever Rojas had kept himself upon the former advance was not clear; but he certainly was prominently in sight now. He made a gaudy, almost a dashing figure. Gale did not recognize the white sombrero, the crimson scarf, the velvet jacket, nor any feature of the dandy's costume; but their general effect, the whole ensemble, recalled vividly to mind his first sight of the bandit. Rojas dismounted and seemed to be listening. He betrayed none of the excitement Gale had seen in him that night at the Del Sol. Evidently this composure struck Ladd and Lash as unusual in a Mexican supposed to be laboring under stress of feeling. Belding made gestures, vehemently bobbed his big head, appeared to talk with his body as much as with his tongue. Then Rojas was seen to reply, and after that it was clear that the talk became painful and difficult. It ended finally in what appeared to be mutual understanding. Rojas mounted and rode away with his men, while Belding came tramping back to the house.

As he entered the door his eyes were shining, his big hands were clenched, and he was breathing audibly.

"You can rope me if I'm not locoed!" he burst out. "I went out to conciliate a red-handed little murderer, and damn me if I didn't meet a—a—well, I've no suitable name handy. I started my bluff and got along pretty well, but I forgot to mention that Mercedes was Thorne's wife. And what do you think? Rojas swore he loved Mercedes—swore he'd marry her right here in Forlorn River—swore he would give up robbing and killing people, and take her away from Mexico. He has gold—jewels. He swore if he didn't get her nothing mattered. He'd die anyway without her.... And here's the strange thing. I believe him! He was cold as ice, and all hell inside. Never saw a Greaser like him. Well, I pretended to be greatly impressed. We got to talking friendly, I suppose, though I didn't understand half he said, and I imagine he gathered less what I said. Anyway, without my asking he said for me to think it over for a day and then we'd talk again."

"Shore we're born lucky!" ejaculated Ladd.

"I reckon Rojas'll be smart enough to string his outfit across the few trails leadin' out of Forlorn River," remarked Jim.

"That needn't worry us. All we want is dark to come," replied Belding. "Yaqui will slip through. If we thank any lucky stars let it be for the Indian.... Now, boys, put on your thinking caps. You'll take eight horses, the pick of my bunch. You must pack all that's needed for a possible long trip. Mind, Yaqui may lead you down into some wild Sonora valley and give Rojas the slip. You may get to Yuma in six days, and maybe in six weeks. Yet you've got to pack light—a small pack in saddles—larger ones on the two free horses. You may have a big fight. Laddy, take the .405. Dick will pack his Remington. All of you go gunned heavy. But the main thing is a pack that'll be light enough for swift travel, yet one that'll keep you from starving on the desert."

The rest of that day passed swiftly. Dick had scarcely a word with Nell, and all the time, as he chose and deliberated and worked over his little pack, there was a dull pain in his heart.

The sun set, twilight fell, then night closed down, fortunately a night slightly overcast. Gale saw the white

horses pass his door like silent ghosts. Even Blanco
Diablo made no sound, and that fact was indeed a tribute
to the Yaqui. Gale went out to put his saddle on Blanco
Sol. The horse rubbed a soft nose against his shoulder.
Then Gale returned to the sitting-room. There was
nothing more to do but wait and say good-by. Mercedes came clad in leather chaps and coat, a slim stripling
of a cowboy, her dark eyes flashing. Her beauty could
not be hidden, and now hope and courage had fired her
blood.

Gale drew Nell off into the shadow of the room. She
was trembling, and as she leaned toward him she was
very different from the coy girl who had so long held
him aloof. He took her into his arms.

"Dearest, I'm going — soon. . . . And maybe I'll
never—"

"Dick, do—don't say it," sobbed Nell, with her head
on his breast.

"I might never come back," he went on, steadily. "I
love you—I've loved you ever since the first moment I
saw you. Do you care for me—a little?"

"Dear Dick—de-dear Dick, my heart is breaking,"
faltered Nell, as she clung to him.

"It might be breaking for Mercedes—for Laddy and
Jim. I want to hear something for myself. Something
to have on long marches—round lonely campfires. Something to keep my spirit alive. Oh, Nell, you can't imagine
that silence out there—that terrible world of sand and
stone!... Do you love me?"

"Yes, yes. Oh, I love you so! I never knew it till
now. I love you so. Dick, I'll be safe and I'll wait—
and hope and pray for your return."

"If I come back—no—*when* I come back, will you
marry me?"

"I—I—oh yes!" she whispered, and returned his kiss.
Belding was in the room speaking softly.

"Nell, darling, I must go," said Dick.

"I'm a selfish little coward," cried Nell. "It's so splendid of you all. I ought to glory in it, but I can't. ... Fight if you must, Dick. Fight for that lovely persecuted girl. I'll love you—the more.... Oh! Goodby! Good-by!"

With a wrench that shook him Gale let her go. He heard Belding's soft voice.

"Yaqui says the early hour's best. Trust him, Laddy. Remember what I say—Yaqui's a godsend."

Then they were all outside in the pale gloom under the trees. Yaqui mounted Blanco Diablo; Mercedes was lifted upon White Woman; Thorne climbed astride Queen; Jim Lash was already upon his horse, which was as white as the others but bore no name; Ladd mounted the stallion Blanco Torres, and gathered up the long halters of the two pack horses; Gale came last with Blanco Sol.

As he toed the stirrup, hand on mane and pommel, Gale took one more look in at the door. Nell stood in the gleam of light, her hair shining, face like ashes, her eyes dark, her lips parted, her arms outstretched. That sweet and tragic picture etched its cruel outlines into Gale's heart. He waved his hand and then fiercely leaped into the saddle.

Blanco Sol stepped out.

Before Gale stretched a line of moving horses, white against dark shadows. He could not see the head of that column; he scarcely heard a soft hoofbeat. A single star shone out of a rift in thin clouds. There was no wind. The air was cold. The dark space of desert seemed to yawn. To the left across the river flickered a few campfires. The chill night, silent and mystical, seemed to close in upon Gale; and he faced the wide, quivering, black level with keen eyes and grim intent, and an awakening of that wild rapture which came like a spell to him in the open desert.

XI

ACROSS CACTUS AND LAVA

BLANCO SOL showed no inclination to bend his head to the alfalfa which swished softly about his legs. Gale felt the horse's sensitive, almost human alertness. Sol knew as well as his master the nature of that flight.

At the far corner of the field Yaqui halted, and slowly the line of white horses merged into a compact mass. There was a trail here leading down to the river. The campfires were so close that the bright blazes could be seen in movement, and dark forms crossed in front of them. Yaqui slipped out of his saddle. He ran his hand over Diablo's nose and spoke low, and repeated this action for each of the other horses. Gale had long ceased to question the strange Indian's behavior. There was no explaining or understanding many of his manœuvers. But the results of them were always thought-provoking. Gale had never seen horses stand so silently as in this instance; no stamp—no champ of bit—no toss of head—no shake of saddle or pack—no heave or snort! It seemed they had become imbued with the spirit of the Indian.

Yaqui moved away into the shadows as noiselessly as if he were one of them. The darkness swallowed him. He had taken a direction parallel with the trail. Gale wondered if Yaqui meant to try to lead his string of horses by the rebel sentinels. Ladd had his head bent low, his ear toward the trail. Jim's long neck had the arch of a listening deer. Gale listened, too, and as the slow, silent moments went by his faculty of hearing grew more acute from strain. He heard Blanco Sol breathe; he heard the pound of his own heart; he heard the silken rustle of the alfalfa; he heard a faint, far-off sound of voice, like a lost echo. Then his ear seemed to register a movement of air, a disturbance so soft as to be nameless. Then followed long, silent moments.

Yaqui appeared as he had vanished. He might have been part of the shadows. But he was there. He started off down the trail leading Diablo. Again the white line stretched slowly out. Gale fell in behind. A bench of ground, covered with sparse greasewood, sloped gently down to the deep, wide arroyo of Forlorn River. Blanco Sol shied a few feet out of the trail. Peering low with keen eyes, Gale made out three objects—a white sombrero, a blanket, and a Mexican lying face down. The Yaqui had stolen upon this sentinel like a silent wind of death. Just then a desert coyote wailed, and the wild cry fitted the darkness and the Yaqui's deed.

Once under the dark lee of the river bank Yaqui caused another halt, and he disappeared as before. It seemed to Gale that the Indian started to cross the pale level sand-bed of the river, where stones stood out gray, and the darker line of opposite shore was visible. But he vanished, and it was impossible to tell whether he went one way or another. Moments passed. The horses held heads up, looked toward the glimmering campfires and listened. Gale thrilled with the meaning of it all—the night—the silence—the flight—and the wonderful Indian stealing with the slow inevitableness of doom upon another sentinel. An hour passed and Gale seemed to have become deadened to all sense of hearing. There were no more sounds in the world. The desert was as silent as it was black. Yet again came that strange change in the tensity of Gale's ear-strain, a check, a break, a vibration—and this time the sound did not go nameless. It might have been moan of wind or wail of far-distant wolf, but Gale imagined it was the strangling death-cry of another guard, or that strange, involuntary utterance of the Yaqui. Blanco Sol trembled in all his great frame, and then Gale was certain the sound was not imagination.

That certainty, once for all, fixed in Gale's mind the mood of his flight. The Yaqui dominated the horses and the rangers. Thorne and Mercedes were as persons under a spell. The Indian's strange silence, the feeling of mystery and power he seemed to create, all that was incomprehensible about him were emphasized in the light of his slow, sure, and ruthless action. If he dominated the others, surely he did more for Gale—colored his thoughts —presaged the wild and terrible future of that flight. If Rojas embodied all the hatred and passion of the peon —scourged slave for a thousand years—then Yaqui embodied all the darkness, the cruelty, the white, sun-heated blood, the ferocity, the tragedy of the desert.

Suddenly the Indian stalked out of the gloom. He mounted Diablo and headed across the river. Once more the line of moving white shadows stretched out. The soft sand gave forth no sound at all. The glimmering campfires sank behind the western bank. Yaqui led the way into the willows, and there was faint swishing of leaves; then into the mesquite, and there was faint rustling of branches. The glimmering lights appeared again, and grotesque forms of *saguaros* loomed darkly. Gale peered sharply along the trail, and, presently, on the pale sand under a cactus, there lay a blanketed form, prone, outstretched, a carbine clutched in one hand, a cigarette, still burning, in the other.

The cavalcade of white horses passed within five hundred yards of campfires, around which dark forms moved in plain sight. Soft pads in sand, faint metallic tickings of steel on thorns, low, regular breathing of horses—these were all the sounds the fugitives made, and they could not have been heard at one-fifth the distance. The lights disappeared from time to time, grew dimmer, more flickering, and at last they vanished altogether. Belding's fleet and tireless steeds were out in front; the desert opened ahead wide, dark, vast. Rojas and his rebels were behind, eating, drinking, careless. The somber shadow lifted from Gale's heart. He held now an unquenchable faith in the Yaqui. Belding would be listening back there along the river. He would know of the escape. He would tell Nell, and then hide her safely. As Gale had accepted a strange and fatalistic foreshadowing of toil, blood, and agony in this desert journey, so he believed in Mercedes's ultimate freedom and happiness, and his own return to the girl who had grown dearer than life.

A cold, gray dawn was fleeing before a rosy sun when Yaqui halted the march at Papago Well. The horses were taken to water, then led down the arroyo into the grass. Here packs were slipped, saddles removed. Mercedes was cold, lame, tired, but happy. It warmed Gale's blood to look at her. The shadow of fear still lay in her eyes, but it was passing. Hope and courage shone there, and affection for her ranger protectors and the Yaqui, and unutterable love for the cavalryman. Jim Lash remarked how cleverly they had fooled the rebels.

"Shore they'll be comin' along," replied Ladd.

They built a fire, cooked and ate. The Yaqui spoke only one word: "Sleep." Blankets were spread. Mercedes dropped into a deep slumber, her head on Thorne's shoulder. Excitement kept Thorne awake. The two rangers dozed beside the fire. Gale shared the Yaqui's watch. The sun began to climb and the icy edge of dawn to wear away. Rabbits bobbed their cotton tails under the mesquite. Gale climbed a rocky wall above the arroyo bank, and there, with command over the miles of the back-trail, he watched.

It was a sweeping, rolling, wrinkled, and streaked range of desert that he saw, ruddy in the morning sunlight, with patches of cactus and mesquite rough-etched in shimmering gloom. No Name Mountains split the eastern sky,

towering high, gloomy, grand, with purple veils upon
their slopes. They were forty miles away and looked five.
Gale thought of the girl who was there under their shadow.

Yaqui kept the horses bunched, and he led them from
one little park of galleta grass to another. At the end of
three hours he took them to water. Upon his return Gale
clambered down from his outlook, the rangers grew active,
Mercedes was awakened; and soon the party faced westward, their long shadows moving before them. Yaqui
led with Blanco Diablo in a long, easy lope. The arroyo
washed itself out into flat desert, and the greens began
to shade into gray, and then the gray into red. Only
sparse cactus and weathered ledges dotted the great low
roll of a rising escarpment. Yaqui suited the gait of his
horse to the lay of the land, and his followers accepted his
pace. There were canter and trot, and swift walk and
slow climb, and long swing—miles up and down and forward. The sun soared hot. The heated air lifted, and
incoming currents from the west swept low and hard over
the barren earth. In the distance, all around the horizon,
accumulations of dust seemed like ranging, mushrooming
yellow clouds.

Yaqui was the only one of the fugitives who never
looked back. Mercedes did it the most. Gale felt what
compelled her, he could not resist it himself. But it was
a vain search. For a thousand puffs of white and yellow
dust rose from that backward sweep of desert, and any
one of them might have been blown from under horses'
hoofs. Gale had a conviction that when Yaqui gazed
back toward the well and the shining plain beyond, there
would be reason for it. But when the sun lost its heat
and the wind died down Yaqui took long and careful sur-
veys westward from the high points on the trail. Sunset
was not far off, and there in a bare, spotted valley lay
Coyote Tanks, the only waterhole between Papago Well
and the Sonoyta Oasis. Gale used his glass, told Yaqui
there was no smoke, no sign of life; still the Indian fixed

his falcon eyes on distant spots and looked long. It was as if his vision could not detect what reason or cunning, or intuition, perhaps an instinct, told him was there. Presently in a sheltered spot, where blown sand had not obliterated the trail, Yaqui found the tracks of horses. The curve of the iron shoes pointed westward. An intersecting trail from the north came in here. Gale thought the tracks either one or two days old. Ladd said they were one day. The Indian shook his head.

No farther advance was undertaken. The Yaqui headed south and traveled slowly, climbing to the brow of a bold height of weathered mesa. There he sat his horse and waited. No one questioned him. The rangers dismounted to stretch their legs, and Mercedes was lifted to a rock, where she rested. Thorne had gradually yielded to the desert's influence for silence. He spoke once or twice to Gale, and occasionally whispered to Mercedes. Gale fancied his friend would soon learn that necessary speech in desert travel meant a few greetings, a few words to make real the fact of human companionship, a few short, terse terms for the business of day or night, and perhaps a stern order or a soft call to a horse.

The sun went down, and the golden, rosy veils turned to blue and shaded darker till twilight was there in the valley. Only the spurs of mountains, spiring the near and far horizon, retained their clear outline. Darkness approached, and the clear peaks faded. The horses stamped to be on the move.

"*Malo!*" exclaimed the Yaqui.

He did not point with arm, but his falcon head was outstretched, and his piercing eyes gazed at the blurring spot which marked the location of Coyote Tanks.

"Jim, can you see anything?" asked Ladd.

"Nope, but I reckon he can."

Darkness increased momentarily till night shaded the deepest part of the valley.

Then Ladd suddenly straightened up, turned to his horse, and muttered low under his breath.

"I reckon so," said Lash, and for once his easy, good-natured tone was not in evidence. His voice was harsh.

Gale's eyes, keen as they were, were last of the rangers to see tiny needle-points of light just faintly perceptible in the blackness.

"Laddy! Campfires?" he asked, quickly.

"Shore's you're born, my boy."

"How many?"

Ladd did not reply; but Yaqui held up his hand, his fingers wide. Five campfires! A strong force of rebels or raiders or some other desert troop was camping at Coyote Tanks.

Yaqui sat his horse for a moment, motionless as stone, his dark face immutable and impassive. Then he stretched wide his right arm in the direction of No Name Mountains, now losing their last faint traces of the afterglow, and he shook his head. He made the same impressive gesture toward the Sonoyta Oasis with the same somber negation.

Thereupon he turned Diablo's head to the south and started down the slope. His manner had been decisive, even stern. Lash did not question it, nor did Ladd. Both rangers hesitated, however, and showed a strange, almost a sullen reluctance which Gale had never seen in them before. Raiders were one thing, Rojas was another; Camino del Diablo still another; but that vast and desolate and unwatered waste of cactus and lava, the Sonora Desert, might appall the stoutest heart. Gale felt his own sink—felt himself flinch.

"Oh, where is he going?" cried Mercedes. Her poignant voice seemed to break a spell.

"Shore, lady, Yaqui's goin' home," replied Ladd gently. "An' considerin' our troubles I reckon we ought to thank God he knows the way."

ACROSS CACTUS AND LAVA

They mounted and rode down the slope toward the darkening south.

Not until night travel was obstructed by a wall of cactus did the Indian halt to make a dry camp. Water and grass for the horses and fire to cook by were not to be had. Mercedes bore up surprisingly; but she fell asleep almost the instant her thirst had been allayed. Thorne laid her upon a blanket and covered her. The men ate and drank. Diablo was the only horse that showed impatience; but he was angry, and not in distress. Blanco Sol licked Gale's hand and stood patiently. Many a time had he taken his rest at night without a drink. Yaqui again bade the men sleep. Ladd said he would take the early watch; but from the way the Indian shook his head and settled himself against a stone, it appeared if Ladd remained awake he would have company. Gale lay down weary of limb and eye. He heard the soft thump of hoofs, the sough of wind in the cactus—then no more.

When he awoke there was bustle and stir about him. Day had not yet dawned, and the air was freezing cold. Yaqui had found a scant bundle of greasewood which served to warm them and to cook breakfast. Mercedes was not aroused till the last moment.

Day dawned with the fugitives in the saddle. A picketed wall of cactus hedged them in, yet the Yaqui made a tortuous path, that, zigzag as it might, in the main always headed south. It was wonderful how he slipped Diablo through the narrow aisles of thorns, saving the horse and saving himself. The others were torn and clutched and held and stung. The way was a flat, sandy pass between low mountain ranges. There were open spots and aisles and squares of sand; and hedging rows of prickly pear and the huge spider-legged *ocatillo* and hummocky masses of clustered *bisnagi*. The day grew dry and hot. A fragrant wind blew through the pass. Cactus flowers bloomed, red and yellow and magenta. The sweet, pale Ajo lily gleamed in shady corners.

Ten miles of travel covered the length of the pass. It opened wide upon a wonderful scene, an arboreal desert, dominated by its pure light green, yet lined by many merging colors. And it rose slowly to a low dim and dark-red zone of lava, spurred, peaked, domed by volcano cones, a wild and ragged region, illimitable as the horizon.

The Yaqui, if not at fault, was yet uncertain. His falcon eyes searched and roved, and became fixed at length at the southwest, and toward this he turned his horse. The great, fluted *saguaros,* fifty, sixty feet high, raised columnal forms, and their branching limbs and curving lines added a grace to the desert. It was the low-bushed cactus that made the toil and pain of travel. Yet these thorny forms were beautiful.

In the basins between the ridges, to right and left along the floor of low plains the mirage glistened, wavered, faded, vanished—lakes and trees and clouds. Inverted mountains hung suspended in the lilac air and faint tracery of white-walled cities.

At noon Yaqui halted the cavalcade. He had selected a field of *bisnagi* cactus for the place of rest. Presently his reason became obvious. With long, heavy knife he cut off the tops of these barrel-shaped plants. He scooped out soft pulp, and with stone and hand then began to pound the deeper pulp into a juicy mass. When he threw this out there was a little water left, sweet, cool water which man and horse shared eagerly. Thus he made even the desert's fiercest growths minister to their needs.

But he did not halt long. Miles of gray-green spiked walls lay between him and that line of ragged, red lava which manifestly he must reach before dark. The travel became faster, straighter. And the glistening thorns clutched and clung to leather and cloth and flesh. The horses reared, snorted, balked, leaped—but they were sent on. Only Blanco Sol, the patient, the plodding, the indomitable, needed no goad or spur. Waves and scarfs and wreaths of heat smoked up from the sand. Mercedes reeled in her saddle. Thorne bade her drink, bathed her face, supported her, and then gave way to Ladd, who took the girl with him on Torres's broad back. Yaqui's unflagging purpose and iron arm were bitter and hateful to the proud and haughty spirit of Blanco Diablo. For once Belding's great white devil had met his master. He fought rider, bit, bridle, cactus, sand—and yet he went on and on, zigzagging, turning, winding, crashing through the barbed growths. The middle of the afternoon saw Thorne reeling in his saddle, and then, wherever possible, Gale's powerful arm lent him strength to hold his seat.

The giant cactus came to be only so in name. These *saguaros* were thinning out, growing stunted, and most of them were single columns. Gradually other cactus forms showed a harder struggle for existence, and the spaces of sand between were wider. But now the dreaded, glistening *choya* began to show pale and gray and white upon the rising slope. Round-topped hills, sunset-colored above, blue-black below, intervened to hide the distant spurs and peaks. Mile and mile long tongues of red lava streamed out between the hills and wound down to stop abruptly upon the slope.

The fugitives were entering a desolate, burned-out world. It rose above them in limitless, gradual ascent and spread wide to east and west. Then the waste of sand began to yield to cinders. The horses sank to their fetlocks as they toiled on. A fine, choking dust blew back from the leaders, and men coughed and horses snorted. The huge, round hills rose smooth, symmetrical, colored as if the setting sun was shining on bare, blue-black surfaces. But the sun was now behind the hills. In between ran the streams of lava. The horsemen skirted the edge between slope of hill and perpendicular ragged wall. This red lava seemed to have flowed and hardened there only yesterday. It was broken, sharp, dull rust color, full of cracks and caves and crevices, and everywhere upon its jagged surface grew the white-thorned *choya.*

Again twilight encompassed the travelers. But there was still light enough for Gale to see the constricted passage open into a wide, deep space where the dull color was relieved by the gray of gnarled and dwarfed mesquite. Blanco Sol, keenest of scent, whistled his welcome herald of water. The other horses answered, quickened their gait. Gale smelled it, too, sweet, cool, damp on the dry air.

Yaqui turned the corner of a pocket in the lava wall. The file of white horses rounded the corner after him. And Gale, coming last, saw the pale, glancing gleam of a pool of water beautiful in the twilight.

Next day the Yaqui's relentless driving demand on the horses was no longer in evidence. He lost no time, but he did not hasten. His course wound between low cinder dunes which limited their view of the surrounding country. These dunes finally sank down to a black floor as hard as flint with tongues of lava to the left, and to the right the slow descent into the cactus plain. Yaqui was now traveling due west. It was Gale's idea that the Indian was skirting the first sharp-toothed slope of a vast volcanic plateau which formed the western half of the Sonora Desert and extended to the Gulf of California. Travel was slow, but not exhausting for rider or beast. A little sand and meager grass gave a grayish tinge to the strip of black ground between lava and plain.

That day, as the manner rather than the purpose of the Yaqui changed, so there seemed to be subtle differences in the others of the party. Gale himself lost a certain sickening dread, which had not been for himself, but for Mercedes and Nell, and Thorne and the rangers. Jim, good-natured again, might have been patrolling the boundary line. Ladd lost his taciturnity and his gloom change.

to a cool, careless air. A mood that was almost defiance began to be manifested in Thorne. It was in Mercedes, however, that Gale marked the most significant change. Her collapse the preceding day might never have been. She was lame and sore; she rode her saddle sidewise, and often she had to be rested and helped; but she had found a reserve fund of strength, and her mental condition was not the same that it had been. Her burden of fear had been lifted. Gale saw in her the difference he always felt in himself after a few days in the desert. Already Mercedes and he, and all of them, had begun to respond to the desert spirit. Moreover, Yaqui's strange influence must have been a call to the primitive.

Thirty miles of easy stages brought the fugitives to another waterhole, a little round pocket under the heaved-up edge of lava. There was spare, short, bleached grass for the horses, but no wood for a fire. This night there were question and reply, conjecture, doubt, opinion, and conviction expressed by the men of the party. But the Indian, who alone could have told where they were, where they were going, what chance they had to escape, maintained his stoical silence. Gale took the early watch, Ladd the midnight one, and Lash that of the morning.

The day broke rosy, glorious, cold as ice. Action was necessary to make useful benumbed hands and feet. Mercedes was fed while yet wrapped in blankets. Then, while the packs were being put on and horses saddled, she walked up and down, slapping her hands, warming her ears. The rose color of the dawn was in her cheeks, and the wonderful clearness of desert light in her eyes. Thorne's eyes sought her constantly. The rangers watched her. The Yaqui bent his glance upon her only seldom; but when he did look it seemed that his strange, fixed, and inscrutable face was about to break into a smile. Yet that never happened. Gale himself was surprised to find how often his own glance found the slender, dark, beautiful Spaniard. Was this because of her beauty? he wondered. He thought not altogether. Mercedes was a woman. She represented something in life that men of all races for thousands of years had loved to see and own, to revere and debase, to fight and die for.

It was a significant index to the day's travel that Yaqui should keep a blanket from the pack and tear it into strips to bind the legs of the horses. It meant the dreaded *choya* and the knife-edged lava. That Yaqui did not mount Diablo was still more significant. Mercedes must ride; but the others must walk.

The Indian led off into one of the gray notches between the tumbled streams of lava. These streams were about thirty feet high, a rotting mass of splintered lava, rougher than any other kind of roughness in the world. At the apex of the notch, where two streams met, a narrow gully wound and ascended. Gale caught sight of the dim, pale shadow of a one-time trail. Near at hand it was invisible; he had to look far ahead to catch the faint tracery. Yaqui led Diablo into it, and then began the most laborious and vexatious and painful of all slow travel.

Once up on top of that lava bed, Gale saw stretching away, breaking into millions of crests and ruts, a vast, red-black field sweeping onward and upward, with ragged, low ridges and mounds and spurs leading higher and higher to a great, split escarpment wall, above which dim peaks shone hazily blue in the distance.

He looked no more in that direction. To keep his foothold, to save his horse, cost him all energy and attention. The course was marked out for him in the tracks of the other horses. He had only to follow. But nothing could have been more difficult. The disintegrating surface of a lava bed was at once the roughest, the hardest, the meanest, the cruelest, the most deceitful kind of ground to travel.

It was rotten, yet it had corners as hard and sharp as pikes. It was rough, yet as slippery as ice. If there was a foot of level surface, that space would be one to break through under a horse's hoofs. It was seamed, lined, cracked, ridged, knotted iron. This lava bed resembled a tremendously magnified clinker. It had been a running sea of molten flint, boiling, bubbling, spouting, and it had burst its surface into a million sharp facets as it hardened. The color was dull, dark, angry red, like no other red, inflaming to the eye. The millions of minute crevices were dominated by deep fissures and holes, ragged and rough beyond all comparison.

The fugitives made slow progress. They picked a cautious, winding way to and fro in little steps here and there along the many twists of the trail, up and down the unavoidable depressions, round and round the holes. At noon, so winding back upon itself had been their course, they appeared to have come only a short distance up the lava slope.

It was rough work for them; it was terrible work for the horses. Blanco Diablo refused to answer to the power of the Yaqui. He balked, he plunged, he bit and kicked. He had to be pulled and beaten over many places. Mercedes's horse almost threw her, and she was put upon Blanco Sol. The white charger snorted a protest, then, obedient to Gale's stern call, patiently lowered his noble head and pawed the lava for a footing that would hold.

The lava caused Gale toil and worry and pain, but he hated the *choyas.* As the travel progressed this species of cactus increased in number of plants and in size. Everywhere the red lava was spotted with little round patches of glistening frosty white. And under every bunch of *choya,* along and in the trail, were the discarded joints, like little frosty pine cones covered with spines. It was utterly impossible always to be on the lookout for these, and when Gale stepped on one, often as not the steel-like thorns pierced leather and flesh. Gale came almost to believe what he had heard claimed by desert travelers—that the *choya* was alive and leaped at man or beast. Certain it was when Gale passed one, if he did not put all attention to avoiding it, he was hooked through his chaps and held by barbed thorns. The pain was almost unendurable. It was like no other. It burned, stung, beat—almost seemed to freeze. It made useless arm or leg. It made him bite his tongue to keep from crying out. It made the sweat roll off him. It made him sick.

Moreover, bad as the *choya* was for man, it was infinitely worse for beast. A jagged stab from this poisoned cactus was the only thing Blanco Sol could not stand. Many times that day, before he carried Mercedes, he had wildly snorted, and then stood trembling while Gale picked broken thorns from the muscular legs. But after Mercedes had been put upon Sol Gale made sure no *choya* touched him.

The afternoon passed like the morning, in ceaseless winding and twisting and climbing along this abandoned trail. Gale saw many waterholes, mostly dry, some containing water, all of them catch-basins, full only after rainy season. Little ugly bunched bushes, that Gale scarcely recognized as mesquites, grew near these holes; also stunted greasewood and prickly pear. There was no grass, and the *choya* alone flourished in that hard soil.

Darkness overtook the party as they unpacked beside a pool of water deep under an overhanging shelf of lava. It had been a hard day. The horses drank their fill, and then stood patiently with drooping heads. Hunger and thirst were appeased, and a warm fire cheered the weary and foot-sore fugitives. Yaqui said, "Sleep." And so another night passed.

Upon the following morning, ten miles or more up the slow-ascending lava slope, Gale's attention was called from his somber search for the less rough places in the trail.

"Dick, why does Yaqui look back?" asked Mercedes.

ACROSS CACTUS AND LAVA

Gale was startled.

"Does he?"

"Every little while," replied Mercedes.

Gale was in the rear of all the other horses, so as to take, for Mercedes's sake, the advantage of the broken trail. Yaqui was leading Diablo, winding around a break. His head was bent as he stepped slowly and unevenly upon the lava. Gale turned to look back, the first time in several days. The mighty hollow of the desert below seemed wide strip of red—wide strip of green—wide strip of gray—streaking to purple peaks. It was all too vast, too mighty to grasp any little details. He thought, of course, of Rojas in certain pursuit; but it seemed absurd to look for him.

Yaqui led on, and Gale often glanced up from his task to watch the Indian. Presently he saw him stop, turn, and look back. Ladd did likewise, and then Jim and Thorne. Gale found the desire irresistible. Thereafter he often rested Blanco Sol, and looked back the while. He had his field-glass, but did not choose to use it.

"Rojas will follow," said Mercedes.

Gale regarded her in amaze. The tone of her voice had been indefinable. If there were fear then he failed to detect it. She was gazing back down the colored slope, and something about her, perhaps the steady, falcon gaze of her magnificent eyes, reminded him of Yaqui.

Many times during the ensuing hour the Indian faced about, and always his followers did likewise. It was high noon, with the sun beating hot and the lava radiating heat, when Yaqui halted for a rest. The place selected was a ridge of lava, almost a promontory, considering its outlook. The horses bunched here and drooped their heads. The rangers were about to slip the packs and remove saddles when Yaqui restrained them.

He fixed a changeless, gleaming gaze on the slow descent; but did not seem to look afar.

Suddenly he uttered his strange cry—the one Gale considered involunta.y, or else significant of some tribal trait or feeling. It was incomprehensible, but no one could have doubted its potency. Yaqui pointed down the lava slope, pointing with finger and arm and neck and head—his whole body was instinct with direction. His whole being seemed to have been animated and then frozen. His posture could not have been misunderstood, yet his expression had not altered. Gale had never seen the Indian's face change its hard, red-bronze calm. It was the color and the flintiness and the character of the lava at his feet.

"Shore he sees somethin'," said Ladd. "But my eyes are no good."

"I reckon I ain't sure of mine," replied Jim. "I'm bothered by a dim movin' streak down there."

Thorne gazed eagerly down as he stood beside Mercedes, who sat motionless facing the slope. Gale looked and looked till he hurt his eyes. Then he took his glass out of its case on Sol's saddle.

There appeared to be nothing upon the lava but the innumerable dots of *choya* shining in the sun. Gale swept his glass slowly forward and back. Then into a nearer field of vision crept a long white-and-black line of horses and men. Without a word he handed the glass to Ladd. The ranger used it, muttering to himself.

"They're on the lava fifteen miles down in an air line," he said, presently. "Jim, shore they're twice that an' more accordin' to the trail."

Jim had his look and replied: "I reckon we're a day an' a night in the lead."

"Is it Rojas?" burst out Thorne, with set jaw.

"Yes, Thorne. It's Rojas and a dozen men or more," replied Gale, and he looked up at Mercedes.

She was transformed. She might have been a medieval princess embodying all the Spanish power and passion of that time, breathing revenge, hate, unquenchable spirit of fire. If her beauty had been wonderful in her helpless and appealing moments, now, when she looked back white-faced and flame-eyed, it was transcendant.

Gale drew a long, deep breath. The mood which had presaged pursuit, strife, blood on this somber desert, returned to him tenfold. He saw Thorne's face corded by black veins, and his teeth exposed like those of a snarling wolf. These rangers, who had coolly risked death many times, and had dealt it often, were white as no fear or pain could have made them. Then, on the moment, Yaqui raised his hand, not clenched or doubled tight, but curled rigid like an eagle's claw; and he shook it in a strange, slow gesture which was menacing and terrible.

It was the woman that called to the depths of these men. And their passion to kill and to save was surpassed only by the wild hate which was yet love, the unfathomable emotion of a peon slave. Gale marveled at it, while he felt his whole being cold and tense, as he turned once more to follow in the tracks of his leaders. The fight predicted by Belding was at hand. What a fight that must be! Rojas was traveling light and fast. He was gaining. He had bought his men with gold, with extravagant promises, perhaps with offers of the body and blood of an aristocrat hateful to their kind. Lastly, there was the wild, desolate environment, a tortured wilderness of jagged lava and poisoned *choya*, a lonely, fierce, and repellant world, a red stage most somberly and fittingly colored for a supreme struggle between men.

Yaqui looked back no more. Mercedes looked back no more. But the others looked, and the time came when Gale saw the creeping line of pursuers with naked eyes.

A level line above marked the rim of the plateau. Sand began to show in the little lava pits. On and upward toiled the cavalcade, still very slowly advancing. At last Yaqui reached the rim. He stood with his hand on Blanco Diablo; and both were silhouetted against the sky. That was the outlook for a Yaqui. And his great horse, dazzlingly white in the sunlight, with head wildly and proudly erect, mane and tail flying in the wind, made a magnificent picture. The others toiled on and upward, and at last Gale led Blanco Sol over the rim. Then all looked down the red slope.

But shadows were gathering there and no moving line could be seen.

Yaqui mounted and wheeled Diablo away. The others followed. Gale saw that the plateau was no more than a vast field of low, ragged circles, levels, mounds, cones, and whirls of lava. The lava was of a darker red than that down upon the slope, and it was harder than flint. In places fine sand and cinders covered the uneven floor. Strange varieties of cactus vied with the omnipresent *choya*. Yaqui, however, found ground that his horse covered at a swift walk.

But there was only an hour, perhaps, of this comparatively easy going. Then the Yaqui led them into a zone of craters. The top of the earth seemed to have been blown out in holes from a few rods in width to large craters, some shallow, others deep, and all red as fire. Yaqui circled close to abysses which yawned sheer from a level surface, and he appeared always to be turning upon his course to avoid them.

The plateau had now a considerable dip to the west. Gale marked the slow heave and ripple of the ocean of lava to the south, where high, rounded peaks marked the center of this volcanic region. The uneven nature of the slope westward prevented any extended view, until suddenly the fugitives emerged from a rugged break to come upon a sublime and awe-inspiring spectacle.

They were upon a high point of the western slope of the plateau. It was a slope, but so many leagues long in its descent that only from a great height could any slant have been perceptible. Yaqui and his white horse stood upon the brink of a crater miles in circumference, a thousand feet deep, with its red walls patched in frost-colored spots by the silvery *choya*. The giant tracery of lava streams waved down the slope to disappear in undulating sand dunes. And these bordered a seemingly endless arm of blue sea. This was the Gulf of California. Beyond the Gulf rose dim, bold mountains, and above them hung the setting sun, dusky red, flooding all that barren empire with a sinister light.

It was strange to Gale then, and perhaps to the others, to see their guide lead Diablo into a smooth and well-worn trail along the rim of the awful crater. Gale looked down into that red chasm. It resembled an inferno. The dark cliffs upon the opposite side were veiled in blue haze that seemed like smoke. Here Yaqui was at home. He moved and looked about him as a man coming at last into his own. Gale saw him stop and gaze out over that red-ribbed void to the Gulf.

Gale divined that somewhere along this crater of hell the Yaqui would make his final stand; and one look into his strange, inscrutable eyes made imagination picture a fitting doom for the pursuing Rojas.

XII

THE CRATER OF HELL

THE trail led along a gigantic fissure in the side of the crater, and then down and down into a red-walled, blue-hazed labyrinth.

Presently Gale, upon turning a sharp corner, was utterly amazed to see that the split in the lava sloped out and widened into an arroyo. It was so green and soft and beautiful in all the angry, contorted red surrounding that Gale could scarcely credit his sight. Blanco Sol whistled his welcome to the scent of water. Then Gale saw a great hole, a pit in the shiny lava, a dark, cool, shady well. There was evidence of the fact that at flood seasons the water had an outlet into the arroyo. The soil appeared to be a fine sand, in which a reddish tinge predominated; and it was abundantly covered with a long grass, still partly green. Mesquites and *palo verdes* dotted the arroyo and gradually closed in thickets that obstructed the view.

"Shore it all beats me," exclaimed Ladd. "What a place to hole-up in! We could have hid here for a long time. Boys, I saw mountain sheep, the real old genuine Rocky Mountain bighorn. What do you think of that?"

"I reckon it's a Yaqui hunting-ground," replied Lash. "That trail we hit must be hundreds of years old. It's worn deep and smooth in the iron lava."

"Well, all I got to say is—Beldin' was shore right about the Indian. An' I can see Rojas's finish somewhere up along that awful hell-hole."

THE CRATER OF HELL

Camp was made on a level spot. Yaqui took the horses to water, and then turned them loose in the arroyo. It was a tired and somber group that sat down to eat. The strain of suspense equaled the wearing effects of the long ride. Mercedes was calm, but her great dark eyes burned in her white face. Yaqui watched her. The others looked at her with unspoken pride. Presently Thorne wrapped her in his blankets, and she seemed to fall asleep at once. Twilight deepened. The campfire blazed brighter. A cool wind played with Mercedes's black hair, waving strands across her brow.

Little of Yaqui's purpose or plan could be elicited from him. But the look of him was enough to satisfy even Thorne. He leaned against a pile of wood, which he had collected, and his gloomy gaze pierced the campfire, and at long intervals strayed over the motionless form of the Spanish girl.

The rangers and Thorne, however, talked in low tones. It was absolutely impossible for Rojas and his men to reach the waterhole before noon of the next day. And long before that time the fugitives would have decided on a plan of defense. What that defense would be, and where it would be made, were matters over which the men considered gravely. Ladd averred the Yaqui would put them into an impregnable position, that at the same time would prove a death-trap for their pursuers. They exhausted every possibility, and then, tired as they were, still kept on talking.

"What stuns me is that Rojas stuck to our trail," said Thorne, his lined and haggard face expressive of dark passion. "He has followed us into this fearful desert. He'll lose men, horses, perhaps his life. He's only a bandit, and he stands to win no gold. If he ever gets out of here it 'll be by herculean labor and by terrible hardship. All for a poor little helpless woman—just a woman! My God, I can't understand it."

"Shore--just a woman," replied Ladd, solemnly nodding his head.

Then there was a long silence during which the men .zed into the fire. Each, perhaps, had some vague conception of the enormity of Rojas's love or hate—some faint and amazing glimpse of the gulf of human passion. Those were cold, hard, grim faces upon which the light flickered.

"Sleep," said the Yaqui.

Thorne rolled in his blanket close beside Mercedes. Then one by one the rangers stretched out, feet to the fire. Gale found that he could not sleep. His eyes were weary, but they would not stay shut; his body ached for rest, yet he could not lie still. The night was so somber, so gloomy, and the lava-encompassed arroyo full of shadows. The dark velvet sky, fretted with white fire, seemed to be close. There was an absolute silence, as of death. Nothing moved—nothing outside of Gale's body appeared to live. T e Yaqui sat like an image carved out of lava. The others lay prone and quiet. Would another night see any of them lie that way, quiet forever? Gale felt a ripple pass over him that was at once a shudder and a contraction of muscles. Used as he was to the desert and its oppression, why should he feel to-night as if the weight of its lava and the burden of its mystery were bearing him down?

He sat up after a while and again watched the fire. Nell's sweet face floated like a wraith in the pale smoke —glowed and flushed and smiled in the embers. Other faces shone there—his sister's—that of his mother. Gale shook off the tender memories. This desolate wilderness with its forbidding silence and its dark promise of hell on the morrow—this was not the place to unnerve oneself with thoughts of love and home. But the torturing paradox of the thing was that this was just the place and just the night for a man to be haunted.

By and by Gale rose and walked down a shadowy

aisle between the mesquites. On his way back the Yaqui joined him. Gale was not surprised. He had become used to the Indian's strange guardianship. But now, perhaps because of Gale's poignancy of thought, the contending tides of love and regret, the deep, burning premonition of deadly strife, he was moved to keener scrutiny of the Yaqui. That, of course, was futile. The Indian was impenetrable, silent, strange. But suddenly, inexplicably, Gale felt Yaqui's human quality. It was aloof, as was everything about this Indian; but it was there. This savage walked silently beside him, without glance or touch or word. His thought was as inscrutable as if mind had never awakened in his race. Yet Gale was conscious of greatness, and, somehow, he was reminded of the Indian's story. His home had been desolated, his people carried off to slavery, his wife and children separated from him to die. What had life meant to the Yaqui? What had been in his heart? What was now in his mind? Gale could not answer these questions. But the difference between himself and Yaqui, which he had vaguely felt as that between savages and civilized men, faded out of his mind forever. Yaqui might have considered he owed Gale a debt, and, with a Yaqui's austere and noble fidelity to honor, he meant to pay it. Nevertheless, this was not the thing Gale found in the Indian's silent presence. Accepting the desert with its subtle and inconceivable influence, Gale felt that the savage and the white man had been bound in a tie which was no less brotherly because it could not be comprehended.

Toward dawn Gale managed to get some sleep. Then the morning broke with the sun hidden back of the uplift of the plateau. The horses trooped up the arroyo and snorted for water. After a hurried breakfast the packs were hidden in holes in the lava. The saddles were left where they were, and the horses allowed to graze and wander at will. Canteens were filled, a small bag of food was packed, and blankets made into a bundle. Then Yaqui faced the steep ascent of the lava slope.

The trail he followed led up on the right side of the fissure, opposite to the one he had come down. It was a steep climb, and encumbered as the men were they made but slow progress. Mercedes had to be lifted up smooth steps and across crevices. They passed places where the rims of the fissure were but a few yards apart. At length the rims widened out and the red, smoky crater yawned beneath. Yaqui left the trail and began clambering down over the rough and twisted convolutions of lava which formed the rim. Sometimes he hung sheer over the precipice. It was with extreme difficulty that the party followed him. Mercedes had to be held on narrow, foot-wide ledges. The *choya* was there to hinder passage. Finally the Indian halted upon a narrow bench of flat, smooth lava, and his followers worked with exceeding care and effort down to his position.

At the back of this bench, between bunches of *choya*, was a niche, a shallow cave with floor lined apparently with mold. Ladd said the place was a refuge which had been inhabited by mountain sheep for many years. Yaqui spread blankets inside, left the canteen and the sack of food, and with a gesture at once humble, yet that of a chief, he invited Mercedes to enter. A few more gestures and fewer words disclosed his plan. In this inaccessible nook Mercedes was to be hidden. The men were to go around upon the opposite rim, and block the trail leading down to the waterhole.

Gale marked the nature of this eyrie. It was the wildest and most rugged place he had ever stepped upon. Only a sheep could have climbed up the wall above or along the slanting shelf of lava beyond. Below glistened a whole bank of *choya*, frosty in the sunlight, and it overhung an apparently bottomless abyss.

Ladd chose the smallest gun in the party and gave it to Mercedes.

THE CRATER OF HELL

"Shore it's best to go the limit on bein' ready," he said, simply. "The chances are you'll never need it. But if you do—"

He left off there, and his break was significant. Mercedes answered him with a fearless and indomitable flash of eyes. Thorne was the only one who showed any shaken nerve. His leave-taking of his wife was affecting and hurried. Then he and the rangers carefully stepped in the tracks of the Yaqui.

They climbed up to the level of the rim and went along the edge. When they reached the fissure and came upon its narrowest point, Yaqui showed in his actions that he meant to leap it. Ladd restrained the Indian. They then continued along the rim till they reached several bridges of lava which crossed it. The fissure was deep in some parts, choked in others. Evidently the crater had no direct outlet into the arroyo below. Its bottom, however, must have been far beneath the level of the waterhole.

After the fissure was crossed the trail was soon found. Here it ran back from the rim. Yaqui waved his hand to the right, where along the corrugated slope of the crater there were holes and crevices and coverts for a hundred men. Yaqui strode on up the trail toward a higher point, where presently his dark figure stood motionless against the sky. The rangers and Thorne selected a deep depression, out of which led several ruts deep enough for cover. According to Ladd it was as good a place as any, perhaps not so hidden as others, but freer from the dreaded *choya*. Here the men laid down rifles and guns, and, removing their heavy cartridge belts, settled down to wait.

Their location was close to the rim wall and probably five hundred yards from the opposite rim, which was now seen to be considerably below them. The glaring red cliff presented a deceitful and baffling appearance. It had a thousand ledges and holes in its surfaces, and one moment it looked perpendicular and the next there seemed to be a long slant. Thorne pointed out where he thought Mercedes was hidden; Ladd selected another place, and Lash still another. Gale searched for the bank of the *choya* he had seen under the bench where Mercedes's retreat lay, and when he found it the others disputed his opinion. Then Gale brought his field glass into requisition, proving that he was right. Once located and fixed in sight, the white patch of *choya,* the bench, and the sheep eyrie stood out from the other features of that rugged wall. But all the men were agreed that Yaqui had hidden Mercedes where only the eyes of a vulture could have found her.

Jim Lash crawled into a little strip of shade and bided the time tranquilly. Ladd was restless and impatient and watchful, every little while rising to look up the far-reaching slope, and then to the right, where Yaqui's dark figure stood out from a high point of the rim. Thorne grew silent, and seemed consumed by a slow, sullen rage. Gale was neither calm nor free of a gnawing suspense nor of a waiting wrath. But as best he could he put the pending action out of mind.

It came over him all of a sudden that he had not grasped the stupendous nature of this desert setting. There was the measureless red slope, its lower ridges finally sinking into white sand dunes toward the blue sea. The cold, sparkling light, the white sun, the deep azure of sky, the feeling of boundless expanse all around him —these meant high altitude. Southward the barren red simply merged into distance. The field of craters rose in high, dark wheels toward the dominating peaks. When Gale withdrew his gaze from the magnitude of these spaces and heights the crater beneath him seemed dwarfed. Yet while he gazed it spread and deepened and multiplied its ragged lines. No, he could not grasp the meaning of size or distance here. There was too much to stun the sight. But the mood in which nature had created this convulsed world of lava seized hold upon him.

Meanwhile the hours passed. As the sun climbed the clear, steely lights vanished, the blue hazes deepened, and slowly the glistening surfaces of lava turned redder. Ladd was concerned to discover that Yaqui was missing from his outlook upon the high point. Jim Lash came out of the shady crevice, and stood up to buckle on his cartridge belt. His narrow, gray glance slowly roved from the height of lava down along the slope, paused in doubt, and then swept on to resurvey the whole vast eastern dip of the plateau.

"I reckon my eyes are pore," he said. "Mebbe it's this damn red glare. Anyway, what's them creepin' spots up there?"

"Shore I seen them. Mountain sheep," replied Ladd.

"Guess again, Laddy. Dick, I reckon you'd better flash the glass up the slope."

Gale adjusted the field glass and began to search the lava, beginning close at hand and working away from him. Presently the glass became stationary.

"I see half a dozen small animals, brown in color. They look like sheep. But I couldn't distinguish mountain sheep from antelope."

"Shore they're bighorn," said Laddy.

"I reckon if you'll pull around to the east an' search under that long wall of lava—there—you'll see what I see," added Jim.

The glass climbed and circled, wavered an instant, then fixed steady as a rock. There was a breathless silence.

"Fourteen horses — two packed — some mounted — others without riders, and lame," said Gale, slowly.

Yaqui appeared far up the trail, coming swiftly. Presently he saw the rangers and halted to wave his arms and point. Then he vanished as if the lava had opened beneath him.

"Lemme that glass," suddenly said Jim Lash. "I'm seein' red, I tell you. . . . Well, pore as my eyes are they had it right. Rojas an' his outfit have left the trail."

"Jim, you ain't meanin' they've taken to that awful slope?" queried Ladd.

"I sure do. There they are—still comin', but goin' down, too."

"Mebbe Rojas is crazy, but it begins to look like he—"

"Laddy, I'll be danged if the Greaser bunch hasn't vamoosed. Gone out of sight! Right there not a half mile away, the whole caboodle—gone!"

"Shore they're behind a crust or have gone down into a rut," suggested Ladd. "They'll show again in a minute. Look sharp, boys, for I'm figgerin' Rojas 'll spread his men."

Minutes passed, but nothing moved upon the slope. Each man crawled up to a vantage point along the crest of rotting lava. The watchers were careful to peer through little notches or from behind a spur, and the constricted nature of their hiding-place kept them close together. Ladd's muttering grew into a growl, then lapsed into the silence that marked his companions. From time to time the rangers looked inquiringly at Gale. The field glass, however, like the naked sight, could not catch the slightest moving object out there upon the lava. A long hour of slow, mounting suspense wore on.

"Shore it's all goin' to be as queer as the Yaqui," said Ladd.

Indeed, the strange mien, the silent action, the somber character of the Indian had not been without effect upon the minds of the men. Then the weird, desolate, tragic scene added to the vague sense of mystery. And now the disappearance of Rojas's band, the long wait in the silence, the boding certainty of invisible foes crawling, circling closer and closer, lent to the situation a final touch that made it unreal.

"I'm reckonin' there's a mind behind them Greasers," replied Jim. "Or mebbe we ain't done Rojas credit. . . . If somethin' would only come off!"

That Lash, the coolest, most provokingly nonchalant

THE CRATER OF HELL

of men in times of peril, should begin to show a nervous strain was all the more indicative of a subtle pervading unreality.

"Boys, look sharp!" suddenly called Lash. "Low down to the left—mebbe three hundred yards. See, along by them seams of lava—behind the *choyas*. First off I thought it was a sheep. But it's the Yaqui! . . . Crawlin' swift as a lizard! Can't you see him?"

It was a full moment before Jim's companions could locate the Indian. Flat as a snake Yaqui wound himself along with incredible rapidity. His advance was all the more remarkable for the fact that he appeared to pass directly under the dreaded *choyas*. Sometimes he paused to lift his head and look. He was directly in line with a huge whorl of lava that rose higher than any point on the slope. This spur was a quarter of a mile from the position of the rangers.

"Shore he's headin' for that high place," said Ladd. "He's going slow now. There, he's stopped behind some *choyas*. He's gettin' up—no' he's kneelin'. . . . Now what the hell!"

"Laddy, take a peek at the side of that lava ridge," sharply called Jim. "I guess mebbe somethin' ain't comin' off. See! There's Rojas an' his outfit climbin'. Don't make out no hosses. . . . Dick, use your glass an' tell us what's doin'. I'll watch Yaqui an' tell you what his move means."

Clearly and distinctly, almost as if he could have touched them, Gale had Rojas and his followers in sight. They were toiling up the rough lava on foot. They were heavily armed. Spurs, chaps, jackets, scarfs were not in evidence. Gale saw the lean, swarthy faces, the black straggly hair, the ragged, soiled garments which had once been white.

"They're almost up now," Gale was saying. "There! They halt on top. I see Rojas. He looks wild. By——! fellows, an Indian! . . . It's a Papago. Belding's old herder! . . . The Indian points—this way—then down. He's showing Rojas the lay of the trail."

"Boys, Yaqui's in range of that bunch," said Jim, swiftly. "He's raisin' his rifle slow—Lord, how slow he is! . . . He's covered some one. Which one I can't say. But I think he'll pick Rojas."

"The Yaqui can shoot. He'll pick Rojas," added Gale, grimly.

"Rojas—yes—yes!" cried Thorne, in passion of suspense.

"Not on your life!" Ladd's voice cut in with scorn. "Gentlemen, you can gamble Yaqui'll kill the Papago. That traitor Indian knows these sheep haunts. He's tellin' Rojas—"

A sharp rifle shot rang out.

"Laddy's right," called Gale. "The Papago's hit— his arm falls— There, he tumbles!"

More shots rang out. Yaqui was seen standing erect firing rapidly at the darting Mexicans. For all Gale could make out no second bullet took effect. Rojas and his men vanished behind the bulge of lava. Then Yaqui deliberately backed away from his position. He made no effort to run or hide. Evidently he watched cautiously for signs of pursuers in the ruts and behind the *choyas*. Presently he turned and came straight toward the position of the rangers, sheered off perhaps a hundred paces below it, and disappeared in a crevice. Plainly his intention was to draw pursuers within rifle shot.

"Shore, Jim, you had your wish. Somethin' come off," said Ladd. "An' I'm sayin' thank God for the Yaqui! That Papago'd have ruined us. Even so, mebbe he's told Rojas more'n enough to make us sweat blood."

"He had a chance to kill Rojas," cried out the drawn-faced, passionate Thorne. "He didn't take it! . . . He didn't take it!"

Only Ladd appeared to be able to answer the cavalryman's poignant cry.

THE CRATER OF HELL

"Listen, son," he said, and his voice rang. "We-all know how you feel. An' if I'd had that one shot never in the world could I have picked the Papago guide. I'd have had to kill Rojas. That's the white man of it. But Yaqui was right. Only an Indian could have done it. You can gamble the Papago alive meant slim chance for us. Because he'd led straight to where Mercedes is hidden, an' then we'd have left cover to fight it out. . . . When you come to think of the Yaqui's for Greasers, when you just seen him pass up a shot at one—well, I don't know how to say what I mean, but damn me, my som-brer-ro is off to the Indian!"

"I reckon so, an' I reckon the ball's opened," rejoined Lash, and now that former nervous impatience so un-natural to him was as if it had never been. He was smil-ingly cool, and his voice had almost a caressing note. He tapped the breach of his Winchester with a sinewy brown hand, and he did not appear to be addressing any one in particular. "Yaqui's opened the ball. Look up your pardners there, gents, an' get ready to dance."

Another wait set in then, and judging by the more di-rect rays of the sun and a receding of the little shadows cast by the *choyas,* Gale was of the opinion that it was a long wait. But it seemed short. The four men were lying under the bank of a half circular hole in the lava. It was notched and cracked, and its rim was fringed by *choyas.* It sloped down and opened to an unobstructed view of the crater. Gale had the upper position, farthest to the right, and therefore was best shielded from possible fire from the higher ridges of the rim, some three hun-dred yards distant. Jim came next, well hidden in a crack. The positions of Thorne and Ladd were most exposed. They kept sharp lookout over the uneven ram-part of their hiding-place.

The sun passed the zenith, began to slope westward, and to grow hotter as it sloped. The men waited and waited. Gale saw no impatience even in Thorne. The sultry air seemed to be laden with some burden or quality that was at once composed of heat, menace, color, and silence. Even the light glancing up from the lava seemed red and the silence had substance. Sometimes Gale felt that it was unbearable. Yet he made no effort to break it.

Suddenly this dead stillness was rent by a shot, clear and stinging, close at hand. It was from a rifle, not a carbine. With startling quickness a cry followed—a cry that pierced Gale—it was so thin, so high-keyed, so different from all other cries. It was the involuntary human shriek of death.

"Yaqui's called out another pardner," said Jim Lash, laconically.

Carbines began to crack. The reports were quick, light, like sharp spats without any ring. Gale peered from behind the edge of his covert. Above the ragged wave of lava floated faint whitish clouds, all that was visible of smokeless powder. Then Gale made out round spots, dark against the background of red, and in front of them leaped out small tongues of fire. Ladd's .405 began to "spang" with its beautiful sound of power. Thorne was firing, somewhat wildly Gale thought. Then Jim Lash pushed his Winchester over the rim under a *choya,* and between shots Gale could hear him singing: "Turn the lady, turn—turn the lady, turn! . . . Alaman left! Swing your pardners! . . . Forward an' back! . . . Turn the lady, turn!" Gale got into the fight himself, not so sure that he hit any of the round, bobbing objects he aimed at, but growing sure of himself as action liberated something forced and congested within his breast.

Then over the position of the rangers came a hail of steel bullets. Those that struck the lava hissed away into the crater; those that came biting through the *choyas* made a sound which resembled a sharp ripping of silk. Bits of cactus stung Gale's face, and he dreaded the flying thorns more than he did the flying bullets.

THE CRATER OF HELL

"Hold on, boys," called Ladd, as he crouched down to reload his rifle. "Save your shells. The Greasers are spreadin' on us, some goin' down below Yaqui, others movin' up for that high ridge. When they get up there I'm damned if it won't be hot for us. There ain't room for all of us to hide here."

Ladd raised himself to peep over the rim. Shots were now scattering, and all appeared to come from below. Emboldened by this he rose higher. A shot from in front, a rip of bullet through the *choya,* a spat of something hitting Ladd's face, a steel missile hissing onward —these inseparably blended sounds were all registered by Gale's sensitive ear.

With a curse Ladd tumbled down into the hole. His face showed a great gray blotch, and starting blood. Gale felt a sickening assurance of desperate injury to the ranger. He ran to him calling: "Laddy! Laddy!"

"Shore I ain't plugged. It's a damn *choya* burr. The bullet knocked it in my face. Pull it out!"

The oval, long-spiked cone was firmly imbedded in Ladd's cheek. Blood streamed down his face and neck. Carefully, yet with no thought of pain to himself, Gale tried to pull the cactus joint away. It was as firm as if it had been nailed there. That was the damnable feature of the barbed thorns: once set, they held on as that strange plant held to its desert life. Ladd began to writhe, and sweat mingled with the blood on his face. He cursed and raved, and his movements made it almost impossible for Gale to do anything.

"Put your knife-blade under an' tear it out!" shouted Ladd, hoarsely.

Thus ordered, Gale slipped a long blade in between the imbedded thorns, and with a powerful jerk literally tore the *choya* out of Ladd's quivering flesh. Then, where the rangers face was not red and raw, it certainly was white.

A volley of shots from a different angle was followed

by the quick ring of steel bullets striking the lava all around Gale. His first idea, as he heard the projectiles sing and hum and whine away into the air, was that they were coming from above him. He looked up to see a number of low, white and dark knobs upon the high point of lava. They had not been there before. Then he saw little, pale, leaping tongues of fire. As he dodged down he distinctly heard a bullet strike Ladd. At the same instant he seemed to hear Thorne cry out and fall, and Lash's boots scrape rapidly away.

Ladd fell backward still holding the .405. Gale dragged him into the shelter of his own position, and dreading to look at him, took up the heavy weapon. It was with a kind of savage strength that he gripped the rifle; and it was with a cold and deadly intent that he aimed and fired. The first Greaser huddled low, let his carbine go clattering down, and then crawled behind the rim. The second and third jerked back. The fourth seemed to flop up over the crest of lava. A dark arm reached for him, clutched his leg, tried to drag him up. It was in vain. Wildly grasping at the air the bandit fell, slid down a steep shelf, rolled over the rim, to go hurtling down out of sight.

Fingering the hot rifle with close-pressed hands, Gale watched the sky line along the high point of lava. It remained unbroken. As his passion left him he feared to look back at his companions, and the cold chill returned to his breast.

"Shore—I'm damn glad—them Greasers ain't usin' soft-nose bullets," drawled a calm voice.

Swift as lightning Gale whirled.

"Laddy! I thought you were done for," cried Gale, with a break in his voice.

"I ain't a-mindin' the bullet much. But that *choya* joint took my nerve, an' you can gamble on it. Dick, this hole's pretty high up, ain't it?"

The ranger's blouse was open at the neck, and on his

right shoulder under the collar bone was a small hole just beginning to bleed.

"Sure it's high, Laddy," replied Gale, gladly. "Went clear through, clean as a whistle!"

He tore a handkerchief into two parts, made wads, and pressing them close over the wounds he bound them there with Ladd's scarf.

"Shore it's funny how a bullet can floor a man an' then not do any damage," said Ladd. "I felt a zip of wind an' somethin' like a pat on my chest an' down I went. Well, so much for the small caliber with their steel bullets. Supposin' I'd connected with a .405!"

"Laddy, I—I'm afraid Thorne's done for," whispered Gale. "He's lying over there in that crack. I can see part of him. He doesn't move."

"I was wonderin' if I'd have to tell you that. Dick, he went down hard hit, fallin', you know, limp an' soggy. It was a moral cinch one of us would get it in this fight; but God! I'm sorry Thorne had to be the man."

"Laddy, maybe he's not dead," replied Gale. He called aloud to his friend. There was no answer.

Ladd got up, and, after peering keenly at the height of lava, he strode swiftly across the space. It was only a dozen steps to the crack in the lava where Thorne had fallen in head first. Ladd bent over, went to his knees, so that Gale saw only his head. Then he appeared rising with arms round the cavalryman. He dragged him across the hole to the sheltered corner that alone afforded protection. He had scarcely reached it when a carbine cracked and a bullet struck the flinty lava, striking sparks, then singing away into the air.

Thorne was either dead or unconscious, and Gale, with a contracting throat and numb heart, decided for the former. Not so Ladd, who probed the bloody gash on Thorne's temple, and then felt his breast.

"He's alive an' not bad hurt. That bullet hit him glancin'. Shore them steel bullets are some lucky for us. Dick, you needn't look so glum. I tell you he ain't bad hurt. I felt his skull with my finger. There's no hole in it. Wash him off an' tie— Wow! did you get the wind of that one? An' mebbe it didn't sing off the lava! . . . Dick, look after Thorne now while I—"

The completion of his speech was the stirring ring of the .405, and then he uttered a laugh that was unpleasant.

"Shore, Greaser, there's a man's size bullet for you. No slim, sharp-point, steel-jacket nail! I'm takin' it on me to believe you're appreciatin' of the .405, seein' as you don't make no fuss."

It was indeed a joy to Gale to find that Thorne had not received a wound necessarily fatal, though it was serious enough. Gale bathed and bound it, and laid the cavalryman against the slant of the bank, his head high to lessen the probability of bleeding.

As Gale straightened up Ladd muttered low and deep, and swung the heavy rifle around to the left. Far along the slope a figure moved. Ladd began to work the lever of the Winchester and to shoot. At every shot the heavy firearm sprang up, and the recoil made Ladd's shoulder give back. Gale saw the bullets strike the lava behind, beside, before the fleeing Mexican, sending up dull puffs of dust. On the sixth shot he plunged down out of sight, either hit or frightened into seeking cover.

"Dick, mebbe there's one or two left above; but we needn't figger much on it," said Ladd, as, loading the rifle, he jerked his fingers quickly from the hot breech. "Listen! Jim an' Yaqui are hittin' it up lively down below. I'll sneak down there. You stay here an' keep about half an eye peeled up yonder, an' keep the rest my way."

Ladd crossed the hole, climbed down into the deep crack where Thorne had fallen, and then went stooping along with only his head above the level. Presently he disappeared. Gale, having little to fear from the high ridge, directed most of his attention toward the point beyond which Ladd had gone. The firing had become desultory, and the light carbine shots outnumbered the sharp rifle shots five to one. Gale made a note of the fact that for some little time he had not heard the unmistakable report of Jim Lash's automatic. Then ensued a long interval in which the desert silence seemed to recover its grip. The .405 ripped it asunder—*spang—spang—spang.* Gale fancied he heard yells. There were a few pattering shots still farther down the trail. Gale had an uneasy conviction that Rojas and some of his band might go straight to the waterhole. It would be hard to dislodge even a few men from that retreat.

There seemed a lull in the battle. Gale ventured to stand high, and, screened behind *choyas,* he swept the three-quarter circle of lava with his glass. In the distance he saw horses, but no riders. Below him, down the slope along the crater rim and the trail, the lava was bare of all except tufts of *choya.* Gale gathered assurance. It looked as if the day was favoring his side. Then Thorne, coming partly to consciousness, engaged Gale's care. The cavalryman stirred and moaned, called for water, and then for Mercedes. Gale held him back with a strong hand, and presently he was once more quiet.

For the first time in hours, as it seemed, Gale took note of the physical aspect of his surroundings. He began to look upon them without keen gaze strained for crouching form, or bobbing head, or spouting carbine. Either Gale's sense of color and proportion had become deranged during the fight, or the encompassing air and the desert had changed. Even the sun had changed. It seemed lowering, oval in shape, magenta in hue, and it had a surface that gleamed like oil on water. Its red rays shone through red haze. Distances that had formerly been clearly outlined were now dim, obscured. The yawning chasm was not the same. It circled wider, redder, deeper. It was a weird, ghastly mouth of hell. Gale stood fascinated, unable to tell how much he saw was real, how much the exaggeration of overwrought emotions. There was no beauty here, but an unparalleled grandeur, a sublime scene of devastation and desolation which might have had its counterpart upon the burned-out moon. The mood that gripped Gale now added to its somber portent an unshakable foreboding of calamity.

He wrestled with the spell as if it were a physical foe. Reason and intelligence had their voices in his mind; but the moment was not one wherein these things could wholly control. He felt life strong within his breast, yet there, a step away, was death, yawning, glaring, smoky, red. It was a moment—an hour for a savage, born, bred, developed in this scarred and blasted place of jagged depths and red distances and silences never meant to be broken. Since Gale was not a savage he fought that call of the red gods which sent him back down the long ages toward his primitive day. His mind combated his sense of sight and the hearing that seemed useless; and his mind did not win all the victory. Something fatal was here, hanging in the balance, as the red haze hung along the vast walls of that crater of hell.

Suddenly harsh, prolonged yells brought him to his feet, and the unrealities vanished. Far down the trails where the crater rims closed in the deep fissure he saw moving forms. They were three in number. Two of them ran nimbly across the lava bridge. The third staggered far behind. It was Ladd. He appeared hard hit. He dragged at the heavy rifle which he seemed unable to raise. The yells came from him. He was calling the Yaqui.

Gale's heart stood still momentarily. Here, then, was the catastrophe! He hardly dared sweep that fissure with his glass. The two fleeing figures halted—turned to fire at Ladd. Gale recognized the foremost one—small, compact, gaudy—Rojas! The bandit's arm was outstretched. Puffs of white smoke rose, and shots rapped out. When Ladd went down Rojas threw his gun aside and with a wild yell bounded over the lava. His companion followed.

A tide of passion, first hot as fire, then cold as ice, rushed over Gale when he saw Rojas take the trail toward Mercedes's hiding-place. The little bandit appeared to have the sure-footedness of a mountain sheep. The Mexican following was not so sure or fast. He turned back. Gale heard the trenchant bark of the .405. Ladd was kneeling. He shot again—again. The retreating bandit seemed to run full into an invisible obstacle, then fell lax, inert, lifeless. Rojas sped on unmindful of the spurts of dust about him. Yaqui, high above Ladd, was also firing at the bandit. Then both rifles were emptied. Rojas turned at a high break in the trail. He shook a defiant hand, and his exulting yell pealed faintly to Gale's ears. About him there was something desperate, magnificent, Then he clambered down the trail.

Ladd dropped the .405, and rising, gun in hand, he staggered toward the bridge of lava. Before he had crossed it Yaqui came bounding down the slope, and in one splendid leap he cleared the fissure. He ran beyond the trail and disappeared on the lava above. Rojas had not seen this sudden, darting move of the Indian.

Gale felt himself bitterly powerless to aid in that pursuit. He could only watch. He wondered, fearfully, what had become of Lash. Presently, when Rojas came out of the cracks and ruts of lava there might be a chance of disabling him by a long shot. His progress was now slow. But he was making straight for Mercedes's hiding-place. What was it leading him there—an eagle eye, or hate, or instinct? Why did he go on when there could be no turning back for him on that trail? Ladd was slow, heavy, staggering on the trail; but he was relentless. Only death could stop the ranger now. Surely Rojas must have known that when he chose the trail. From time to time Gale caught glimpses of Yaqui's dark figure stealing along the higher rim of the crater. He was making for a point above the bandit.

Moments—endless moments dragged by. The lowering sun colored only the upper half of the crater walls. Far down the depths were murky blue. Again Gale felt the insupportable silence. The red haze became a transparent veil before his eyes. Sinister, evil, brooding, waiting, seemed that yawning abyss. Ladd staggered along the trail, at times he crawled. The Yaqui gained; he might have had wings; he leaped from jagged crust to jagged crust; his sure-footedness was a wonderful thing.

But for Gale the marvel of that endless period of watching was the purpose of the bandit Rojas. He had now no weapon. Gale's glass made this fact plain. There was death behind him, death below him, death before him, and though he could not have known it, death above him. He never faltered—never made a misstep upon the narrow, flinty trail. When he reached the lower end of the level ledge Gale's poignant doubt became a certainty. Rojas had seen Mercedes. It was incredible, yet Gale believed it. Then, his heart clamped as in an icy vise, Gale threw forward the Remington, and sinking on one knee, began to shoot. He emptied the magazine. Puffs of dust near Rojas did not even make him turn.

As Gale began to reload he was horror-stricken by a low cry from Thorne. The cavalryman had recovered consciousness. He was half raised, pointing with shaking hand at the opposite ledge. His distended eyes were riveted upon Rojas. He was trying to utter speech that would not come.

Gale wheeled, rigid now, steeling himself to one last forlorn hope—that Mercedes could defend herself. She had a gun. He doubted not at all that she would use it. But, remembering her terror of this savage, he feared for her.

Rojas reached the level of the ledge. He halted. He

crouched. It was the act of a panther. Manifestly he saw Mercedes within the cave. Then faint shots patted the air, broke in quick echo. Rojas went down as if struck a heavy blow. He was hit. But even as Gale yelled in sheer madness the bandit leaped erect. He seemed too quick, too supple to be badly wounded. A slight, dark figure flashed out of the cave. Mercedes! She backed against the wall. Gale saw a puff of white—heard a report. But the bandit lunged at her. Mercedes ran, not to try to pass him, but straight for the precipice. Her intention was plain. But Rojas outstripped her, even as she reached the verge. Then a piercing scream pealed across the crater—a scream of despair.

Gale closed his eyes. He could not bear to see more.

Thorne echoed Mercedes's scream. Gale looked round just in time to leap and catch the cavalryman as he staggered, apparently for the steep slope. And then, as Gale dragged him back, both fell. Gale saved his friend, but he plunged into a *choya*. He drew his hands away full of the great glistening cones of thorns.

"For God's sake, Gale, shoot! Shoot! *Kill her! Kill her!* . . . Can't—you—see—Rojas—"

Thorne fainted.

Gale, stunned for the instant, stood with uplifted hands, and gazed from Thorne across the crater. Rojas had not killed Mercedes. He was overpowering her. His actions seemed slow, wearing, purposeful. Hers were violent. Like a trapped she-wolf, Mercedes was fighting. She tore, struggled, flung herself.

Rojas's intention was terribly plain.

In agony now, both mental and physical, cold and sick and weak, Gale gripped his rifle and aimed at the struggling forms on the ledge. He pulled the trigger. The bullet struck up a cloud of red dust close to the struggling couple. Again Gale fired, hoping to hit Rojas, praying to kill Mercedes. The bullet struck high. A third—fourth—fifth time the Remington spoke—in vain! The rifle fell from Gale's racked hands.

How horribly plain that fiend's intention! Gale tried to close his eyes, but could not. He prayed wildly for a sudden blindness—to faint as Thorne had fainted. But he was transfixed to the spot with eyes that pierced the red light.

Mercedes was growing weaker, seemed about to collapse.

"Oh, Jim Lash, are you dead?" cried Gale. "Oh, Laddy! . . . Oh, Yaqui!"

Suddenly a dark form literally fell down the wall behind the ledge where Rojas fought the girl. It sank in a heap, then bounded erect.

"Yaqui!" screamed Gale, and he waved his bleeding hands till the blood bespattered his face. Then he choked. Utterance became impossible.

The Indian bent over Rojas and flung him against the wall. Mercedes, sinking back, lay still. When Rojas got up the Indian stood between him and escape from the ledge. Rojas backed the other way along the narrowing shelf of lava. His manner was abject, stupefied. Slowly he stepped backward.

It was then that Gale caught the white gleam of a knife in Yaqui's hand. Rojas turned and ran. He rounded a corner of wall where the footing was precarious. Yaqui followed slowly. His figure was dark and menacing. But he was not in a hurry. When he passed off the ledge Rojas was edging farther and farther along the wall. He was clinging now to the lava, creeping inch by inch. Perhaps he had thought to work around the buttress or climb over it. Evidently he went as far as possible, and there he clung, an unscalable wall above, the abyss beneath.

The approach of the Yaqui was like a slow dark shadow of gloom. If it seemed so to the stricken Gale what must it have been to Rojas? He appeared to sink against the wall. The Yaqui stole closer and closer. He was the savage now, and for him the moment must have been glorified. Gale saw him gaze up at the great circling walls of the crater, then down into the depths. Perhaps the red haze hanging above him, or the purple haze below, or the deep caverns in the lava, held for Yaqui spirits of the desert, his gods to whom he called. Perhaps he invoked shadows of his loved ones and his race, calling them in this moment of vengeance.

Gale heard—or imagined he heard—that wild, strange Yaqui cry.

Then the Indian stepped close to Rojas, and bent low, keeping out of reach. How slow were his motions! Would Yaqui never—never end it? . . . A wail drifted across the crater to Gale's ears.

Rojas fell backward and plunged sheer. The bank of white *choyas* caught him, held him upon their steel spikes. How long did the dazed Gale sit there watching Rojas wrestling and writhing in convulsive frenzy? The bandit now seemed mad to win the delayed death.

When he broke free he was a white patched object no longer human, a ball of *choya* burrs, and he slipped off the bank to shoot down and down into the purple depths of the crater.

XIII

CHANGES AT FORLORN RIVER

THE first of March saw the federal occupation of the garrison at Casita. After a short, decisive engagement the rebels were dispersed into small bands and driven eastward along the boundary line toward Nogales.

It was the destiny of Forlorn River, however, never to return to the slow, sleepy tenor of its former existence. Belding's predictions came true. That straggling line of home-seekers was but a forerunner of the real invasion of Altar Valley. Refugees from Mexico and from Casita spread the word that water and wood and grass and land were to be had at Forlorn River; and as if by magic the white tents and red adobe houses sprang up to glisten in the sun.

Belding was happier than he had been for a long time. He believed that evil days for Forlorn River, along with the apathy and lack of enterprise, were in the past. He hired a couple of trustworthy Mexicans to ride the boundary line, and he settled down to think of ranching and irrigation and mining projects. Every morning he expected to receive some word from Sonoyta or Yuma, telling him that Yaqui had guided his party safely across the desert.

Belding was simple-minded, a man more inclined to action than reflection. When the complexities of life hemmed him in, he groped his way out, never quite understanding. His wife had always been a mystery to him. Nell was sunshine most of the time, but, like the sun-dominated desert, she was subject to strange changes, wilful, stormy, sudden. It was enough for Belding now to find his wife in a lighter, happier mood, and to see Nell dreamily turning a ring round and round the third finger of her left hand and watching the west. Every day both mother and daughter appeared farther removed from the past darkly threatening days. Belding was hearty in his affections, but undemonstrative. If there was any sentiment in his make-up it had an outlet in his memory of Blanco Diablo and a longing to see him. Often Belding stopped his work to gaze out over the desert toward the west. When he thought of his rangers and Thorne and Mercedes he certainly never forgot his horse. He wondered if Diablo was running, walking, resting; if Yaqui was finding water and grass.

In March, with the short desert winter over, the days began to grow warm. The noon hours were hot, and seemed to give promise of the white summer blaze and blasting furnace wind soon to come. No word was received from the rangers. But this caused Belding no concern, and it seemed to him that his women folk considered no news good news.

Among the many changes coming to pass in Forlorn River were the installing of post-office service and the building of a mescal drinking-house. Belding had worked hard for the post-office, but he did not like the idea of a saloon for Forlorn River. Still, that was an inevitable evil. The Mexicans would have mescal. Belding had kept the little border hamlet free of an establishment for distillation of the fiery cactus drink. A good many Americans drifted into Forlorn River—miners, cowboys, prospectors, outlaws, and others of nondescript character; and these men, of course, made the saloon, which was also an inn, their headquarters. Belding, with Carter and other old residents, saw the need of a sheriff for Forlorn River.

One morning early in this spring month, while Belding was on his way from the house to the corrals, he saw Nell running Blanco José down the road at a gait that amazed him. She did not take the turn of the road to come in by the gate. She put José at a four-foot wire fence, and came clattering into the yard.

"Nell must have another tantrum," said Belding. "She's long past due."

Blanco José, like the other white horses, was big of frame and heavy, and thunder rolled from under his great hoofs. Nell pulled him up, and as he pounded and slid to a halt in a cloud of dust she swung lightly down.

It did not take more than half an eye for Belding to see that she was furious.

"Nell, what's come off now?" asked Belding.

"I'm not going to tell you," she replied, and started away, leading José toward the corral.

Belding leisurely followed. She went into the corral, removed José's bridle, and led him to the watering-trough. Belding came up, and without saying anything began to unbuckle José's saddle girths. But he ventured a look at Nell. The red had gone from her face, and he was surprised to see her eyes brimming with tears. Most assuredly this was not one of Nell's tantrums. While taking off José's saddle and hanging it in the shed Belding pondered in his slow way. When he came back to the corral Nell had her face against the bars, and she was crying. He slipped a big arm around her and waited. Although it was not often expressed, there was a strong attachment between them.

"Dad, I don't want you to think me a—a baby any more," she said. "I've been insulted."

With a specific fact to make clear thought in Belding's mind he was never slow.

"I knew something unusual had come off. I guess you'd better tell me."

"Dad, I will, if you promise."

"What?"

"Not to mention it to mother, not to pack a gun down there, and never, never tell Dick."

Belding was silent. Seldom did he make promises readily.

"Nell, sure something must have come off, for you to ask all that."

"If you don't promise I'll never tell, that's all," she declared, firmly.

Belding deliberated a little longer. He knew the girl.

"Well, I promise not to tell mother," he said, presently; "and seeing you're here safe and well, I guess I won't go packing a gun down there, wherever that is. But I won't promise to keep anything from Dick that perhaps he ought to know."

"Dad, what would Dick do if—if he were here and I were to tell him I'd—I'd been horribly insulted?"

"I guess that'd depend. Mostly, you know, Dick does what you want. But you couldn't stop him—nobody could—if there was reason, a man's reason, to get started. Remember what he did to Rojas! . . . Nell, tell me what's happened."

Nell, regaining her composure, wiped her eyes and smoothed back her hair.

"The other day, Wednesday," she began, "I was coming home, and in front of that mescal drinking-place there was a crowd. It was a noisy crowd. I didn't want to walk out into the street or seem afraid. But I had to do both. There were several young men, and if they weren't drunk they certainly were rude. I never saw them before, but I think they must belong to the mining company that was run out of Sonora by rebels. Mrs. Carter was telling me. Anyway, these young fellows were Americans. They stretched themselves across the walk and smiled at me. I had to go out in the road. One of them, the rudest, followed me. He was a big fellow, red-faced, with prominent eyes and a bold look. He came up beside me and spoke to me. I ran home. And as I ran I heard his companions jeering.

"Well, to-day, just now, when I was riding up the valley road I came upon the same fellows. They had instruments and were surveying. Remembering Dick, and how he always wished for an instrument to help work out his plan for irrigation, I was certainly surprised to see these strangers surveying—and surveying upon Laddy's plot of land. It was a sandy road there, and José happened to be walking. So I reined in and asked these engineers what they were doing. The leader, who was that same bold fellow who had followed me, seemed much pleased at being addressed. He was swaggering—too friendly; not my idea of a gentleman at all. He said he was glad to tell me he was going to run water all over Altar Valley. Dad, you can bet that made me wild. That was Dick's plan, his discovery, and here were surveyors on Laddy's claim.

"Then I told him that he was working on private land and he'd better get off. He seemed to forget his flirty proclivities in amazement. Then he looked cunning. I read his mind. It was news to him that all the land along the valley had been taken up.

"He said something about not seeing any squatters on the land, and then he shut up tight on that score. But he began to be flirty again. He got hold of José's bridle, and before I could catch my breath he said I was a peach, that he wanted to make a date with me, that his name was Chase, that he owned a gold mine in Mexico. He said a lot more I didn't gather, but when he called me 'Dearie' I—well, I lost my temper.

"I jerked on the bridle and told him to let go. He held on and rolled his eyes at me. I dare say he imagined he was a gentleman to be infatuated with. He seemed sure of conquest. One thing was certain, he didn't know the least bit about horses. It scared me the way he got in front of José. I thanked my stars I wasn't up on Blanco Diablo. Well, Dad, I'm a little ashamed now, but I was mad. I slashed him across the face with my quirt.

José jumped and knocked Mr. Chase into the sand. I didn't get the horse under control till I was out of sight of those surveyors, and then I let him run home."

"Nell, I guess you punished the fellow enough. Maybe he's only a conceited softy. But I don't like that sort of thing. It isn't Western. I guess he won't be so smart next time. Any fellow would remember being hit by Blanco José. If you'd been up on Diablo we'd have to bury Mr. Chase."

"Thank goodness I wasn't! I'm sorry now, Dad. Perhaps the fellow was hurt. But what could I do? Let's forget all about it, and I'll be careful where I ride in the future. . . . Dad, what does it mean, this surveying around Forlorn River?"

"I don't know, Nell," replied Belding, thoughtfully. "It worries me. It looks good for Forlorn River, but bad for Dick's plan to irrigate the valley. Lord, I'd hate to have some one forestall Dick on that!"

"No, no, we won't let anybody have Dick's rights," declared Nell.

"Where have I been keeping myself not to know about these surveyors?" muttered Belding. "They must have just come."

"Go see Mrs. Carter. She told me there were strangers in town, Americans, who had mining interests in Sonora, and were run out by Orozco. Find out what they're doing, Dad."

Belding discovered that he was, indeed, the last man of consequence in Forlorn River to learn of the arrival of Ben Chase and son, mine owners and operators in Sonora. They, with a force of miners, had been besieged by rebels and finally driven off their property. This property was not destroyed, but held for ransom. And the Chases, pending developments, had packed outfits and struck for the border. Casita had been their objective point, but, for some reason which Belding did not learn, they had arrived instead at Forlorn River. It had taken Ben Chase just one day to see the possibilities of Altar Valley, and in three days he had men at work.

Belding returned home without going to see the Chases and their operations. He wanted to think over the situation. Next morning he went out to the valley to see for himself. Mexicans were hastily erecting adobe houses upon Ladd's one hundred and sixty acres, upon Dick Gale's, upon Jim Lash's and Thorne's. There were men staking the valley floor and the river bed. That was sufficient for Belding. He turned back toward town and headed for the camp of these intruders.

In fact, the surroundings of Forlorn River, except on the river side, reminded Belding of the mushroom growth of a newly discovered mining camp. Tents were everywhere; adobe shacks were in all stages of construction; rough clapboard houses were going up. The latest of this work was new and surprising to Belding, all because he was a busy man, with no chance to hear village gossip. When he was directed to the headquarters of the Chase Mining Company he went thither in slow-growing wrath.

He came to a big tent with a huge canvas fly stretched in front, under which sat several men in their shirt sleeves. They were talking and smoking.

"My name's Belding. I want to see this Mr. Chase," said Belding, gruffly.

Slow-witted as Belding was, and absorbed in his own feelings, he yet saw plainly that his advent was disturbing to these men. They looked alarmed, exchanged glances, and then quickly turned to him. One of them, a tall, rugged man with sharp face and shrewd eyes and white hair, got up and offered his hand.

"I'm Chase, senior," he said. "My son Radford Chase is here somewhere. You're Belding, the line inspector, I take it? I meant to call on you."

He seemed a rough-and-ready, loud-spoken man, withal cordial enough.

"Yes, I'm the inspector," replied Belding, ignoring the

proffered hand, "and I'd like to know what in the hell you mean by taking up land claims—staked ground that belongs to my rangers?"

"Land claims?" slowly echoed Chase, studying his man. "We're taking up only unclaimed land."

"That's a lie. You couldn't miss the stakes."

"Well, Mr. Belding, as to that, I think my men did run across some staked ground. But we recognize only squatters. If your rangers think they've got property just because they drove a few stakes in the ground they're much mistaken. A squatter has to build a house and live on his land so long, according to law, before he owns it."

This argument was unanswerable, and Belding knew it.

"According to law!" exclaimed Belding. "Then you own up; you've jumped our claims."

"Mr. Belding, I'm a plain business man. I come along. I see a good opening. Nobody seems to have tenable grants. I stake out claims, locate squatters, start to build. It seems to me your rangers have overlooked certain precautions. That's unfortunate for them. I'm prepared to hold my claim and to back all the squatters who work for me. If you don't like it you can carry the matter to Tucson. The law will uphold me."

"The law? Say, on this southwest border we haven't any law except a man's word and a gun."

"Then you'll find United States law has come along with Ben Chase," replied the other, snapping his fingers. He was still smooth, outspoken, but his mask had fallen.

"You're not a Westerner?" queried Belding.

"No, I'm from Illinois."

"I thought the West hadn't bred you. I know your kind. You'd last a long time on the Texas border; now, wouldn't you? You're one of the land and water hogs that has come to root in the West. You're like the timber sharks—take it all and leave none for those who follow. Mr. Chase, the West would fare better and last longer if men like you were driven out."

"You can't drive me out."

"I'm not so sure of that. Wait till my rangers come back. I wouldn't be in your boots. Don't mistake me. I don't suppose you could be accused of stealing another man's ideas or plan, but sure you've stolen these four claims. Maybe the law might uphold you. But the spirit, not the letter counts with us bordermen."

"See here, Belding, I think you're taking the wrong view of the matter. I'm going to develop this valley. You'd do better to get in with me. I've a proposition to make you about that strip of land of yours facing the river."

"You can't make any deals with me. I won't have anything to do with you."

Belding abruptly left the camp and went home. Nell met him, probably intended to question him, but one look into his face confirmed her fears. She silently turned away. Belding realized he was powerless to stop Chase, and he was sick with disappointment for the ruin of Dick's hopes and his own.

XIV

A LOST SON

TIME passed. The population of Forlorn River grew apace. Belding, who had once been the head of the community, found himself a person of little consequence. Even had he desired it he would not have had any voice in the selection of postmaster, sheriff, and a few other officials. The Chases divided their labors between Forlorn River and their Mexican gold mine, which had been restored to them. The desert trips between these two places were taken in automobiles. A month's time made the motor cars almost as familiar a sight in Forlorn River as they had been in Casita before the revolution.

Belding was not so busy as he had been formerly. As he lost ambition he began to find less work to do. His wrath at the usurping Chases increased as he slowly realized his powerlessness to cope with such men. They were promoters, men of big interests and wide influence in the Southwest. The more they did for Forlorn River the less reason there seemed to be for his own grievance. He had to admit that it was personal; that he and Gale and the rangers would never have been able to develop the resources of the valley as these men were doing it.

All day long he heard the heavy booming blasts and the rumble of avalanches up in the gorge. Chase's men were dynamiting the cliffs in the narrow box cañon. They were making the dam just as Gale had planned to make it. When this work of blasting was over Belding experienced a relief. He would not now be continually reminded of

233

his and Gale's loss. Resignation finally came to him. But he could not reconcile himself to misfortune for Gale.

Moreover, Belding had other worry and strain. April arrived with no news of the rangers. From Casita came vague reports of raiders in the Sonoyta country—reports impossible to verify until his Mexican rangers returned. When these men rode in, one of them, Gonzales, an intelligent and reliable halfbreed, said he had met prospectors at the oasis. They had just come in on the Camino del Diablo, reported a terrible trip of heat and drought, and not a trace of the Yaqui's party.

"That settles it," declared Belding. "Yaqui never went to Sonoyta. He's circled round to the Devil's Road, and the rangers, Mercedes, Thorne, the horses—they—I'm afraid they have been lost in the desert. It's an old story on Camino del Diablo."

He had to tell Nell that, and it was an ordeal which left him weak.

Mrs. Belding listened to him, and was silent for a long time while she held the stricken Nell to her breast. Then she opposed his convictions with that quiet strength so characteristic of her arguments.

"Well, then," decided Belding, "Rojas headed the rangers at Papago Well or the Tanks."

"Tom, when you are down in the mouth you use poor judgment," she went on. "You know only by a miracle could Rojas or anybody have headed those white horses. Where's your old stubborn confidence? Yaqui was up on Diablo. Dick was up on Sol. And there were the other horses. They could not have been headed or caught. Miracles don't happen."

"All right, mother, it's sure good to hear you," said Belding. She always cheered him, and now he grasped at straws. "I'm not myself these days, don't mistake that. Tell us what you think. You always say you feel things when you really don't know them."

"I can say little more than what you said yourself the

night Mercedes was taken away. You told Laddy to trust Yaqui, that he was a godsend. He might go south into some wild Sonora valley. He might lead Rojas into a trap. He would find water and grass where no Mexican or American could."

"But mother, they're gone seven weeks. Seven weeks! At the most I gave them six weeks. Seven weeks in the desert!"

"How do the Yaquis live?" she asked.

Belding could not reply to that, but hope revived in him. He had faith in his wife, though he could not in the least understand what he imagined was something mystic in her.

"Years ago when I was searching for my father I learned many things about this country," said Mrs. Belding. "You can never tell how long a man may live in the desert. The fiercest, most terrible and inaccessible places often have their hidden oasis. In his later years my father became a prospector. That was strange to me, for he never cared for gold or money. I learned that he was often gone in the desert for weeks, once for months. Then the time came when he never came back. That was years before I reached the southwest border and heard of him. Even then I did not for long give up hope of his coming back. I know now—something tells me—indeed, it seems his spirit tells me—he was lost. But I don't have that feeling for Yaqui and his party. Yaqui has given Rojas the slip or has ambushed him in some trap. Probably that took time and a long journey into Sonora. The Indian is too wise to start back now over dry trails. He'll curb the rangers; he'll wait. I seem to know this, dear Nell, so be brave, patient. Dick Gale will come back to you."

"Oh, mother!" cried Nell. "I can't give up hope while I have you."

That talk with the strong mother worked a change in Nell and in Belding. Nell, who had done little but brood and watch the west and take violent rides, seemed to settle into a waiting patience that was sad, yet serene. She helped her mother more than ever; she was a comfort to Belding; she began to take active interest in the affairs of the growing village. Belding, who had been breaking under the strain of worry, recovered himself so that to outward appearance he was his old self. He alone knew, however, that his humor was forced, and that the slow burning wrath he felt for the Chases was flaming into hate. Belding argued with himself that if Ben Chase and his son, Radford, had turned out to be big men in other ways than in the power to carry on great enterprises he might have become reconciled to them. But the father was greedy, grasping, hard, cold; the son added to those traits an overbearing disposition to rule, and he showed a fondness for drink and cards. These men were developing the valley, to be sure, and a horde of poor Mexicans and many Americans were benefiting from that development; nevertheless, these Chases were operating in a way which proved they cared only for themselves.

Belding shook off a lethargic spell and decided he had better set about several by no means small tasks, if he wanted to get them finished before the hot months. He made a trip to the Sonoyta Oasis. He satisfied himself that matters along the line were favorable, and that there was absolutely no trace of his rangers. Upon completing this trip he went to Casita with a number of his white thoroughbreds and shipped them to ranchers and horse-breeders in Texas. Then, being near the railroad, and having time, he went up to Tucson. There he learned some interesting particulars about the Chases. They had an office in the city; influential friends in the Capitol. They were powerful men in the rapidly growing finance of the West. They had interested the Southern Pacific Railroad, and in the near future a branch line was to be constructed from San Felipe to Forlorn River. These details of the Chase development were insignificant when compared to a matter striking close home to Belding. His responsibility had been subtly attacked. A doubt had been cast upon his capability of executing the duties of immigration inspector to the best advantage of the state. Belding divined that this was only an entering wedge. The Chases were bent upon driving him out of Forlorn River; but, perhaps to serve better their own ends, they were proceeding at leisure. Belding returned home consumed by rage. But he controlled it. For the first time in his life he was afraid of himself. He had his wife and Nell to think of; and the old law of the West had gone forever.

"Dad, there's another Rojas round these diggings," was Nell's remark, after the greetings were over and the usual questions and answers passed.

Belding's exclamation was cut short by Nell's laugh. She was serious with a kind of amused contempt.

"Mr. Radford Chase!"

"Now Nell, what the—" roared Belding.

"Hush, Dad! Don't swear," interrupted Nell. "I only meant to tease you."

"Humph! Say, my girl, that name Chase makes me see red. If you must tease me hit on some other way. *Sabe,* señorita?"

"*Si, si,* Dad."

"Nell, you may as well tell him and have it over," said Mrs. Belding, quietly.

"You promised me once, Dad, that you'd not go packing a gun off down there, didn't you?"

"Yes, I remember," replied Belding; but he did not answer her smile.

"Will you promise again?" she asked, lightly. Here was Nell with arch eyes, yet not the old arch eyes, so full of fun and mischief. Her lips were tremulous; her cheeks seemed less round.

"Yes," rejoined Belding; and he knew why his voice was a little thick.

"Well, if you weren't such a good old blind Dad you'd have seen long ago the way Mr. Radford Chase ran round after me. At first it was only annoying, and I did not want to add to your worries. But these two weeks you've been gone I've been more than annoyed. After that time I struck Mr. Chase with my quirt he made all possible efforts to meet me. He did meet me wherever I went. He sent me letters till I got tired of sending them back.

"When you left home on your trips I don't know that he grew bolder, but he had more opportunity. I couldn't stay in the house all the time. There were mama's errands and sick people and my Sunday school, and what not. Mr. Chase waylaid me every time I went out. If he works any more I don't know when, unless it's when I'm asleep. He followed me until it was less embarrassing for me to let him walk with me and talk his head off. He made love to me. He begged me to marry him. I told him I was already in love and engaged to be married. He said that didn't make any difference. Then I called him a fool.

"Next time he saw me he said he must explain. He meant I was being true to a man who, everybody on the border knew, had been lost in the desert. That—that hurt. Maybe—maybe it's true. Sometimes it seems terribly true. Since then, of course, I have stayed in the house to avoid being hurt again.

"But, Dad, a little thing like a girl sticking close to her mother and her room doesn't stop Mr. Chase. I think he's crazy. Anyway, he's a most persistent fool. I want to be charitable, because the man swears he loves me, and maybe he does, but he is making me nervous. I don't sleep. I'm afraid to be in my room at night. I've gone to mother's room. He's always hanging round. Bold! Why, that isn't the thing to call Mr. Chase. He's absolutely without a sense of decency. He bribes our servants. He comes into our patio. Think of that! He makes the most ridiculous excuses. He bothers mother to death. I feel like a poor little rabbit holed by a hound. And I daren't peep out."

Somehow the thing struck Belding as funny, and he laughed. He had not had a laugh for so long that it made him feel good. He stopped only at sight of Nell's surprise and pain. Then he put his arms round her.

"Never mind dear. I'm an old bear. But it tickled me, I guess. I sure hope Mr. Radford Chase *has* got it bad.... Nell, it's only the old story. The fellows fall in love with you. It's your good looks, Nell. What a price women like you and Mercedes have to pay for beauty! I'd a d— a good deal rather be ugly as a mud fence."

"So would I, Dad, if—if Dick would still love me."

"He wouldn't, you can gamble on that, as Laddy says. ... Well, the first time I catch this locoed Romeo sneaking round here I'll—I'll—"

"Dad, you promised."

"Confound it, Nell, I promised not to pack a gun. That's all. I'll only shoo this fellow off the place, gently, mind you, gently. I'll leave the rest for Dick Gale!"

"*Oh, Dad!*" cried Nell; and she clung to him wistful, frightened, yet something more.

"Don't mistake me, Nell. You have you own way, generally. You pull the wool over mother's eyes, and you wind me round your little finger. But you can't do either with Dick Gale. You're tender-hearted; you overlook the doings of this hound, Chase. But when Dick comes back, you just make up your mind to a little hell in the Chase camp. Oh, he'll find it out. And I sure want to be round when Dick hands Mr. Radford the same as he handed Rojas!"

Belding kept a sharp lookout for young Chase, and then, a few days later, learned that both son and father had gone off upon one of their frequent trips to Casa Grandes, near where their mines were situated.

April grew apace, and soon gave way to May. One

morning Belding was called from some garden work by the whirring of an automobile and a "Holloa!" He went forward to the front yard and there saw a car he thought resembled one he had seen in Casita. It contained a familiar-looking driver, but the three figures in gray coats and veils were strange to him. By the time he had gotten to the road he decided two were women and the other a man. At the moment their faces were emerging from dusty veils. Belding saw an elderly, sallow-faced, rather frail-appearing man who was an entire stranger to him; a handsome dark-eyed woman whose hair showed white through her veil; and a superbly built girl, whose face made Belding at once think of Dick Gale.

"Is this Mr. Tom Belding, inspector of immigration?" inquired the gentleman, courteously.

"I'm Belding, and I know who you are," replied Belding in hearty amaze, as he stretched forth his big hand. "You're Dick Gale's Dad—the Governor, Dick used to say. I'm sure glad to meet you."

"Thank you. Yes, I'm Dick's governor, and here, Mr. Belding—Dick's mother and his sister Elsie."

Beaming his pleasure, Belding shook hands with the ladies, who showed their agitation clearly.

"Mr. Belding, I've come west to look up my lost son," said Mr. Gale. "His sister's letters were unanswered. We haven't heard from him in months. Is he still here with you?"

"Well, now, sure I'm awful sorry," began Belding, his slow mind at work. "Dick's away just now—been away for a considerable spell. I'm expecting him back any day.... Won't you come in? You're all dusty and hot and tired. Come in, and let mother and Nell make you comfortable. Of course you'll stay. We've a big house. You must stay till Dick comes back. Maybe that 'll be— Aw, I guess it won't be long.... Let me handle the baggage, Mr. Gale.... Come in. I sure am glad to meet you all."

A LOST SON

Eager, excited, delighted, Belding went on talking as he ushered the Gales into the sitting-room, presenting them in his hearty way to the astounded Mrs. Belding and Nell. For the space of a few moments his wife and daughter were bewildered. Belding did not recollect any other occasion when a few callers had thrown them off their balance. But of course this was different. He was a little flustered himself—a circumstance that dawned upon him with surprise. When the Gales had been shown to rooms, Mrs. Belding gained the poise momentarily lost; but Nell came rushing back, wilder than a deer, in a state of excitement strange even for her.

"Oh! Dick's mother, his sister!" whispered Nell.

Belding observed the omission of the father in Nell's exclamation of mingled delight and alarm.

"His mother!" went on Nell. "Oh, I knew it! I always guessed it! Dick's people are proud, rich; they're somebody. I thought I'd faint when she looked at me. She was just curious—curious, but so cold and proud. She was wondering about me. Dick has never written her that he's—he's engaged to me. I'm wearing his ring. It was his mother's, he said. I won't—I can't take it off. And I'm scared.... But the sister—oh, she's lovely and sweet—proud, too. I felt warm all over when she looked at me. I—I wanted to kiss her. She looks like Dick when he first came to us. But he's changed. They'll hardly recognize him.... To think they've come! And I had to be looking a fright, when of all times on earth I'd want to look my best."

Nell, out of breath, ran away evidently to make herself presentable, according to her idea of the exigency of the case. Belding caught a glimpse of his wife's face as she went out, and it wore a sad, strange, anxious expression. Then Belding sat alone, pondering the contracting emotions of his wife and daughter. It was beyond his understanding. Women were creatures of feeling. Belding saw reason to be delighted to entertain Dick's family; and for the time being no disturbing thought entered his mind.

Presently the Gales came back into the sitting-room, looking very different without the long gray cloaks and veils. Belding saw distinction and elegance. Mr. Gale seemed a grave, troubled, kindly person, ill in body and mind. Belding received the same impression of power that Ben Chase had given him, only here it was minus any harshness or hard quality. He gathered that Mr. Gale was a man of authority. Mrs. Gale rather frightened Belding, but he could not have told why. The girl was just like Dick as he used to be.

Their manner of speaking also reminded Belding of Dick. They talked of the ride from Ash Fork down to the border, of the ugly and torn-up Casita, of the heat and dust and cactus along the trail. Presently Nell came in, now cool and sweet in white, with a red rose at her breast. Belding had never been so proud of her. He saw that she meant to appear well in the eyes of Dick's people, and began to have a faint perception of what the ordeal was for her. Belding imagined the sooner the Gales were told that Dick was to marry Nell the better for all concerned, and especially for Nell. In the general conversation that ensued he sought for an opening in which to tell this important news, but he was kept so busy answering questions about his position on the border, the kind of place Forlorn River was, the reason for so many tents, etc., that he was unable to find opportunity.

"It's interesting, very interesting," said Mr. Gale. "At another time I want to learn all you'll tell me about the West. It's new to me. I'm surprised, amazed, sir, I may say.... But, Mr. Belding, what I want to know most is about my son. I'm broken in health. I've worried myself ill over him. I don't mind telling you, sir, that we quarreled. I laughed at his threats. He went away. And I've come to see I didn't know Richard. I was wrong to upbraid him. For a year we've known nothing of his doings, and now for almost six months we've not heard from him at all. Frankly, Mr. Belding, I weakened first, and I've come to hunt him up. My fear is that I didn't start soon enough. The boy will have a great position some day—God knows, perhaps soon! I should not have allowed him to run over this wild country for so long. But I hope, though I hardly believed, that he might find himself. Now I'm afraid he's—"

Mr. Gale paused, and the white hand he raised expressively shook a little.

Belding was not so thick-witted where men were concerned. He saw how the matter lay between Dick Gale and his father.

"Well, Mr. Gale, sure most young bucks from the East go to the bad out here," he said, bluntly.

"I've been told that," replied Mr. Gale, and a shade overspread his worn face.

"They blow their money, then go to punching cows, take to whisky."

"Yes," rejoined Mr. Gale, feebly nodding.

"Then they get to gambling, lose their jobs," went on Belding.

Mr. Gale lifted haggard eyes.

"Then it's bumming around, regular tramps, and to the bad generally." Belding spread wide his big arms, and when one of them dropped round Nell, who sat beside him, she squeezed his hand tight. "Sure, it's the regular thing," he concluded, cheerfully.

He rather felt a little glee at Mr. Gale's distress, and Mrs. Gale's crushed I-told-you-so woe in no wise bothered him; but the look in the big, dark eyes of Dick's sister was too much for Belding.

He choked off his characteristic oath when excited and blurted out, "Say, but *Dick Gale* never went to the bad! ...Listen!"

Belding had scarcely started Dick Gale's story when he perceived that never in his life had he such an absorbed and breathless audience. Presently they were awed, and at the conclusion of that story they sat white-faced, still, amazed beyond speech. Dick Gale's advent in Casita, his rescue of Mercedes, his life as a border ranger certainly lost no picturesque or daring or even noble detail in Belding's telling. He kept back nothing but the present doubt of Dick's safety.

Dick's sister was the first of the three to recover herself.

"Oh, father!" she cried; and there was a glorious light in her eyes. "Deep down in my heart I knew Dick was a man!"

Mr. Gale rose unsteadily from his chair. His frailty was now painfully manifest.

"Mr. Belding, do you mean my son—Richard Gale—has done all that you told us?" he asked, incredulously.

"I sure do," replied Belding, with hearty good will.

"Martha, do you hear?" Mr. Gale turned to question his wife. She could not answer. Her face had not yet regained its natural color.

"He faced that bandit and his gang alone—he *fought* them?" demanded Mr. Gale, his voice stronger.

"Dick mopped up the floor with the whole outfit!"

"He rescued a Spanish girl, went into the desert without food, weapons, anything but his hands? Richard Gale, whose hands were always useless?"

Belding nodded with a grin.

"He's a ranger now—riding, fighting, sleeping on the sand, preparing his own food?"

"Well, I should smile," rejoined Belding.

"He cares for his horse, with his own hands?" This query seemed to be the climax of Mr. Gale's strange hunger for truth. He had raised his head a little higher, and his eye was brighter.

Mention of a horse fired Belding's blood.

"Does Dick Gale *care* for his horse? Say, there are not many *men* as well loved as that white horse of Dick's. Blanco Sol he is, Mr. Gale. That's Mex for White Sun.

A LOST SON

Wait till you see Blanco Sol! Bar one, the whitest, biggest, strongest, fastest, grandest horse in the Southwest!"

"So he loves a horse! I shall not know my own son. ... Mr. Belding, you say Richard works for you. May I ask, at what salary?"

"He gets forty dollars, board and outfit," replied Belding, proudly.

"Forty dollars?" echoed the father. "By the day or week?"

"The month, of course," said Belding, somewhat taken aback.

"Forty dollars a month for a young man who spent five hundred in the same time when he was at college, and who ran it into thousands when he got out!"

Mr. Gale laughed for the first time, and it was the laugh of a man who wanted to believe what he heard yet scarcely dared to do it.

"What does he do with so much money—money earned by peril, toil, sweat, and blood? Forty dollars a month!"

"He saves it," replied Belding.

Evidently this was too much for Dick Gale's father, and he gazed at his wife in sheer speechless astonishment. Dick's sister clapped her hands like a little child.

Belding saw that the moment was propitious.

"Sure he saves it. Dick's engaged to marry Nell here. My stepdaughter, Nell Burton."

"Oh-h, Dad!" faltered Nell; and she rose, white as her dress.

How strange it was to see Dick's mother and sister rise, also, and turn to Nell with dark, proud, searching eyes. Belding vaguely realized some blunder he had made. Nell's white, appealing face gave him a pang. What had he done? Surely this family of Dick's ought to know his relation to Nell. There was a silence that positively made Belding nervous.

Then Elsie Gale stepped close to Nell.

"Miss Burton, are you really Richard's betrothed?"

Nell's tremulous lips framed an affirmative, but never uttered it. She held out her hand, showing the ring Dick had given her. Miss Gale's recognition was instant, and her response was warm, sweet, gracious.

"I think I am going to be very, very glad," she said, and kissed Nell.

"Miss Burton, we are learning wonderful things about Richard," added Mr. Gale, in an earnest though shaken voice. "If you have had to do with making a man of him—and now I begin to see, to believe so—may God bless you!... My dear girl, I have not really looked at you. Richard's fiancée!...Mother, we have not found him yet, but I think we've found his secret. We believed him a lost son. But here is his sweetheart!"

It was only then that the pride and hauteur of Mrs. Gale's face broke into an expression of mingled pain and joy. She opened her arms. Nell, uttering a strange little stifled cry, flew into them.

Belding suddenly discovered an unaccountable blur in his sight. He could not see perfectly, and that was why, when Mrs. Belding entered the sitting-room, he was not certain that her face was as sad and white as it seemed.

XV

FAR away from Forlorn River Dick Gale sat stunned, gazing down into the purple depths where Rojas had plunged to his death. The Yaqui stood motionless upon the steep red wall of lava from which he had cut the bandit's hold. Mercedes lay quietly where she had fallen. From across the depths there came to Gale's ear the Indian's strange, wild cry.

Then silence, hollow, breathless, stony silence enveloped the great abyss and its upheaved lava walls. The sun was setting. Every instant the haze reddened and thickened.

Action on the part of the Yaqui loosened the spell which held Gale as motionless as his surroundings. The Indian was edging back toward the ledge. He did not move with his former lithe and sure freedom. He crawled, slipped, dragged himself, rested often, and went on again. He had been wounded. When at last he reached the ledge where Mercedes lay Gale jumped to his feet, strong and thrilling, spurred to meet the responsibility that now rested upon him.

Swiftly he turned to where Thorne lay. The cavalryman was just returning to consciousness. Gale ran for a canteen, bathed his face, made him drink. The look in Thorne's eyes was hard to bear.

"Thorne! Thorne! it's all right, it's all right!" cried Gale, in piercing tones. "Mercedes is safe! Yaqui saved her! Rojas is done for! Yaqui jumped down the wall and drove the bandit off the ledge. Cut him loose

247

from the wall, foot by foot, hand by hand! We've won the fight, Thorne."

For Thorne these were marvelous strength-giving words. The dark horror left his eyes, and they began to dilate, to shine. He stood up, dizzily but unaided, and he gazed across the crater. Yaqui had reached the side of Mercedes, was bending over her. She stirred. Yaqui lifted her to her feet. She appeared weak, unable to stand alone. But she faced across the crater and waved her hand. She was unharmed. Thorne lifted both arms above his head, and from his lips issued a cry. It was neither call nor holloa nor welcome nor answer. Like the Yaqui's, it could scarcely be named. But it was deep, husky, prolonged, terribly human in its intensity. It made Gale shudder and made his heart beat like a trip hammer. Mercedes again waved a white hand. The Yaqui waved, too, and Gale saw in the action an urgent signal.

Hastily taking up canteen and rifles, Gale put a supporting arm around Thorne.

"Come, old man. Can you walk? Sure you can walk! Lean on me, and we'll soon get out of this. Don't look across. Look where you step. We've not much time before dark. Oh, Thorne, I'm afraid Jim has cashed in! And the last I saw of Laddy he was badly hurt."

Gale was keyed up to a high pitch of excitement and alertness. He seemed to be able to do many things. But once off the ragged notched lava into the trail he had not such difficulty with Thorne, and could keep his keen gaze shifting everywhere for sight of enemies.

"Listen, Thorne! What's that?" asked Gale, halting as they came to a place where the trail led down through rough breaks in the lava. The silence was broken by a strange sound, almost unbelievable considering the time and place. A voice was droning: "Turn the lady, turn! Turn the lady, turn! Alamon left. All swing; turn the lady, turn!"

BOUND IN THE DESERT

"Hello, Jim," called Gale, dragging Thorne round the corner of lava. "Where are you? Oh, you son of a gun! I thought you were dead. Oh, I'm glad to see you! Jim, are you hurt?"

Jim Lash stood in the trail leaning over the butt of his rifle, which evidently he was utilizing as a crutch. He was pale but smiling. His hands were bloody. A scarf had been bound tightly round his left leg just above the knee. The leg hung limp, and the foot dragged.

"I reckon I ain't injured much," replied Jim. "But my leg hurts like hell, if you want to know."

"Laddy! Oh, where's Laddy?"

"He's just across the crack there. I was trying to get to him. We had it hot an' heavy down here. Laddy was pretty bad shot up before he tried to head Rojas off the trail.... Dick, did you see the Yaqui go after Rojas?"

"Did I!" exclaimed Gale, grimly.

"The finish was all that saved me from runnin' loco plumb over the rim. You see I was closer'n you to where Mercedes was hid. When Rojas an' his last Greaser started across, Laddy went after them, but I couldn't. Laddy did for Rojas's man, then went down himself. But he got up an' fell, got up, went on, an' fell again. Laddy kept doin' that till he dropped for good. I reckon our chances are against findin' him alive.... I tell you, boys, Rojas was hell-bent. An' Mercedes was game. I saw her shoot him. But mebbe bullets couldn't stop him then. If I didn't sweat blood when Mercedes was fightin' him on the cliff! Then the finish! Only a Yaqui could have done that.... Thorne, you didn't miss it?"

"Yes, I was down and out," replied the cavalryman.

"It's a shame. Greatest stunt I ever seen! Thorne, you're standin' up pretty fair. How about you? Dick, is he bad hurt?"

"No, he's not. A hard knock on the skull and a scalp wound," replied Dick. "Here, Jim, let me help you over this place."

Step by step Gale got the two injured men down the uneven declivity and then across the narrow lava bridge over the fissure. Here he bade them rest while he went along the trail on that side to search for Laddy. Gale found the ranger stretched out, face downward, a reddened hand clutching a gun. Gale thought he was dead. Upon examination, however, it was found that Ladd still lived, though he had many wounds. Gale lifted him and carried him back to the others.

"He's alive, but that's all," said Dick, as he laid the ranger down. "Do what you can. Stop the blood. Laddy's tough as cactus, you know. I'll hurry back for Mercedes and Yaqui."

Gale, like a fleet, sure-footed mountain sheep, ran along the trail. When he came across the Mexican, Rojas's last ally, Gale had evidence of the terrible execution of the .405. He did not pause. On the first part of that descent he made faster time than had Rojas. But he exercised care along the hard, slippery, ragged slope leading to the ledge. Presently he came upon Mercedes and the Yaqui. She ran right into Dick's arms, and there her strength, if not her courage, broke, and she grew lax.

"Mercedes, you're safe! Thorne's safe. It's all right now."

"Rojas!" she whispered.

"Gone! To the bottom of the crater! A Yaqui" vengeance, Mercedes."

He heard the girl whisper the name of the Virgin. Then he gathered her up in his arms.

"Come, Yaqui."

The Indian grunted. He had one hand pressed close over a bloody place in his shoulder. Gale looked keenly at him. Yaqui was inscrutable, as of old, yet Gale somehow knew that wound meant little to him. The Indian followed him.

Without pausing, moving slowly in some places, very carefully in others, and swiftly on the smooth part of the trail, Gale carried Mercedes up to the rim and along to the others. Jim Lash worked awkwardly over Ladd. Thorne was trying to assist. Ladd, himself, was conscious, but he was a pallid, apparently a death-stricken man. The greeting between Mercedes and Thorne was calm— strangely so, it seemed to Gale. But he was now calm himself. Ladd smiled at him, and evidently would have spoken had he the power. Yaqui then joined the group, and his piercing eyes roved from one to the other, lingering longest over Ladd.

"Dick, I'm figger'n' hard," said Jim, faintly. "In a minute it'll be up to you an' Mercedes. I've about shot my bolt.... Reckon you'll do—best by bringin' up blankets — water — salt — firewood. Laddy's got — one chance—in a hundred. Fix him up—first. Use hot salt water. If my leg's broken—set it best you can. That hole in Yaqui—only'll bother him a day. Thorne's bad hurt. . . . Now rustle—Dick, old—boy."

Lash's voice died away in a husky whisper, and he quietly lay back, stretching out all but the crippled leg. Gale examined it, assured himself the bones had not been broken, and then rose ready to go down the trail.

"Mercedes, hold Thorne's head up, in your lap—so. Now I'll go."

On the moment Yaqui appeared to have completed the binding of his wounded shoulder, and he started to follow Gale. He paid no attention to Gale's order for him to stay back. But he was slow, and gradually Gale forged ahead. The lingering brightness of the sunset lightened the trail, and the descent to the arroyo was swift and easy. Some of the white horses had come in for water. Blanco Sol spied Gale and whistled and came pounding toward him. It was twilight down in the arroyo. Yaqui appeared and began collecting a bundle of mesquite sticks. Gale hastily put together the things he needed; and, packing them all in a tarpaulin, he turned to retrace his steps up the trail.

DESERT GOLD

Darkness was setting in. The trail was narrow, exceedingly steep, and in some places fronted on precipices. Gale's burden was not very heavy, but its bulk made it unwieldy, and it was always overbalancing him or knocking against the wall side of the trail. Gale found it necessary to wait for Yaqui to take the lead. The Indian's eyes must have seen as well at night as by day. Gale toiled upward, shouldering, swinging, dragging the big pack; and, though the ascent of the slope was not really long, it seemed endless. At last they reached a level, and were soon on the spot with Mercedes and the injured men.

Gale then set to work. Yaqui's part was to keep the fire blazing and the water hot, Mercedes's to help Gale in what way she could. Gale found Ladd had many wounds, yet not one of them was directly in a vital place. Evidently, the ranger had almost bled to death. He remained unconscious through Gale's operations. According to Jim Lash, Ladd had one chance in a hundred, but Gale considered it one in a thousand. Having done all that was possible for the ranger, Gale slipped blankets under and around him, and then turned his attention to Lash.

Jim came out of his stupor. A mushrooming bullet had torn a great hole in his leg. Gale, upon examination, could not be sure the bones had been missed, but there was no bad break. The application of hot salt water made Jim groan. When he had been bandaged and laid beside Ladd, Gale went on to the cavalryman. Thorne was very weak and scarcely conscious. A furrow had been plowed through his scalp down to the bone. When it had been dressed, Mercedes collapsed. Gale laid her with the three in a row and covered them with blankets and the tarpaulin.

Then Yaqui submitted to examination. A bullet had gone through the Indian's shoulder. To Gale it appeared serious. Yaqui said it was a flea bite. But he allowed

BOUND IN THE DESERT

Gale to bandage it, and obeyed when he was told to lie quiet in his blanket beside the fire.

Gale stood guard. He seemed still calm, and wondered at what he considered a strange absence of poignant feeling. If he had felt weariness it was now gone. He coaxed the fire with as little wood as would keep it burning; he sat beside it; he walked to and fro close by; sometimes he stood over the five sleepers, wondering if two of them, at least, would ever awaken.

Time had passed swiftly, but as the necessity for immediate action had gone by, the hours gradually assumed something of their normal length. The night wore on. The air grew colder, the stars brighter, the sky bluer, and, if such could be possible, the silence more intense. The fire burned out, and for lack of wood could not be rekindled. Gale patrolled his short beat, becoming colder and damper as dawn approached. The darkness grew so dense that he could not see the pale faces of the sleepers. He dreaded the gray dawn and the light. Slowly the heavy black belt close to the lava changed to a pale gloom, then to gray, and after that morning came quickly.

The hour had come for Dick Gale to face his great problem. It was natural that he hung back a little at first; natural that when he went forward to look at the quiet sleepers he did so with a grim and stern force urging him. Yaqui stirred, roused, yawned, got up; and, though he did not smile at Gale, a light shone swiftly across his dark face. His shoulder drooped and appeared stiff, otherwise he was himself. Mercedes lay in deep slumber. Thorne had a high fever, and was beginning to show signs of restlessness. Ladd seemed just barely alive. Jim Lash slept as if he was not much the worse for his wound.

Gale rose from his examination with a sharp breaking of his cold mood. While there was life in Thorne and Ladd there was hope for them. Then he faced his problem, and his decision was instant.

He awoke Mercedes. How wondering, wistful, beautiful was that first opening flash of her eyes! Then the dark, troubled thought came. Swiftly she sat up.

"Mercedes—come. Are you all right? Laddy is alive. Thorne's not—not so bad. But we've got a job on our hands! You must help me."

She bent over Thorne and laid her hands on his hot face. Then she rose—a woman such as he had imagined she might be in an hour of trial.

Gale took up Ladd as carefully and gently as possible.

"Mercedes, bring what you can carry and follow me," he said. Then, motioning for Yaqui to remain there, he turned down the slope with Ladd in his arms.

Neither pausing nor making a misstep nor conscious of great effort, Gale carried the wounded man down into the arroyo. Mercedes kept at his heels, light, supple, lithe as a panther. He left her with Ladd and went back. When he had started off with Thorne in his arms he felt the tax on his strength. Surely and swiftly, however, he bore the cavalryman down the trail to lay him beside Ladd. Again he started back, and when he began to mount the steep lava steps he was hot, wet, breathing hard. As he reached the scene of that night's camp a voice greeted him. Jim Lash was sitting up.

"Hello, Dick. I woke some late this mornin'. Where's Laddy? Dick, you ain't a-goin' to say—"

"Laddy's alive—that's about all," replied Dick.

"Where's Thorne an' Mercedes? Look here, man! I reckon you ain't packin' this crippled outfit down that awful trail?"

"Had to, Jim. An hour's sun—would kill—both Laddy and Thorne. Come on now."

For once Jim Lash's cool good nature and careless indifference gave precedence to amaze and concern.

"Always knew you was a husky chap. But, Dick, you're no hoss! Get me a crutch an' give me a lift on one side."

"Come on," replied Gale. "I've no time to monkey."

BOUND IN THE DESERT

He lifted the ranger, called to Yaqui to follow with some of the camp outfit, and once more essayed the steep descent. Jim Lash was the heaviest man of the three, and Gale's strength was put to enormous strain to carry him on that broken trail. Nevertheless, Gale went down, down, walking swiftly and surely over the bad places; and at last he staggered into the arroyo with bursting heart and red-blinded eyes. When he had recovered he made a final trip up the slope for the camp effects which Yaqui had been unable to carry.

Then he drew Jim and Mercedes and Yaqui, also, into an earnest discussion of ways and means whereby to fight for the life of Thorne. Ladd's case Gale now considered hopeless, though he meant to fight for him, too, as long as he breathed.

In the labor of watching and nursing it seemed to Gale that two days and two nights slipped by like a few hours. During that time the Indian recovered from his injury, and became capable of performing all except heavy tasks. Then Gale succumbed to weariness. After his much-needed rest he relieved Mercedes of the care and watch over Thorne which, up to that time, she had absolutely refused to relinquish. The cavalryman had high fever, and Gale feared he had developed blood poisoning. He required constant attention. His condition slowly grew worse, and there came a day which Gale thought surely was the end. But that day passed, and the night, and the next day, and Thorne lived on, ghastly, stricken, raving. Mercedes hung over him with jealous, passionate care and did all that could have been humanly done for a man. She grew wan, absorbed, silent. But suddenly, and to Gale's amaze and thanksgiving, there came an abatement of Thorne's fever. With it some of the heat and redness of the inflamed wound disappeared. Next morning he was conscious, and Gale grasped some of the hope that Mercedes had never abandoned. He forced her to rest while he attended to Thorne. That day he saw that the crisis was past. Recovery for Thorne was now possible, and would perhaps depend entirely upon the care he received.

Jim Lash's wound healed without any aggravating symptoms. It would be only a matter of time until he had the use of his leg again. All these days, however, there was little apparent change in Ladd's condition, unless it was that he seemed to fade away as he lingered. At first his wounds remained open; they bled a little all the time outwardly, perhaps internally also; his blood did not seem to clot, and so the bullet holes did not close. Then Yaqui asked for the care of Ladd. Gale yielded it with opposing thoughts—that Ladd would waste slowly away till life ceased, and that there never was any telling what might lie in the power of this strange Indian. Yaqui absented himself from camp for a while, and when he returned he carried the roots and leaves of desert plants unknown to Gale. From these the Indian brewed an ointment. Then he stripped the bandages from Ladd and applied the mixture to his wounds. That done, he let him lie with the wounds exposed to the air, at night covering him. Next day he again exposed the wounds to the warm, dry air. Slowly they closed, and Ladd ceased to bleed externally.

Days passed and grew into what Gale imagined must have been weeks. Yaqui recovered fully. Jim Lash began to move about on a crutch; he shared the Indian's watch over Ladd. Thorne lay a haggard, emaciated ghost of his former rugged self, but with life in the eyes that turned always toward Mercedes. Ladd lingered and lingered. The life seemingly would not leave his bullet-pierced body. He faded, withered, shrunk till he was almost a skeleton. He knew those who worked and watched over him, but he had no power of speech. His eyes and eyelids moved; the rest of him seemed stone. All those days nothing except water was given him. It was marvelous how tenaciously, however feebly, he clung to life. Gale imagined it was the Yaqui's spirit that held back death. That tireless, implacable, inscrutable savage was ever at the ranger's side. His great somber eyes burned. At length he went to Gale, and, with that strange light flitting across the hard bronzed face, he said Ladd would live.

The second day after Ladd had been given such thin nourishment as he could swallow he recovered the use of his tongue.

"Shore—this's—hell," he whispered.

That was a characteristic speech for the ranger, Gale thought; and indeed it made all who heard it smile while their eyes were wet.

From that time forward Ladd gained, but he gained so immeasurably slowly that only the eyes of hope could have seen any improvement. Jim Lash threw away his crutch, and Thorne was well, if still somewhat weak, before Ladd could lift his arm or turn his head. A kind of long, immovable gloom passed, like a shadow, from his face. His whispers grew stronger. And the day arrived when Gale, who was perhaps the least optimistic, threw doubt to the winds and knew the ranger would get well. For Gale that joyous moment of realization was one in which he seemed to return to a former self long absent. He experienced an elevation of soul. He was suddenly overwhelmed with gratefulness, humility, awe. A gloomy black terror had passed by. He wanted to thank the faithful Mercedes, and Thorne for getting well, and the cheerful Lash, and Ladd himself, and that strange and wonderful Yaqui, now such a splendid figure. He thought of home and Nell. The terrible encompassing red slopes lost something of their fearsomeness, and there was a good spirit hovering near.

"Boys, come round," said Ladd, in his low voice. "An' you, Mercedes. An' call the Yaqui."

Ladd lay in the shade of the brush shelter that had been

erected. His head was raised slightly on a pillow. There seemed little of him but long lean lines, and if it had not been for his keen, thoughtful, kindly eyes, his face would have resembled a death mask of a man starved.

"Shore I want to know what day is it an' what month?" asked Ladd.

Nobody could answer him. The question seemed a surprise to Gale, and evidently was so to the others.

"Look at that cactus," went on Ladd.

Near the wall of lava a stunted *saguaro* lifted its head. A few shriveled blossoms that had once been white hung along the fluted column.

"I reckon according to that giant cactus it's somewheres along the end of March," said Jim Lash, soberly.

"Shore it's April. Look where the sun is. An' can't you feel it's gettin' hot?"

"Supposin' it is April?" queried Lash, slowly.

"Well, what I'm drivin' at is it's about time you all was hittin' the trail back to Forlorn River, before the waterholes dry out."

"Laddy, I reckon we'll start soon as you're able to be put on a hoss."

"Shore that 'll be too late."

A silence ensued, in which those who heard Ladd gazed fixedly at him and then at one another. Lash uneasily shifted the position of his lame leg, and Gale saw him moisten his lips with his tongue.

"Charlie Ladd, I ain't reckonin' you mean we're to ride off an' leave you here?"

"What else is there to do? The hot weather's close. Pretty soon most of the waterholes will be dry. You can't travel then. . . . I'm on my back here, an' God only knows when I could be packed out. Not for weeks, mebbe. I'll never be any good again, even if I was to get out alive. . . . You see, shore this sort of case comes round sometimes in the desert. It's common enough. I've heard of several cases where men had to go an' leave a feller behind. It's reasonable. If you're fightin' the desert you can't afford to be sentimental.... Now, as I said, I'm all in. So what's the sense of you waitin' here, when it means the old desert story? By goin' now mebbe you'll get home. If you wait on a chance of takin' me, you'll be too late. Pretty soon this lava'll be one roastin' hell. Shore now, boys, you'll see this the right way? Jim, old pard?"

"No, Laddy, an' I can't figger how you could ever ask me."

"Shore then leave me here with Yaqui an' a couple of the hosses. We can eat sheep meat. An' if the water holds out—"

"No!" interrupted Lash, violently.

Ladd's eyes sought Gale's face.

"Son, you ain't bull-headed like Jim. You'll see the sense of it. There's Nell a-waitin' back at Forlorn River. Think what it means to her! She's a damn fine girl, Dick, an' what right have you to break her heart for an old worn-out cowpuncher? Think how she's watchin' for you with that sweet face all sad an' troubled, an' her eyes turnin' black. You'll go, son, won't you?"

Dick shook his head.

The ranger turned his gaze upon Thorne, and now the keen, glistening light in his gray eyes had blurred.

"Thorne, it's different with you. Jim's a fool, an' young Gale has been punctured by *choya* thorns. He's got the desert poison in his blood. But you now—you've no call to stick—you can find that trail out. It's easy to follow, made by so many shod hosses. Take your wife an' go.... Shore you'll go, Thorne?"

Deliberately and without an instant's hesitation the cavalryman replied "No."

Ladd then directed his appeal to Mercedes. His face was now convulsed, and his voice, though it had sunk to a whisper, was clear, and beautiful with some rich quality that Gale had never before heard in it.

"Mercedes, you're a woman. You're the woman we fought for. An' some of us are shore goin' to die for you. Don't make it all for nothin'. Let us feel we saved the woman. Shore you can make Thorne go. He'll have to go if you say. They'll all have to go. Think of the years of love an' happiness in store for you. A week or so an' it'll be too late. Can you stand for me seein' you? ... Let me tell you, Mercedes, when the summer heat hits the lava we'll all wither an' curl up like shavin's near a fire. A wind of hell will blow up this slope. Look at them mesquites. See the twist in them. That's the torture of heat an' thirst. Do you want me or all us men seein' you like that? ... Mercedes, don't make it all for nothin'. Say you'll persuade Thorne, if not the others."

For all the effect his appeal had to move her Mercedes might have possessed a heart as hard and fixed as the surrounding lava.

"Never!"

White-faced, with great black eyes flashing, the Spanish girl spoke the word that bound her and her companions in the desert.

The subject was never mentioned again. Gale thought that he read a sinister purpose in Ladd's mind. To his astonishment, Lash came to him with the same fancy. After that they made certain there never was a gun within reach of Ladd's clutching, clawlike hands.

Gradually a somber spell lifted from the ranger's mind. When he was entirely free of it he began to gather strength daily. Then it was as if he had never known patience—he who had shown so well how to wait. He was in a frenzy to get well. His appetite could not be satisfied.

The sun climbed higher, whiter, hotter. At midday a wind from gulfward roared up the arroyo, and now only the *palo verdes* and the few *saguaros* were green. Every day the water in the lava hole sank an inch.

The Yaqui alone spent the waiting time in activity. He made trips up on the lava slope, and each time he re-

BOUND IN THE DESERT

turned with guns or boots or sombreros, or something belonging to the bandits that had fallen. He never fetched in a saddle or bridle, and from that the rangers concluded Rojas's horses had long before taken their back trail. What speculation, what consternation those sad-dled horses would cause if they returned to Forlorn River!

As Ladd improved there was one story he had to hear every day. It was the one relating to what he had missed —the sight of Rojas pursued and plunged to his doom. The thing had a morbid fascination for the sick ranger. He reveled in it. He tortured Mercedes. His gentle-ness and consideration, heretofore so marked, were in abeyance to some sinister, ghastly joy. But to humor him Mercedes racked her soul with the sensations she had suffered when Rojas hounded her out on the ledge; when she shot him; when she sprang to throw herself over the precipice; when she fought him; when with half-blinded eyes she looked up to see the merciless Yaqui reaching for the bandit. Ladd fed his cruel longing with Thorne's poignant recollections, with the keen, clear, never-to-be-forgotten shocks to Gale's eye and ear. Jim Lash, for one at least, never tired of telling how he had seen and heard the tragedy, and every time in the telling it gathered some more tragic and gruesome detail. Jim believed in satiating the ranger. Then in the twilight, when the camp-fire burned, Ladd would try to get the Yaqui to tell his side of the story. But this the Indian would never do. There was only the expression of his fathomless eyes and the set passion of his massive face.

Those waiting days grew into weeks. Ladd gained very slowly. Nevertheless, at last he could walk about, and soon he averred that, strapped to a horse, he could last out the trip to Forlorn River.

There was rejoicing in camp, and plans were eagerly suggested. The Yaqui happened to be absent. When he returned the rangers told him they were now ready to undertake the journey back across lava and cactus.

Yaqui shook his head. They declared again their intention.

"No!" replied the Indian, and his deep, sonorous voice rolled out upon the quiet of the arroyo. He spoke briefly then. They had waited too long. The smaller water-holes back in the trail were dry. The hot summer was upon them. There could be only death waiting down in the burning valley. Here was water and grass and wood and shade from the sun's rays, and sheep to be killed on the peaks. The water would hold unless the season was that dreaded *ano seco* of the Mexicans.

"Wait for rain," concluded Yaqui, and now as never before he spoke as one with authority. "If no rain—" Silently he lifted a speaking hand.

XVI

MOUNTAIN SHEEP

WHAT Gale might have thought an appalling situation, if considered from a safe and comfortable home away from the desert, became, now that he was shut in by the red-ribbed lava walls and great dry wastes, a matter calmly accepted as inevitable. So he imagined it was accepted by the others. Not even Mercedes uttered a regret. No word was spoken of home. If there was thought of loved ones, it was locked deep in their minds. In Mercedes there was no change in womanly quality, perhaps because all she had to love was there in the desert with her.

Gale had often pondered over this singular change in character. He had trained himself, in order to fight a paralyzing something in the desert's influence, to oppose with memory and thought an insidious primitive retrogression to what was scarcely consciousness at all, merely a savage's instinct of sight and sound. He felt the need now of redoubled effort. For there was a sheer happiness in drifting. Not only was it easy to forget, it was hard to remember. His idea was that a man laboring under a great wrong, a great crime, a great passion might find the lonely desert a fitting place for either remembrance or oblivion, according to the nature of his soul. But an ordinary, healthy, reasonably happy mortal who loved the open with its blaze of sun and sweep of wind would have a task to keep from going backward to the natural man as he was before civilization.

By tacit agreement Ladd again became the leader of

the party. Ladd was a man who would have taken all the responsibility whether or not it was given him. In moments of hazard, of uncertainty, Lash and Gale, even Belding, unconsciously looked to the ranger. He had that kind of power.

The first thing Ladd asked was to have the store of food that remained spread out upon a tarpaulin. Assuredly, it was a slender enough supply. The ranger stood for long moments gazing down at it. He was groping among past experiences, calling back from his years of life on range and desert that which might be valuable for the present issue. It was impossible to read the gravity of Ladd's face, for he still looked like a dead man, but the slow shake of his head told Gale much. There was a grain of hope, however, in the significance with which he touched the bags of salt and said, "Shore it was sense packin' all that salt!"

Then he turned to face his comrades.

"That's little grub for six starvin' people corralled in the desert. But the grub end ain't worryin' me. Yaqui can get sheep up the slopes. Water! That's the beginnin' an' middle an' end of our case."

"Laddy, I reckon the waterhole here never goes dry," replied Jim.

"Ask the Indian."

Upon being questioned, Yaqui repeated what he had said about the dreaded *ano seco* of the Mexicans. In a dry year this waterhole failed.

"Dick, take a rope an' see how much water's in the hole."

Gale could not find bottom with a thirty foot lasso. The water was as cool, clear, sweet as if it had been kept in a shaded iron receptacle.

Ladd welcomed this information with surprise and gladness.

"Let's see. Last year was shore pretty dry. Mebbe this summer won't be. Mebbe our wonderful good luck'll hold. Ask Yaqui if he thinks it'll rain."

MOUNTAIN SHEEP

Mercedes questioned the Indian.

"He says no man can tell surely. But he thinks the rain will come," she replied.

"Shore it'll rain, you can gamble on that now," continued Ladd. "If there's only grass for the hosses! We can't get out of here without hosses. Dick, take the Indian an' scout down the arroyo. To-day I seen the hosses were gettin' fat. Gettin' fat in this desert! But mebbe they've about grazed up all the grass. Go an' see, Dick. An' may you come back with more good news!"

Gale, upon the few occasions when he had wandered down the arroyo, had never gone far. The Yaqui said there was grass for the horses, and until now no one had given the question more consideration. Gale found that the arroyo widened as it opened. Near the head, where it was narrow, the grass lined the course of the dry stream bed. But farther down this stream bed spread out. There was every indication that at flood seasons the water covered the floor of the arroyo. The farther Gale went the thicker and larger grew the gnarled mesquites and *palo verdes,* the more cactus and greasewood there were, and other desert growths. Patches of gray grass grew everywhere. Gale began to wonder where the horses were. Finally the trees and brush thinned out, and a mile-wide gray plain stretched down to reddish sand dunes. Over to one side were the white horses, and even as Gale saw them both Blanco Diablo and Sol lifted their heads and, with white manes tossing in the wind, whistled clarion calls. Here was grass enough for many horses; the arroyo was indeed an oasis.

Ladd and the others were awaiting Gale's report, and they received it with calmness, yet with a joy no less evident because it was restrained. Gale, in his keen observation at the moment, found that he and his comrades turned with glad eyes to the woman of the party.

"Señor Laddy, you think—you—believe—we shall—"
she faltered, and her voice failed. It was the woman in her,
weakening in the light of real hope, of the happiness now
possible beyond that desert barrier.

"Mercedes, no white man can tell what'll come to pass
out here," said Ladd, earnestly. "Shore I have hopes
now I never dreamed of. I was pretty near a dead man.
The Indian saved me. Queer notions have come into
my head about Yaqui. I don't understand them. He
seems when you look at him only a squalid, sullen, vengeful savage. But Lord! that's far from truth. Mebbe
Yaqui's different from most Indians. He *looks* the same,
though. Mebbe the trouble is we white folks never knew
the Indian. Anyway, Beldin' had it right. Yaqui's
our godsend. Now as to the future, I'd like to know
mebbe as well as you if we're ever to get home. Only
bein' what I am, I say *Quien sabe?* But somethin' tells
me Yaqui knows. Ask him, Mercedes. Make him tell.
We'll all be the better for knowin'. We'd be stronger for
havin' more'n our faith in him. He's a silent Indian, but
make him tell."

Mercedes called to Yaqui. At her bidding there was
always a suggestion of hurry, which otherwise was never
manifest in his actions. She put a hand on his bared
muscular arm and began to speak in Spanish. Her voice
was low, swift, full of deep emotion, sweet as the sound
of a bell. It thrilled Gale, though he understood scarcely
a word she said. He did not need translation to know that
here spoke the longing of a woman for life, love, home,
the heritage of a woman's heart.

Gale doubted his own divining impression. It was that
the Yaqui understood this woman's longing. In Gale's
sight the Indian's stoicism, his inscrutability, the lavalike
hardness of his face, although they did not change, seemed
to give forth light, gentleness, loyalty. For an instant
Gale seemed to have a vision; but it did not last, and he
failed to hold some beautiful illusive thing.

MOUNTAIN SHEEP

"Si!" rolled out the Indian's reply, full of power and depth.

Mercedes drew a long breath, and her hand sought Thorne's.

"He says yes," she whispered. "He answers he'll save us; he'll take us all back—he knows!"

The Indian turned away to his tasks, and the silence that held the little group was finally broken by Ladd.

"Shore I said so. Now all we've got to do is use sense. Friends, I'm the commissary department of this outfit, an' what I say goes. You all won't eat except when I tell you. Mebbe it'll not be so hard to keep our health. Starved beggars don't get sick. But there's the heat comin', an' we can all go loco, you know. To pass the time! Lord, that's our problem. Now if you all only had a hankerin' for checkers. Shore I'll make a board an' make you play. Thorne, you're the luckiest. You've got your girl, an' this can be a honeymoon. Now with a few tools an' little material see what a grand house you can build for your wife. Dick, you're lucky, too. You like to hunt, an' up there you'll find the finest bighorn huntin' in the West. Take Yaqui and the .405. We need the meat, but while you're gettin' it have your sport. The same chance will never come again. I wish we all was able to go. But crippled men can't climb the lava. Shore you'll see some country from the peaks. There's no wilder place on earth, except the poles. An' when you're older, you an' Nell, with a couple of fine boys, think what it'll be to tell them about bein' lost in the lava, an' about huntin' sheep with a Yaqui. Shore I've hit it. You can take yours out in huntin' and thinkin'. Now if I had a girl like Nell I'd never go crazy. That's your game, Dick. Hunt, an' think of Nell, an' how you'll tell those fine boys about it all, an' about the old cowman you knowed, Laddy, who'll by then be long past the divide. Rustle now, son. Get some enthusiasm. For shore you'll need it for yourself an' us."

DESERT GOLD

Gale climbed the lava slope, away round to the right of the arroyo, along an old trail that Yaqui said the Papagos had made before his own people hunted there. Part way it led through spiked, crested, upheaved lava that would have been almost impassable even without its silver coating of *choya* cactus. There were benches and ledges and ridges bare and glistening in the sun. From the crests of these Yaqui's searching falcon gaze roved near and far for signs of sheep, and Gale used his glass on the reaches of lava that slanted steeply upward to the corrugated peaks, and down over endless heave and roll and red-waved slopes. The heat smoked up from the lava, and this, with the red color and shiny *choyas*, gave the impression of a world of smoldering fire.

Farther along the slope Yaqui halted and crawled behind projections to a point commanding a view over an extraordinary section of country. The peaks were off to the left. In the foreground were gullies, ridges, cañons, arroyos, all glistening with *choyas* and some other and more numerous white bushes, and here and there towered a green cactus. This region was only a splintered and more devastated part of the volcanic slope, but it was miles in extent. Yaqui peeped over the top of a blunt block of lava and searched the sharp-billowed wilderness. Suddenly he grasped Gale and pointed across a deep wide gully.

With the aid of his glass Gale saw five sheep. They were much larger than he had expected, dull brown in color, and two of them were rams with great curved horns. They were looking in his direction. Remembering what he had heard about the wonderful eyesight of these mountain animals, Gale could only conclude that they had seen the hunters.

Then Yaqui's movements attracted and interested him. The Indian had brought with him a red scarf and a mesquite branch. He tied the scarf on the stick, and propped this up in a crack of the lava. The scarf waved in the wind. That done, the Indian bade Gale watch.

Once again he leveled the glass at the sheep. All five now were motionless, standing like statues, heads pointed across the gully. They were more than a mile distant. When Gale looked without his glass they merged into the roughness of the lava. He was intensely interested. Did the sheep see the red scarf? It seemed incredible, but nothing else could account for that statuesque alertness. The sheep held this rigid position for perhaps fifteen minutes. Then the leading ram started to approach. The others followed. He took a few steps, then halted. Always he held his head up, nose pointed.

"By George, they're coming!" exclaimed Gale. "They see that flag. They're hunting us. They're curious. If this doesn't beat me!"

Evidently the Indian understood, for he grunted.

Gale found difficulty in curbing his impatience. The approach of the sheep was slow. The advances of the leader and the intervals of watching had a singular regularity. He worked like a machine. Gale followed him down the opposite wall, around holes, across gullies, over ridges. Then Gale shifted the glass back to find the others. They were coming also, with exactly the same pace and pause of their leader. What steppers they were! How sure-footed! What leaps they made! It was thrilling to watch them. Gale forgot he had a rifle. The Yaqui pressed a heavy hand down upon his shoulder. He was to keep well hidden and to be quiet. Gale suddenly conceived the idea that the sheep might come clear across to investigate the puzzling red thing fluttering in the breeze. Strange, indeed, would that be for the wildest creatures in the world.

The big ram led on with the same regular persistence, and in half an hour's time he was in the bottom of the great gulf, and soon he was facing up the slope. Gale knew then that the alluring scarf had fascinated him.

It was no longer necessary now for Gale to use his glass. There was a short period when an intervening crest of lava hid the sheep from yiew. After that the two rams and their smaller followers were plainly in sight for perhaps a quarter of an hour. Then they disappeared behind another ridge. Gale kept watching, sure they would come out farther on. A tense period of waiting passed, then a sudden electrifying pressure of Yaqui's hand made Gale tremble with excitement.

Very cautiously he shifted his position. There, not fifty feet distant upon a high mound of lava, stood the leader of the sheep. His size astounded Gale. He seemed all horns. But only for a moment did the impression of horns overbalancing body remain with Gale. The sheep was graceful, sinewy, slender, powerfully built, and in poise magnificent. As Gale watched, spellbound, the second ram leaped lightly upon the mound, and presently the three others did likewise.

Then, indeed, Gale feasted his eyes with a spectacle for a hunter. It came to him suddenly that there had been something he expected to see in this Rocky Mountain bighorn, and it was lacking. They were beautiful, as wonderful as even Ladd's encomiums had led him to suppose. He thought perhaps it was the contrast these soft, sleek, short-furred, graceful animals afforded to what he imagined the barren, terrible lava mountains might develop.

The splendid leader stepped closer, his round, protruding amber eyes, which Gale could now plainly see, intent upon that fatal red flag. Like automatons the other four crowded into his tracks. A few little slow steps, then the leader halted.

At this instant Gale's absorbed attention was directed by Yaqui to the rifle, and so to the purpose of the climb. A little cold shock affronted Gale's vivid pleasure. With it dawned a realization of what he had imagined was lacking in these animals. They did not look wild! The so-called wildest of wild creatures appeared tamer than sheep he had followed on a farm. It would be little less than murder to kill them. Gale regretted the need of slaughter. Nevertheless, he could not resist the desire to show himself and see how tame they really were.

He reached for the .405, and as he threw a shell into the chamber the slight metallic click made the sheep jump. Then Gale rose quickly to his feet.

The noble ram and his band simply stared at Gale. They had never seen a man. They showed not the slightest indication of instinctive fear. Curiosity, surprise, even friendliness, seemed to mark their attitude of attention. Gale imagined that they were going to step still closer. He did not choose to wait to see if this were true. Certainly it already took a grim resolution to raise the heavy .405.

His shot killed the big leader. The others bounded away with remarkable nimbleness. Gale used up the remaining four shells to drop the second ram, and by the time he had reloaded the others were out of range.

The Yaqui's method of hunting was sure and deadly and saving in energy, but Gale never would try it again. He chose to stalk the game. This entailed a great expenditure of strength, the eyes and the lungs of a mountaineer, and, as Gale put it to Ladd, the need of seven-league boots. After being hunted a few times and shot at, the sheep became exceedingly difficult to approach. Gale learned to know that their fame as the keenest-eyed of all animals was well founded. If he worked directly toward a flock, crawling over the sharp lava, always a sentinel ram espied him before he got within range. The only method of attack that he found successful was to locate sheep with his glass, work round to windward of them, and then, getting behind a ridge or buttress, crawl like a lizard to a vantage point. He failed often. The stalk called forth all that was in him of endurance, cunning, speed. As the days grew hotter he hunted in the early morning hours and a while before the sun went down. More than one night he lay out on the lava, with the great stars close overhead and the immense void all beneath him. This pursuit he learned to love. Upon those scarred and blasted slopes the wild spirit that was in him had free rein. And like a shadow the faithful Yaqui tried ever to keep at his heels.

One morning the rising sun greeted him as he surmounted the higher cone of the volcano. He saw the vastness of the east aglow with a glazed rosy whiteness, like the changing hue of an ember. At this height there was a sweeping wind, still cool. The western slopes of lava lay dark, and all that world of sand and gulf and mountain barrier beyond was shrouded in the mystic cloud of distance. Gale had assimilated much of the loneliness and the sense of ownership and the love of lofty heights that might well belong to the great condor of the peak. Like this wide-winged bird, he had an unparalleled range of vision. The very corners whence came the winds seemed pierced by Gale's eyes.

Yaqui spied a flock of sheep far under the curved broken rim of the main crater. Then began the stalk. Gale had taught Yaqui something—that speed might win as well as patient cunning. Keeping out of sight, Gale ran over the spike-crusted lava, leaving the Indian far behind. His feet were magnets, attracting supporting holds, and he passed over them too fast to fall. The wind, the keen air of the heights, the red lava, the boundless surrounding blue, all seemed to have something to do with his wildness. Then, hiding, slipping, creeping, crawling, he closed in upon his quarry until the long rifle grew like stone in his grip, and the whipping "spang" ripped the silence, and the strange echo boomed deep in the crater, and rolled around, as if in hollow mockery at the hopelessness of escape.

Gale's exultant yell was given as much to free himself

of some bursting joy of action as it was to call the slower Yaqui. Then he liked the strange echoes. It was a maddening whirl of sound that bored deeper and deeper along the whorled and caverned walls of the crater. It was as if these aged walls resented the violating of their silent sanctity. Gale felt himself a man, a thing alive, something superior to all this savage, dead, upflung world of iron, a master even of all this grandeur and sublimity because he had a soul.

He waited beside his quarry, and breathed deep, and swept the long slopes with searching eyes of habit.

When Yaqui came up they set about the hardest task of all, to pack the best of that heavy sheep down miles of steep, ragged, *choya*-covered lava. But even in this Gale rejoiced. The heat was nothing, the millions of little pits which could hold and twist a foot were nothing; the blade-edged crusts and the deep fissures and the choked cañons and the tangled, dwarfed mesquites, all these were as nothing but obstacles to be cheerfully overcome. Only the *choya* hindered Dick Gale.

When his heavy burden pulled him out of sure-footedness, and he plunged into a *choya,* or when the strange, deceitful, uncanny, almost invisible frosty thorns caught and pierced him, then there was call for all of fortitude and endurance. For this cactus had a malignant power of torture. Its pain was a stinging, blinding, burning, sickening poison in the blood. If thorns pierced his legs he felt the pain all over his body; if his hands rose from a fall full of the barbed joints, he was helpless and quivering till Yaqui tore them out.

But this one peril, dreaded more than dizzy height of precipice or sunblindness on the glistening peak, did not daunt Gale. His teacher was the Yaqui, and always before him was an example that made him despair of a white man's equality. Color, race, blood, breeding— what were these in the wilderness? Verily, Dick Gale had come to learn the use of his hands.

So in a descent of hours he toiled down the lava slope, to stalk into the arroyo like a burdened giant, wringing wet, panting, clear-eyed and dark-faced, his ragged clothes and boots white with *choya* thorns.

The gaunt Ladd rose from his shaded seat, and removed his pipe from smiling lips, and turned to nod at Jim, and then looked back again.

The torrid summer heat came imperceptibly, or it could never have been borne by white men. It changed the lives of the fugitives, making them partly nocturnal in habit. The nights had the balmy coolness of spring, and would have been delightful for sleep, but that would have made the blazing days unendurable.

The sun rose in a vast white flame. With it came the blasting, withering wind from the gulf. A red haze, like that of earlier sunsets, seemed to come sweeping on the wind, and it roared up the arroyo, and went bellowing into the crater, and rushed on in fury to lash the peaks.

During these hot, windy hours the desert-bound party slept in deep recesses in the lava; and if necessity brought them forth they could not remain out long. The sand burned through boots, and a touch of bare hand on lava raised a blister.

A short while before sundown the Yaqui went forth to build a campfire, and soon the others came out, heat-dazed, half blinded, with parching throats to allay and hunger that was never satisfied. A little action and a cooling of the air revived them, and when night set in they were comfortable round the campfire.

As Ladd had said, one of their greatest problems was the passing of time. The nights were interminably long, but they had to be passed in work or play or dream—anything except sleep. That was Ladd's most inflexible command. He gave no reason. But not improbably the ranger thought that the terrific heat of the day spent in slumber lessened a wear and strain, if not a real danger of madness.

MOUNTAIN SHEEP

Accordingly, at first the occupations of this little group were many and various. They worked if they had something to do, or could invent a pretext. They told and re-told stories until all were wearisome. They sang songs. Mercedes taught Spanish. They played every game they knew. They invented others that were so trivial children would scarcely have been interested, and these they played seriously. In a word, with intelligence and passion, with all that was civilized and human, they fought the ever-infringing loneliness, the savage solitude of their environment.

But they had only finite minds. It was not in reason to expect a complete victory against this mighty Nature, this abounding horizon of death and desolation and decay. Gradually they fell back upon fewer and fewer occupations, until the time came when the silence was hard to break.

Gale believed himself the keenest of the party, the one who thought most, and he watched the effect of the desert upon his companions. He imagined that he saw Ladd grow old sitting around the campfire. Certain it was that the ranger's gray hair had turned white. What had been at times hard and cold and grim about him had strangely vanished in sweet temper and a vacant-mindedness that held him longer as the days passed. For hours, it seemed, Ladd would bend over his checkerboard and never make a move. It mattered not now whether or not he had a partner. He was always glad of being spoken to, as if he were called back from some vague region of mind. Jim Lash, the calmest, coolest, most nonchalant, best-humored Westerner Gale had ever met, had by slow degrees lost that cheerful character which would have been of such infinite good to his companions, and always he sat brooding, silently brooding. Jim had no ties, few memories, and the desert was claiming him.

Thorne and Mercedes, however, were living, wonderful proof that spirit, mind, and heart were free—free to soar in scorn of the colossal barrenness and silence and space of that terrible hedging prison of lava. They were young; they loved; they were together; and the oasis was almost a paradise. Gale believed he helped himself by watching them. Imagination had never pictured real happiness to him. Thorne and Mercedes had forgotten the outside world. If they had been existing on the burned-out desolate moon they could hardly have been in a harsher, grimmer, lonelier spot than this red-walled arroyo. But it might have been a statelier Eden than that of the primitive day.

Mercedes grew thinner, until she was a slender shadow of her former self. She became hard, brown as the rangers, lithe and quick as a panther. She seemed to live on water and the air—perhaps, indeed, on love. For of the scant fare, the best of which was continually urged upon her, she partook but little. She reminded Gale of a wild brown creature, free as the wind on the lava slopes. Yet, despite the great change, her beauty remained undiminished. Her eyes, seeming so much larger now in her small face, were great black, starry gulfs. She was the life of that camp. Her smiles, her rapid speech, her low laughter, her quick movements, her playful moods with the rangers, the dark and passionate glance, which rested so often on her lover, the whispers in the dusk as hand in hand they paced the campfire beat—these helped Gale to retain his loosening hold on reality, to resist the lure of a strange beckoning life where a man stood free in the golden open, where emotion was not, nor troub'e, nor sickness, nor anything but the savage's rest and sleep and action and dream.

Although the Yaqui was as his shadow, Gale reached a point when he seemed to wander alone at twilight, in the night, at dawn. Far down the arroyo, in the deepen'ng red twilight, when the heat rolled away on slow-dying wind, Blanco Sol raised his splendid head and whistled for his master. Gale reproached himself for neg'ect of the noble horse. Blanco Sol was always the same. He loved four things—his master, a long drink of cool water, to graze at will, and to run. Time and place, Gale thought, meant little to Sol if he could have those four things. Gale put his arm over the great arched neck and laid his cheek against the long white mane, and then even as he stood there forgot the horse. What was that dull, red-tinged, horizon-wide mantle creeping up the slope? Through it the copper sun glowed, paled, died. Was it only twilight? Was it gloom? If he thought about it he had a feeling that it was the herald of night, and the night must be a vigil, and that made him tremble.

At night he had formed a habit of climbing up the lava slope as far as the smooth trail extended, and there on a promontory he paced to and fro, and watched the stars, and sat stone-still for hours looking down at the vast void with its moving, changing shadows. From that promontory he gazed up at a velvet-blue sky, deep and dark, bright with millions of cold, distant, blinking stars, and he grasped a little of the meaning of infinitude. He gazed down into the shadows, which, black as they were and impenetrable, yet gave a conception of immeasurable space.

Then the silence! He was dumb, he was awed, he bowed his head, he trembled, he marveled at the desert silence. It was the one thing always present. Even when the wind roared there seemed to be silence. But at night, in this lava world of ashes and canker, he waited for this terrible strangeness of nature to come to him with the secret. He seemed at once a little child and a strong man, and something very old. What tortured him was the incomprehensibility that the vaster the space the greater the silence! At one moment Gale felt there was only death here, and that was the secret; at another he heard the slow beat of a mighty heart.

He came at length to realize that the desert was a teacher. He did not realize all that he had learned, but he was a different man. And when he decided upon that, he was not thinking of the slow, sure call to the primal instincts of man; he was thinking that the desert, as much as he had experienced and no more, would absolutely overturn the whole scale of a man's values, break old habits, form new ones, remake him. More of desert experience, Gale believed, would be too much for intellect. The desert did not breed civilized man, and that made Gale ponder over a strange thought: after all, was the civilized man inferior to the savage?

Yaqui was the answer to that. When Gale acknowledged this he always remembered his present strange manner of thought. The past, the old order of mind, seemed as remote as this desert world was from the haunts of civilized men. A man must know a savage as Gale knew Yaqui before he could speak authoritatively, and then something stilled his tongue. In the first stage of Gale's observation of Yaqui he had marked tenaciousness of life, stoicism, endurance, strength. These were the attributes of the desert. But what of that second stage wherein the Indian had loomed up a colossal figure of strange honor, loyalty, love? Gale doubted his convictions and scorned himself for doubting.

There in the gloom sat the silent, impassive, inscrutable Yaqui. His dark face, his dark eyes were plain in the light of the stars. Always he was near Gale, unobtrusive, shadowy, but there. Why? Gale absolutely could not doubt that the Indian had heart as well as mind. Yaqui had from the very first stood between Gale and accident, toil, peril. It was his own choosing. Gale could not change him or thwart him. He understood the Indian's idea of obligation and sacred duty. But there was more, and that baffled Gale. In the night hours, alone on the slope, Gale felt in Yaqui, as he felt the mighty throb of that desert pulse, a something that drew him irresistibly to the Indian. Sometimes he looked around to find the Indian, to dispel these strange, pressing thoughts of unreality, and it was never in vain.

MOUNTAIN SHEEP

Thus the nights passed, endlessly long, with Gale fighting for his old order of thought, fighting the fascination of that infinite sky, and the gloomy insulating whirl of the wide shadows, fighting for belief, hope, prayer, fighting against that terrible ever-recurring idea of being lost, lost, lost in the desert, fighting harder than any other thing the insidious, penetrating, tranquil, unfeeling self that was coming between him and his memory.

He was losing the battle, losing his hold on tangible things, losing his power to stand up under this ponderous, merciless weight of desert space and silence.

He acknowledged it in a kind of despair, and the shadows of the night seemed whirling fiends. Lost! Lost! Lost! What are you waiting for? *Rain?* . . . Lost! Lost! Lost in the desert! So the shadows seemed to scream in voiceless mockery.

At the moment he was alone on the promontory. The night was far spent. A ghastly moon haunted the black volcanic spurs. The winds blew silently. Was he alone? No, he did not seem to be alone. The Yaqui was there. Suddenly a strange, cold sensation crept over Gale. It was new. He felt a presence. Turning, he expected to see the Indian, but instead, a slight shadow, pale, almost white, stood there, not close nor yet distant. It seemed to brighten. Then he saw a woman who resembled a girl he had seemed to know long ago. She was white-faced, golden-haired, and her lips were sweet, and her eyes were turning black. *Nell!* He had forgotten her. Over him flooded a torrent of memory. There was tragic woe in this sweet face. Nell was holding out her arms— she was crying aloud to him across the sand and the cactus and the lava. She was in trouble, and he had been forgetting.

That night he climbed the lava to the topmost cone, and never slipped on a ragged crust nor touched a *choya* thorn. A voice had called to him. He saw Nell's eyes in the stars, in the velvet blue of sky, in the blackness of the engulfing shadows. She was with him, a slender shape, a spirit, keeping step with him, and memory was strong, sweet, beating, beautiful. Far down in the west, faintly golden with light of the sinking moon, he saw a cloud that resembled her face. A cloud on the desert horizon! He gazed and gazed. Was that a spirit face like the one by his side? No—he did not dream.

In the hot, sultry morning Yaqui appeared at camp, after long hours of absence, and he pointed with a long, dark arm toward the west. A bank of clouds was rising above the mountain barrier.

"Rain!" he cried; and his sonorous voice rolled down the arroyo.

Those who heard him were as shipwrecked mariners at sight of a distant sail.

Dick Gale, silent, grateful to the depths of his soul, stood with arm over Blanco Sol and watched the transforming west, where clouds of wondrous size and hue piled over one another, rushing, darkening, spreading, sweeping upward toward that white and glowing sun.

When they reached the zenith and swept round to blot out the blazing orb, the earth took on a dark, lowering aspect. The red of sand and lava changed to steely gray. Vast shadows, like ripples on water, sheeted in from the gulf with a low, strange moan. Yet the silence was like death. The desert was awaiting a strange and hated visitation—storm! If all the endless torrid days, the endless mystic nights had seemed unreal to Gale, what, then, seemed this stupendous spectacle?

"Oh! I felt a drop of rain on my face!" cried Mercedes; and, whispering the name of a saint, she kissed her husband.

The white-haired Ladd, gaunt, old, bent, looked up at the maelstrom of clouds, and he said, softly, "Shore we'll get in the hosses, an' pack light, an' hit the trail, an' make night marches!"

Then up out of the gulf of the west swept a be'lowing wind and a black pall and terrible flashes of lightning and thunder like the end of the world—fury, blackness, chaos, the desert storm.

XVII

THE WHISTLE OF A HORSE

AT the ranch-house at Forlorn River Belding stood
alone in his darkened room. It was quiet there and
quiet outside; the sickening midsummer heat, like a hot
heavy blanket, lay upon the house.

He took up the gun belt from his table and with slow
hands buckled it around his waist. He seemed to feel
something familiar and comfortable and inspiring in the
weight of the big gun against his hip. He faced the door
as if to go out, but hesitated, and then began a slow,
plodding walk up and down the length of the room.
Presently he halted at the table, and with reluctant hands
he unbuckled the gun belt and laid it down.

The action did not have an air of finality, and Belding
knew it. He had seen border life in Texas in the early
days; he had been a sheriff when the law in the West de-
pended on a quickness of wrist; he had seen many a man
lay down his gun for good and all. His own action was
not final. Of late he had done the same thing many times,
and this last time it seemed a little harder to do, a little
more indicative of vacillation. There were reasons why
Belding's gun held for him a gloomy fascination.

The Chases, those grasping and conscienceless agents
of a new force in the development of the West, were bent
upon Belding's ruin, and, so far as his fortunes at Forlorn
River were concerned, had almost accomplished it. One
by one he lost points for which he contended with them.
He carried into the Tucson courts the matter of the staked
claims, and mining claims, and water claims, and he lost

all. Following that he lost his government position as inspector of immigration; and this fact, because of what he considered its injustice, had been a hard blow. He had been made to suffer a humiliation equally as great. It came about that he actually had to pay the Chases for water to irrigate his alfalfa fields. The never-failing spring upon his land answered for the needs of household and horses, but no more.

These matters were unfortunate for Belding, but not by any means wholly accountable for his worry and unhappiness and brooding hate. He believed Dick Gale and the rest of the party taken into the desert by the Yaqui had been killed or lost. Two months before a string of Mexican horses, riderless, saddled, starved for grass and wild for water, had come in to Forlorn River. They were a part of the horses belonging to Rojas and his band. Their arrival complicated the mystery and strengthened convictions of the loss of both pursuers and pursued. Belding was wont to say that he had worried himself gray over the fate of his rangers.

Belding's unhappiness could hardly be laid to material loss. He had been rich and was now poor, but change of fortune such as that could not have made him unhappy. Something more somber and mysterious and sad than the loss of Dick Gale and their friends had come into the lives of his wife and Nell. He dated the time of this change back to a certain day when Mrs. Belding recognized in the elder Chase an old schoolmate and a rejected suitor. It took time for slow-thinking Belding to discover anything wrong in his household, especially as the fact of the Gales lingering there made Mrs. Belding and Nell, for the most part, hide their real and deeper feelings. Gradually, however, Belding had forced on him the fact of some secret cause for grief other than Gale's loss. He was sure of it when his wife signified her desire to make a visit to her old home back in Peoria. She did not give many reasons, but she did show him a letter that had found its way from old friends. This letter contained news that may or may not have been authentic; but it was enough, Belding thought, to interest his wife. An old prospector had returned to Peoria, and he had told relatives of meeting Robert Burton at the Sonoyta Oasis fifteen years before, and that Burton had gone into the desert never to return. To Belding this was no surprise, for he had heard that before his marriage. There appeared to have been no doubts as to the death of his wife's first husband. The singular thing was that both Nell's father and grandfather had been lost somewhere in the Sonora Desert.

Belding did not oppose his wife's desire to visit her old home. He thought it would be a wholesome trip for her, and did all in his power to persuade Nell to accompany her. But Nell would not go.

It was after Mrs. Belding's departure that Belding discovered in Nell a condition of mind that amazed and distressed him. She had suddenly become strangely wretched, so that she could not conceal it from even the Gales, who, of all people, Belding imagined, were the ones to make Nell proud. She would tell him nothing. But after a while, when he had thought it out, he dated this further and more deplorable change in Nell back to a day on which he had met Nell with Radford Chase. This indefatigable wooer had not in the least abandoned his suit. Something about the fellow made Belding grind his teeth. But Nell grew not only solicitously, but now strangely, entreatingly earnest in her importunities to Belding not to insult or lay a hand on Chase. This had bound Belding so far; it had made him think and watch. He had never been a man to interfere with his women folk. They could do as they liked, and usually that pleased him. But a slow surprise gathered and grew upon him when he saw that Nell, apparently, was accepting young Chase's attentions. At least, she no longer hid from him. Belding could not account for this, because he was sure Nell cordially despised the fellow. And toward the end he divined, if he did not actually know, that these Chases possessed some strange power over Nell, and were using it. That stirred a hate in Belding—a hate he had felt at the first and had manfully striven against which now gave him over to dark brooding thoughts.

Midsummer passed, and the storms came late. But when they arrived they made up for tardiness. Belding did not remember so terrible a storm of wind and rain as that which broke the summer's drought.

In a few days, it seemed, Altar Valley was a bright and green expanse, where dust clouds did not rise. Forlorn River ran, a slow, heavy, turgid torrent. Belding never saw the river in flood that it did not give him joy; yet now, desert man as he was, he suffered a regret when he thought of the great Chase reservoir full and overflowing. The dull thunder of the spillway was not pleasant. It was the first time in his life that the sound of falling water jarred upon him.

Belding noticed workmen once more engaged in the fields bounding his land. The Chases had extended a main irrigation ditch down to Belding's farm, skipped the width of his ground, then had gone on down through Altar Valley. They had exerted every influence to obtain right to connect these ditches by digging through his land, but Belding had remained obdurate. He refused to have any dealings with them. It was therefore with some curiosity and suspicion that he saw a gang of Mexicans once more at work upon these ditches.

At daylight next morning a tremendous blast almost threw Belding out of his bed. It cracked the adobe walls of his house and broke windows and sent pans and crockery to the floor with a crash. Belding's idea was that the store of dynamite kept by the Chases for blasting had blown up. Hurriedly getting into his clothes, he went to Nell's room to reassure her; and, telling her to have a thought for their guests, he went out to see what had happened.

DESERT GOLD

The villagers were pretty badly frightened. Many of the poorly constructed adobe huts had crumbled almost into dust. A great yellow cloud, like smoke, hung over the river. This appeared to be at the upper end of Belding's plot, and close to the river. When he reached his fence the smoke and dust were so thick he could scarcely breathe, and for a little while he was unable to see what had happened. Presently he made out a huge hole in the sand just about where the irrigation ditch had stopped near his line. For some reason or other, not clear to Belding, the Mexicans had set off an extraordinarily heavy blast at that point.

Belding pondered. He did not now for a moment consider an accidental discharge of dynamite. But why had this blast been set off? The loose sandy soil had yielded readily to shovel; there were no rocks; as far as construction of a ditch was concerned such a blast would have done more harm than good.

Slowly, with reluctant feet, Belding walked toward a green hollow, where in a cluster of willows lay the never-failing spring that his horses loved so well, and, indeed, which he loved no less. He was actually afraid to part the drooping willows to enter the little cool, shady path that led to the spring. Then, suddenly seized by suspense, he ran the rest of the way.

He was just in time to see the last of the water. It seemed to sink as in quicksand. The shape of the hole had changed. The tremendous force of the blast had obstructed or diverted the underground stream of water.

Belding's never-failing spring had been ruined. What had made this little plot of ground green and sweet and fragrant was now no more. Belding's first feeling was for the pity of it. The pale Ajo lilies would bloom no more under those willows. The willows themselves would soon wither and die. He thought how many times in the middle of hot summer nights he had come down to the spring to drink. Never again!

THE WHISTLE OF A HORSE

Suddenly he thought of Blanco Diablo. How the great white thoroughbred had loved this spring! Belding straightened up and looked with tear-blurred eyes out over the waste of desert to the west. Never a day passed that he had not thought of the splendid horse; but this moment, with its significant memory, was doubly keen, and there came a dull pang in his breast.

"Diablo will never drink here again!" muttered Belding.

The loss of Blanco Diablo, though admitted and mourned by Belding, had never seemed quite real until this moment.

The pall of dust drifting over him, the din of the falling water up at the dam, diverted Belding's mind to the Chases. All at once he was in the harsh grip of a cold certainty. The blast had been set off intentionally to ruin his spring. What a hellish trick! No Westerner, no Indian or Mexican, no desert man could have been guilty of such a crime. To ruin a beautiful, clear, cool, never-failing stream of water in the desert!

It was then that Belding's worry and indecision and brooding were as if they had never existed. As he strode swiftly back to the house, his head, which had long been bent thoughtfully and sadly, was held erect. He went directly to his room, and with an air that was now final he buckled on his gun belt. He looked the gun over and tried the action. He squared himself and walked a little more erect. Some long-lost individuality had returned to Belding.

"Let's see," he was saying. "I can get Carter to send the horses I've got left back to Waco to my brother. I'll make Nell take what money there is and go hunt up her mother. The Gales are ready to go—to-day, if I say the word. Nell can travel with them part way East. That's your game, Tom Belding, don't mistake me."

As he went out he encountered Mr. Gale coming up the walk. The long sojourn at Forlorn River, despite the fact that it had been laden with a suspense which was gradually changing to a sad certainty, had been of great benefit to Dick's father. The dry air, the heat, and the quiet had made him, if not entirely a well man, certainly stronger than he had been in many years.

"Belding, what was that terrible roar?" asked Mr. Gale. "We were badly frightened until Miss Nell came to us. We feared it was an earthquake."

"Well, I'll tell you, Mr. Gale, we've had some quakes here, but none of them could hold a candle to this jar we just had."

Then Belding explained what had caused the explosion, and why it had been set off so close to his property.

"It's an outrage, sir, an unspeakable outrage," declared Mr. Gale, hotly. "Such a thing would not be tolerated in the East. Mr. Belding, I'm amazed at your attitude in the face of all this trickery."

"You see—there was mother and Nell," began Belding, as if apologizing. He dropped his head a little and made marks in the sand with the toe of his boot. "Mr. Gale, I've been sort of half hitched, as Laddy used to say. I'm planning to have a little more elbow room round this ranch. I'm going to send Nell East to her mother. Then I'll— See here, Mr. Gale, would you mind having Nell with you part way when you go home?"

"We'd all be delighted to have her go all the way and make us a visit," replied Mr. Gale.

"That's fine. And you'll be going soon? Don't take that as if I wanted to—" Belding paused, for the truth was that he did want to hurry them off.

"We would have been gone before this, but for you," said Mr. Gale. "Long ago we gave up hope of—of Richard ever returning. And I believe, now we're sure he was lost, that we'd do well to go home at once. You wished us to remain till the heat was broken—till the rains came to make traveling easier for us. Now I see no need for further delay. My stay here has greatly benefited my health. I shall never forget your hospitality. This

Western trip would have made me a new man if—only—Richard—"

"Sure. I understand," said Belding, gruffly. "Let's go in and tell the women to pack up."

Nell was busy with the servants preparing breakfast. Belding took her into the sitting-room while Mr. Gale called his wife and daughter.

"My girl, I've some news for you," began Belding. "Mr. Gale is leaving to-day with his family. I'm going to send you with them—part way, anyhow. You're invited to visit them. I think that'd be great for you—help you to forget. But the main thing is—you're going East to join mother."

Nell gazed at him, white-faced, without uttering a word.

"You see, Nell, I'm about done in Forlorn River," went on Belding. "That blast this morning sank my spring. There's no water now. It was the last straw. So we'll shake the dust of Forlorn River. I'll come on a little later—that's all."

"Dad, you're packing your gun!" exclaimed Nell, suddenly pointing with a trembling finger. She ran to him, and for the first time in his life Belding put her away from him. His movements had lost the old slow gentleness.

"Why, so I am," replied Belding, coolly, as his hand moved down to the sheath swinging at his hip. "Nell, I'm that absent-minded these days!"

"Dad!" she cried.

"That 'll do from you," he replied, in a voice he had never used to her. "Get breakfast now, then pack to leave Forlorn River."

"Leave Forlorn River!" whispered Nell, with a thin white hand stealing up to her breast. How changed the girl was! Belding reproached himself for his hardness, but did not speak his thought aloud. Nell was fading here, just as Mercedes had faded before the coming of Thorne.

Nell turned away to the west window and looked out

across the desert toward the dim blue peaks in the distance. Belding watched her; likewise the Gales; and no one spoke. There ensued a long silence. Belding felt a lump rise in his throat. Nell laid her arm against the window frame, but gradually it dropped, and she was leaning with her face against the wood. A low sob broke from her. Elsie Gale went to her, embraced her, took the drooping head on her shoulder.

"We've come to be such friends," she said. "I believe it 'll be good for you to visit me in the city. Here—all day you look out across that awful lonely desert.... Come, Nell."

Heavy steps sounded outside on the flagstones, then the door rattled under a strong knock. Belding opened it. The Chases, father and son, stood beyond the threshold.

"Good morning, Belding," said the elder Chase. "We were routed out early by that big blast and came up to see what was wrong. All a blunder. The Greaser foreman was drunk yesterday, and his ignorant men made a mistake. Sorry if the blast bothered you."

"Chase, I reckon that's the first of your blasts I was ever glad to hear," replied Belding, in a way that made Chase look blank.

"So? Well, I'm glad you're glad," he went on, evidently puzzled. "I was a little worried—you've always been so touchy—we never could get together. I hurried over, fearing maybe you might think the blast—you see, Belding—"

"I see this, Mr. Ben Chase," interrupted Belding, in curt and ringing voice. "The blast *was* a mistake, the biggest you ever made in your life."

"What do you mean?" demanded Chase.

"You'll have to excuse me for a while, unless you're dead set on having it out right now. Mr. Gale and his family are leaving, and my daughter is going with them. I'd rather you'd wait a little."

"Nell going away!" exclaimed Radford Chase. He

reminded Belding of an overgrown boy in disappointment.

"Yes. But—*Miss Burton* to you, young man—"

"Mr. Belding, I certainly would prefer a conference with you right now," interposed the elder Chase, cutting short Belding's strange speech. "There are other matters—important matters to discuss. They've got to be settled. May we step in, sir?"

"No, you may not," replied Belding, bluntly. "I'm sure particular who I invite into my house. But I'll go with you."

Belding stepped out and closed the door. "Come away from the house so the women won't hear the—the talk."

The elder Chase was purple with rage, yet seemed to be controlling it. The younger man looked black, sullen, impatient. He appeared not to have a thought of Belding. He was absolutely blind to the situation, as considered from Belding's point of view. Ben Chase found his voice about the time Belding halted under the trees out of earshot from the house.

"Sir, you've insulted me—my son. How dare you? I want you to understand that you're—"

"Chop that kind of talk with me, you——— ——— ——— ———!" interrupted Belding. He had always been profane, and now he certainly did not choose his language. Chase turned livid, gasped, and seemed about to give way to fury. But something about Belding evidently exerted a powerful quieting influence. "If you talk sense I'll listen," went on Belding.

Belding was frankly curious. He did not think any argument or inducement offered by Chase could change his mind on past dealings or his purpose of the present. But he believed by listening he might get some light on what had long puzzled him. The masterly effort Chase put forth to conquer his aroused passions gave Belding another idea of the character of this promoter.

"I want to make a last effort to propitiate you," began

Chase, in his quick, smooth voice. That was a singular change to Belding—the dropping instantly into an easy flow of speech. "You've had losses here, and naturally you're sore. I don't blame you. But you can't see this thing from my side of the fence. Business is business. In business the best man wins. The law upheld those transactions of mine the honesty of which you questioned. As to mining and water claims, you lost on this technical point—that you had nothing to prove you had held them for five years. Five years is the time necessary in law. A dozen men might claim the source of Forlorn River, but if they had no house or papers to prove their squatters' rights any man could go in and fight them for the water. ... Now I want to run that main ditch along the river, through your farm. Can't we make a deal? I'm ready to be liberal—to meet you more than halfway. I'll give you an interest in the company. I think I've influence enough up at the Capitol to have you reinstated as inspector. A little reasonableness on your part will put you right again in Forlorn River, with a chance of growing rich. There's a big future here. ... My interest, Belding, has become personal. Radford is in love with your stepdaughter. He wants to marry her. I'll admit now if I had foreseen this situation I wouldn't have pushed you so hard. But we can square the thing. Now let's get together not only in business, but in a family way. If my son's happiness depends upon having this girl, you may rest assured I'll do all I can to get her for him. I'll absolutely make good all your losses. Now what do you say?"

"No," replied Belding. "Your money can't buy a right of way across my ranch. And Nell doesn't want your son. That settles that."

"But you could persuade her."

"I won't, that's all."

"May I ask why?" Chase's voice was losing its suave quality, but it was even swifter than before.

THE WHISTLE OF A HORSE

"Sure. I don't mind your asking," replied Belding, in slow deliberation. "I wouldn't do such a low-down trick. Besides, if I would, I'd want it to be a man I was persuading for. I know Greasers—I know a Yaqui I'd rather give Nell to than your son."

Radford Chase began to roar in inarticulate rage. Belding paid no attention to him; indeed, he never glanced at the young man. The elder Chase checked a violent start. He plucked at the collar of his gray flannel shirt, opened it at the neck.

"My son's offer of marriage is an honor—more an honor, sir, than you perhaps are aware of."

Belding made no reply. His steady gaze did not turn from the long lane that led down to the river. He waited coldly, sure of himself.

"Mrs. Belding's daughter has no right to the name of Burton," snapped Chase. "Did you know that?"

"I did not," replied Belding, quietly.

"Well, you know it now," added Chase, bitingly.

"Sure you can prove what you say?" queried Belding, in the same cool, unemotional tone. It struck him strangely at the moment what little knowledge this man had of the West and of Western character.

"Prove it? Why, yes, I think so, enough to make the truth plain to any reasonable man. I come from Peoria—was born and raised there. I went to school with Nell Warren. That was your wife's maiden name. She was a beautiful, gay girl. All the fellows were in love with her. I knew Bob Burton well. He was a splendid fellow, but wild. Nobody ever knew for sure, but we all supposed he was engaged to marry Nell. He left Peoria, however, and soon after that the truth about Nell came out. She ran away. It was at least a couple of months before Burton showed up in Peoria. He did not stay long. Then for years nothing was heard of either of them. When word did come Nell was in Oklahoma, Burton was in Denver. There's a chance, of course, that

Burton followed Nell and married her. That would account for Nell Warren taking the name of Burton. But it isn't likely. None of us ever heard of such a thing and wouldn't have believed it if we had. The affair seemed destined to end unfortunately. But Belding, while I'm at it, I want to say that Nell Warren was one of the sweetest, finest, truest girls in the world. If she drifted to the Southwest and kept her past a secret that was only natural. Certainly it should not be held against her. Why, she was only a child—a girl—seventeen—eighteen years old.... In a moment of amazement—when I recognized your wife as an old schoolmate—I blurted the thing out to Radford. You see now how little it matters to me when I ask your stepdaughter's hand in marriage for my son."

Belding stood listening. The genuine emotion in Chase's voice was as strong as the ring of truth. Belding knew truth when he heard it. The revelation did not surprise him. Belding did not soften, for he divined that Chase's emotion was due to the probing of an old wound, the recalling of a past both happy and painful. Still, human nature was so strange that perhaps kindness and sympathy might yet have a place in this Chase's heart. Belding did not believe so, but he was willing to give Chase the benefit of the doubt.

"So you told my wife you'd respect her secret—keep her dishonor from husband and daughter?" demanded Belding, his dark gaze sweeping back from the lane.

"What! I—I—" stammered Chase.

"You made your son swear to be a man and die before he'd hint the thing to Nell?" went on Belding, and his voice rang louder.

Ben Chase had no answer. The red left his face. His son slunk back against the fence.

"I say you never held this secret over the heads of my wife and her daughter?" thundered Belding.

He had his answer in the gray faces, in the lips that fear

made mute. Like a flash Belding saw the whole truth of Mrs. Belding's agony, the reason for her departure; he saw what had been driving Nell; and it seemed that all the dogs of hell were loosed within his heart. He struck out blindly, instinctively in his pain, and the blow sent Ben Chase staggering into the fence corner. Then he stretched forth a long arm and whirled Radford Chase back beside his father.

"I see it all now," went on Belding, hoarsely. "You found the woman's weakness—her love for the girl. You found the girl's weakness—her pride and fear of shame. So you drove the one and hounded the other. God, what a base thing to do! To *teli* the girl was bad enough, but to *threaten* her with betrayal; there's no name for that!"

Belding's voice thickened, and he paused, breathing heavily. He stepped back a few paces; and this, an ominous action for an armed man of his kind, instead of adding to the fear of the Chases, seemed to relieve them. If there had been any pity in Belding's heart he would have felt it then.

"And now, gentlemen," continued Belding, speaking low and with difficulty, "seeing I've turned down your proposition, I suppose you think you've no more call to keep your mouths shut?"

The elder Chase appeared fascinated by something he either saw or felt in Belding, and his gray face grew grayer. He put up a shaking hand. Then Radford Chase, livid and snarling, burst out: "I'll talk till I'm black in the face. You can't stop me!"

"You'll go black in the face, but it won't be from talking," hissed Belding.

His big arm swept down, and when he threw it up the gun glittered in his hand. Simultaneously with the latter action pealed out a shrill, penetrating whistle.

The whistle of a horse! It froze Belding's arm aloft. For an instant he could not move even his eyes. The familiarity of that whistle was terrible in its power to rob him of strength. Then he heard the rapid, heavy pound of hoofs, and again the piercing whistle.

"*Blanco Diablo!*" he cried, huskily.

He turned to see a huge white horse come thundering into the yard. A wild, gaunt, terrible horse; indeed, the loved Blanco Diablo. A bronzed, long-haired Indian bestrode him. More white horses galloped into the yard, pounded to a halt, whistling home. Belding saw a slim shadow of a girl who seemed all great black eyes.

Under the trees flashed Blanco Sol, as dazzling white, as beautiful as if he had never been lost in the desert. He slid to a halt, then plunged and stamped. His rider leaped, throwing the bridle. Belding saw a powerful, spare, ragged man, with dark, gaunt face and eyes of flame.

Then Nell came running from the house, her golden hair flying, her hands outstretched, her face wonderful.

"Dick! Dick! Oh-h-h, Dick!" she cried. Her voice seemed to quiver in Belding's heart.

Belding's eyes began to blur. He was not sure he saw clearly. Whose face was this now close before him—a long thin, shrunken face, haggard, tragic in its semblance of torture, almost of death? But the eyes were keen and kind. Belding thought wildly that they proved he was not dreaming.

"I shore am glad to see you all," said a well-remembered voice in a slow, cool drawl.

XVIII

REALITY AGAINST DREAMS

LADD, Lash, Thorne, Mercedes, they were all held tight in Belding's arms. Then he ran to Blanco Diablo. For once the great horse was gentle, quiet, glad. He remembered this kindest of masters and reached for him with warm, wet muzzle.

Dick Gale was standing bowed over Nell's slight form, almost hidden in his arms. Belding hugged them both. He was like a boy. He saw Ben Chase and his son slip away under the trees, but the circumstance meant nothing to him then.

"Dick! Dick!" he roared. "Is it you? ... Say, who do you think's here—here, in Forlorn River?"

Gale gripped Belding with a hand as rough and hard as a file and as strong as a vise. But he did not speak a word. Belding thought Gale's eyes would haunt him forever.

It was then three more persons came upon the scene—Elsie Gale, running swiftly, her father assisting Mrs. Gale, who appeared about to faint.

"Belding! Who on earth's that?" cried Dick, hoarsely.

"*Quien sabe,* my son," replied Belding; and now his voice seemed a little shaky. "Nell, come here. Give him a chance."

Belding slipped his arm round Nell, and whispered in her ear. "This 'll be great!"

Elsie Gale's face was white and agitated, a face expressing extreme joy.

"Oh, brother! Mama saw you—Papa saw you, and

never knew you! But I knew you when you jumped quick—that way—off your horse. And now I don't know you. You wild man! You giant! You splendid barbarian!... Mama, Papa, hurry! It *is* Dick! Look at him. Just look at him! Oh-h, thank God!"

Belding turned away and drew Nell with him. In another second she and Mercedes were clasped in each other's arms. Then followed a time of joyful greetings all round.

The Yaqui stood leaning against a tree watching the welcoming home of the lost. No one seemed to think of him, until Belding, ever mindful of the needs of horses, put a hand on Blanco Diablo and called to Yaqui to bring the others. They led the string of whites down to the barn, freed them of wet and dusty saddles and packs, and turned them loose in the alfalfa, now breast-high. Diablo found his old spirit; Blanco Sol tossed his head and whistled his satisfaction; White Woman pranced to and fro; and presently they all settled down to quiet grazing. How good it was for Belding to see those white shapes against the rich background of green! His eyes glistened. It was a sight he had never expected to see again. He lingered there many moments when he wanted to hurry back to his rangers.

At last he tore himself away from watching Blanco Diablo and returned to the house. It was only to find that he might have spared himself the hurry. Jim and Ladd were lying on the beds that had not held them for so many months. Their slumber seemed as deep and quiet as death. Curiously Belding gazed down upon them. They had removed only boots and chaps. Their clothes were in tatters. Jim appeared little more than skin and bones, a long shape, dark and hard as iron. Ladd's appearance shocked Belding. The ranger looked an old man, blasted, shriveled, starved. Yet his gaunt face, though terrible in its records of tortures, had something fine and noble, even beautiful to Belding, in its strength, its victory.

REALITY AGAINST DREAMS

Thorne and Mercedes had disappeared. The low murmur of voices came from Mrs. Gale's room, and Belding concluded that Dick was still with his family. No doubt he, also, would soon seek rest and sleep. Belding went through the patio and called in at Nell's door. She was there sitting by her window. The flush of happiness had not left her face, but she looked stunned, and a shadow of fear lay dark in her eyes. Belding had intended to talk. He wanted some one to listen to him. The expression in Nell's eyes, however, silenced him. He had forgotten. Nell read his thought in his face, and then she lost all her color and dropped her head. Belding entered, stood beside her with a hand on hers. He tried desperately hard to think of the right thing to say, and realized so long as he tried that he could not speak at all.

"Nell—Dick's back safe and sound," he said, slowly. "That's the main thing. I wish you could have seen his eyes when he held you in his arms out there.... Of course, Dick's coming knocks out your trip East and changes plans generally. We haven't had the happiest time lately. But now it 'll all be different. Dick's as true as a Yaqui. He'll chase that Chase fellow, don't mistake me.... Then mother will be home soon. She'll straighten out this—this mystery. And Nell—however it turns out —I know Dick Gale will feel just the same as I feel. Brace up now, girl."

Belding left the patio and traced thoughtful steps back toward the corrals. He realized the need of his wife. If she had been at home he would not have come so close to killing two men. Nell would never have fallen so low in spirit. Whatever the real truth of the tragedy of his wife's life, it would not make the slightest difference to him. What hurt him was the pain mother and daughter had suffered, were suffering still. Somehow he must put an end to that pain.

He found the Yaqui curled up in a corner of the barn in as deep a sleep as that of the rangers. Looking down at him, Belding felt again the rush of curious thrilling eagerness to learn all that had happened since the dark night when Yaqui had led the white horses away into the desert. Belding curbed his impatience and set to work upon tasks he had long neglected. Presently he was interrupted by Mr. Gale, who came out, beside himself with happiness and excitement. He flung a hundred questions at Belding and never gave him time to answer one, even if that had been possible. Finally, when Mr. Gale lost his breath, Belding got a word in. "See here, Mr. Gale, you know as much as I know. Dick's back. They're all back—a hard lot, starved, burned, torn to pieces, worked out to the limit I never saw in desert travelers, but they're alive—alive and well, man! Just wait. Just gamble I won't sleep or eat till I hear that story. But *they've* got to sleep and eat."

Belding gathered with growing amusement that besides the joy, excitement, anxiety, impatience expressed by Mr. Gale there was something else which Belding took for pride. It pleased him. Looking back, he remembered some of the things Dick had confessed his father thought of him. Belding's sympathy had always been with the boy. But he had learned to like the old man, to find him kind and wise, and to think that perhaps college and business had not brought out the best in Richard Gale. The West had done that, however, as it had for many a wild youngster; and Belding resolved to have a little fun at the expense of Mr. Gale. So he began by making a few remarks that appeared to rob Dick's father of both speech and breath.

"And don't mistake me," concluded Belding, "just keep out of earshot when Laddy tells us the story of that desert trip, unless you're hankering to have your hair turn *pure* white and stand *curled* on end and *freeze* that way."

About the middle of the forenoon on the following day the rangers hobbled out of the kitchen to the porch.

REALITY AGAINST DREAMS

"I'm a sick man, I tell you," Ladd was complaining, "an' I gotta be fed. Soup! Beef tea! That ain't so much as wind to me. I want about a barrel of bread an' butter, an' a whole platter of mashed potatoes with gravy an' green stuff—all kinds of green stuff—an' a whole big apple pie. Give me everythin' an' anythin' to eat but meat. Shore I never, never want to taste meat again, an' sight of a piece of sheep meat would jest about finish me.... Jim, you used to be a human bein' that stood up for Charlie Ladd."

"Laddy, I'm lined up beside you with both guns," replied Jim, plaintively. "Hungry? Say, the smell of breakfast in that kitchen made my mouth water so I near choked to death. I reckon we're gettin' most onhuman treatment."

"But I'm a sick man," protested Ladd, "an' I'm agoin' to fall over in a minute if somebody doesn't feed me. Nell, you *used* to be fond of me."

"Oh, Laddy, I am yet," replied Nell.

"Shore I don't believe it. Any girl with a tender heart just couldn't let a man starve under her eyes.... Look at Dick, there. I'll bet he's had something to eat, mebbe potatoes an' gravy, an' pie an'—"

"Laddy, Dick has had no more than I gave you—indeed, not nearly so much."

"Shore he's had a lot of kisses then, for he hasn't hollered onct about this treatment."

"Perhaps he has," said Nell, with a blush; "and if you think that—they would help you to be reasonable I might—I'll—"

"Well, powerful fond as I am of you, just now kisses'll have to run second to bread an' butter."

"Oh, Laddy, what a gallant speech!" laughed Nell. "I'm sorry, but I've Dad's orders."

"Laddy," interrupted Belding, "you've got to be broke in gradually to eating. Now you know that. You'd be the severest kind of a boss if you had some starved beggars on your hands."

"But I'm sick—I'm dyin'," howled Ladd.

"You were never sick in your life, and if all the bullet holes I see in you couldn't kill you, why, you never will die."

"Can I smoke?" queried Ladd, with sudden animation. "My Gawd, I used to smoke. Shore I've forgot. Nell, if you want to be reinstated in my gallery of angels, just find me a pipe an' tobacco."

"I've hung onto my pipe," said Jim, thoughtfully. "I reckon I had it empty in my mouth for seven years or so, wasn't it, Laddy? A long time! I can see the red lava an' the red haze, an' the red twilight creepin' up. It was hot an' some lonely. Then the wind, and always that awful silence! An' always Yaqui watchin' the west, an' Laddy with his checkers, an' Mercedes burnin' up, wastin' away to nothin' but eyes! It's all there—I'll never get rid—"

"Chop that kind of talk," interrupted Belding, bluntly. "Tell us where Yaqui took you—what happened to Rojas —why you seemed lost for so long."

"I reckon Laddy can tell all that best; but when it comes to Rojas's finish I'll tell what I seen, an' so'll Dick an' Thorne. Laddy missed Rojas's finish. Bar none, that was the—"

"I'm a sick man, but I can talk," put in Ladd, "an' shore I don't want the whole story exaggerated none by Jim."

Ladd filled the pipe Nell brought, puffed ecstatically at it, and settled himself upon the bench for a long talk. Nell glanced appealingly at Dick, who tried to slip away. Mercedes did go, and was followed by Thorne. Mr. Gale brought chairs, and in subdued excitement called his wife and daughter. Belding leaned forward, rendered all the more eager by Dick's reluctance to stay, the memory of the quick tragic change in the expression of Mercedes's beautiful eyes, by the strange gloomy cast stealing over Ladd's face.

REALITY AGAINST DREAMS

The ranger talked for two hours—talked till his voice weakened to a husky whisper. At the conclusion of his story there was an impressive silence. Then Elsie Gale stood up, and with her hand on Dick's shoulder, her eyes bright and warm as sunlight, she showed the rangers what a woman thought of them and of the Yaqui. Nell clung to Dick, weeping silently. Mrs. Gale was overcome, and Mr. Gale, very white and quiet, helped her up to her room.

"The Indian! the Indian!" burst out Belding, his voice deep and rolling. "What did I tell you? Didn't I say he'd be a godsend? Remember what I said about Yaqui and some gory Aztec knifework? So he cut Rojas loose from that awful crater wall, foot by foot, finger by finger, slow and terrible? And Rojas didn't hang long on the *choya* thorns? Thank the Lord for that!... Laddy, no story of Camino del Diablo can hold a candle to yours. The flight and the fight were jobs for men. But living through this long hot summer and coming out—that's a miracle. Only the Yaqui could have done it. The Yaqui! the Yaqui!"

"Shore. Charlie Ladd looks up at an Indian these days. But Beldin', as for the comin' out, don't forget the hosses. Without grand old Sol an' Diablo, who I don't hate no more, an' the other Blancos, we'd never have got here. Yaqui *an'* the hosses, that's my story!"

Early in the afternoon of the next day Belding encountered Dick at the water barrel.

"Belding, this is river water, and muddy at that," said Dick. "Lord knows I'm not kicking. But I've dreamed some of our cool running spring, and I want a drink from it."

"Never again, son. The spring's gone, faded, sunk, dry as dust."

"Dry!" Gale slowly straightened. "We've had rains. The river's full. The spring ought to be overflowing. What's wrong? Why is it dry?"

"Dick, seeing you're interested, I may as well tell you that a big charge of nitroglycerin choked my spring."

"Nitroglycerin?" echoed Gale. Then he gave a quick start. "My mind's been on home, Nell, my family. But all the same I felt something was wrong here with the ranch, with you, with Nell.... Belding, that ditch there is dry. The roses are dead. The little green in that grass has come with the rains. What's happened? The ranch's run down. Now I look around I see a change."

"Some change, yes," replied Belding, bitterly. "Listen, son."

Briefly, but not the less forcibly for that, Belding related his story of the operations of the Chases.

Astonishment appeared to be Gale's first feeling. "Our water gone, our claims gone, our plans forestalled! Why, Belding, it's unbelievable. Forlorn River with promoters, business, railroad, bank, and what not!"

Suddenly he became fiery and suspicious. "These Chases—did they do all this on the level?"

"Barefaced robbery! Worse than a Greaser holdup," replied Belding, grimly.

"You say the law upheld them?"

"Sure. Why, Ben Chase has a pull as strong as Diablo's on a down grade. Dick, we're jobbed, outfigured, beat, tricked, and we can't do a thing."

"Oh, I'm sorry, Belding, most of all for Laddy," said Gale, feelingly. "He's all in. He'll never ride again. He wanted to settle down here on the farm he thought he owned, grow grass and raise horses, and take it easy. Oh, but it's tough! Say, he doesn't know it yet. He was just telling me he'd like to go out and look the farm over. Who's going to tell him? What's he going to do when he finds out about this deal?"

"Son, that's made me think some," replied Belding, with keen eyes fast upon the young man. "And I was kind of wondering how you'd take it."

"I? Well, I'll call on the Chases. Look here, Belding, I'd better do some forestalling myself. If Laddy gets started now there'll be blood spilled. He's not just right in his mind yet. He talks in his sleep sometimes about how Yaqui finished Rojas. If it's left to him— he'll kill these men. But if I take it up—"

"You're talking sense, Dick. Only here, I'm not so sure of you. And there's more to tell. Son, you've Nell to think of and your mother."

Belding's ranger gave him a long and searching glance.

"You can be sure of me," he said.

"All right, then; listen," began Belding. With deep voice that had many a break and tremor he told Gale how Nell had been hounded by Radford Chase, how her mother had been driven by Ben Chase—the whole sad story.

"So that's the trouble! Poor little girl!" murmured Gale, brokenly. "I felt something was wrong. Nell wasn't natural, like her old self. And when I begged her to marry me soon, while Dad was here, she couldn't talk. She could only cry."

"It *was* hard on Nell," said Belding, simply. "But it 'll be better now you're back. Dick, I know the girl. She'll refuse to marry you and you'll have a hard job to break her down, as hard as the one you just rode in off of. I think I know you, too, or I wouldn't be saying—"

"Belding, what 're you hinting at?" demanded Gale. "Do you dare insinuate that—that—if the thing were true it 'd make any difference to me?"

"Aw, come now, Dick; I couldn't mean that. I'm only awkward at saying things. And I'm cut pretty deep—"

"For God's sake, you don't *believe* what Chase said?" queried Gale, in passionate haste. "It's a lie. I swear it's a lie. I know it's a lie. And I've got to tell Nell this minute. Come on in with me. I want you, Belding. Oh, why didn't you tell me sooner?"

Belding felt himself dragged by an iron arm into the sitting-room, out into the patio, and across that to where

Nell sat in her door. At sight of them she gave a little cry, drooped for an instant, then raised a pale, still face, with eyes beginning to darken.

"Dearest, I know now why you are not wearing my mother's ring," said Gale, steadily and low-voiced.

"Dick, I am not worthy," she replied, and held out a trembling hand with the ring lying in the palm.

Swift as light Gale caught her hand and slipped the ring back upon the third finger.

"Nell! Look at me. It is your engagement ring.... Listen. I don't believe this—this thing that's been torturing you. I know it's a lie. I am absolutely sure your mother will prove it a lie. She must have suffered once—perhaps there was a sad error—but the thing you fear is not true. But, hear me, dearest; even if it *was* true it wouldn't make the slightest difference to me. I'd promise you on my honor I'd never think of it again. I'd love you all the more because you'd suffered. I want you all the more to be my wife—to let me make you forget—to—"

She rose swiftly with the passionate abandon of a woman stirred to her depths, and she kissed him.

"Oh, Dick, you're good—so good! You'll never know—just what those words mean to me. They've saved me—I think."

"Then, dearest, it's all right?" Dick questioned, eagerly. "You will keep your promise? You will marry me?"

The glow, the light faded out of her face, and now the blue eyes were almost black. She drooped and shook her head.

"Nell!" exclaimed Gale, sharply catching his breath.

"Don't ask me, Dick. I—I won't marry you."

"Why?"

"You know. It's true that I—"

"It's a lie," interrupted Gale, fiercely. "But even if it's true—why—why won't you marry me? Between you and me love is the thing. Love, and nothing else! Don't you love me any more?"

REALITY AGAINST DREAMS

They had forgotten Belding, who stepped back into the shade.

"I love you with my whole heart and soul. I'd die for you," whispered Nell, with clenching hands. "But I won't disgrace you."

"Dear, you have worried over this trouble till you're morbid. It has grown out of all proportion. I tell you that I'll not only be the happiest man on earth, but the luckiest, if you marry me."

"Dick, you give not one thought to your family. Would they receive me as your wife?"

"They surely would," replied Gale, steadily.

"No! oh no!"

"You're wrong, Nell. I'm glad you said that. You give me a chance to prove something. I'll go this minute and tell them all. I'll be back here in less than—"

"Dick, you will not tell her—your mother?" cried Nell, with her eyes streaming. "You will not? Oh, I can't bear it! She's so proud! And Dick, I love her. Don't tell her! Please, please don't! She'll be going soon. She needn't ever know—about me. I want her always to think well of me. Dick, I beg of you. Oh, the fear of her knowing has been the worst of all! Please don't go!"

"Nell, I'm sorry. I hate to hurt you. But you're wrong. You can't see things clearly. This is your happiness I'm fighting for. And it's my life. . . . Wait here, dear. I won't be long."

Gale ran across the patio and disappeared. Nell sank to the doorstep, and as she met the question in Belding's eyes she shook her head mournfully. They waited without speaking. It seemed a long while before Gale returned. Belding thrilled at sight of him. There was more boy about him than Belding had ever seen. Dick was coming swiftly, flushed, glowing, eager, erect, almost smiling.

"I told them. I swore it was a lie, but I wanted them

DESERT GOLD

to decide as if it were true. I didn't have to waste a
minute on Elsie. She loves you, Nell. The Governor
is crazy about you. I didn't have to waste two minutes
on him. Mother used up the time. She wanted to
know all there was to tell. She is proud, yes; but, Nell,
I wish you could have seen how she took the—the story
about you. Why, she never thought of me at all, until
she had cried over you. Nell, she loves you, too. They
all love you. Oh, it's so good to tell you. I think
mother realizes the part you have had in the—what shall
I call it?—the regeneration of Richard Gale. Doesn't
that sound fine? Darling, mother not only consents,
she wants you to be my wife. Do you hear that? And
listen—she had me in a corner and, of course, being my
mother, she put on the screws. She made me promise
that we'd live in the East half the year. That means
Chicago, Cape May, New York—you see, I'm not exactly
the lost son any more. Why, Nell, dear, you'll have to
learn who Dick Gale really is. But I always want to be
the ranger you helped me become, and ride Blanco Sol,
and see a little of the desert. Don't let the idea of big
cities frighten you. We'll always love the open places
best. Now, Nell, say you'll forget this trouble. I know
it 'll come all right. Say you'll marry me soon.... Why,
dearest, you're crying... Nell!"

"My—heart—is broken," sobbed Nell, "for—I—I can't
marry you."

The boyish brightness faded out of Gale's face. Here,
Belding saw, was the stern reality arrayed against his
dreams.

"That devil Radford Chase—he'll tell my secret,"
panted Nell. "He swore if you ever came back and married me he'd follow us all over the world to tell it."

Belding saw Gale grow deathly white and suddenly
stand stock-still.

"Chase threatened you, then?" asked Dick; and the
forced naturalness of his voice struck Belding.

"Threatened me? He made my life a nightmare," replied Nell, in a rush of speech. "At first I wondered how he was worrying mother sick. But she wouldn't tell me. Then when she went away he began to hint things. I hated him all the more. But when he told me—I was frightened, shamed. Still I did not weaken. He was pretty decent when he was sober. But when he was half drunk he was a devil. He laughed at me and my pride. I didn't dare shut the door in his face. After a while he found out that your mother loved me and that I loved her. Then he began to threaten me. If I didn't give in to him he'd see she learned the truth. That made me weaken. It nearly killed me. I simply could not bear the thought of Mrs. Gale knowing. But I couldn't marry him. Besides, he got so half the time, when he was drunk, he didn't want or ask me to be his wife. I was about ready to give up and go mad when you—you came home."

She ended in a whisper, looking up wistfully and sadly at him. Belding was a raging fire within, cold without. He watched Gale, and believed he could foretell that young man's future conduct. Gale gathered Nell up into his arms and held her to his breast for a long moment.

"Dear Nell, I'm sure the worst of your trouble is over," he said, gently. "I *will not* give you up. Now, won't you lie down, try to rest and calm yourself. Don't grieve any more. This thing isn't so bad as you make it. Trust me. I'll shut Mr. Radford Chase's mouth."

As he released her she glanced quickly up at him, then lifted appealing hands.

"Dick, you won't hunt for him—go after him?"

Gale laughed, and the laugh made Belding jump.

"Dick, I beg of you. Please don't make trouble. The Chases have been hard enough on us. They are rich, powerful. Dick, say you will not make matters worse. Please promise me you'll not go to him."

"You ask me that?" he demanded.

"Yes. Oh yes!"

"But you know it's useless. What kind of a man do you want me to be?"

"It's only that I'm afraid. Oh, Dick, he'd shoot you in the back."

"No, Nell, a man of his kind wouldn't have nerve enough even for that."

"You'll go?" she cried, wildly.

Gale smiled, and the smile made Belding cold.

"Dick, I cannot keep you back?"

"No,'' he said.

Then the woman in her burst through instinctive fear, and with her eyes blazing black in her white face she lifted parted quivering lips and kissed him.

Gale left the patio, and Belding followed closely at his heels. They went through the sitting-room. Outside upon the porch sat the rangers, Mr. Gale, and Thorne. Dick went into his room without speaking.

"Shore somethin's comin' off," said Ladd, sharply; and he sat up with his keen eyes narrowing.

Belding spoke a few words; and, remembering an impression he had wished to make upon Mr. Gale, he made them strong. But now it was with a grim humor that he spoke.

"Better stop that boy," he concluded, looking at Mr. Gale. "He'll do some mischief. He's wilder'n hell."

"Stop him? Why, assuredly," replied Mr. Gale, rising with nervous haste.

Just then Dick came out of his door. Belding eyed him keenly. The only change he could see was that Dick had put on a hat and a pair of heavy gloves.

"Richard, where are you going?" asked his father.

"I'm going over here to see a man."

"No. It is my wish that you remain. I forbid you to go," said Mr. Gale, with a hand on his son's shoulder.

Dick put Mr. Gale aside gently, respectfully, yet forcibly. The old man gasped.

"Dad, I haven't gotten over my bad habit of disobeying you. I'm sorry. Don't interfere with me now. And don't follow me. You might see something unpleasant."

"But my son! What are you going to do?"

"I'm going to beat a dog."

Mr. Gale looked helplessly from this strangely calm and cold son to the restless Belding. Then Dick strode off the porch.

"Hold on!" Ladd's voice would have stopped almost any man. "Dick, you wasn't agoin' without me?"

"Yes, I was. But I'm thoughtless just now, Laddy."

"Shore you was. Wait a minute, Dick. I'm a sick man, but at that nobody can pull any stunts round here without me."

He hobbled along the porch and went into his room. Jim Lash knocked the ashes out of his pipe, and, humming his dance tune, he followed Ladd. In a moment the rangers appeared, and both were packing guns.

Not a little of Belding's grim excitement came from observation of Mr. Gale. At sight of the rangers with their guns the old man turned white and began to tremble.

"Better stay behind," whispered Belding. "Dick's going to beat that two-legged dog, and the rangers get excited when they're packing guns."

"I will not stay behind," replied Mr. Gale, stoutly. "I'll see this affair through. Belding, I've guessed it. Richard is going to fight the Chases, those robbers who have ruined you."

"Well, I can't guarantee any fight on *their* side," returned Belding, dryly. "But maybe there'll be Greasers with a gun or two."

Belding stalked off to catch up with Dick, and Mr. Gale came trudging behind with Thorne.

"Where will we find these Chases?" asked Dick of Belding.

"They've got a place down the road adjoining the inn. They call it their club. At this hour Radford will be there sure. I don't know about the old man. But his office is now just across the way."

They passed several houses, turned a corner into the main street, and stopped at a wide, low adobe structure. A number of saddled horses stood haltered to posts. Mexicans lolled around the wide doorway.

"There's Ben Chase now over on the corner," said Belding to Dick. "See, the tall man with the white hair, and leather band on his hat. He sees us. He knows there's something up. He's got men with him. They'll come over. We're after the young buck, and sure he'll be in here."

They entered. The place was a hall, and needed only a bar to make it a saloon. There were two rickety pool tables. Evidently Chase had fitted up this amusement room for his laborers as well as for the use of his engineers and assistants, for the crowd contained both Mexicans and Americans. A large table near a window was surrounded by a noisy, smoking, drinking circle of card-players.

"Point out this Radford Chase to me," said Gale.

"There! The big fellow with the red face. His eyes stick out a little. See! He's dropped his cards and his face isn't red any more."

Dick strode across the room.

Belding grasped Mr. Gale and whispered hoarsely: "Don't miss anything. It'll be great. Watch Dick and watch Laddy! If there's any gun play, dodge behind me."

Belding smiled with a grim pleasure as he saw Mr. Gale's face turn white.

Dick halted beside the table. His heavy boot shot up, and with a crash the table split, and glasses, cards, chips flew everywhere. As they rattled down and the chairs of the dumfounded players began to slide Dick called out: "My name is Gale. I'm looking for Mr. Radford Chase."

REALITY AGAINST DREAMS

A tall, heavy-shouldered fellow rose, boldly enough, even swaggeringly, and glowered at Gale.

"I'm Radford Chase," he said. His voice betrayed the boldness of his action.

It was over in a few moments. The tables and chairs were tumbled into a heap; one of the pool tables had been shoved aside; a lamp lay shattered, with oil running dark upon the floor. Ladd leaned against a post with a smoking gun in his hand. A Mexican crouched close to the wall moaning over a broken arm. In the far corner upheld by comrades another wounded Mexican cried out in pain. These two had attempted to draw weapons upon Gale, and Ladd had crippled them.

In the center of the room lay Radford Chase, a limp, torn, hulking, bloody figure. He was not seriously injured. But he was helpless, a miserable beaten wretch, who knew his condition and felt the eyes upon him. He sobbed and moaned and howled. But no one offered to help him to his feet.

Backed against the door of the hall stood Ben Chase, for once stripped of all authority and confidence and courage. Gale confronted him, and now Gale's mien was in striking contrast to the coolness with which he had entered the place. Though sweat dripped from his face, it was white as chalk. Like dark flames his eyes seemed to leap and dance and burn. His lean jaw hung down and quivered with passion. He shook a huge gloved fist in Chase's face.

"Your gray hairs save you this time. But keep out of my way! And when that son of yours comes to, tell him every time I meet him I'll add some more to what he got to-day!"

XIX

I N the early morning Gale, seeking solitude where he
could brood over his trouble, wandered alone. It was
not easy for him to elude the Yaqui, and just at the
moment when he had cast himself down in a secluded
shady corner the Indian appeared, noiseless, shadowy,
mysterious as always.

"*Malo,*" he said, in his deep voice.

"Yes, Yaqui, it's bad—very bad," replied Gale.

The Indian had been told of the losses sustained by
Belding and his rangers.

"Go—me!" said Yaqui, with an impressive gesture
toward the lofty lilac-colored steps of No Name Mountains.

He seemed the same as usual, but a glance on Gale's
part, a moment's attention, made him conscious of the
old strange force in the Yaqui.

"Why does my brother want me to climb the nameless
mountains with him?" asked Gale.

"*Lluvia d'oro,*" replied Yaqui, and he made motions
that Gale found difficult of interpretation.

"Shower of Gold," translated Gale. That was the
Yaqui's name for Nell. What did he mean by using it in
connection with a climb into the mountains? Were his
motions intended to convey an idea of a shower of golden
blossoms from that rare and beautiful tree, or a golden
rain? Gale's listlessness vanished in a flash of thought.
The Yaqui meant gold. Gold! He meant he could
retrieve the fallen fortunes of the white brother who had

saved his life that evil day at the Papago Well. Gale thrilled as he gazed piercingly into the wonderful eyes of this Indian. Would Yaqui never consider his debt paid?

"Go—me?" repeated the Indian, pointing with the singular directness that always made this action remarkable in him.

"Yes, Yaqui."

Gale ran to his room, put on hobnailed boots, filled a canteen, and hurried back to the corral. Yaqui awaited him. The Indian carried a coiled lasso and a short stout stick. Without a word he led the way down the lane, turned up the river toward the mountains. None of Belding's household saw their departure.

What had once been only a narrow mesquite-bordered trail was now a well-trodden road. A deep irrigation ditch, full of flowing muddy water, ran parallel with the road. Gale had been curious about the operations of the Chases, but a bitterness he could not help had kept him from going out to see the work. He was not surprised to find that the engineers who had constructed the ditches and dam had anticipated him in every particular. The dammed-up gulch made a magnificent reservoir, and Gale could not look upon the long narrow lake without a feeling of gladness. The dreaded *ano seco* of the Mexicans might come again and would come, but never to the inhabitants of Forlorn River. That stone-walled, stone-floored gulch would never leak, and already it contained water enough to irrigate the whole of Altar Valley for two dry seasons.

Yaqui led swiftly along the lake to the upper end, where the stream roared down over unscalable walls. This point was the farthest Gale had ever penetrated into the rough foothills, and he had Belding's word for it that no white man had ever climbed No Name Mountains from the west.

But a white man was not an Indian. The former might have stolen the range and valley and mountain, even the desert, but his possessions would ever remain mysteries. Gale had scarcely faced the great gray ponderous wall of cliff before the old strange interest in the Yaqui seized him again. It recalled the tie that existed between them, a tie almost as close as blood. Then he was eager and curious to see how the Indian would conquer those seemingly insurmountable steps of stone.

Yaqui left the gulch and clambered up over a jumble of weathered slides and traced a slow course along the base of the giant wall. He looked up and seemed to select a point for ascent. It was the last place in that mountain-side where Gale would have thought climbing possible. Before him the wall rose, leaning over him, shutting out the light, a dark mighty mountain mass. Innumerable cracks and crevices and caves roughened the bulging sides of dark rock.

Yaqui tied one end of his lasso to the short, stout stick and, carefully disentangling the coils, he whirled the stick round and round and threw it almost over the first rim of the shelf, perhaps thirty feet up. The stick did not lodge. Yaqui tried again. This time it caught in a crack. He pulled hard. Then, holding to the lasso, he walked up the steep slant, hand over hand on the rope. When he reached the shelf he motioned for Gale to follow. Gale found that method of scaling a wall both quick and easy. Yaqui pulled up the lasso, and threw the stick aloft into another crack. He climbed to another shelf, and Gale followed him. The third effort brought them to a more rugged bench a hundred feet above the slides. The Yaqui worked round to the left, and turned into a dark fissure. Gale kept close at his heels. They came out presently into lighter space, yet one that restricted any extended view. Broken sections of cliff were on all sides.

Here the ascent became toil. Gale could distance Yaqui going downhill; on the climb, however, he was hard put to it to keep the Indian in sight. It was not a ques-

tion of strength or lightness of foot. These Gale had
beyond the share of most men. It was a matter of lung
power, and the Yaqui's life had been spent scaling the
desert heights. Moreover, the climbing was infinitely
slow, tedious, dangerous. On the way up several times
Gale imagined he heard a dull roar of falling water. The
sound seemed to be under him, over him, to this side and
to that. When he was certain he could locate the direction from which it came then he heard it no more until he
had gone on. Gradually he forgot it in the physical sensations of the climb. He burned his hands and knees. He
grew hot and wet and winded. His heart thumped so
that it hurt, and there were instants when his sight was
blurred. When at last he had toiled to where the Yaqui
sat awaiting him upon the rim of that great wall, it was
none too soon.

Gale lay back and rested for a while without note of
anything except the blue sky. Then he sat up. He was
amazed to find that after that wonderful climb he was only
a thousand feet or so above the valley. Judged by the
nature of his effort, he would have said he had climbed a
mile. The village lay beneath him, with its new adobe
structures and tents and buildings in bright contrast
with the older habitations. He saw the green alfalfa
fields, and Belding's white horses, looking very small and
motionless. He pleased himself by imagining he could
pick out Blanco Sol. Then his gaze swept on to the
river.

Indeed, he realized now why some one had named it
Forlorn River. Even at this season when it was full of
water it had a forlorn aspect. It was doomed to fail out
there on the desert—doomed never to mingle with the
waters of the Gulf. It wound away down the valley,
growing wider and shallower, encroaching more and more
on the gray flats, until it disappeared on its sad journey
toward Sonoyta. That vast shimmering, sun-governed
waste recognized its life only at this flood season, and was

already with parched tongue and insatiate fire licking and burning up its futile waters.

Yaqui put a hand on Gale's knee. It was a bronzed, scarred, powerful hand, always eloquent of meaning. The Indian was listening. His bent head, his strange dilating eyes, his rigid form, and that close-pressing hand, how these brought back to Gale the terrible lonely night hours on the lava!

"What do you hear, Yaqui?" asked Gale. He laughed a little at the mood that had come over him. But the sound of his voice did not break the spell. He did not want to speak again. He yielded to Yaqui's subtle nameless influence. He listened himself, heard nothing but the scream of an eagle. Often he wondered if the Indian could hear things that made no sound. Yaqui was beyond understanding.

Whatever the Indian had listened to or for, presently he satisfied himself, and, with a grunt that might mean anything, he rose and turned away from the rim. Gale followed, rested now and eager to go on. He saw that the great cliff they had climbed was only a stairway up to the huge looming dark bulk of the plateau above.

Suddenly he again heard the dull roar of falling water. It seemed to have cleared itself of muffled vibrations. Yaqui mounted a little ridge and halted. The next instant Gale stood above a bottomless cleft into which a white stream leaped. His astounded gaze swept backward along this narrow swift stream to its end in a dark, round, boiling pool. It was a huge spring, a bubbling well, the outcropping of an underground river coming down from the vast plateau above.

Yaqui had brought Gale to the source of Forlorn River.

Flashing thoughts in Gale's mind were no swifter than the thrills that ran over him. He would stake out a claim here and never be cheated out of it. Ditches on the benches and troughs on the steep walls would carry water down to the valley. Ben Chase had built a great dam which would be useless if Gale chose to turn Forlorn River from its natural course. The fountain head of that mysterious desert river belonged to him.

His eagerness, his mounting passion, was checked by Yaqui's unusual action. The Indian showed wonder, hesitation, even reluctance. His strange eyes surveyed this boiling well as if they could not believe the sight they saw. Gale divined instantly that Yaqui had never before seen the source of Forlorn River. If he had ever ascended to this plateau, probably it had been to some other part, for the water was new to him. He stood gazing aloft at peaks, at lower ramparts of the mountain, and at nearer landmarks of prominence. Yaqui seemed at fault. He was not sure of his location.

Then he strode past the swirling pool of dark water and began to ascend a little slope that led up to a shelving cliff. Another object halted the Indian. It was a pile of stones, weathered, crumbled, fallen into ruin, but still retaining shape enough to prove it had been built there by the hands of men. Round and round this the Yaqui stalked, and his curiosity attested a further uncertainty. It was as if he had come upon something surprising. Gale wondered about the pile of stones. Had it once been a prospector's claim?

"Ugh!" grunted the Indian; and, though his exclamation expressed no satisfaction, it surely put an end to doubt. He pointed up to the roof of the sloping yellow shelf of stone. Faintly outlined there in red were the imprints of many human hands with fingers spread wide. Gale had often seen such paintings on the walls of the desert caverns. Manifestly these told Yaqui he had come to the spot for which he had aimed.

Then his actions became swift—and Yaqui seldom moved swiftly. The fact impressed Gale. The Indian searched the level floor under the shelf. He gathered up handfuls of small black stones, and he thrust them at Gale. Their weight made Gale start, and then he trembled. The

Indian's next move was to pick up a piece of weathered rock and throw it against the wall. It broke. He snatched up parts, and showed the broken edges to Gale. They contained yellow streaks, dull glints, faint tracings of green. It was gold.

Gale found his legs shaking under him; and he sat down, trying to take all the bits of stone into his lap. His fingers were all thumbs as with knife blade he dug into the black pieces of rock. He found gold. Then he stared down the slope, down into the valley with its river winding forlornly away into the desert. But he did not see any of that. Here was reality as sweet, as wonderful, as saving as a dream come true. Yaqui had led him to a ledge of gold. Gale had learned enough about mineral to know that this was a rich strike. All in a second he was speechless with the joy of it. But his mind whirled in thought about this strange and noble Indian, who seemed never to be able to pay a debt. Belding and the poverty that had come to him! Nell, who had wept over the loss of a spring! Laddy, who never could ride again! Jim Lash, who swore he would always look after his friend! Thorne and Mercedes! All these people, who had been good to him and whom he loved, were poor. But now they would be rich. They would one and all be his partners. He had discovered the source of Forlorn River, and was rich in water. Yaqui had made him rich in gold. Gale wanted to rush down the slope, down into the valley, and tell his wonderful news.

Suddenly his eyes cleared and he saw the pile of stones. His blood turned to ice, then to fire. That was the mark of a prospector's claim. But it was old, very old. The ledge had never been worked. The slope was wild. There was not another single indication that a prospector had ever been there. Where, then, was he who had first staked this claim? Gale wondered with growing hope, with the fire easing, with the cold passing.

The Yaqui uttered the low, strange, involuntary cry so

rare with him, a cry somehow always associated with death. Gale shuddered.

The Indian was digging in the sand and dust under the shelving wall. He threw out an object that rang against the stone. It was a belt buckle. He threw out old shrunken, withered boots. He came upon other things, and then he ceased to dig.

The grave of desert prospectors! Gale had seen more than one. Ladd had told him many a story of such gruesome finds. It was grim, hard fact.

Then the keen-eyed Yaqui reached up to a little projecting shelf of rock and took from it a small object. He showed no curiosity and gave the thing to Gale.

How strangely Gale felt when he received into his hands a flat oblong box! Was it only the influence of the Yaqui, or was there a nameless and unseen presence beside that grave? Gale could not be sure. But he knew he had gone back to the old desert mood. He knew something hung in the balance. No accident, no luck, no debt-paying Indian could account wholly for that moment. Gale knew he held in his hands more than gold.

The box was a tin one, and not at all rusty. Gale pried open the reluctant lid. A faint old musty odor penetrated his nostrils. Inside the box lay a packet wrapped in what once might have been oilskin. He took it out and removed this covering. A folded paper remained in his hands.

It was growing yellow with age. But he described a dim tracery of words. A crabbed scrawl, written in blood, hard to read! He held it more to the light, and slowly he deciphered its content.

> *"We, Robert Burton and Jonas Warren, give half of this gold claim to the man who finds it and half to Nell Burton, daughter and granddaughter."*

DESERT GOLD

Gasping, with a bursting heart, overwhelmed by an unutterable joy of divination, Gale fumbled with the paper until he got it open.

It was a certificate twenty-one years old, and recorded the marriage of Robert Burton and Nellie Warren.

XX

DESERT GOLD

A SUMMER day dawned on Forlorn River, a beautiful, still, hot, golden day with huge sail clouds of white motionless over No Name Peaks and the purple of clear air in the distance along the desert horizon.

Mrs. Belding returned that day to find her daughter happy and the past buried forever in two lonely graves. The haunting shadow left her eyes. Gale believed he would never forget the sweetness, the wonder, the passion of her embrace when she called him her boy and gave him her blessing.

The little wrinkled padre who married Gale and Nell performed the ceremony as he told his beads, without interest or penetration, and went his way, leaving happiness behind.

"Shore I *was* a sick man," Ladd said, "an' darn near a dead one, but I'm agoin' to get well. Mebbe I'll be able to ride again some day. Nell, I lay it to you. An' I'm agoin' to kiss you an' wish you all the joy there is in this world. An' Dick, as Yaqui says, she's shore your Shower of Gold."

He spoke of Gale's finding love—spoke of it with the deep and wistful feeling of the lonely ranger who had always yearned for love and had never known it. Belding, once more practical, and important as never before with mining projects and water claims to manage, spoke of Gale's great good fortune in the finding of gold—he called it desert gold.

"Ah, yes. *Desert Gold!*" exclaimed Dick's father,

323

softly, with eyes of pride. Perhaps he was glad Dick
had found the rich claim; surely he was happy that Dick
had won the girl he loved. But it seemed to Dick himself
that his father meant something very different from love
and fortune in his allusion to desert gold.

That beautiful happy day, like life or love itself, could
not be wholly perfect.

Yaqui came to Dick to say good-by. Dick was startled,
grieved, and in his impulsiveness forgot for a moment the
nature of the Indian. Yaqui was not to be changed.

Belding tried to overload him with gifts. The Indian
packed a bag of food, a blanket, a gun, a knife, a canteen,
and no more. The whole household went out with him
to the corrals and fields from which Belding bade him
choose a horse—any horse, even the loved Blanco Diablo.
Gale's heart was in his throat for fear the Indian might
choose Blanco Sol, and Gale hated himself for a selfish-
ness he could not help. But without a word he would
have parted with the treasured Sol.

Yaqui whistled the horses up—for the last time. Did
he care for them? It would have been hard to say. He
never looked at the fierce and haughty Diablo, nor at
Blanco Sol as he raised his noble head and rang his piercing blast. The Indian did not choose one of Belding's
whites. He caught a lean and wiry broncho, strapped a
blanket on him, and fastened on the pack.

Then he turned to these friends, the same emotionless,
inscrutable dark and silent Indian that he had always
been. This parting was nothing to him. He had stayed
to pay a debt, and now he was going home.

He shook hands with the men, swept a dark fleeting
glance over Nell, and rested his strange eyes upon Mercedes's beautiful and agitated face. It must have been
a moment of intense feeling for the Spanish girl. She
owed it to him that she had life and love and happiness.
She held out those speaking slender hands. But Yaqui

did not touch them. Turning away, he mounted the broncho and rode down the trail toward the river.

"He's going home," said Belding.

"Home!" whispered Ladd; and Dick knew the ranger had felt the resurging tide of memory. Home—across the cactus and lava, through solemn lonely days, the silent, lonely nights, into the vast and red-hazed world of desolation.

"Thorne, Mercedes, Nell, let's climb the foothill yonder and watch him out of sight," said Dick.

They climbed while the others returned to the house. When they reached the summit of the hill Yaqui was riding up the far bank of the river.

"He will turn to look—to wave good-by?" asked Nell.

"Dear, he is an Indian," replied Gale.

From that height they watched him ride through the mesquites, up over the river bank to enter the cactus. His mount showed dark against the green and white, and for a long time he was plainly in sight. The sun hung red in a golden sky. The last the watchers saw of Yaqui was when he rode across a ridge and stood silhouetted against the gold of desert sky—a wild, lonely, beautiful picture. Then he was gone.

Strangely it came to Gale then that he was glad. Yaqui had returned to his own—the great spaces, the desolation, the solitude—to the trails he had trodden when a child, trails haunted now by ghosts of his people, and ever by his gods. Gale realized that in the Yaqui he had known the spirit of the desert, that this spirit had claimed all which was wild and primitive in him.

Tears glistened in Mercedes's magnificent black eyes, and Thorne kissed them away—kissed the fire back to them and the flame to her cheeks.

That action recalled Gale's earlier mood, the joy of the present, and he turned to Nell's sweet face. The desert was there, wonderful, constructive, ennobling, beautiful, terrible, but it was not for him as it was for the Indian. In the light of Nell's tremulous returning smile that strange, deep, clutching shadow faded, lost its hold forever; and he leaned close to her, whispering: *"Lluvia d'oro"*—"Shower of Gold."

THE END